CW01080858

A Richer Dust Concealed

R P Nathan

CASSIOPEIA
PUBLISHING

First published in 2021 by Cassiopeia Publishing
Cover art and typesetting by Cabochon Design

All rights reserved, © R P Nathan 2021

The right of R P Nathan to be identified as
author of this work has been asserted in
accordance with Section 77 of the Copyright,
Designs and Patents Act 1988

ISBN: 9798734042311

This book is sold subject to the condition that it
shall not, by way of trade or otherwise, be lent,
resold, hired out or otherwise circulated without
the author's prior consent in any form of binding
or cover other than that in which it is published
and without a similar condition including this
condition being imposed on the subsequent
purchaser.

This book is a work of fiction. Many of the
historical characters are real but the detail of their
actions is imagined. Other characters and events
are entirely imaginary and any resemblance to
actual persons, living or dead, or actual events is
purely coincidental. This might seem at odds
with the book's Foreword in which the narrator
claims everything written here is true. Well, as
always in life, you're going to have to decide
whom to believe.

For

Paola *and* Beppe,
Alessandro, Anna *and* Camilla

And of course for

Hilary

without whom
I would never have met them
in the first place

.

If I should die, think only this of me:
That there's some corner of a foreign field
That is for ever England. There shall be
In that rich earth a richer dust concealed;
A dust whom England bore, shaped, made aware,
Gave, once, her flowers to love, her ways to roam,
A body of England's, breathing English air,
Washed by the rivers, blest by suns of home.

The Soldier, Rupert Brooke, 1915

July 2020, London

John

Foreword

The first thing to say is that this book is all true.

Just because it's taken me a few years to get it out there doesn't mean I made any of it up.

In fact soon after the events it covers had occurred I did try to warn a few people. But the "authorities" weren't the slightest bit interested in our story. You've got to remember it was 2002 and they had more important things to worry about post 9/11 than a group of Venetian terrorists.

(Although even back then I wasn't sure "terrorists" was the right word for Them.)

But the main point I'm trying to get across is that I'm not lying about any of this stuff. Which was certainly not the impression given by the frowning and puzzled faces at the Police station, and the Home Office, and the Italian Consulate, when I went there to tell them about it. About what had happened and what I thought might happen next. They neither believed me nor felt the need to do anything about any of it.

And to be fair nothing *did* happen next. And though I scanned the Italian press, looking for stray news items about the main protagonists, I neither saw their names pop up nor heard of any atrocities which might be linked to Them.

(Not that atrocities ever seemed to be Her kind of style.)

So anyway, that's where I was: nobody believed me; and nothing happened.

But I was determined not to let all this fade. It had

already been my life for several years after all. So I decided to write it down. Well my bits anyway and then to pull together everyone else's versions of events – from the ones who were still alive – and to combine them with the older pieces of the story, the ones that had got us into all this in the first place. I figured that way at least I'd have it documented should anyone become interested in it some day.

Or if something untoward was to befall one of us…

Anyway, I'd not really written anything before so it took me a while to get the book together.

But it didn't take eighteen years.

In truth it probably only took about two. But soon after I was done – despite the lack of any hint of surveillance or reprisal – I suddenly got cold feet about doing anything with it. I became convinced that if I published these memoirs that They would come after me – after *us* – and I really didn't want that.

Unlike in 2002, I now had something to lose, a life I wasn't willing to give up.

By the time that feeling of danger was past, however, and I tried to get a publisher interested, it was already too late. The literary world was far more interested in fictional adventures like the *Da Vinci Code* than a true story like mine.

By then things had moved on for me in any case. We had a family; work was hectic; and time passed the way it does. I gave up trying to get the book I'd written – or perhaps assembled would be more accurate – published and it lay in the attic: a couple of print copies and a digital version on an old laptop.

Like so many people, though, this year – the pandemic year – has brought everything to a crashing halt. We've both been furloughed and the twins – teenagers now – have been off from school for what already seems like an eternity. The novelty of us all being together wore off pretty quickly and the long days we spend together drag by.

The weather at least has been good.

And it was on one of those baking days when I was meant to be using some of the enforced downtime to clear out the attic that I found this book again. One of the hard copies. A sheaf of 400 A4 pages still encircled by the string I'd so proudly tied it with all those years ago; ready to send – and re-send – to publishers until I lost interest at the lack of theirs.

I abandoned my clear-out and stumbled downstairs and out into the garden. Pulled a deckchair into the shade of the lilac tree and began to leaf through the pages.

And as I started reading it reminded me not just of those events but of that *time*.

Of being just out of university; and then of being in my early thirties. By comparison to now those days seemed so care free. It reminded me of *then*: the places, the warmth, the light. I sat in our small garden and read the pages and even though there was danger and heartbreak contained within that story, there was laughter and camaraderie too. I longed to be back there, to be away from the claustrophobia of Lockdown London, and back into the heat and sounds and vivid colours of Rome and Venice and Cyprus; and back to the London of my past.

It struck me as I was reading it that everything that had happened – even our own contribution – was now long ago. And maybe that was fitting. The past is where we live. It's what makes us. It's less another country, more an archipelago, each island a fragment of time entire unto itself; yet detached. There's no continuum in memory and seldom agreement or objectivity. Soon today will be yesterday in any case; and my own story will gather dust like the other, older, books which are so central to it.

And that's as it should be.

So anyway, over the last month I've been re-reading these pages, whiling away the endless languor of furlough while the rest of the family have been otherwise occupied. I've corrected a few typos but otherwise left the book unchanged. I want to present what it felt to be 21 and 31 so there's no point trying to rewrite anything of it now, when I'm nearly 50.

Ugh.

Even writing that makes me depressed. But there we go.

Anyway I've done a light edit and now the book is finally out there.

This book.

And it feels like a relief to be telling the story at last. Even more than a memoir it's a warning first and foremost; in case They ever re-surface. Though as I've said there's been nothing in the news about Them recently; or ever really. It was like They'd just disappeared.

As though none of it had ever happened.

Except it *did* happen.

Like I said at the start: it's all true.

Every single word of it.

Part One

A Foreign Field

14 September 1570, Cyprus

Girolamo Polidoro

Prologue

My master Count Bugon told me that we should be needing two horses that very evening and that I was to squire him and should ensure his armour was polished and his flintlock pistols were in readiness and that I myself should be prepared with mail tunic and sword. I thought at first that the Turk must be already hard upon us but he told me we had a special duty to perform for all Venice that night and would be riding with the Captain General himself.

At close to midnight and after eating a small morsel, my master and I saddled up and we rode together into the main square. There were eleven others there horsed, their faces shown by torchlight: five noblemen – which were Captain General Marc'Antonio Bragadino; Lorenzo Tiepolo, who was Captain of the City of Baffo; Astorre Baglione, General of the Militia; Count Sigismondo da Casoldo, and Captain Bernadino da Gubio – their five squires, one of whom was my great friend Giuseppe, and another man, Alvise, who was the head servant of Captain Bragadino's household. This last was bearing a flat wooden box in front of him, rested on the pommel of his saddle.

On our arrival the company was complete and with the Captain General's squire, whose name was Zani, taking the lead, we thirteen rode through the streets of Famagusta and left the city by the Limisso gate. The moon had risen, so though we had extinguished our torches as precaution, there was glimmer enough to be able to see. We rode slowly and with care but there was no sign of the Turks who had been raiding ever closer to the city walls in recent weeks.

We rode some three hours by my reckoning with but one brief stop, until at last a halt was called on the edge of some trees. We dismounted and were told to leave our horses there in the care of the

Captain General's squire, and that we were to continue on foot. However, before we moved off, Captain Bragadino instructed his servant Alvise to blindfold us other servants and squires so that we would not see the path we were about to walk.

We were greatly surprised at this. Alvise explained to us, however, that we were to act as witnesses to a deed of great importance and that it was desirous that the exact location of this should be revealed to as few as possible.

Blindfolded then, we walked down a gentle incline, each of us five servants guided by his master. After about twenty minutes we came out into some open place where the ground was stone paved and around us was the sound of many buzzing bees. We were given cool water to drink and were halted there for some time whilst a discussion was had amongst the captains and then once consensus was reached we set off again walking on a long path through forest. The fragrance of resin was strong about us, and tree roots underfoot tripped us, slowing our blind progress. Almost an hour we walked until from the sounds we heard and the smell of salt we knew we approached the sea. We descended a short scree slope and almost immediately came out onto a beach of fine sand. The sun was just rising, for we could feel the warmth and light of it come through the cloth we wore over our eyes, and this was welcome indeed after the hard night's ride and the walk through the dark.

Captain Bragadino shouted an order and our blindfolds were removed. We had been stood so that we looked along the shoreline, the sea and sun on our left, the beach to our right, but we were told as our blindfolds were removed not to turn our heads on pain of death.

Standing directly before us on the sand was Marc'Antonio Bragadino himself. At his feet was the box that Alvise had brought with him, and in the Captain General's hands was a sackcloth covered bundle taken from it. It was bulky, some four feet long by two feet wide, and from the way he held it, it had weight also. He stood with the sun shining on him, gilding the side of his noble face. Then, raising the bundle high, he cried out,

"Behold the Most Holy Cross of Saint Peter and Saint Paul! Of all the treasures taken from Constantinople this is the greatest."

He let slip the rags from the bundle and suddenly was revealed a cross of gold encrusted as though with the stars of heaven. I had never before in my life seen anything of such beauty. It gleamed with the fresh sun like fire itself. The face of the cross was lustrous yellow gold unadorned with any engraving, but set into it were gems from all the earth it seemed: white diamonds, blood rubies, green emeralds and purple amethysts. At the base was a single enamelled panel pricked again with smaller gems and emanating light and colour. But it was to the centre of the cross that my eye was drawn. For at its heart where the arms met was a stone of the clearest, most vivid blue, a blue which was at once the beauty of the sky yet the majesty of the sea, a blue of splendour but which held the gaze in a tender embrace. I saw with clarity and I looked with love at the blue eye on my heart. And, without being in control of my actions, I found myself walking forward to the cross, my hand outstretching. There was a sudden barked warning and Alvise stepped before me, scowling, his sword half drawn from its sheath. I shook my head from its mesmeris and looked away.

Captain Bragadino laughed loud, a high ringing laugh, and said in a voice as though intoxicated with heady wine, "I see what your servant desires, Bugon. Do not be angry with him. And you," he addressed me, "do not be ashamed neither. For this is the most beautiful of treasures and the most precious, for behind the panel in the base are the holiest of relics: a thorn from Christ's crown, a splinter from the True Cross, and a lock each of the hair of the Apostles Peter and Paul. And at the heart of the cross is a stone they call Tranquillity. It was brought by traders from the ends of the East to be set in the cross. It is a single perfect sapphire set at the heart of a work of man wrought to honour God. It is in its whole a work of perfection and is symbol of the full glory of Venice."

He was addressing us all again now and I felt confident to look up once more. I found the sapphire drawing my eye and I stared deep into it. For me it was as though my whole life previous had dissolved and existed only within the gaze of the stone. And whilst I looked into it I was at peace.

"This cross used to sit on the altar of Santa Sophia in Nicosia but it was removed to Famagusta to ensure its safety. It is the most

precious treasure in the whole maritime empire and some would say it is more precious even than the Pala d'Oro in Venice because of the relics it contains. Whatever happens in the war with the Turk on our island of Cyprus we cannot allow this treasure to fall into their hands; to let it become but another bauble of the Sultan. But the sea lanes are no longer safe, and so we must hide the cross here. We will bury it in the sand. You five knights before me, along with my servant Alvise, will know the place. You five servants will be witness to this act."

My lord Francesco Bugon stepped forward. "But why hide it sire?" he said, his eyes as transfixed by the beauty of the cross as we all were. "We will win the fight with the Turk. Help is near at hand. When the siege comes Famagusta will not fall."

"No doubt, Bugon. But in that event we have nothing to fear. We shall return in one week or one month or one year: whenever it is that the siege is lifted and the Turk defeated on land and sea. Then shall we recover this precious and holy relic. But if for some reason God wills that the Turks are victorious and we suffer the same fate as at Nicosia..." He paused to give us time to think upon that which had been anyway uppermost in all our minds since we had heard of the fall of that great city. "Then this will have been a wise precaution. And one day hence, any of us who should survive shall return and recover this for the greater glory of Venice and of God."

"And if none of us survives?" asked Count Sigismondo.

"Then better the cross is lost forever than be ceded to the Turk."

There was a murmur of agreement. "And now shall the cross be buried. Alvise see to this and you knights will note the place. But first please bind again the eyes of your servants." He addressed us five. "You have seen this and will bear witness if necessary to whichever authority of Venice commands."

My master stood behind me and took the band to blindfold me. I stared for one moment more at the centre of the cross before the strip of cloth covered my eyes and I was left in darkness. But the image of that jewel was burned into my mind and into my soul and I resolved that one day, though it might take me my whole life, I would look into its blue heart again.

Summer 1992, Rome/Venice

John

1

Of course I didn't know any of that stuff then.

Sitting there in the backpackers' bar on that hot summer's night in Rome, I had yet to hear of Polidoro or Bragadino or the Cross of St Peter and Paul. Surrounded by dark walls and cheap art posters, Amstel on tap and low denomination bank notes of various currencies stapled to the beams, I had no knowledge of Venetian Cyprus and was oblivious to the sieges of Famagusta and Nicosia. Surrounded by young Scandinavians and Germans and even a few other British, all travelling round Europe, here for a few days and wanting to party, I knew or cared about as much as a recent sciences graduate would be expected to about any of those subjects: a big fat nothing.

It was all about to change of course – within minutes in fact – when I was to meet her for the first time and all of that history stuff started to matter. But at that precise moment I couldn't have cared less. Because all I could think about was that – yet again – Julius and Duncan were doing my head in.

"So-*oooo*," said Duncan, opening his eyes wide and sending his drawly American accent into overdrive. "Are they *babes?*"

Patrick looked embarrassed. "I'm not sure. I haven't actually met Maya. And Sarah's my cousin so it's hard to say. I *think* she's good-looking..." He shrugged. "What do you think, Julius?"

"Sarah was fifteen when I last saw her."

"You know what they say: sweet fifteen."

"That's *sixteen*, Duncan."

"Whatever. Anyway, what was she *like?*"

"Spotty. With a brace."

"Ugh," said Duncan making a face.

"Well, I bet they'll both be really nice." I gave Patrick a supportive smile.

"Well, I guess you'll be looking after them then," said Julius, grinning in a way that made me want to punch him even more than normal. "I just don't see why we had to meet them at a touristy student place like this when we could have gone somewhere more properly Italian."

"Because we're touristy students perhaps..?" I said.

"I'm just trying to broaden your horizons. Personally I think we should have gone to that little *enoteca* by Piazza Navona. That's a *wine bar* John," he said smiling at me condescendingly.

I glowered. "Yes. You told me."

"Well I know you have trouble with the language."

I felt Patrick's hand on my arm. The holiday hadn't actually come to blows yet but it felt oh so close at times.

"Well thanks for agreeing to come here," said Patrick hurriedly before I could say anything. "Sarah had suggested it."

"It's tolerable," said Julius. "But in future don't say I'm always deciding where we're going."

I felt the blood rise in me. "You *are* always—"

"Whoa!" said Duncan in awe. "Look at those girls over there. Are they Italian? They are bell-issi-maaa."

"Bellisime..." said Julius thoughtfully, following his pointing arm. "I'm not sure if they are Italian. But come on Duncan," he said getting up. "Let's go and find out."

I scowled at Julius's back as he disappeared into the crowd by the bar. Took a sip of my lager and looked over at Patrick in annoyance. "What time were they meant to be here?"

"Half an hour ago."

Somehow it was always like this. Patrick and me sitting together, saving the table, while Julius and Duncan were off having fun. I was wondering – not very nobly – whether I should abandon my friend and go and join the other two – who, however loathsome, were at least talking to girls – when Patrick suddenly stood up and waved. "There they are!"

I looked round and choked on my beer.

Two girls were jostling their way towards us. The one in front, waving back to Patrick, was five-eight with short spiky blonde hair. She wore a thigh-length flowery summer dress, her legs and arms bare and tanned. The girl behind was taller and wore an elegant black top and shorts. Her skin was deep brown, her legs long and lightly muscled, her hair cut into a sleek black bob. This second girl was objectively beautiful, and Patrick gazed helplessly at her. But I was drawn back to the one in front: her eyes almond shaped and nose deliciously straight. Her friend may have been beautiful, but she was *cute*.

"Hi Cuzz," she said giving Patrick a kiss, her voice rasping hoarse and gorgeous. "Isn't it cool meeting up in Rome? This is my best friend Maya. You remember me telling you about her?"

"Of course." He blushed. "And this is my friend John."

"Hi John. I'm Sarah." She held out a slender bronzed arm and I felt a jolt juice through me as I shook her hand. "Let me get some drinks," I croaked happily. By the time I got back to the table, Patrick was sitting by Maya, leaving a place for me next to Sarah. Sarah smiled a gleaming white smile at me. "So how long have you been over so far?"

"Two weeks," I said, smiling back.

"We've done almost three. And are you enjoying it?"

"Oh we're having a really good time," said Patrick enthusiastically.

He looked at me and I looked at the girls and nodded

vigorously. It was amazing how Julius and Duncan not being around really lifted my spirits and made me forget that the last fortnight had actually been pretty rubbish. "It's been brilliant."

"So where've you been?"

"Well," said Patrick, more talkative than he'd been on the entire holiday. "We started in France obviously. Paris, then down to Nice and Cannes."

"All those beaches," said Maya longingly. *"Yum."* She had a broad Lancashire accent and the combination of this and the classical beauty of her face made anything she said kind of mesmerising. Patrick had to give his head a little shake before he was able to continue.

"After France we came to Italy. Milan, Pisa, Florence and here. How about you?" His eyes were locked onto Maya but it was Sarah who answered.

"Well we skipped through Paris," she said. "Only spent a couple of days there because it was really expensive. We didn't even get to go to the Louvre." She looked accusingly at Maya; but her friend just shrugged so that her hair shivered and fell about her shoulders.

"I think we had a pretty good time in Paris," Maya said decidedly.

"What did you do?" Patrick asked, his eyes wide.

She gave him an enigmatic smile. "We went to Père-Lachaise cemetery."

"The *cemetery?*"

"Well, it was free. And I'd always wanted to see where Jim Morrison was buried."

"Who's Jim Morrison?"

"How can you not know Jim Morrison? Lead singer of The Doors?"

Patrick shook his head.

"You must know them. *Riders on the Storm?*" She started to sing it.

"Anyway," Sarah interrupted, giving her a look. "We

14

were trying to save our money for later. So after that we just hung out in Montmartre."

"That's where we met those Canadian guys." They looked at each other and giggled.

Patrick and I exchanged a men-of-the-world kind of glance.

"Then where?"

"After that," said Sarah. "We kept going east into Germany. Frankfurt. Berlin. That was amazing. Are you guys going there?"

Patrick and I looked at each other uncertainly. "Maybe…" I said, knowing full well that it wasn't on the itinerary Julius had planned for us.

"Well you should. Just to see the Wall. It was really moving."

"It were *OK*…" said Maya with a strained expression. "But it were crawling with loads of other skanky inter-railers. And most of the time we had to live off jaffa cakes. Bloody hell, Germans eat a lot of meat."

"We're both vegetarian," explained Sarah.

"I'm veggie too," I said happily.

"Are you?" She smiled at me and I felt a shiver run down my spine. "It's not easy is it? Europe isn't designed for people like us. Anyway," she said taking a sip of beer, "after that we went down to Prague, then Greece for a few days on the beach. Took the ferry over to Bari and then here." She was momentarily distracted as she rummaged in her bag. "I don't suppose either of you have got a cigarette?"

"I thought you were giving up?" said Maya. Sarah shrugged and smiled at us appealingly.

"Sorry," I said. "I don't smoke."

"Wow," said Sarah looking straight at me, so that I felt my heart bang in my chest. "Veggie *and* a non-smoker: your body really is a temple isn't it?"

I laughed and was about to give her a suitably worldly

yet extremely funny riposte when—

"Were you asking for cigarettes?"

I swivelled round and found to my horror that Julius had materialised at my shoulder. "Marlboro Lights OK?" At the same time a large tanned hand appeared on the table between Patrick and Maya.

"Hi," said Duncan in his deepest voice.

"Blimey," said Maya appreciatively. "You're a tall lad aren't you?"

Sarah stood up. "Hi, Julius," she said breathlessly. "You probably don't remember me."

"Of course I remember you, Sarah," he said smiling at her and she grinned back at him. We went through the whole introduction thing once more and somehow, when we'd all sat down again, Duncan was between Patrick and Maya and Julius had inserted himself next to Sarah.

"So what have you ladies been up to tonight?" asked Duncan sitting square on to Maya, baring his big pearly teeth at her.

"We were at a lecture," said Maya, tossing her head, her hair transforming to a shimmering black waterfall.

Duncan gagged. "A *lecture?* On *holiday?*"

"About Venice. It were Sarah's idea."

"It's not as bad as it sounds," said Sarah hurriedly. "It was part of a series on the history of Italian cities."

"Any good?"

"I'm the wrong person to ask. I'm a sucker for anything to do with Venice. What did you think, Maya?"

"Oh it were too gruesome for me. Loads of stories about people getting impaled or dropped in canals or that one about the guy in Cyprus—"

"Bragadino? Oh, I loved that story," sighed Sarah.

"That's because you're gross," said Maya.

"What's it about?" I said trying to get Sarah's attention again.

"Oh it's fantastic." Her eyes shone as she looked at me.

"It was 1570 and the Venetian Republic was still really powerful: Venice controlled a big chunk of mainland Italy called the *Terraferma* – places like Verona and Padua – and loads of Greek islands including Crete and Cyprus. But the Ottoman Empire – that's the Turks – wanted Cyprus because it was strategic and fertile and the usual blah-blah-blah. So they invaded and surrounded the capital, Nicosia. But it didn't put up much of a fight and they broke through and massacred everyone inside. Like *20,000* people."

"Sarah." Maya had visibly paled. "I don't want to hear this again."

"And then they moved on to Famagusta, which was the main port, where this guy Marcantonio Bragadino was the captain—"

"*Sarah*—"

"And they laid siege to it for almost a year and at the end of it—"

"*Sarah, stop it!*" Maya's voice was sharp, serious.

"Don't be so delicate."

"I'm not being delicate." She made a face. "It's horrible what happened to them and I don't want to have to hear it again. *I mean it.*"

Sarah looked at her friend for a moment then gave her an apologetic smile. "*Sorry,*" she mouthed. "So anyway," she continued after a second's awkward silence, looking around, changing the subject. "How long are you in Rome for?"

"A couple more days," said Julius. "Then we're heading further south to Naples. I really want to show the guys Pompeii and then go and climb Vesuvius to put it in context for them."

I choked on my beer. He wanted us to do *what?*

"That sounds like fun," said Sarah wistfully. "But Pompeii will have to be in the next trip for us. This time we're going up to Venice."

"When?"

"Tomorrow. Via Bologna. We've got a friend from Uni

who's au pairing there."

"You know," said Julius clearing his throat, making sure everyone was listening. "You're making a mistake going to Venice."

Sarah was taken aback. "How come?"

"Because a) we're headed in the opposite direction." He smiled at her and – infuriatingly – she blushed in return. "And b) because Venice is massively overrated."

"Is that so?" said Sarah grinning. "Well a) perhaps we could meet up later on: maybe Paris just before we all go back? And b)," she said adjusting her seat a little and, fixing Julius with a stare I would have gladly been the recipient of, "Just what is so overrated about Venice?"

We left the bar at one but I'd lost track of their conversation a long time before that.

I tended to tune out Julius's voice whenever he started talking about art or history… or anything really. But clearly Sarah did not possess the same filter. She hung on his every word, smiling when he smiled, enthralled by his anecdotes, and wasting her own husky, lovely voice on discussions about Titian and Veronese when she could have been talking to me about… well about other stuff.

I had nothing to contribute to their discussion, so I just sat back, drank my Amstel and watched Sarah's face, animated, wonderful and increasingly a touch blurred.

"I need a pizza," said Duncan as we milled in the street afterwards.

"Me too," said Maya.

Duncan regarded her with a look of respect. "*All right.*"

"OK," shrugged Julius. "Let's go to that pizzeria we saw on the way up here. That seemed pretty authentic." Patrick shrugged and nodded.

"Fine," I said woozily, starting to walk the other way. "I'll see you all back at the room."

"Well, where are you going?"

"McDonalds."

Julius looked like he was going to be sick. "You don't go to McDonalds in Italy. Just come for a pizza and stop being such a geek."

I hated it when he called me a geek. "I want some fries. Is that OK? You want me to bring you some back?"

"No of course not—"

"I'll have some," said Duncan. "And maybe a Big Mac too?"

Julius looked at him wide eyed.

"Well, I'm hungry," he said unabashed.

"Let's just go," said Julius. "Enjoy your *food.*"

"I will."

"Hey wait, I'm coming too."

Both Julius and I turned in surprise.

It was Sarah.

"I love their salad bar," she explained.

"Well maybe," Julius said, his voice suddenly shaky. "Maybe we should all stick together and—"

"No that's cool," she said. "Let's have our food and then meet up back at your hotel. Come on John."

I blinked happily, not quite sure how this turn of events had occurred.

"Chop, chop!"

I hurried after her.

We didn't talk. We just concentrated on getting to Piazza di Spagna as soon as possible. And even though I'd had too much to drink, and even though it was clearly Julius she liked, it still gave me a thrill to be with her in the warm dark of the Roman night. It flowed around us as we moved, liquid black surrounding us, filling the space between us. I luxuriated in her proximity, the clatter of her shoes on the cobbles, and the faint scent of her perfume. The mellow buzz of the alcohol in my head and the heat of the night combined, folding in with the rhythm of our footsteps, faster, faster.

But when we got to the Spanish Steps the McDonalds was shut as were the bars and cafés around it. The place was only dotted with the travelling students and young lovers who normally crowded there, and in their place was a strew of cardboard and polystyrene cartons.

Sarah sat down on one of the steps with a sigh. "Shall we go and get pizza with the others?"

I regarded her for a moment. The others meant Julius and I didn't need any more of him tonight. I shrugged. "If you want, I'll walk you there. But after that I'm just heading back to the hotel." I pulled out a tatty map from my jeans and tried to orientate myself.

"Have you got food and drink back in your room?"

"Some."

"Then, let's go to yours."

I lifted my eyes from the map. She was stretching out a leg, poking a toe at a piece of litter. The leg was long and shapely. She looked up as I watched her and wrinkled her nose at me. "If that's OK?"

Of course it was OK.

We set off but after only a couple of minutes I stopped again and looked around in confusion. We'd ended up on a street which wasn't marked on the map. I squinted at the crumpled paper but it made no difference. The street just didn't exist. I gave the map a hopeful quarter turn and Sarah burst into laughter.

"What's so funny?"

"You don't know where your hotel is do you?"

"Of course I do. We just need to backtrack a little…"

"Look, your place is near the station isn't it?"

"So?"

"Well the station is north and north is in that direction."

"And what are you? A homing pigeon? How do you know where north is?"

"How do you not know?"

I frowned at her but we started walking, and after only a

20

minute I said in surprise, "Oh hang on, this is our road coming up now…"

"You see. You should have believed me."

"Well I would have, but I assumed you were wrong. Here's our hotel."

"Oh one star," she grinned looking at the sign. "Luxury."

We trudged up the three flights of stairs to the top. I opened our door and turned on the light and even I was a little shocked at the mess in the room.

"We were going to tidy up tomorrow," I said hurriedly. "Look, that's my bed. Just clear the stuff off it and make yourself at home.

"Thanks," she said sweeping a pile of clothes onto the floor. "It's just like home." She sat down on the edge of the bed and gave it an exploratory bounce.

I held up a bar of Toblerone and a bag of Ruffles. "You choose."

"Toblerone." I threw it to her and opened the crisps; sat down on the hard wooden chair opposite her.

"What have you got to drink?" she said after a few minutes of silent munching.

"Bacardi or gin."

"With what?"

"Er... Tomato juice."

"Gin and tomato juice? Yuk."

"Well I'm going to have one." I grabbed a mug and poured in half a cup of warm tomato juice and a good heft of gin. Took a swig and almost threw up. "It's great," I said, my eyes watering.

"You liar." She snatched the cup from me and tasted it herself. "Oh God that's disgusting." She screwed her face up. "I'm going to try one with rum."

She poured herself four fingers of Bacardi and added a splash of tomato juice. Took a gulp. Winced. "Cheers?" she said smiling, holding up her cup.

I grinned at her and we clinked mugs. "Cheers." We took another draught each and sat back to recover.

"I don't fancy him by the way," she said.

"Who?"

"Julius."

I blinked at her.

"I know you think I do," she continued breezily.

"It's none of my business…"

She giggled. "Whatever."

I looked at my drink wishing I hadn't had so much of it. I felt like I ought to say something. "So… how come you like Venice so much?"

"I'm doing history of art. And my director of studies *loves* Venice." She tilted her head to one side. "I do fancy him."

I gagged on my drink. "Your director of studies?"

"Yeah. Why not?"

"Well," I said feeling a sudden twinge of jealousy. "I'm assuming he's a bit old for you?"

"He isn't old. He's only twenty-five."

"And you're what? Nineteen? He's practically your granddad."

"Oh don't be silly. That's only a few years older than you. Or do you think you're too old for me as well?" Her face was flushed and I felt suddenly flushed too. She had stood up, hands on hips. The thin straps of her dress hung loose over her shoulders, over the cream tan of her skin. Her small breasts pressed against the flowery material and her short skirt swished against her thighs.

I thought,

This is one of those moments that either happens or it doesn't.

When you're alone with someone you think is God-wonderful.

And you have as long as it takes for that drop of sweat to trickle from under her chin all the way down the smooth curve of her neck.

You have that long.

I leaned forward and kissed her and immediately she pressed herself into me, her arms going round my neck, her hands into my hair and then we were on the bed and she was on top of me under me on top of me. Her arms reached out and pushed onto my chest forcing my shirt buttons open, kneading me and I reached up and slipped the straps of her dress down, one, two, needing her and the dress fell about her waist. I stroked the backs of my hands down her breasts and she arched away from me and then fell forward onto me, her mouth on my mouth and face and chest and arms and my mouth traversing the same salt sweet journey over her. "I really want you," I said, and she ground herself into me and her tongue found mine and we lay pressed together.

She rolled from under me and kicked her legs up in the air and slipped her dress off. She lay there in front of me in just her skimpy white panties. Her thumbs went down to the elastic at either hip, and began to tease them down, watching me watching her, enjoying my enjoyment, lifting her bottom off the bed as she slid the material free—

Bang!

I felt the sound almost before I heard it. But when I heard it, I almost jumped out of my skin.

Bang! Bang! Bang!

The sound of a fist repeatedly hitting a door.

Our door.

"John, open up man! I need the bathroom."

Duncan.

I fell off the bed. Clambered to my feet and senses, yanking on the underpants that I hadn't even realised I'd shed.

"Come on dude!"

I pulled on my trousers. Searched desperately for my shirt and put it on. Sarah was smoothing the dress back over her. I leaned down and kissed her. "We will get a chance to finish this won't we?" I said desperately.

"Dude I'm going to just pee right here."

She giggled and pushed me away. I felt suddenly conscious that she hadn't answered me, so I moved in close to her. She held me back with a finger on my lips. "You better let him in."

I walked to the door, surveyed myself – trousers on, pants on, shirt done up – looked back over my shoulder and saw Sarah was now sitting on a chair in the corner. She stroked the material of her skirt down against her thighs, looked up, winked, and then started flicking through the pages of a GQ.

I took a deep breath and opened the door. Duncan fell into the room on top of me. He lay on the floor a moment one hand on his fly the other on a dusty vase he had picked up in the hallway. He got to his feet and handed the vase to me. "Thanks dude," he said staggering to the bathroom. "I was getting desperate there."

The bathroom light pinged on and immediately we could hear the gushing sound of urine hitting water, the constant musical jangle, cascading, never-ending... The guy had a bladder the size of a beach ball.

My eyes wandered to Sarah. I watched her cross one leg over the other, and felt a shiver of anticipation at the thought of our next time together, of how I would start by kissing her ankles, before turning my attentions higher, tracing the inside line up her calf, higher and… *Sweet Jesus.* Was he still peeing?

Finally came the sound of the toilet being flushed. Duncan re-emerged and threw himself on his bed. "Did you get those fries?" he asked hopefully.

There were noises in the hallway, the door opened and Patrick, Julius and Maya came into the room. Sarah jumped to her feet.

"Hey M, we need to get going."

"Already?" said Julius ambushed by disappointment. "What time are you heading off tomorrow?"

Sarah gave him a kiss on both cheeks then Patrick and Duncan. Maya was following the same circuit. "Shall we talk tomorrow about meeting up in Paris? We'll drop by on our way to the station."

I followed them to the door. Maya went out first into the corridor.

"Goodnight, Maya," Duncan called after her. "I hope you're not up all night thinking about me."

"Me too," she called back laughing.

I stood in the doorway with Sarah. "I wish you weren't heading off just yet."

"We have to. We promised our friend. And we're going to see each other in Paris."

"But what about before then?" I said in a low voice. "Why don't I come up and see you in Venice? I'll meet you there in a couple of days time. When you've finished in Bologna."

"I thought you were going down to Naples?"

"Screw Naples. I want to see Venice and I want to see you again."

"Come on," Maya yawned at her from down the hallway. "I'm knackered."

"Coming." She turned back to me, put her head to one side and then nodded. "OK. See you in Venice. Thursday. Midday at St Mark's."

"Midday at St Mark's," I repeated faithfully, happily and then I remembered my earlier unanswered question. "This is going to happen isn't it?"

She arched an eyebrow at me. "What do you think?"

I leant forward to kiss her on the lips but she ducked so that I caught her on the cheek.

"They're all watching," she hissed. "Goodnight guys," she said in general to the room and then slinked down the corridor after her friend.

2

When I woke, I woke with a jolt.

I sat up in bed blinking at the sunlight streaming over the tops of the shutters. My mouth was dry and I was gripped with a feeling close to nausea. At first I assumed it *was* nausea: my stomach was cramping and I had a heightened sense of smell – gin everywhere. But I felt cold too, a static shiver in the midst of the surrounding warmth; and a sense of panic, the feeling of a lost dream: an emptiness and a need to remember at all costs. I stared around me, scared and sick, unable to comprehend why I was feeling quite so lousy. And then it came to me in a flash of sunshine and dust motes.

Sarah.

I sank back in bed basking at the thought of her; stared up at the ceiling and glimpsed her face projected there so that she filled my field of view. I could still feel her touch and sense her skin and the beat of her heart and mine. "What do you think?" she said with an invitingly arched eyebrow as she slipped out of her dress again.

I breathed a happy sigh and allowed myself a recollection of her legs and neck and breasts. But just momentarily. I didn't want to dilute the memory through overuse. It was there after all, it had happened, would happen again. *"What do you think?"* she grinned. I opened my eyes and allowed the startling white brilliance of spilled sunlight on the ceiling burn the vision away.

I sat up again and looked round the room. I was the only one awake. Duncan was sprawled out on his front in his boxer shorts, snoring and snuffling. Julius was lying on his back a sheet drawn up over him, his arms neatly down by his sides. And Patrick was curled into a tight ball lying on the bare mattress, sheet kicked off in the hot night.

Duncan, an incongruous history of art student, was the

biggest character of the group. In fact he was big in every way. Six foot four and filled out at twenty-one in a way that the other three of us, the same age, were not; his American footballer's body topped off with a mop of blond curls and a tanned handsome face, forever split with his dazzling grin.

Julius also studied history of art yet could have been drawn as his antithesis. Eight inches shorter, his hair dark and close cropped, his frame slight, his face pale even after a fortnight of high summer. And yet his features had an animation and a magnetic quality that attracted people – girls mostly – just as surely as Duncan. Where in Duncan there was a good-natured ebullience, in Julius there was an evident and deep-seated intelligence, artistic, and intense, which proved every bit as alluring to the opposite sex as Duncan's All American charm.

By contrast, Patrick and I were pretty average. Maybe that was why we had become such good friends. We did similar subjects, him maths, me physics. We were both about six feet, brown hair, bluish eyes, still a little scrawny after three years of student life. Both kind of good looking in an understated way.

It was only by chance that we'd all ended up on holiday together. I'd already been planning an inter-rail trip with Patrick for much of our last term at university when he realised Julius and Duncan were doing the same. Patrick had known Julius since school so it had seemed only natural for us all to link up. I had even thought I might finally warm to Julius having sustained a mutually held indifference towards him throughout my three years at College. But I didn't; and instead of indifference I now loathed him with a passion that bordered on the pathological and had done since the start of the holiday and the very first argument over where to eat and his first peals of patronising laughter at my attempted Italian pronunciation. Still, it all seemed to matter a whole lot less this morning. I thought again of Sarah and grinned. Then checked my watch and sat upright once more.

It was nine-thirty. The others often didn't get up till midday and usually I'd be left lying in bed reading, waiting for them. But not today. Today I had things to do. Sarah would be coming round at noon and before she did I wanted to get her a present, something small, something she'd like. Which was easier said than done, since I knew next to nothing about her. All I could remember from the previous night was that she liked Venice. And the fragments of a story she had started to tell.

None of them stirred as I scrambled out of bed. I pulled on jeans and T-shirt and trainers then picked my way through the mess on the floor. I slipped out onto the landing, letting the door click quietly shut behind me.

But I was only halfway down the stairs when I heard a voice. Patrick was standing in our doorway, his hair on end, a sheet wrapped round him. "Are you going for a walk?" he stage whispered down to me, and before I could reply he continued, "I'll come with you. I'll only be five minutes." And he disappeared back into the room.

I walked slowly down to the foyer and as I waited there the doubts set in. What had happened last night was like a dream now. Perhaps no more than a dream. *"What do you think?"* Maybe the moment was gone now. Maybe it was last night or never? But no. She wanted to meet me in Venice. She had said so. And a couple of words or a shared smile when I saw her later would be enough to settle me. *"What do you think?"* she said, decisively, pulling me to her. I stepped outside and the sun was bright and strong and the air just the right side of hot, and all felt right again.

A second later Patrick came dashing out to join me, apologising profusely for keeping me waiting.

"Where are we going?" he asked as we set off down the road. Our hotel was in Termini, the district surrounding the railway station. The neighbourhood here was crammed full of hostels and cheap hotels and low-end restaurants and cafés. At this time of day it was noisy with garbage trucks. It felt generally down at heel in a way that made it good to be walking out of it.

"Nowhere really," I lied.

"Did you have a good time last night?"

I tried to keep my voice as neutral as possible. "Yeah, it was good."

"You seemed to be getting on really well with Sarah."

"You think so?" I blurted and then, recovering, "Yes she was nice." I was wondering when I should tell him what had happened. She was his cousin after all. I thought on balance that later might be better… "What about you and Maya?"

"Oh," he said, wistfully. "She was wonderful."

I nodded. "A complete babe."

"But she had an inner kind of beauty about her as well," he said earnestly.

"I guess so…" I definitely got the outer beauty anyway.

We stepped out into the street as we passed a shopkeeper hosing down his stretch of pavement. "Do you think they will want to meet up in Paris?" he asked.

"You can ask them when we see them," I said feeling guilty. I hadn't told him about going up to Venice yet either. I looked across at him and saw he was smiling happily, gazing up at the morning blue bar of sky between the building tops, savouring the cool shadows. The moment passed and we walked on. Through the Piazza della Republica then across the busy Via Nazionale and a left onto Via Quattro Fontane walking along in amicable silence until we reached a crossroads with elaborate fountains cut into niches at each of the four corners.

"That way kind of leads towards the Spanish Steps," I said consulting my guide book. "Why don't we head over there and then go on to the Trevi Fountain."

"Sure."

"And then on the way," I said, like I'd just thought of it,

"we could pop into one of the bookshops we saw the other day."

"What are you after?"

"Oh nothing really," I said casually. "Perhaps a book on Venetian history."

"Like what Sarah was talking about? Are you interested in that stuff too?"

"Yes." I nodded, my face flushed, warm. "Quite interested."

We continued down the road and as it became Via Sistina we saw what we wanted on the left hand side: a narrow street with bookshops on either side. I stared vacantly at them, panicked by the choice, but then I pointed at a sign, gold on black in an antique script. "What about that one?"

"Amici della Venezia," read Patrick. "That means 'Friends of Venice' doesn't it?"

"Something like that," I said vaguely. "Do you think they speak English?"

We walked up the steps and into the shop. Compared with the faded exterior, the inside of the shop was light and airy with a blond wood floor. Everything was clearly labelled and easy to find and there was even a small section of English language magazines. But we couldn't see any books on Venice.

Behind the counter was a man in his mid-twenties. "Hi," he said in an American accent. "I'm Giovanni. Can I help you?" He was tall in a casual shirt and trousers, his hair close-cropped and dyed blonde. He wore a name tag: Giovanni Galbaio.

"Hi," I said nervously. "I was looking for a history book about Venice. About a guy called... Braga-din?"

He looked at me blankly.

"To do with Cyprus and the Turks? Braga-*din*." I gave the end of the name a kind of rising note which I thought sounded quite authentic.

"Oh, *Bragadino*," said Galbaio. "Apologies, your accent... Yes we may well have a book, but we wouldn't keep it in the front of the store. Books on Venice don't sell real well in Rome."

"The sign—"

"Oh, I know. It's an old sign. My father didn't want it removed when I took over. Luckily he's here today. He knows the old stock back-to-front. *Papa! Cliente!*" We heard the sound of footsteps on the stairs and an older figure emerged into the shop, mid-fifties, but unmistakably the other's father. Tall like his son and the same handsome face though his hair was a mass of dark curls. I noticed that he must have had a streak of grey because the hair there was dyed and it showed up a subtly different shade of brown under the lights. The younger man spoke rapidly in Italian and then smiled at us. "My father will look after you now," he said, and turned to another customer.

The older man gestured with his hand and we walked round to the end of the counter. He studied us and then said in a heavy Italian accent, "My son says you want a book about Bragadino and the siege of Famagusta."

"The siege of Famagusta," I echoed remembering what Sarah had said. "Yes, that's right."

"I got a book for you," he grunted. "It's by Girolamo Polidoro. You know who he was?"

I shook my head

"He was there during the siege. He was the one that saved Bragadino's skin." He gave a throaty and not particularly pleasant chuckle. "I have his journal which gives an account of the siege."

My eyes widened. Sarah would love that. "Is it in English?"

"No, in Italian. But I also have an English translation. An *amateur* English translation only, you understand. Handwritten in a notebook by a British soldier who was killed in the First World War."

"Oh right. And how come you've got something like that?"

"You would have to ask my father or my grandfather a question like that," he said briskly. "They knew the stories of all the books in the shop but not me. Since I have been here these two have always been together: the journal and the notebook. Are you interested?"

"They sound great."

He sniffed and shrugged. "Fine. Then I go get them." He returned after only a few moments with a pair of books, laying them carefully on the counter before us. Both were slim volumes, the size of a paperback. The journal was bound in brown leather. He opened it, turning the pages with care, revealing large printed text inside broken up with dates. The book was a hundred or so pages long but at the end, for the last six pages the shape of the text suddenly changed, paragraphs and indents replaced by solid blocks of printing: row after row of equally spaced capital letters.

"A code," he said.

He closed the journal and turned his attention to the other book, black and clothbound. He opened it and we could see it too was set out like a diary, handwritten, the script a perfectly legible copperplate, filling about half the pages on one side only.

"Now look," he said and turned the notebook upside down and over and there was more of the same neat script. "This is the translation of Polidoro's journal."

We craned and read the words: *This is the journal of Girolamo Polidoro, servant to Count Francesco Bugon of Verona and most loyal subject of Venice. I set these thoughts down so that a record might exist—*

He snapped the notebook shut and placed it on top of the journal.

"Why's the end of the journal in code?" I asked.

"It holds a secret. It tells where a great treasure is hidden."

I started to laugh but the sound choked in me almost immediately as I realised he was serious.

"What kind of code is it?" asked Patrick.

"You know about codes?"

"I studied them as part of my maths degree."

"I did physics," I piped up.

Galbaio ignored me, fixing Patrick with a stare. "If you've studied mathematics then perhaps you will be able to break the code."

Patrick blinked back at him in surprise. "Perhaps. Has no one broken it already?"

"Not in four hundred years."

"And what's the treasure?" I asked eagerly.

"Read the book," he said patting them both with the palm of his hand. "They will tell you. So you will buy them?"

"Definitely," I said.

"Fine. I will wrap them." He pulled a paper bag from under the counter. "That will be 300,000 Lire."

My jaw dropped open and I could feel Patrick staring at me.

"That's over a hundred quid," he hissed. "Did you mean to spend that much?"

I looked back at him helplessly. All I wanted was to get her a present. Something that she'd like. But a hundred quid? *A hundred quid?*

The bookshop owner had paused, the books halfway into the bag. He gave me an icy look. "There is a problem?"

"No problem." I was feeling light headed. "They just seem quite expensive."

"Expensive? These books are old books. This one is eighty years old and this one is four hundred years old. You understand? *Four hundred years* and you say it is expensive." He shook his head in disgust. "And what do *you* want?" His son had come over and was looking at the books anxiously.

"These books, Papa. Uncle Lori won't be very happy if

you sell them."

"It's none of his business," he growled.

"But he's been working on them for a long time—"

"Then maybe it's time someone else looked at them!" He thumped the counter. "He thinks he can always do what he wants. Running around, causing trouble. Hurting people—"

"No one's actually got hurt."

"Yet. *Yet.* It's just a matter of time. Which will mean trouble for all of us. Well, while he's playing with fireworks, someone has to keep things going. Keep us from going under. Loredan needs to remember who is in charge." He turned back to us with a terrifying expression on his face. "So, you want them or you don't want them?"

"Yes," I squeaked, not wanting to catch his eye. "I want them." I didn't look at Patrick either. I just pulled out the credit card I carried for emergencies. "It's fine. I'll pay with that."

"Thank you," he said suddenly smiling again, taking the card and getting an imprint of it. "Now please sign this slip and this is your receipt and this is mine and here are your books." And before we knew it we were out on the street again.

"What was all that about?" said Patrick as we stood blinking at each another.

"I have no idea."

"You know…" His voice was gentle. "You know you've just bought an old notebook and a journal you can't even read for a *hundred* pounds."

"I know, Patrick. You've said that already."

"Sorry."

A strange jittery sensation started fluttering inside me. I didn't have a lot of money like Julius and Duncan or even Patrick for that matter and the enormity of what I'd done was only just sinking in.

"Do you think they're even genuine?"

I suddenly felt sick. "Come on. Let's go and find a piazza somewhere and have a drink."

It was fully twenty minutes later sitting in a corner of Piazza Navona that we plucked up the courage to look at the books again.

"You know it doesn't really seem that old," said Patrick of the brown leather bound journal. "Certainly not four hundred years anyway. *Sorry—*"

"It's OK," I said resignedly. "Somehow it seemed older in the shop."

"I think it was the bookseller's patter."

"Yeah, all that stuff about some other guy wanting it," I said glumly. "He really suckered me in."

"We could always go and ask for your money back."

I thought of the bookseller again and it made me shiver. "No way." I held up the clothbound notebook. "Well this one seems reasonably old anyway." I opened it. Handwritten inside the front cover was: *The diary of Henry Arthur Shaeffer*. On the facing page the diary started immediately.

3 January 1915
My darling Anna

At the beginning of this new year, I have resolved to keep a diary for I fear I will go mad otherwise from the lack of practised thought and intelligent conversation. If but once a day, a week or even a month I set down my thoughts to you then I can imagine them examined by your trained mind, my words and deeds questioned and quizzed as though you were before me. And once I have returned to you, you will be able to read this diary and gauge that I have indeed missed you, and that I wish with my whole heart to have you and Frances beside me once again.

I know you have received my letters and am glad to

have received yours. But as you know all mine are read first by the <u>wonderful</u> Captain Hargreaves and, estimable man that he is, I feel that there is no need to make his blood pound stronger by committing my innermost thoughts for his perusal. No, better I keep these thoughts, and my views on the war – which has left me frustratingly uninvolved so far – and my views on <u>him</u> and, most of all, my deepest thoughts for you, a secret between you and me.

When I do finally see you again (and Colonel Roberts has told me that I will be back with you for June at the latest) I will be able to present this journal to you in person and you can catalogue and order my thoughts to your heart's content, abstract them to nothing, and reduce my meanderings to but one drop of sense, that drop being my intense desire for you and my eternal love for Frances.

"It's quite *personal* isn't it," I said disappointed. "Why don't we take a look at the translation instead." I turned to the back of the book.

This is the journal of Girolamo Polidoro, servant to Count Francesco Bugon of Verona and most loyal subject of the Republic of Venice. I set these thoughts down so that a record might exist of these dark days in Famagusta and so that should the same fate befall us here as in Nicosia then others might know of all that the murderous Turk hath wrought against the followers of Christ in this fair city. And should the fight go against us and we are laid waste then it will be known that we fought with our hands and our hearts and, if God will allow, these dishonours that are sure to be heaped upon us may one day be avenged one thousand times one thousand fold.

14 September 1570
A Greek peasant arrived this morning sent by the Turks from Nicosia bearing news to our Captain General Marc'Antonio

Bragadino, and carrying the head of Nicolo Dandolo in a basin. His arrival and tidings had a disquieting effect upon the populace in Famagusta. Aware that the news was abroad, the Captain General and Captain of the Militia, Astorre Baglione, walked through the town and made a show of consulting with all the fighting men and captains to raise heart. Of the Captain General many good things are said by my lord and master Count Bugon who has spoken with him several times in the past weeks and considers him to have an able brain and a cool nerve. My lord had criticised Dandolo, who had been invested with the defence of Nicosia, as a weak man and not suitable for such a task and though it is not right to speak ill of the fallen, I believe his conduct exhibited many deficiencies.

The loss of Nicosia and twenty thousand Christian souls causes a great sadness to fall upon me. But it does not bring me fear for the defences of Famagusta are stronger than at Nicosia and our position on the sea will enable reinforcements and supplies to arrive more easily. But our great strength will lie in the organisation of our leaders and the bravery of those within the walls of the city, which is second to none.

"Well that's more interesting isn't it," I said breathing a sigh of relief. "Let's read for just another ten minutes and then head back. The girls'll be dropping by soon."

My master Count Bugon told me that we should be needing two horses that very evening...

3

When we got back to the room the shutters had been opened but Julius and Duncan were still lying undressed in bed, propped up against their pillows, smoking and chatting.

"Hi guys," said Duncan cheerily. "Where'd you go?"

"Over to Piazza Navona," I said casually.

"Any good?" He gave a huge yawn and dropped his cigarette butt into the empty Coke can by his bed.

"Yeah. You should check it out."

"Is it on the agenda Julio?"

"Maybe this evening. I think we should head off to the Forum this afternoon. What have you got there?"

Patrick and I exchanged an excited smile.

"A couple of books I picked up. This one's a notebook written by a soldier who died in the First World War. And *this* is a journal from the sixteenth century."

Julius eyes widened. "Let me see that."

I handed it to him carefully. "It's an account of the siege of Famagusta by Girolamo Polidoro. Sarah was talking about it last night. It's amazing. It begins with the hiding of a gold cross and then the end contains the exact location but it's in code—"

"Let's have a look at the notebook," said Duncan. I gave it to him and shot a triumphant glance at Patrick as the two of them pored over the books.

"How much did you pay for this?" asked Julius eventually.

"About a hundred quid."

He looked up at me in awe.

"Why?" My heart was racing. "Do you think it's worth a lot more than that?"

"More?" He started laughing. "No not *more*. This is toilet paper."

It was like he'd hit me.

"This isn't four hundred years old, you geek. It isn't even a *hundred* years old. Can't you tell anything? The leather's almost brand new and there are no printer's marks or anything."

"Who are you to say? You're no expert—"

"No I'm not. The only *expert* is the guy who took a hundred pounds off you for this fake. He must have seen you coming."

"You don't know anything." But even to me my voice sounded weak and uncertain.

Duncan let out a sudden guffaw. "Ha ha! It's fucking porn man. Listen to this." He put on an upper class English accent and read from the notebook:

...I said yes we would make love, but perhaps just once, starting with a kiss and an embrace, undressing, feeling your gentle touch on my skin, which is like electricity to me, and then falling together, caressing, and moving, slowly at first—

"Give me that!" I snatched the book from him. He rolled on his bed consumed with hilarity.

"The boys bought old bad porn!"

"Don't forget your *sixteenth century manuscript*," Julius sneered and threw the journal at me so that the pages caught the air and splayed out. "*Expert*."

I bit my lip in fury.

"It's a shame," said Duncan sitting up again, tears of laughter rolling down his face. "It's a shame the girls aren't coming by. They'd wet their cute little panties at this. Hey no offence Patrick."

Patrick was staring at him and I was staring at Patrick, anger and bewilderment swirling together inside me.

"What do you mean, they're not coming by?" I said.

"You know. Like: *not – coming – by*."

"But they were going to drop in on the way to the station." My chest tightened. Each breath and word was suddenly an ordeal. "They were coming at lunchtime."

"Sure, but they're not now. They rang and told us about an hour ago. They've taken an earlier train." He shrugged; then a slow smile spread over his face. "Hey Patrick. Why didn't you let on how hot your cousin's little friend was? Were you saving her for yourself?"

Patrick was taken by surprise. "*No.*"

"You sly dog."

"She certainly was very pretty," said Julius coolly.

"I don't understand," I said, my face screwed up in frustration.

"Understand what?" Julius arched an eyebrow.

"Why would they want to catch an earlier train?"

"How should I know?"

"But didn't they say anything when they rang? Didn't they leave a message?"

"Not for you dude," said Duncan. "They did tell us to say goodbye to Patrick though."

"Did they mention about meeting up in Paris?" Patrick looked hopeful.

Duncan and Julius exchanged a quick glance. "No, actually," said Julius. "Paris wasn't mentioned. They said we might meet up again in London or something… When we get back."

"But that's ages away." Patrick made a face.

"Hey," said Duncan. "Look on the plus side: it's not like you really stood a chance with Maya anyway." He smiled. He was being reassuring. Kind even. "Because she was *wanting* her Uncle Dunc."

"Patrick was getting on with her just as well as you were!"

"Yeah, sure he was," said Duncan indulgently. He chuckled to himself. "And what about you Julio? You and Sarah made quite an item."

"They did *not!*"

"Dude, they were seriously digging each other. There was *massive* chemistry between them."

"I've got to say we did get on very well." Julius sat straight up against the wall, his arms crossed over his pale torso, evidently savouring the memory. "And Patrick, you said she's always had a soft spot for me."

I froze.

"Well..." He looked over at me guiltily. "I'm not sure."

"It doesn't matter," Julius said smugly. "She was certainly interested last night. She practically snogged me when we said goodbye."

"She couldn't have!"

"John," he said, blinking at me superciliously. "I think I know when a girl's got her tongue in my mouth."

"But we'd have seen it if she snogged you—"

"I pretty much saw it," said Duncan nodding.

"But… she can't have."

"Why not?" said Julius frowning.

"Because she'd already got off with me!"

"Hey!" said Duncan sounding impressed.

"She did not."

"She did *what?*" Patrick's eyes widened. "You *and* Julius."

"I'm sorry Pat. I was going to tell you."

"What do you mean: *got off with her?*" said Julius.

"None of your business."

"I thought so."

"Hang on—"

"Look," said Duncan to me. "I heard Sarah on the phone this morning and she was *hot* for Julius."

"She couldn't have been." My head was swirling. "I know what happened."

"Evidently not," smiled Julius. "And in any case I talked to her last so I think I'm in the best position to judge."

Suddenly I'd had enough. "Fine. *Whatever.* I'm sick of listening to your crap. I'm out of here."

"What do you mean?" said Patrick. He looked utterly spun out.

"I'm sorry, Patrick, but it's just not working."

"I agree," yawned Julius. "I've been thinking that for a while. Duncan and I had been planning to go our separate way as well."

"You *had?*" said Patrick.

"Don't worry, Pat," I said scowling at Julius. "I want you to come with me."

"Sorry," said Julius. "But you understand. I just don't think we can keep up the pretence any longer." He swung his legs round and sat up on the edge of his bed in his boxer shorts. Scratched a surprisingly hairy leg. "We should get up now," he said to Duncan. "I'm starving."

Patrick and I watched them in shell-shocked silence as they dressed.

"Right," said Julius when they were done. "Do you guys fancy some lunch?"

"We've already eaten," I said sourly.

"Suit yourself. See you later then. Or will you already be gone? If so can you leave some cash for the room?"

"Catch you back in England," said Duncan cheerfully.

Julius gave a little shrug to Patrick – *you know how it is, doesn't change anything between us* – and then he and Duncan were gone.

"Enjoy Naples!" I yelled down the stairs after them and then felt like an idiot. I clumped back into the room, pulled out my rucksack and started retrieving clothes from the floor. "Can you believe them?"

Patrick sat down on his bed.

"The cheek of them." I was furiously stuffing trousers, shirts, and underwear into my pack in any old order. "And he did *not* get off with Sarah. She doesn't even fancy him." I cleared my toiletries into my washbag and crammed it into the infeasibly small space remaining at the top of the rucksack. It was me she liked. I yanked the webbing straps as hard as I could to get it closed, to hold it together. I mean we'd almost had sex for Pete's sake.

But then why hadn't she dropped by or left a message?

Why had she left without saying goodbye?

I looked up feeling crosser than ever and then saw that Patrick was still just sitting there. "Come on, we need to get going."

He raised his face from his hands. "But where? Are we still going to Naples?"

"No, of course not. We're going to Venice."

"Venice?"

I hesitated and then realised it was a little late to be coy. "I agreed with Sarah that I'd meet her there in a couple of days."

"You did?" He didn't even sound that surprised any more.

"Yeah. So, I thought we could go up to Venice, get a nice pad and wait for the girls to arrive. Just the two of us and the two of them."

He made a face. "What's the point? Maya doesn't like me."

"Of course she does."

He looked at me and sighed. "I really like *her* you know."

"I know. And I really like Sarah. And if we meet up with them we've got a chance to do something about it. So why don't you get your stuff together and start thinking about what you're going to say to Maya when you see her in St Mark's Square."

4

There was a train at 1.30. It was reservations only but by the time we got to the station it was already twenty past so we thought we'd wing it.

We shuffled under the weight of our rucksacks straight to the platform. The train was there and we walked past first class and squeezed on where second began. Patrick stayed with our packs and I walked unhindered through the carriages to find a seat. But it was completely packed, and I ended up rejoining him in the connecting area between cars 5 and 6, along with a couple of young Italian women who'd just done the same tour of the carriages as me.

The doors closed and we moved smoothly away. A pair of ticket inspectors came by almost immediately and remonstrated that we needed reservations. But we just remonstrated back that we didn't speak Italian, safe in the knowledge that the next stop was Florence and we couldn't get kicked off till then. Eventually, one of the Italian girls stepped in and said a few calming words. The inspectors sighed and shrugged, clipped her ticket and her companion's, glared at our inter-rail passes and then left us alone.

"Thanks," I said.

"You're welcome." She was mid-twenties with thick brown curly hair. Now I looked closer, I saw her companion was much younger, maybe only sixteen, mousy blonde. "I told them you were medical students on your way to a conference on cancer," she continued smiling. "They were more understanding then."

"And what do you do?"

"I'm a medical student on the way to a conference on cancer."

Patrick and I laughed.

We all sat down on the floor, making ourselves as

comfortable as we could against the vibrating metal walls.

"I'm Carlotta Contarini," she said.

"John."

"Patrick."

I looked at the seventeen year old encouragingly. She stared back stony faced. *"Non parlo inglese,"* she said eventually, pointedly.

"Her name is Fran," said Carlotta. "She's my cousin." Fran just shrugged at us uninterestedly.

"Are you from Venice?" I asked.

"My family is and Fran lives there. I work and study in Rome. Now I must be rude and read through some of the notes I have brought with me." She pulled out a handful of papers and a pair of reading glasses. She said something to her cousin who huffed out a sigh, then stood up again and stared out of the window. Carlotta exchanged an amused glance with us and then settled down to read, putting her fingers in her ears.

I knew if we just sat there with nothing to do we'd spend the whole journey fretting about Sarah and Maya and the bust up with Julius, so I retrieved the two books I'd bought from my rucksack. I caught Carlotta's eye as she was looking up, thinking about a passage she had read. She smiled at me then concentrated on her paper again.

I opened Shaeffer's notebook to the translation at the back, looked at Patrick who nodded and I held it between us so that we could both see.

15 September 1570

We walked back from the beach retracing the steps by which we had come until we reached our horses. It being close to eleven o'clock, and the sun high, we servants, our blindfolds by now removed, proceeded to prepare some small repast from the victuals we had brought with us, and we ate them there and then, just some pieces of meat, and some cheese and bread and a draft of sweet Cyprus wine.

Our meal over, we saddled up to return to the city. We rode in silence and I fancy every man and not just this unworthy servant was thinking upon the sight he had seen. I felt even more certain of this as my master had not reproached me for my behaviour on the beach. And I was glad that there were no harsh words from him in the light of what was to follow.

We rode without break taking the same path we had the previous night but now we rode faster for we had the benefit of light, and in less than an hour we had covered the distance to the outskirts of the city. We approached from the south where the land though flat was strewn about with rocks and boulders. Although the previous night we had seen no sign of the Turks we made our approach with care for their scouts were already active in the area, and we knew that Mustafa Pasha's army would soon be making the march up from Nicosia.

Thus when we were yet half a league from the walls we stopped in a sheltered place and my master and I and Count Sigismondo and my friend Giuseppe, who was his servant, dismounted and leaving our horses with the remainder of the company, we walked forwards as an advance party to spy the land and to ensure our way was clear.

We made our way some two hundred yards through a rocky approach and then moved cautiously into the open on the other side, keeping low amongst the scrubby bushes and the blowing dust. We surveyed carefully but there was no sign of the Turk and the way over to the Limisso gate, some mile away, seemed clear. We stood up straight and signalled to the rest of our party with the wave of a red pennant. They signalled back and began to ride to us.

The four of us walked on a little further into the open still scanning the countryside for movement. The sun was high in the sky now and beat down on us, its light flashing from my master's polished breastplate. Suddenly over to my right, but a hundred yards distant, I caught the same glint amidst a clump of low rocks there. I turned and cried a warning but even as I did so there was a puff of smoke and my master fell to the ground with a musket ball smashed into him. As I ran to him more shots rang out and I threw myself to the ground crawling to his side. But the musket ball had blown a hole in his armour, a clean shot right in the centre of the breastplate guided by the faithless sun. His head was to one side and blood came from his mouth and I kissed him and closed his eyes for he was already dead.

There was continued fire onto us and the Count Sigismondo had also fallen. I could see from the continuing puffs of smoke that there were perhaps only ten Turks attacking us. I looked round to our horsemen and saw that they had assessed the situation the same and were riding on the Turks' position, fearless of their muskets. I saw the Turks stand up and wave empty hands signalling their cowards' surrender. Our company slowed accordingly but suddenly musket shots came from the left hitting two of our horses immediately. At the same time the Turks in front picked up their weapons again and began to fire now at close range and I realised a trap had been set for us and our lords were caught in a deadly cross fire.

From my position I could do nothing so I helped Giuseppe to drag Count Sigismondo towards the closest rocks which provided what cover there was. The Count was badly injured though still breathing. He bore a wound to his side where a ball had ripped through the seam of his armour but Giuseppe thanked God for the ball had not lodged inside him. He carefully removed his master's upper garments and cleaned the wound as best he could. Meanwhile I tore my linen shirt into strips and Giuseppe used them to bind the Count's side to staunch his blood.

About us the dust whipped into a cloud, the sun blazed down and all was confusion. Our horse had been split and two were galloping away riderless from the mayhem. On the ground I could see three bodies of our company. The remainder were still circling, reining their horses to control them, undecided whether they should press forward or retire to their original cover. But then Captain Bragadino spurred his mount and drew his sabre from its scabbard and cried aloud an exhortation to Venice and to God; and the others, encouraged, drew swords also and charged with him. They smashed into the enemy and my heart leapt as I saw the Turks cut down, their raised musket butts no match for the fury of Venetian steel. Our company broke them entirely and rode on through the flashing sun and the dust and the blood to the Limisso gate and safety.

I looked to Giuseppe with relief for their escape, but with a shared knowledge of what was to come next. For the Turks who had lain in

47

ambush whilst their fellows had allowed themselves to draw fire were now advancing upon us. There were a dozen of them and having fired off their muskets they now drew their cruel scimitars and ran forward through the dust.

Giuseppe and I drew swords also. And we sat Count Sigismondo up against a stone, for he was a little recovered, and drew his long knife for him and he was grateful and he held it before him determined to sell his life dear. Then Giuseppe and I embraced. For we were old friends from the same quarter in Verona, and we had played together when we were boys along with my brother Antonio. And we told each other that we would see each other in heaven that very day where we would be welcomed by St Mark and our good masters, mine already gone there. And Count Sigismondo laughed to hear us, for it raised all our spirits, though we could see that the effort pained him.

And then the Turks were upon us wielding their crescent blades high so that the sun shone along them like star gleams. We jumped back and onto the rocks. Two came at me at once and I swung my blade killing the first outright, clashing steels with the second. My arm jarred with the force but my higher ground told and I turned him and kicked him away. I felt a sharp pain in my back and twisted round. Another Turk had jumped onto the rock behind me but he struck before he was at balance and missed me. I jumped down and swung at his legs as he made to chop down onto me. I caught him first and he fell dead to the ground.

The Turks fell back, surprised by the fury of our resistance. I looked round and saw Giuseppe, his left arm thick with blood, standing over his master. The count was slumped, a scimitar thrust into him. Giuseppe wept openly out of love for him and anger too.

I called to him and we scrambled back onto the rocks and stood there together, our chests heaving, burning with the effort, our brows encrusted with dirt and blood and baked under the sun's high heat. "My master is dead," he said grimly. "And I will die with him rather than subject myself to the mastery of the Turk." I nodded and we embraced once more and stood there back to back now as the Turks came charging through the dust at us for the final time. All of them together, their scimitars aloft and yelling in their language terrible *impious words. They closed around us and though we fought back bravely, too soon they forced us from the rocks. I saw Giuseppe fall to the ground and then I was struck on the shoulder and fell also. I was on all fours and held out my sword one last time. To strike a final blow for my master and for Venice and for Giuseppe before I was killed. But my sword was knocked away and I was without defence. I closed my eyes and prayed to God and waited for the blow to fall.*

But it did not come, for blessed, uncalled for, my assailant was suddenly thrown aside in a clattering of hooves, his chest speared through by a lance and from it like some miracle of God appeared a banner bearing the winged lion of St Mark and it had not been touched by his bloody entrails or the dirt and was on a virgin white background still and he fell with the mighty power of Venice shown to him.

Captain Bragadino, for it was he who had returned to save us, most blessed of all captains which have ever served Venice, dropped the lance and drew his sabre and cut down two Turks with a blow this way and that. And my heart leaped for his charge had put our enemies into chaos. Looking round, I saw that Giuseppe that I had thought dead was alive still and I helped him to his feet for he was weak from his wounds. Captain Bragadino and his faithful horseman Zani wheeled their horses and cantered to us. I helped Giuseppe onto Zani's horse and then I clambered up behind Captain Bragadino himself and we galloped towards the gate. He had let none others risk themselves save him and his squire, and I almost cried in gratitude; and then I did cry in anguish as I thought of my dead master.

"What ails thee?" he inquired of me.

"My master, the Count Bugon, is dead, sire."

"Ah, this has proved a bitter day indeed. We have lost five by my reckoning. And there have been greater men, but one was my servant Alvise and I loved him. What is your name?"

"Girolamo Polidoro, sire."

"Polidoro, since you have lost a master today and I a servant, what say you to serving me?"

I was so overwhelmed that I could but nod and I struggled to hold back my tears. He looked over his shoulder at me and nodded also in satisfaction. "I will need a brave man with me in the days to come, Polidoro."

"Yes, sire," I blurted now. "And I vow to you that I will save you one day as you have saved me."

He laughed. "There will be plenty of occasion for that. The Pasha's army is almost upon us and the siege of Famagusta will begin in but a matter of days. Now hold to me tight, Polidoro. We must cross this open space to get to the walls and the enemy might be lurking for another attack." So I held close to my new master; he spurred his horse and we rode like the wind.

5

At Florence some seats came free and Patrick and I settled down at a table with Carlotta and Fran sitting opposite. Carlotta continued to read her papers. Her cousin took a pack of playing cards from her pocket and started to shuffle. It looked at first like she was going to deal them out for a game of patience but she didn't; she just kept shuffling, her hands moving lazily but precisely, her face toward the window, her bored expression turned away from us. The motif on the back of the cards was unusual and I inclined my head to see it more clearly: a blue-green background with a winged lion sitting above an *X*.

There were voices from down the corridor and the ticket inspectors appeared again. This time though they just glared at us and walked past.

On returning safe within the city walls I wanted no more than to lay down and sleep. But many things had to be done and were immediately asked of me once I was back. Captain Bragadino gave me but one hour to fetch my belongings from the Count Bugon's residence and to bring them and myself to his own servants' quarters. There I dressed myself in the manner of his household and was required almost immediately to attend upon his person.

He was weary after the battle and spoke little but there was one piece of news which was brought to him whilst I was there. The city of Kyrenia has surrendered without a shot being fired, unhappy tidings as Commandant Giovan-Maria Mudazzo and Captain Alfonso Palazzo had previously declared their intention of holding out as long as they could. It is clear that the Turks are now free to overrun the island at their leisure and that the only resistance will come from Famagusta.

16 September 1570
I went to see Giuseppe to take him news and was greatly pleased

to see that he was recovering from his wounds and his fever had passed. It heartened me to see him so well changed and I embraced him fondly. Yet he was still weak and, though able to stand, walking and fighting will surely be beyond him for some time.

17 September 1570

All is change. I have been detailed along with most of the able men and women in the city to work on the fortification of the walls. Hard work but necessary and I have been told to expect my duties will remain as such whilst the enemy is without.

Many Turks were riding to and fro today as we laboured on the battlements. They rode carrying on lances the heads of those killed in Nicosia. A sight that raised not terror but defiance in our hearts. They sent a messenger to parley with our commanders and ask them to surrender the city. This was of course refused and the messenger sent away. In the afternoon Turkish forces moved up in full to the outskirts of Famagusta bringing with them guns and timber and all manner of materials for war.

18 September 1570

We expect the Turks to attack at any time now. We have set in place what defences we can and now must wait upon the mood of the enemy and the mercy of God.

While time still remains to me I shall describe the layout of the city. The lines of fortification form an imperfect square with the harbour on the eastern side. The circuit of the fortress is some two and a half miles and the walls throughout are excellent and of stone. On the land side these are twenty feet thick with a ditch in front of it at least twelve paces broad.

At the four corners of the square are four bastions and overlooking the harbour is a fifth. Of the corner bastions, two face the sea and two the land. Of those facing the land the one in the south-west is a hexagonal tower. This is the Limisso gate and in front of it rises the ravelin which spans the surrounding ditch. Of the towers facing the sea, the Arsenal is on the south-east corner and the Signoria bastion is on the north-east.

Around the fortress the country is all perfectly flat. Only on the northwest and the north does the ground rise into low hills. This area is called the Grottoes and it was assumed that the enemy would base itself here because of its extensive caves in which a large number of men could be safely lodged. But it would seem that the rocky ground does not suit the Turks' fashion of camping and so instead they have spread their whole force on the south side of the city where it stretches for three miles from the city to the sea occupying the area known as the Gardens. This area used to be rich with orange, lemon and other fruit bearing trees, but we cut them down so that they might not profit the enemy. The Pasha himself, who is the leader of the Turkish forces on the island, still waits a league off in Pomo d'Adamo.

19 September 1570

The siege has begun. An advance guard of Turkish horse approached the gates and offered battle. General Astorre Baglione met them with cavalry and infantry at the Grottoes and battle ensued in which the Turks suffered heavy casualties. All is busyness. I will write more when I have time.

* * *

Patrick got up to get some drinks. We were just pulling out of Bologna and I watched from the window as our smooth acceleration left the city centre behind and turned it to suburbs and then green-brown farmland quicker than I thought possible. I gazed out at the flashing wheat fields and felt my eyes grow heavy. I blinked them open again and turned and saw that Carlotta had put her papers down. Her pair of reading glasses, big and brown like her eyes, were pushed up into her hair.

"Tired?" she asked.

I smiled and nodded. "You look tired too."

"Reading scientific papers is always tiring." She smiled and picked up Polidoro's journal. "May I?" She flicked through it. Fran looked round and her eyes flickered with momentary interest as she saw the book. She glanced up at me, looking me fully in the face for the first time. She watched me unblinking and unmoved by the smile I gave her, as though she were sizing me up or committing my face to memory, and then just as coolly, she looked away and started shuffling her cards again. Carlotta replaced the book before me. "Looks interesting. I didn't think you spoke Italian."

"We don't." I tapped Shaeffer's diary. "We have a translation in here."

"Very good." She sighed and looked at her watch. I noticed she had a big gold wedding band on her finger. Maybe I'd be married to Sarah one day. Then I remembered what Julius had said. Maybe not.

"Another hour and a half to go," she said. "You have been to Venice before?"

"No."

"You will enjoy it. Make sure you look out of the window as we come into the city. It's a good view."

"Thanks for the tip."

"Where are you staying?"

"We were going to just turn up and find a place."

"That may work in Rome," she said, "but not in Venice. Certainly not in August—" Her cousin whispered something in her ear. Carlotta smiled at the interruption. "A friend of my husband owns a hotel. If you are having difficulties, you could try it." She wrote the details in black biro in her notepad, ripped out the page and gave it to me. "If you go there, tell the owner he owes me a telephone call."

"I will. Thanks."

"You're welcome," and then she pulled the glasses down from her forehead and started to read again.

Patrick returned presently with a couple of cans of lemon San Pellegrino. He sat back in his seat and took a long draught. But I just played with the ring pull on my can. I couldn't get Sarah out of my head.

"You are OK with it aren't you?" I asked him abruptly. "I mean with me and Sarah. If there *is* a me and Sarah."

He looked at me and shrugged. "I guess so."

It wasn't exactly a ringing endorsement but maybe he was preoccupied with his own thoughts of Maya.

"Cool," I said eventually, uncomfortably.

1 October 1570

In the last week the Turks have built many siege towers around our walls and have begun to pound the city and harbour with heavy shot. The sound is deafening and unceasing. We are already exhausted yet are working continuously to ensure that our defences are full proof and all the people in the town, be they men, women or priests, assist in this regard. Thank God we have suffered only few casualties thus far as our walls are strong and have proved more than a match for even their biggest guns. And indeed today when the enemy moved its cannon round to fire upon the Limisso gate our batteries there returned fire and destroyed them.

3 October 1570

An explosion was heard today which shook all Famagusta. It came from the waters outside the harbour and at first we took this as a sign that the hoped for reinforcements from Venice had arrived. But as the day latened we realised this not to be the case and instead the defenders of the sea wall related that they had seen one of the Pasha's galleys, which had been anchored with the rest of the Turkish fleet blockading the harbour, explode into pieces and set two others alight. In the explosion they had seen a great number of bodies thrown in the air and the boards and oars and stuff of the boat cast to the four winds. We rejoiced greatly at this calamity which had befallen the Turks though we did not understand at this time the cause of it for our guns could not reach them where they were moored.

6 October 1570

We have seen the bulk of the Turkish fleet sail away today leaving just seven galleys to blockade our port. Captain Bragadino fears this is an evil sign that our naval forces are delayed for otherwise the Turks would not feel so free to leave the approaches by sea so lightly guarded. However, we still have hope and pray daily that relief will come, for the Turks have fully surrounded the city and whilst they have yet not made any dent in our stone armour, the chance to turn them and drive them from their camps and from this island would be welcome indeed; and for this we need the fighting power that will be brought by Venice and her allies of Spain and Rome.

10 October 1570

A captured Turk has told the story of the ship which exploded and the news he gave caused all men who heard it to weep openly and beat their breasts that God should allow such events to pass in Christian lands. For the galley was indeed one of the Pasha's and a special one at that for it was intended for the Sultan himself in Constantinople and was laden with booty from Nicosia. But amongst the gold and silver was something more precious by far: Italian and Greek children, enslaved, and being taken to satisfy an ugly greed. They were the sweet flowers of Nicosia, held in chains for the whim of the stinking Turk prince.

Yet for all the weakness shown in the defence of Nicosia, these child captives displayed greater spirit. One of the girls slipped her chains and rather than allow herself and her friends be taken into a life of slavery, set fire to the powder magazine and blew the ship and herself and her companions and the accursed Turks on board into so many pieces.

And though we wept openly for their sad fate we rejoiced at their courage and the fact that their suffering was at an end and that they were already with God in heaven.

As for the Turk who had told us this tale, so aroused were the passions of the men who had captured him that after his story was finished, they cut out his tongue so that he could speak it no more, and then, after many taunts, killed him with swords.

"That's enough for the moment," said Patrick hurriedly.

I nodded feeling a little sick.

"Look out of the window now," Carlotta said to us.

The train was swooping over the lagoon on the Ponte della Libertà from Mestre, and beside us on the road bridge a streak of traffic did the same. The water was wide and green. In the distance and growing steadily larger we could see the island of Venice, a smudge of brick red, but featureless at the moment. We were approaching from the north-west and out of the right hand window the concrete terminals of the modern harbour were the first thing to become distinct, container ships manoeuvring their way slowly around them, into and out of port. And then beyond that, far beyond it on the horizon was the longer shape, low in the water, of the Lido.

On either side we could see the smaller islands, dotting the water: Tessera, Campalto, San Secondo, Tresse, San Giorgio in Alga, and on the left a larger mass on Venice's shoulder: Murano. But still of Venice we could see nothing except the harbour and the Tronchetto car park hanging off it. These grew until they filled the view on the right hand side, whilst on the left there was just a glimpse of faded waterfront and some run down buildings, a dirty blur. And then we were alongside the Tronchetto itself and we caught a glimpse of the mass of cars and coaches and lorries queuing their way in, desperate for space, a mass of bustle without beauty. And then all too quickly the lagoon was behind us and we drew into the silent dark of Santa Lucia station.

"It wasn't quite how I was expecting it," said Patrick voicing my own disappointment.

Carlotta smiled. "You'll see," she said easing her way out into the aisle. "Enjoy your stay."

The younger girl barely glanced at us as she trailed after her cousin. But then at the last minute, just as she was leaving the carriage, she looked back over her shoulder. *"Arriverdeci,"* she mouthed.

We retrieved our rucksacks, helped each other into them and stepped awkwardly from the train, walking down the platform and onto the concourse. Santa Lucia was a modern station, concrete, high clean lines but featureless and ugly to my eyes. Unwelcoming. On the walls were graffitied police posters warning of the explosive dangers of unattended packages along with the grainy mugshot of what seemed to be an active terrorist. The concourse was dirty and packed with people and we had to jostle our way through to the exit and when we got to it my cumbersome pack caught in the long bar handle on the door so I had to spend several frustrating minutes untangling myself.

It had been a long journey and we were tired and hungry and disillusioned plus we still needed to find somewhere to stay that night. We trudged wearily down the concrete steps outside, surveying the featureless grey concrete piazza opening out before us and the grey pigeons and the grey chewing gum blotches underfoot.

And then we came to a halt.

Our eyes had been drawn upwards and we suddenly understood what Carlotta had meant. For there in front of us, coursing through our vision was the Grand Canal, an artery of vivid aquamarine in the afternoon sun, a shimmering plasma bearing corpuscles of vaporetti, motoscafi and traghetti along its vital pulsing length. To our left was the Ponte degli Scalzi, effortlessly spanning the water in a single graceful arch of its stone back. Directly in front, across the canal, rose the immense weathered dome of San Simeone, the stuccoed buildings to either side warm pink and orange and brown. And behind it all, backdrop to our vision, a sky of the deepest blue reared up to infinity.

6

It was almost six o'clock when we dragged ourselves away from the view over the canal and began to think about where to spend the night. We thought we may as well try the place Carlotta had recommended first. It was five minutes away in Campo San Geremia, a hotel called *Casa Tron*, a slightly faded two-star, but it seemed reasonable enough. However, the owner, who proudly announced that he was Signor Tron himself, shook his head when we asked for a room. Completely full, he said.

"But, you were recommended to us by a friend of yours."

"What friend?"

"Carlotta Contarini. She said for you to call her," I added desperately.

His eyes softened and his nose twitched. *"Carlotta, Carlotta…"*

"And there was another girl. Fran? Her cousin I think."

"The Morosini girl?" I shrugged but he was talking to himself. *"La futura,"* he muttered respectfully; then he gestured to us to wait and he had another look through his reservations book. OK, he said. He could give us a room he had been holding for someone else. He shrugged at us: business is business, and Venice is Venice.

He took us up to the room, right at the top of the building. It could best be described as adequate: two beds, basic furniture, no TV, but a small balcony – which was lucky because the room was hot and airless. It wasn't quite the pad we'd hoped for but we'd certainly stayed in worse. The price though made us wince: almost fifty pounds a night but as Signor Tron said again, not amazingly helpfully, *Venice is Venice*. We paid a night in advance and collapsed on our new beds.

We snoozed for a couple of hours until our hunger got

us up and out again. We picked our way through Cannaregio and, halfway along the busy shop-lined Strada Nuova, we found a McDonalds. Having split from Julius it was almost inevitable that we would go there. Patrick had a Big Mac meal and I had some fries and a slice of pizza from the Spizzico counter.

It tasted fantastic.

Patrick had been in a quiet mood since we'd left the hotel but I assumed he was just thinking about Maya. I was happy to be free of Julius's voice and sat there enjoying my simple edible pleasures in silence. I sucked on a huge cup of watery Coke wondering whether I should treat myself to another slice of pizza when Patrick suddenly asked, "What are we going to do later?"

"We could get a drink? There's an Irish Pub—"

"No. *Later*. When the summer's over."

"I don't get you. You know what we're doing. We're starting our PhDs."

"Oh right." He looked like it was news to him.

I shifted uncomfortably in my seat. "Aren't you looking forward to it anymore?"

"I guess so." But then he frowned. "Don't you sometimes feel like this holiday's the end of the safety net? School, degree: they're all finished when we get back home. Then it's like *real life*."

"But we'll still be students. It's not like we'll be working in an office or anything."

"But maybe a PhD won't be any better."

"Of course it will."

He nodded slowly and echoed me. "Of course it will." And then, brightly now, "Yeah, it'll be fine." He scooped up the last of his fries and gulped down some Sprite.

I watched him uneasily. He'd been doing this a lot recently: quiet for long periods followed by bursts of chatter. Although, in a way, he'd always been a bit like that… And he was right: it *was* kind of scary that school and degree were all over; but doing research would be great.

He thumped down his empty cup. "You know what I'm going to do? I'm going to take a look at Polidoro's code. I bet you I'll be able to crack it."

I laughed, pleased to see him positive again.

"You'll see," he said seriously but then he grinned too.

We didn't bother with a drink in the end and decided on an early night. The room was hot so we threw open the doors to the balcony. But the air outside was heavy and still. Patrick began looking at the code but started yawning almost immediately and, mumbling that he'd crack it in the morning, he placed the book carefully on the floor, curled up on top of his sheets and fell asleep.

I lay in my boxer shorts and read more of the translation until midnight and then switched my light off. I'd been tired anyway but I'd wanted to get really exhausted from reading so that I would go straight to sleep. But in the darkness I thought immediately of Sarah. *"What do you think?"* She was naked before me and I felt myself catch my breath; then shook my head. Now we were in Venice, my optimism was starting to subside. *"What do you think?"* I didn't know what I bloody thought. She confused me. Julius confused me.

I tried to block her out but when I was at last having some success and was on the verge of dropping off I became aware of a mosquito flying round the room, the sound of it like a high pitched electric saw, distracting in the extreme, circling around me for hours it seemed.

Eventually though I slept, waking only once, in the middle of the night, when I sat up, my mouth and throat dry in the airless heat. Patrick was standing on the balcony in just his boxer shorts, a dark shape against the night. He stood there for some time, motionless, looking out, perhaps getting a breath of air. He was still standing there when I lay down again and went back to sleep. But when I awoke in the morning he was lying back in the bed next to mine, snoring contentedly and I did not think to mention it.

7

20 April 1571

My master Captain Bragadino spoke today to the men of Famagusta:

"Why, my brave comrades, have you come here from a far distant country, exposing yourselves to great danger in so long a voyage if not to earn the supreme honours of war? Now the chance which you have so eagerly desired is put before you. For this city is assailed and encompassed by foes of great repute, and the result of this siege is watched throughout the world. And my confidence in you, citizens and others who are enrolled among our troops is no less great. Your generous hearts will never allow that in the defence of what is your own – your wives, your children, your goods – that others should take the lead. Do not let the enemy's numbers frighten you. They are certainly less than we hear by report, or than what is indicated by the pompous array of empty tents. Most of them, or at least the bravest of them, are exhausted by toil, or have returned home to enjoy the riches acquired in the siege of Nicosia. What happened in that city should wake in you vigilance rather than alarm, for we know that it was not the valour or industry of the enemy which gave them victory, but the negligence of the besieged, who appear to have thought that walls alone, not the stout hearts of men are the bulwarks of cities. But besides the confidence which rests on mere human resolve, we have a livelier hope of deliverance and victory, in that we are defending a just and pious cause against treacherous foes, to whom God's providence has so far allowed some measure of success, so that with a change in the fortune of war their fall may be the greater. We then have every argument, human and divine, to persuade us to drive fear from our breasts and to hope for a good and prosperous issue to our efforts."

All present greeted his words with loud cheering.

"Backtrack, backtrack," said Patrick. "How did we get to April?"

It was one o'clock and we were on the narrow triangle

of land called the Customs Point which jutted out from Santa Maria della Salute. We sat against the lamppost at the end, looking out onto the water. On the right we could see the end of Giudecca and the island of San Giorgio Maggiore, and on the left the brick red tower of the Campanile in St Mark's Square, where we had been just a couple of hours before.

We had been up by nine and had gone down to breakfast together. Patrick was cheerful and in a talkative mood again, excited about exploring Venice. In Julius's absence we thought we would get the full tourist experience and do what the guidebook recommended and so we caught the Number 1 water bus from outside Santa Lucia station all the way down the Grand Canal, an eye-popping miracle of a journey in which every cliché from film and TV special was suddenly set before us in bobbing sunlit reality: a jaw-dropping blur of boats (speedboats and fishing boats and gondolas and water buses) and palaces (Foscari and Fontana and Dandolo) and churches and houses and museums and bridges and everywhere *glimpses:* of watery alleyways and markets, of terraces and back rooms; glimpses of life and activity, bustle under the blue sky all wrapped in multi-coloured plaster and tile and sparkling ultramarine.

It took forty glorious minutes to reach St Mark's square. We went by it first on the water, averting our eyes in an attempt at delayed gratification, and got off at San Zaccaria and then walked back; past the high-end hotels on the quay (our inter-railing eyes popping enviously), and the colonnaded lower floors of the Doge's Palace and finally passing between the twin columns bearing St Theodore and the winged lion of St Mark into the Piazzetta and the main piazza of San Marco beyond.

We walked around soaking it in: gawping at those taking coffee at Florian's, kicking at the pigeons, and marvelling at the front of the basilica itself with its four horses perched on top. We did not go in as we were saving that for the next day when the girls turned up; but we did join the hour long queue to go up the Campanile and look out over Venice in its entirety, enraptured still by its beauty and entirely satisfied by its spectacle laid out before us.

It was from there that we saw Santa Maria della Salute and the golden ball of the Customs Point glinting in the sun. It seemed like a haven from the bustle of St Mark's, so coming down we made a foray into the interior to buy a few provisions, then returned to San Zaccaria and got the Number 1 going back the other way to Salute.

"How did we get to April?" Patrick asked again. He had been sitting for the last hour with Polidoro's journal in front of him, making notes about the code on scraps of paper.

"Well, between October and March the siege continues. All through the winter the Turks make assaults and the Venetians defend. But the city walls are too strong for the Turks to make any headway. So stalemate. Then in January a relief convoy of ships captained by Marcantonio Quirini manages to get through the Turkish blockade. Sixteen ships bring reinforcements and food and there's huge rejoicing when he arrives. He sets about raiding Turkish positions on the coast and harrying the enemy generally and it puts real heart into the city. In February Quirini sets sail again for Crete, taking the children of the city with him to safety and promising to return with a bigger fleet from the garrison there soon.

"Then what?"

"Oh a few scraps and skirmishes." I flicked through the journal and called out a couple of highlights. "*Fourteenth March: five Turkish galleys are wrecked in a storm within the harbour. Twenty-second March: a magazine of cotton close to the powder store catches fire*. Stuff like that. And all the time they're clinging to the hope of reinforcements from Venice.

"On the 30th March eighty Turkish galleys arrive

bringing massive reinforcements. All through April they build a network of trenches around the city and when they're finished the trenches are so deep that the Turkish cavalry can ride through them unseen. In response the Venetians are doing all they can to strengthen the walls.

The enemy draws closer to the walls, yet we are making preparations daily. The whole city is working together to strengthen the parapets, prepare new shelters and to repair the old. We have thrown ourselves fully into this work: every hour has its toil but every day shows new improvements, new designs. Our batteries are reinforced with guns cast on the spot and chemists have prepared fireworks to be used against the enemy.

"Behind the scenes difficult decisions have to be made. In the middle of April, Bragadino takes an inventory of supplies and then orders 5000 Greek non-combatants to leave the city taking only a day's provisions each. And they get searched on the way out to make sure they're not carrying any extra food."

"A bit harsh."

"Though Polidoro does say the Turks allowed them through their lines and let them go off to their villages. After this full rationing comes into force:

Rations are now under the sole charge of Captain Laurence Tiepolo. All our bread is baked at one oven in the Arsenal. All barley, spelt and straw having being now exhausted, horses of the cavalry are fed on bran. Wine is also being rationed and is very scarce and where available is at such a high price that only the nobles can afford it. We others manage now on a mixture of vinegar and water. Salted meat and rice are prepared in a great central kitchen for all the troops so that they may have full bellies for this great fight. On meatless days they are served beans cooked in oil. During the day oil and vinegar are distributed for refreshment and I assist in this. The city is confident that as long as a crumb of food remains Captain

Bragadino will distribute it and even when it is all gone there will still remain his good will to sustain us.

"Then Bragadino makes that speech to cheer everyone up. Bragadino, Baglione and Tiepolo take up their quarters within the bastions in the perimeter to be close to the troops. Meanwhile the Turks have built huge wooden towers to batter the city walls from close range and even when the defenders manage to destroy one they just repair it within a couple of days. The defence gets ever more desperate:

In the city powder has begun to run short and has to be used with care so that our gunners have been forbidden to fire without express orders from their commanders and these are only given when absolutely necessary. The chief means of harassing the enemy lies in the fireworks which we hurl down on them from the walls, throwing them into disorder and killing many. Iron balls too have been used, full of very fine powder, which when they burst can kill many Turks simultaneously yet despite these devices we cannot keep the enemy away from the walls, and they have begun to dig under them in several places and lay mines there, especially near the Arsenal.

"By the end of June the Turkish bombardments are incessant:

They keep up a never-ending fire from mortars throwing balls of enormous weight high over the walls and into the city where they fall on houses destroying the roofs and killing the inmates. Yesterday they also shot off a shower of arrows aiming high so that they fell perpendicularly on the heads of those who stood within and near the walls. And over the last week they have kept sounding the alarm, especially at night time as though they were coming to attack. In short they have never allowed us an hour's rest.

"New breaches in the walls are appearing daily. The

nights are spent trying to patch them up, so the defenders are exhausted. Polidoro speaks of:

> ... a *creeping tiredness which has permeated everyone so that we walk through the city not greeting or speaking to anyone unless it is to assist in some task which is our next defensive duty.*

"Everyone in the city is involved: the women, the priests, even the bishops. But things just get harder and harder."

"So when does it finally change? When do the Venetians finally send reinforcements?"

"They don't."

He blinked at me. "But I thought the Venetians won the siege?"

I gave him a wan smile. "On the 21st June a mine blows a large gap in the wall by the Arsenal tower. Six assaults are made and all repulsed. On the 29th June another part of the wall is breached and simultaneous assaults are staged. The Venetians fight these off as well. But then on the 7th July the Turks land more heavy guns and even more reinforcements begin a round-the-clock bombardment. On the 9th July comes the all-out assault. It rages all day: wave after wave of Turks throwing themselves into attacks on the walls:

> *The Turks fought furiously, inflamed by their desire to gain the city. But our men kept well together and we have held our ground with desperate courage. I was in the bastion of the Arsenal and the bitterest day it was for much of the fighting was hand to hand and we were weary even at the outset. The assault continued for five full hours but we met it bravely.*
>
> *Because of the fierceness of the fighting we only heard of how the other parts of the defence fared later in the day. The worst news came from the Limisso gate. There our soldiers were thrown into disorder by the enemy's fireworks and were still engaged with the enemy and*

suffering very severe losses when at other sections of the walls the battle was almost done.

At last they had to give way and the Turks coming onto them began to scale the ravelin—

"What's a ravelin?"
"Dunno. Some kind of fortification I suppose…"

—which if they continued would allow them access into the city itself. And so with no other defence available, the commanders took the terrible decision to fire a mine which they had themselves dug under the ravelin against such an emergency. On the ravelin stood crowded together troops from the enemy's camp and our own fine soldiers, charging and retreating, and in an instant as the mine was fired, friend and foe alike were buried in the ruins.

The ravelin lost, there remained between besiegers and besieged only the breadth of the second line of defence constructed of casks and sacks full of earth. But Captain Baglione urged the soldiers to fight and, full of daring and with his own hands, he tore from a Turkish standard bearer a flag taken in the siege of Nicosia on which were blazoned the arms of Venice. And somehow, through dint of our soldiers' blood and a firm belief in the rightness of our cause, the Turks were repulsed.

But still they devised yet a new way to harass our men whose troubles and difficulties were already unbearable. They filled the whole space between the gate and the ravelin with firewood and fascines and set the stuff on fire. Our soldiers at that part of the walls were sorely tormented with the heat and with the stench of a certain wood grown on the island called by the peasants tezza which gives out a strong and most unpleasant odour. This fire has lasted for now many days and there is nothing we can do to extinguish it, try as we might.

"They're really in a bad way now. There are no medicines to tend the wounded and all the food is gone:

We are driven through hunger to eat the flesh of the dogs and the cats and the rats now, even though the taste of them is nauseous to us.

But we have no choice for the pain of hunger gnaws at us constantly and if God in his wisdom were to send a plague of locusts to try us yet further, we would eat them as well.

"It was only now that hope finally died in them and they realised that help from Venice wouldn't come. They knew there was no point resisting further and to fight on would simply be to throw more lives away. So, on the 1st August, a white flag was raised over Famagusta and the City surrendered."

We sat in silence looking out over the water at Venice and beyond. It was three o'clock in the afternoon on a warm August day and the scene before us, the bright water and the beautiful buildings, felt a million miles from Famagusta.

"But why didn't Venice help them?" asked Patrick eventually.

"Maybe they thought the whole thing was hopeless from the start."

"They should have at least *tried*." He sniffed. "So what happens to Polidoro in the end?"

"I'll tell you when I'm done." I flicked the remaining few pages. "How are you getting on with the code?"

"Pretty good. I'm sure I can crack it."

I smiled at him.

"The trick is that it's old so it must have been a relatively simple code. I think it's a straight monoalphabetic cipher."

"And what's that?" I said happy to think about something different.

"It's where each letter in the coded document corresponds to a single letter in the original. So if A is encoded as F, then every time you see an F in the code you know it was an A in the original."

"Aren't they all like that?"

"No. The harder ones are where an A will be sometimes represented by an F, sometimes by a Q or whatever. It changes according to some pattern, which is known as the key. That's called a *poly*alphabetic cipher."

"Oh right," I said vaguely, taking the book from him and looking at the code properly for the first time, at the pages of seemingly random letters stretched out before me. It was difficult to believe there was any order to them at all: *V E L G A S A G A I I...*

"The problem is," said Patrick frowning, "is that if it *were* that simple then someone – this Henry Shaeffer for instance – would already have cracked it and so would have found the treasure."

"If there really was a treasure."

He looked at me in surprise. "Of course there's a treasure. It's just whether anyone's cracked the code and gone and dug it up yet. But in any case *I'll* crack it. And then maybe we should take the girls on a little trip to Cyprus..." He smiled at me and to himself and at his scraps of paper. "Can I borrow Shaeffer's notebook for a bit? There could be some comments in there about the code. Could save me some time."

I handed it to him then turned my face into the warm breeze blowing off the water, closed my eyes, starting to relax at last.

"OK, listen to this," Patrick said, leafing through. "Dum-de-dum – boring, boring – saying what he's doing in Italy—"

I flicked an eye open. "What *is* he doing in Italy?"

Patrick looked at me like I was wasting his time. "I'll tell you," he said grudgingly.

4 January 1915
It is four months since I left you in Cambridge. It was raining that day and it sometimes feels like it has been raining ever since I arrived here in Venice. It has been four weeks since I was moved from Rome and though in geographical theory I am closer to the front

line and therefore closer to action, in reality I am trapped still within this netherworld of diplomacy. Italy dithers. That she chose not to enter the war on the side of her ally Germany naturally gives us cause for thanks as it reduces the pressure on beleaguered France. But why does she not come out and outright declare war on Austria Hungary?

"Are you sure you want to hear all this?"

"It shouldn't take you too long." I stretched out in the sunshine.

In Rome we had spent weeks talking with the generals of the Italian army, talking with the senior admirals of the navy, talking with the Italian minister of war and his staff; in short, talking to all who would listen, or at least allow us to talk (there is unfortunately a distinction to be drawn there my darling) in an attempt to get the powers that be to understand that by attacking Austria Hungary they would have the perfect opportunity to annex the Italian speaking areas of the South Tyrol and Trieste, as well as strengthening her hand in the Adriatic generally. But, alas, so far these compelling arguments have fallen on deaf ears and after another hour's talking we are offered a small cup of strong coffee or a glass of grappa and a smile and a nod that they have heard what we have been saying (again, alas, my darling Anna, all too different to having listened).

And so another day would pass. But at least in Rome there was the Pantheon and the Vatican and the Colosseum and the Forum and any number of places of rich culture. And at least in Rome the sun shone and the heat warmed me through if not right to my heart then at least all other parts of the body. And at least in Rome there was food and drink in rich abundance and variety which could salve my lust for home and my deep desire to see and hold you again.

But now I am here in Venice at the British consulate. Four weeks of unremitting boredom. Ignore what I have told you in my letters. I have been diplomatic about my post as second assistant military attaché here. It is my job to be diplomatic after all so there is no reason why I should not continue as such in my missives. The work here is dull. There are not even the regular meetings to look forward to, however frustrating I found them in Rome. There is simply intelligence (a singularly inappropriate term) to review, translation (which I do with none of your flair) of intercepted telegraph transmissions and some code breaking. This last I do enjoy but there is too little of it to occupy us for very long.

"Oh," said Patrick. "So he's got a background in codes."
"See, I told you it would be interesting."

And the rest of the time we pore over maps of the area so that I believe I really am now an expert on that whole cursed area from the Piave to the Tagliamento to the Isonzo and the Gulf of Trieste.

Oh, how I long that events had taken a different turn and that instead of being seconded here – and if I could not be back with you my darling – at least I could have been with Rupert and the rest of the Royal Naval Division. Though they are back in England now they have at least seen action in Antwerp. If it were not for my facility with Italian I would be with them still.

"Who's Rupert?" I asked yawning. It was warm and entirely pleasant lying there in the sunshine whilst Patrick read from the notebook.
"Some mate of his maybe? I don't think he's mentioned

him before."

And although I would not do anything to risk myself and my chances of seeing you and little Frances again, still I am loath to think that I shall spend this whole war (and it could last a whole year more yet!) in a small consular outpost in Italy whilst on the battlefields of France and Belgium so many are fighting and dying.

And Venice itself reduces me to tears of boredom. When there is little work – which is often – and little conversation to be had – which is oftener still since the consulate is small and Captain Hargreaves is a man of few interests and will not even play a game of cards with me because he does not approve – then I wander abroad in Venice. But what a difference from Rome. Though Ruskin might be besotted with this place I am not. It is drab my darling, grey and stained from the constant wet. And I care not for the canals, which alternately flood and stink and the architecture I find dull and leaden and not to my taste. Where is the music or the food or the laughter of Rome? Where are the fine buildings and hills? Above all, where is the sun? This greyness, wet and unremitting, is making me sick. And in truth, my love, this role I have here and the city and my colleagues and everything that is not your arms and sweet breasts and my daughter's smile is slowly killing me and stealing the energy and life from me.

"I'm getting bored of this now."

"Fine." I forced my self to sit up so that I didn't fall asleep which would have really annoyed him. "But can you just see if there's an explanation of how he got hold of Polidoro's journal?"

He screwed up his face as though this was all taking a

huge effort. "OK. But after that I'm fast forwarding to the code stuff."

7 January 1915
My darling Anna

At last a day of interest for me. I was walking without purpose in Dorsoduro when I happened on a street called Rio Terra Antonio Foscarini which led down to San Agnese. On this street were many bookshops, and books being one of the few things which make Venice (or any other very dull place) bearable, I selected a shop which appeared from the window display to be the oldest and hence to my mind the most interesting, and entered.

Inside I fell into discussion with the owner, a tall and wiry man with a white stripe in his black hair that reminded me of a badger. From his skin he was probably old, perhaps seventy even, but his eyes were bright and alert. He asked me whether I was looking for any book in particular and I told him no, but that I had been in Venice four weeks and that since it had rained every day of that four weeks and seemed likely to continue raining for another four, that I would require something to occupy my mind.

He looked at me inquisitively, his head to one side as though he were sizing me for a suit and then he asked me to tell him something about myself so that he might select something suitable for me. So I told him of my background in Classics at Cambridge. "My specialities are of course Latin and Greek but I have a love for all languages and have found particular pleasure in archaic scripts such as Egyptian hieroglyphs. I find them a challenge."

At that he nodded. "You like codes and puzzles?"

"Of course. You could say they are my business." This was loose talk from me I know, but he seemed harmless.

His eyes were positively dancing now. "I have just the book for you. It is a journal. The Italian is of a slightly old form but you should have no difficulty with it."

"And what is this book?"

"It is by Girolamo Polidoro, one of the minor heroes of Venice past, and present at the siege of Famagusta as servant to Marco Antonio Bragadino. You are aware of the story?" I nodded. "Well, this journal was written by Polidoro during the battle for that city."

"That is interesting," said I not interested in the least. "But I have read much on the history of Venice already. The present of Venice is so damp that it has allowed me to become well acquainted with its past. A noble history to be sure, but I am looking more for a work of fiction, perhaps an adventure—"

"Yes, a noble history," he interrupted, stressing the word "history" strangely and I thought for a moment that I had misunderstood him. "But," he continued, and his eyes were fired with passion, "this journal is more than that. Polidoro's is a first hand account. He was there when the city was besieged." He leaned across the counter to me. "And he was also present when a great treasure was hid before the siege to safeguard it from the Turks. The ending of the journal, written in code, gives the whereabouts to that treasure." He stood up straight again. "So they say."

By this time he had my interest. "What is this treasure?"

"A wondrous piece in gold and gems originally from Constantinople."

"And did Polidoro himself recover this treasure?"

"No. On his final return to Venice in 1588, he was questioned by the Council of Ten but he did not have the treasure with him. After that, so the story goes, he went to live with his brother in Verona and never left the Republic again."

"So the treasure is still in Cyprus somewhere?"

"Perhaps. A treasure that if found would be beyond price." He looked me up and down. "But of course if you would rather have a good adventure or a romance—"

"No. This sounds just what I need to keep me sane in the likely event that the rain does not stop."

"Very good. I will fetch the book for you." He disappeared into the interior of the shop and returned with a thin calfskin bound book. It looked old and the pages were printed in large type, yet the whole thing was no more than one hundred pages. The last six were clearly in code as the letters were all capitalised and arranged with no break.

"I hope you enjoy it, Signor," he said and he wrapped the book and handed it to me with a smile, his eyes again showing bright in his old face.

"Thank you," I said taking it and putting it into my portfolio so that it would be protected from rain. I shook his hand and turned to go.

"Signor," he called after me as I opened the door and paused, confronted with the curtain of relentless water outside. "Remember to return and let me know if you find the treasure."

I laughed and said, "Of course," and bade him farewell. But the light had gone out of his eyes and he was already disappearing again into the interior of the shop.

I took the book home and unwrapped the paper and held it in my hands. The leather binding seemed suitably aged and the papers inside were thick and with uncertain edges as though the paper was handmade. I had no idea by looking at it whether it was genuine or not as I am not an expert in these matters, but if it affords me some diversion then I will not care.

I looked at the first page and began to translate. The Italian is easier than I thought, not Venetian dialect, but a recognisable Italian so I am making good progress. I will copy my translation in full into the back of my journal so that when you receive it you will be able to correct my work and calm my over-florid style; but in brief it does indeed appear to be a journal by one Girolamo Polidoro and refers explicitly to his time in Famagusta in Cyprus. I say appears to be for I must be guarded about the provenance of such a work in printed form. There is no clue on the frontispiece – not even a printer's mark which I would have thought unusual – as to whether Polidoro himself sought to have his thoughts captured for posterity in this way or whether it was some admirer – contemporary or later – who performed the act for him. And whether this admirer has already broken the code which sits at the end and has found this great treasure (if it even exists or ever existed) is yet another question unanswered. I confess I have already looked at these encoded pages since you know I find such things irresistible, the encrypted letters carrying a mysterious beauty of their own: V E L G A S A G A I I... And I have tried a few usual tricks to see how I get on (like shifting each letter by one in the alphabet to see if words drop out) but to no avail. But I realise that I am getting ahead of myself, and that what I must first do is translate Polidoro's words to provide me with a proper context which will no doubt allow me to break the code eventually anyway. (Oh Anna: I am <u>unbearably</u> confident when I am drawn into something, is that not so?)

And so to work. I shall produce a translation and

you shall review it. For the first time since I have been in Venice I feel I have a purpose and that my time can profitably be spent and my mind engaged so that it does not dwell on how much I miss you. To work then, my love. To work.

8

We went to McDonalds again that night and reprised our previous day's meal. But our normal roles were reversed in that Patrick, engrossed in the code, was happy to talk and I was content to listen and think of other things.

I'd finished the last of my fries when I finally asked him the question I'd been mulling all day. "Do you think the girls will show up tomorrow?"

"Did Sarah say she would?"

"Well yes but—"

"Then she'll show up." His mood had been getting more and more upbeat as he shuffled his little slips of paper and pored over Shaeffer's notebook. "Oh yeah, they'll definitely show up. I can't wait to see Maya again. I'm going to tell her all about Polidoro's code and the cross and—"

"How can you be so sure though?"

"Well Sarah got off with you didn't she?"

I felt myself colouring. "Well, *yes*… But what about all that stuff with Julius?"

"Who cares? Julius and Duncan'll be in Naples by now." He chuckled callously but then we both jumped as an alarm started ringing in the restaurant. I looked around and saw the other customers and the waiting staff were hurrying for the door. We'd finished anyway so rushed after them outside into the street. The manager shooed us back from the glass shop front.

"What's going on?" I asked one of the staff, a short dark Italian my kind of age.

"Paura di una bomba," he said. "A bomb scare."

"Really?" I looked around anxiously.

"Yeah. But don't worry."

Patrick and I exchanged a glance. "I mean it's a bit worrying," Patrick said.

"No, no, there have been many recently in Venice. The

American shops like us. A couple of little ones have gone off but no one's been hurt. They just don't like us being here."

"Who's they?"

"Take your pick. Right wing. Left wing. *Mafia.*" He shrugged. "But it's OK. Life goes on. It's not like it was ten years ago. Bologna station. *Mamma mia.*"

At that moment a group of black uniformed Carabinieri turned up. Two started talking urgently to the manager, who beckoned over the employee we'd been speaking with. The other Carabinieri started making a cordon around the McDonalds pushing us back along with the other customers and assorted passers-by who'd stopped to gawp. After a few moments of inactivity though the crowd started to disperse and we went with them, happy to be walking away.

It had been a bit unnerving. It wasn't like we weren't used to bomb scares and actual bombs back home – there had been that big bomb at the Baltic Exchange only a few months before – but somehow it felt different when you were on holiday.

We found ourselves wandering through some back streets, and though we probably could both have done with a drink, we couldn't find a bar nearby. So in the end we just returned to the hotel room. Which felt nice and safe; though I did still allow myself a jolt of spite towards Julius who always seemed to know the right places to go, almost by instinct. I resolved that by the time the girls were with us the following day I would be an expert in these matters too. So after we crashed out I studied my guidebook looking for restaurants and bars that we would impress Sarah and Maya. And all the while Patrick continued to study Henry Shaeffer's notebook for leads on how to break Polidoro's code.

Patrick switched his light off first.

The room was hot and close again and I couldn't sleep.

It wasn't the bomb scare that was keeping me awake. I'd

actually relaxed pretty quickly after we got back to the room. And we certainly hadn't heard any explosions so I just chalked it down to being one of those things.

What was keeping me awake was Sarah.

My heart thumped uncontrollably at the thought of meeting her again. I saw her raised eyebrow and her eyes and her smile. My blood was slamming through me. I heard her voice. Tomorrow seemed a lifetime away.

I got up quietly and tiptoed round to Patrick's bed and picked up Shaeffer's notebook from beside it; then lay down again to read till I fell asleep.

1st August 1571

The Pasha has sent his envoys to negotiate our surrender. The whole city dares to rest a while now and at last we sit in groups and speak in gentle voices without fearing for our lives and without our ears being assaulted by the din of war. When we look at each other we smile for, though we have been defeated, we feel no dishonour and there is just a dull joy that it is over at last.

2nd August 1571

Food has been sent into the city by the Pasha and to eat again of wholesome meat and bread has lifted our spirits immeasurably. All through the city the talk is of the truce. For Mustafa Pasha has shown a noble character and has granted us safe passage from the island and his own ships will bear us to Crete. To this end, forty galleys today entered the harbour and the sick and the wounded have started to embark; though I am glad to say that Giuseppe considered himself well enough to stay in the city for the moment and help me with my works. Of those Greeks amongst us, the Turks have said that they will allow them to stay unmolested on the island if they so wish. It is an honourable settlement and certainly we will not share the same fate as the citizenry of Nicosia.

The Turkish troops who entered the camp were well-behaved for the most part. When they saw our men they were astonished that we had held the city for so long with so small a company. But even more amazing was it for us when we could finally put our heads above the parapets and survey the prodigious numbers that were in the Turkish camp.

Everywhere we looked, for over three miles from the city they stretched in a vast circuit; the area so full of troops that the turbans, which on every side showed white above the trenches, covered the ground like snow flakes.

9

In retrospect it had clearly been a mistake to arrange to meet in St Mark's but it was only when we got there that I realised quite how fundamentally flawed the plan was. Because the Piazza was, of course, completely stuffed with people. Quite why this hadn't occurred to me the previous day when we'd walked through it I'm not sure but it took me by surprise in a way I found almost touching as we stood there and looked out and into and in between some twenty thousand people. Was it twenty thousand? More? Less? I didn't know but at points when they would surge one way and the next like flocking birds it seemed like all the tourists in Venice were packed into St Mark's.

"We'll never find them," said Patrick with an air of finality.

Since this is what both of us had been thinking for the previous fifteen minutes there seemed little to say in response. And indeed we had said little that morning apart from occasional talk about the journal. I assumed he was feeling the same ever-present stomach prickle of nerves as me. I was going to see Sarah again. He was going to see Maya. We didn't speak about it. We didn't need to. And the vague and nagging memory that in the middle of the night I had watched Patrick walk out onto the balcony again I just put down to a dream.

"Will we?"

To add to our difficulties it had also started to drizzle and with those first few spots of rain any meagre sight lines we might have had disappeared in a flurry of rising umbrellas, the Piazza becoming an impenetrable expanse of bobbing black picked out here and highlit there in luminous yellow and Day-Glo red and Burberry check.

"Of course they may not even be here."

I winced. Which would have been worse? That Sarah

was there somewhere in the midst of all those tourists; or that she'd never intended to come in the first place. "Oh where are they?" I ended up saying.

It started to rain more heavily and from the square a thin mist began to rise. As the rain increased so did the numbers of people huddling with us under the arches of the Procuratie Nuove at the southern end of the Piazza, until there were so many that we were being jostled and elbowed from all sides. I bore this reasonably stoically but when someone jabbed their umbrella into my thigh, that was the last straw. I spun round ready to vent my annoyances on whichever cursed tourist was responsible; but saw only Sarah standing there before me. "You two are hopeless," she said pealing with laughter.

A huge surge of relief and happiness washed over me. *"Hi!"* My carefully prepared speeches and cool openings evaporated in the delight which filled me. *"Hi."* I didn't know whether to kiss her or not but she settled that for me by leaning forward and giving me a peck on the cheek.

"Great to see you again," she said. "You enjoying Venice?"

"It's amazing," I gushed. "I'm so glad you came."

"Me too. Hi Cuzz. How are you?" She gave Patrick a kiss as well.

"Where have you been?" he asked in a cross sounding voice.

"Where have I been? I've been right here for the last ten minutes and poking John in the back for the last five. You're either the politest person in the world or you have no sensation in your legs."

"Sorry," I said happily. "I thought you were a tourist."

"I am a tourist." She laughed and brushed a hand through her spiky blonde hair, sending a fine shower of water droplets into the air. I smiled what I hoped was my winning smile at her. She smiled back, but when she looked at Patrick it faded on her face. "What's up with you?"

"Nothing." He coughed. "Where's Maya?"

Sarah's smile returned. "She's back in the room. She's sick."

"Oh…" The breath escaped from him, his sullenness transforming to open disappointment. "Oh."

"She picked up a bug in a restaurant in Bologna. She should be OK by this evening though."

"Oh that's good," I said and then, *not* smoothly, but if I hadn't done it then I'd have lost my nerve, "By the way, I got you a present." I pulled out a small wrapped parcel from my anorak pocket.

"You're kidding me." She looked genuinely touched. She carefully peeled the paper from it, leaving the tan leather of Polidoro's journal in the palms of her hands.

"It's by a guy called Girolamo Polidoro," I said excitedly as she started to turn the pages.

"I know him. He was at Famagusta with Bragadino and after of course—"

"Well then you know all about it!" I looked at Patrick delighted. "It's his account of the siege. I figured you might like it."

"Like it?" She clasped it to her breast. "I love it. It's the most amazing present." She gave me a kiss and a hug.

"It's four hundred years old you know," said Patrick trying to be helpful. "And it was really expensive."

Her eyes flicked up in surprise. "How expensive?"

Patrick looked at me suddenly apologetic.

"Well… it was a hundred quid," I said eventually, reluctantly. "But—"

"Oh, John. I can't accept it." She was already handing it back to me.

"But I bought it for you."

"It wouldn't be right. You keep it and I'll borrow it sometime."

It didn't mean anything I told myself as I put the book back in my pocket. It didn't mean it wasn't going to happen.

"So you're interested in the siege of Famagusta?" she said.

"Yeah it's fascinating," said Patrick chirpily, trying to make amends. "Though we haven't got to the end of the journal yet."

"So you don't actually know what happened to Bragadino?" Sarah looked flabbergasted.

"Well we know the Turks won the siege," I said hurriedly. "We just haven't read the last bit…"

"But that's why the story's so famous. Come on. Let me show you."

* * *

D.O.P
M. ANTONII BRAGADENI DUM PRO FIDE ET PATRIA
BELLO CYPRIO SALAMINAE CONTRA TURCAS CONSTANTER
FORTITERQ. CURAM, PRINICIPEM SUSTINERET LONGA
OBSIDIONE VICTI A PERFIDIA HOSTIS MANU IPSO VIVO AC
INTREPIDE SUFFERENTE DETRACTA
PELLIS

We were in the church of Santi Giovanni e Paolo. Before us and rising some thirty feet above the ground was a memorial in white marble. On the lower part and ten feet wide was the inscription in granite flanked on either side by columns and two heraldic shields each topped by a knight's helmet and a winged lion. Above this on a dark plinth, shaped like a vase and about a foot across, was a marble bust of a bearded figure. Higher still was a monochrome fresco which was difficult to make out sandwiched as it was between two tall windows streaming bright white light into the church.

"It's a great honour for Bragadino's memorial to be here at all," she said. "This is where most of the great doges have their tombs. It shows how highly he was regarded and also perhaps a bit of guilt that Venice didn't do more to help him."

"I've got a bad feeling about this," I said. "What happened?"

"Well, after the city surrendered, the Turkish general – the Pasha – said he wanted to meet with Bragadino in person to congratulate him on his defence of the city. So Bragadino rode out with a company of three hundred men to the Pasha's camp and he was received with great courtesy."

"OK…" I said nervously. "So far so good."

"Yeah. But then the Pasha suddenly went off on one, accusing Bragadino of killing prisoners."

I thought of the journal entry we had read.

"He gave an order and Bragadino's close companions were murdered in front of him and then his unarmed men were massacred in the courtyard."

Patrick visibly blanched. Sarah looked delighted.

"Bragadino was made to kneel down in front of the Pasha who cut off his nose and ears and threw him in a dungeon."

I made a face. "No wonder Maya was so squeamish about this."

"They left him in the dungeon for a week until his wounds had become infected and then they made him walk back to Famagusta carrying heavy sacks of rocks. They made him kiss the ground by the Pasha's feet. Then they took him to the harbour and hoisted him up the mast of one of the ships, to see whether he could see the Venetian fleet coming to save him. Which obviously it wasn't. And then finally they dragged him to the main square, tied him to a pillar in the boiling hot sun, and flayed him alive."

"Oh my God…"

"When Bragadino was finally dead, they took his skin and stuffed it with straw. Then they dressed it in his purple ceremonial robes and put it on the back of a cow and paraded it round town. Later they sailed it round the Mediterranean on one of the Pasha's ships, ending up in Constantinople where it was presented to the Sultan."

I blinked at her and then looked across at Patrick but he was gazing up at the memorial. I cleared my throat. And asked the question I really didn't want to ask. "What happened to Polidoro? Please don't let it be something horrible."

She gave me a kind smile. "Actually he was one of the luckier ones. Well kind of... Polidoro was one of the few people to get out of Famagusta alive. And he did make it back to Venice."

"So he survived?" I was ecstatic; although that turned almost immediately to foolishness. "I suppose he had to have really otherwise we'd never have his journal..."

She laughed. "I suppose so. Anyway he made it safely back to Venice. *But*, years later, Bragadino's brother and sons approached him and asked him to recover the skin. They persuaded him to go to Constantinople and steal it from under the Turks' noses. Which he did, and the skin was returned to Venice where it was placed in an urn. Polidoro, though, got caught by the Turks and only escaped years later."

"But he did escape?"

"As far as we know. And that," she said pointing to the top of the monument, "is the urn up there. And we know it's real because they opened it in the 1960s and lo and behold there was human skin inside."

We peered up at it, a dark stone mass under the bust. And then, a little higher, squinting against the strong sunlight, we finally made out the detail of the fresco: a man being held against a column by turbanned figures whilst another ripped the skin from him.

"So there we go," she said shrugging. "That's everything I know about Bragadino and Polidoro. How far does he describe it in your journal? Up to getting the skin back? Or just the time in Cyprus?"

"Well, like I said, I haven't actually got that far yet. But I'll let you know."

"How come you can even read it? I didn't think you two spoke Italian?"

"Can *you?*" I said affronted at her assumption, however accurate.

"Yeah." She shrugged. "I did it for A Level. It sort of went with History of Art. Plus I had a dreamy Italian teacher…"

"You know there's a pattern there, right? But no, we don't speak Italian. We've got a translation. In a notebook written by a guy called Henry Shaeffer. He died in the First World War."

"Oh, how sad."

"I know. It's his diary as well." I took the books back out of my pocket again and handed the black one to her.

She flicked through the pages. "I love old books," she mused. She handed it back to me but then, almost absent-mindedly, she took Polidoro's journal from me again, turning it over in her hands, caressing the pages. "It does look fascinating," she said a touch wistfully.

"Oh it is! Especially the stuff about the buried treasure."

She raised an eyebrow.

"No really. According to Polidoro a golden cross was hidden before the siege started. He said it had been brought from Nicosia and was originally from Constantinople. Bragadino buried it so it wouldn't fall into the hands of the Turks. Does that sound ridiculous?"

"Completely ridiculous." She put her head to one side. "But… treasure was buried at times of war. And Nicosia was one of the richest cities in Christendom, so it's possible that something like this could have existed. And if it was from Constantinople then it could have been part of the loot from the Fourth Crusade… Sounds possible. Sounds interesting. Does the journal say where the treasure is?"

"Yes, but it's in code."

"More and more fascinating." She opened the journal and inspected the final few pages. "And has the code been broken?"

"We think Shaeffer came close but died before he could complete the work."

"But I'm going to break it," said Patrick.

"Modest as always, cousin dear."

He shrugged. "Well I am."

She grinned. "Well I've got to admit I'm intrigued."

I watched her happily, her eyes shining as she carefully closed the journal. She looked up and saw me watching her. She sighed and reluctantly handed the book back to me once more.

"Please, keep it."

She smiled at me sadly. "I can't." She glanced at her watch. "I need to head off now. I told Maya I'd be back by three."

"D'you think..." I said closing my eyes for an instant, certain she was going to say no. "I mean is it OK if we meet up later on? This evening I mean..."

She looked surprised. "Of course it is. I'd assumed we were all going to be meeting up tonight anyway."

"Oh. Excellent." I grinned in a rush of happy relief. "That's great. Well, shall we come over to your hotel at seven o'clock then?"

"Perfect. Here's where we're staying." She scribbled an address onto my guidebook. "And I'm sure Maya will be really happy to see both of you. Especially you," she said, looking directly at Patrick.

He blushed and she walked away waving and laughing.

10

We headed straight back to our hotel too keyed up to be interested in any more sightseeing at the moment.

"You see," I said. "They were expecting to go out with us this evening. *Us*. Sarah and me. You and Maya. I told you she liked you."

And Sarah liked me. *What do you think?* she had said. What did I think? What I thought – what I *knew* – was that she was as smitten by me as I was with her.

Back in the room I picked out a fancy sounding restaurant from my guidebook and went down to the payphone in the square to book a table for the four of us. The waiter spoke English so the task was easily done and I went back upstairs feeling very pleased with myself. I could do this type of stuff just as well as Julius.

"Listen to this," said Patrick. He was lying on his bed with Shaeffer's diary open in front of him.

25 January 1915
Colonel Roberts informed me that we will be returning to Rome tomorrow. My joy is unbridled. It is thought that Italy will now enter the war though it may be as late as April or May as any attack will be across mountain passes towards their ultimate prize of Trieste. And I have been told I will be rejoining the Royal Naval Division and thus be reunited with Rupert and the others.

My darling Anna, I can't tell you what high spirits we are all in today. Colonel Roberts is practically hopping up and down with pleasure, whilst even the normally staid Captain Hargreaves is walking around with a smile on his face by which you'd think he had just found a diamond in his boot. It is with a light heart that I write this entry: almost my last from this dismal place.

I will be putting my journal aside now for a few days so let me just say that the translation of Polidoro's writings is now complete, albeit a touch weak in places, in others overblown, yet hopefully you will forgive me that. And I am sure you will be able to help me with the questions I have of the text: Why is the closing section of a more formal nature than what has gone before? Why does Polidoro give no detail of when or why Bragadino entrusted the location of the treasure to him? And why if he knew where it was, did he not simply disclose it to the Council of Ten in Venice on his return?

"What did you think of the closing passage?" Patrick asked me.

"I don't know. I haven't read it yet." I too was lying on my bed by now. A fly landed on the bedspread and I shooed it away. Tried not to think about it. "Throw it over." He gently tossed me the notebook and I flicked to the end of the translation. "It *is* more formal. But then maybe that's just down to the way Shaeffer interpreted it…"

I have set down this journal for the glory of Venice and the love of God so that one day, even if I do not survive, the wonderful creation which is the Most Holy Cross of St Peter and St Paul will be recovered by the great and noble Venetian Empire, which was one quarter and one half quarter protector of Byzantium, and that it may be returned to Venice as its final resting place. And to that end I commit to these final pages the cipher which I have devised so that only the eyes of the worthy will be able to read and understand it and that this great treasure might be kept from the enemy. For, though I did not see the place of hiding of this treasure, my master Marc'Antonio Bragadino (may his soul be in heaven with the saints this day) passed word to me of its location. Therefore I say, read this cipher, you sons of

Venice so that the cross of the true Apostles may be returned to Venice where it rightfully belongs. I now lay out the directions below and maintain all I have written in this journal to be true, by this humble servant to the honour of God and the Glory of Venice, Girolamus Polidorus.

"Shaeffer was right. It sounds completely different to the rest…" I turned the notebook over and returned to the section of diary that Patrick had been reading. "Oh!"

Although I have finished the translation, to my disappointment I have not yet managed to break the coded passage at the end.

"Yes!" Patrick punched the air. "He didn't crack it!"

He was delighted but I was more distracted by the fly which had landed on the ceiling now, and was crawling around above us. I hated insects. I passed the notebook back to him.

"Listen to this," he said.

I will set down my trials so far when I have more time. As with all such puzzles, I feel frustration but this will only drive me further to unravel the secrets of those letters. And I know that eventually I will succeed.

Knowing that I would be leaving the next day, I returned to the bookshop to tell the shopkeeper of my progress before setting off for Rome. He seemed eager to hear of it – it being another dreary day and this the only source to enliven it for him no doubt. He asked me to write to him if I should get any further with it. I told him that although I had not cracked it yet, it is only a matter of time as all codes are there to be broken. He pressed his hand into mine and shook it with a vigour which I would have thought beyond one

so old. I smiled at him then walked to the door. I felt uneasy, I cannot say why, and as I tarried in the doorway, I felt certain that the bookseller was staring at me intently; but when I looked round he had gone.

10 February 1915
My darling Anna
This is my first journal entry for two weeks. The work has been busier since the return to Rome and we are seeking to order the papers built up in Venice over the last six months.

Polidoro's journal is translated as I said in my last entry and I have made further attempts at breaking the code in which is written the assumed directions to the treasure. But still with no luck. I am certain of a few things, however: it is not a Caesar shift or a monoalphabetic substitution cipher. I therefore must surmise that it is some type of polyalphabetic substitution cipher. Although very simple to construct – even a child could do it with ease – this would have been an extremely powerful cipher in Polidoro's time. None of the contemporary intelligence services, not even the Ten themselves, would have had the skills to break it.

"Ha, ha," said Patrick rubbing his hands. "If it wasn't polyalphabetic it wouldn't be a challenge. Who are the Ten by the way?"

"No idea. And why are you looking so happy? Doesn't he say the code's unbreakable?"

Patrick's eyes glinted. "*Was* unbreakable."

I was in the Forum, looking for inspiration amongst the ruins when I came to this conclusion that the code had to be polyalphabetic. And I own I felt a surge of energy at the revelation. For though such a code is

devilishly difficult to break it is not impossible. Charles Babbage had indicated the way forward using a form of modified frequency analysis. I remembered seeing a paper he had written on the subject and decided to head back to the embassy and look it up without delay.

"That's fine," I said hurriedly. "I don't want to know what modified frequency analysis is. Just tell me how close did he get to cracking it?"

"Well…" he said sounding a bit hurt, scanning through the pages. "Quite close *he* says though I'm not sure whether to believe him. He says he cracked it but he doesn't actually give the keyword or translate the code. He says he's done it by use of a crib." He eyed my blank look with impatience. And honestly I was more distracted with the relief that came from the fly becoming airborne once more and heading out of the window.

"A crib is a short word which somehow you know in the coded text. It can give you a way in to the whole code. The British used it in the Second World War to help crack the Enigma code, because we knew that messages being sent to submarines would often start with the German word for weather: *wetter.*"

"So what's the crib here?"

"Well that's the thing. He doesn't say. He just alludes to it…" He snapped the diary shut. "It doesn't matter. I can use Babbage's approach. It's much more certain to get results."

I'd completely lost the thread of Patrick's chatter by this time but he seemed happy enough as he lay there on his bed. But then suddenly he sat bolt upright. "And in fact it doesn't matter *what* the code says."

"Why?"

"Because I know where the treasure is."

"Sure: it's in Cyprus buried in a hole in a beach somewhere—"

"*No.* It's not in Cyprus. It's in Venice." His voice became an urgent whisper. "It's in Bragadino's urn. In San Giovanni e Paolo."

I looked at him blankly.

"Isn't it obvious?"

"*No.* And anyway the urn's not big enough. The cross was four foot long—"

"It's just the sapphire that's in there. That's all Polidoro was interested in."

"Right," I said not sure whether I should be humouring him or not. "And how did it get in the urn?"

"Well he put it there of course. Polidoro I mean. He makes a journey to go and get Bragadino's skin. Surely he would have used that trip to recover the sapphire as well. He said he would if it took him his whole life."

"But it doesn't make sense. Why is he hiding it?"

"Because the authorities were after it. They would have searched him for it. In the urn it would have been safe. But somehow he wasn't able to retrieve it…" His eyes widened. "I think it's still in there."

"But Sarah said they opened the urn in the '60s. They would have found it then."

"It must be in a secret compartment at the bottom of the urn."

"Of course." I rolled my eyes. "A secret compartment. How could I have been so stupid? Can we stop this now? You're doing my head in."

"Suit yourself," he said and he turned to face the other way.

I opened my mouth to say something more; but then just shrugged. Let him have his fantasies of treasure. I had fantasies of my own after all. And I lay on my back and stared up at the ceiling, trying my hardest to conjure an image of Sarah into my mind.

11

We both had a nap and afterwards I was relieved that Patrick had forgotten about the urn and was, like me, more preoccupied in finding something presentable to wear from the crumpled and limited selection of clothes in our rucksacks. We settled eventually on a maroon polo top for him and a cornflower blue long sleeved shirt for me. Plus, because we wanted to make an impression, trousers rather than jeans, and shoes instead of trainers.

At seven o'clock we stepped outside feeling if not quite a million dollars, then certainly as close as we could get on an inter-rail budget. The rain of the day had given way to blue sky and warm sunshine and we walked through the early evening streets enjoying the crisp sound of our shoes against the cobbles and despising the tourists around us padding along in their too-white trainers.

The girls' hotel was a few streets away and the route took us past the McDonald's which we approached nervously. But the cordon was gone and everything seemed to be business as usual. We shrugged and carried on to the girls' address. It seemed a bit seedier than our hotel but, I chuckled to myself, if things worked out right, Sarah and Maya would not be sleeping there too often.

We went straight up, climbing four flights of winding, fire-trap stairs to the top floor. We did a last minute inspection of each other and knocked on the door of number 44. We heard movements inside and then the door opened a little. It was Sarah. I noticed with momentary disappointment that she was still wearing jeans and anorak but this evaporated as she leant forward and gave me a kiss. We were both moving at the same time so it ended up on the edge of my lips rather than my cheek, which suited me fine and she just giggled.

"Hi guys. Welcome to our luxurious abode." She

opened the door wider and we could see Maya sitting on the bed directly facing the door. Patrick's face lit up.

"Hi guys," Maya called. Reclining there she reminded me of Manet's Olympia albeit a partially clothed one in a pair of shorts and tight fitting T-shirt.

"Hi," I said casually walking into the room with Patrick, both of us leaning down and giving her a kiss.

"Hi Maya," said Patrick blushing. "Are you feeling better?"

"Much better thanks. Well I haven't chucked me guts up for at least twelve hours anyway."

Patrick grinned and blushed again and nodded and said something; and Sarah started speaking at the same time to apologise for the untidiness of the room; but I didn't listen to either of them because over them both I heard a familiar sound. *Pssht*. Then again.

Pssht.

The sound of a can of drink being opened.

And looking round, I saw for the first time that we weren't alone in the room. There were two more single beds over by the window and sitting on them were Julius and Duncan.

Pssht.

"Hi guys," said Duncan, looking up. "Do you want a beer?"

"But... But you're in Naples."

Duncan reached over and pinched Julius who punched him back. "No, we're here."

"The girls convinced us to meet them in Bologna," said Julius taking a casual sip from his can and holding out another two for Sarah and Maya. "We spoke to them before they left Rome."

"So you... you've been together for the last couple of days?" I stared at him in disbelief.

"That's right. Beer Patrick?" He waved a can at him but Patrick just flopped down on the edge of Maya's bed in a daze.

"But... but you didn't say anything about it."

"Just like you didn't mention that you were meeting Sarah in Venice."

"But…" My mind was doing somersaults as it tried to process the information hurled at it.

"To being together again!" toasted Duncan as he drained his beer and crunched the can. Belched. "Sorry ladies," he said to Patrick and me.

"You two look nice," said Sarah.

"Yeah!" said Duncan coming closer while he popped open another can. "Yeah, you boys look a picture." I felt my colour rising. "Those shoes man. Those are serious shoes."

"Where are you going tonight?" asked Sarah.

"To an interview." Duncan guffawed with laughter.

I blinked my eyes and then looked directly at Sarah, ignoring Duncan as far as was possible. "We thought you and Maya might like to go out for dinner with us."

"Oh. That's so sweet." She looked across at Maya. "But I don't think M's going to be up to it."

The colour had drained from Maya's face at the mention of food. "I'm not having nothing but toast. That's all I can face."

"Sorry," said Sarah giving Patrick and me a rueful smile. "Let's do it tomorrow maybe."

"Well how about having a drink with us." I felt a rising tide of desperation well up inside me.

"Is it OK if we just stay here?" said Sarah. "I'm running a bit low on money and this hotel room's draining us, even when it's split four ways."

I'll pay for you, I didn't say. Patrick'll gladly pay for Maya, I didn't add. Just anything to get them out of that room with us.

"Is that OK?"

"Yes, of course." I forced a smile. But within a second

of seeing Julius lean over and start talking to Sarah I knew I had to get out of there. "Actually," I said walking to the door, "I've just remembered I gave the restaurant my credit card number. They'll charge me unless I go and sort things out."

"I'll come with you," said Patrick hurriedly.

"Fair enough," said Julius looking fairly neutral about whether we stayed or not. "But, anyway, why don't we meet for lunch tomorrow? Just to show there's no hard feelings. There's an authentic little trattoria in Campo San Geremia. That's where you're staying isn't it?"

I nodded at him noncommittally, not trusting myself to say anything. Patrick was the first to the door and was through it even before anyone had said goodbye.

"Thanks for coming over," said Sarah following me out into the corridor. Patrick was already halfway down the stairs by now. "Look," she whispered, letting the door swing closed behind her. "I'm sorry about all that. It wasn't what you were expecting. I thought you knew they were here."

"I guess not," I said shrugging.

"No. I guess not. But it's not how it looks you know."

"How does it look?" I was pleased to see her blush through her tan.

"I mean there's nothing going on. Between Julius and me – or *anyone*. We just couldn't find a room. So we had to take one for all four of us."

"Right."

"And…" She took a breath. "And I'm sorry about the other night as well. I didn't want to give you the wrong idea."

My chest tightened. "Wrong idea about what?" I said trying to sound as calm as I could.

"About me."

"I'm not sure—"

"I mean I *really* like you. Don't get me wrong. I do. But I was so drunk that night. And I was acting like an idiot. Do you know what I mean?"

I knew exactly what she meant. But even her giving me the brush-off was still interaction with her. It was still contact. "I'm not sure…" I said in the end to see her eager brown eyes gazing back at me for a little longer.

"It's just we were both really drunk and it was fun but it wasn't cool. *You* were. But I was super *un*cool. And it's just completely the wrong time because I'm getting over someone at university who used me to get over someone else and I don't want to do the same to you."

I just watched her now. I didn't even blink. To blink would have been to miss an instant of her gorgeous mouth; her pretty nose; her eyes.

"So can we just pretend it never happened?"

"If that's what you want," I heard myself saying.

"I think it's best, don't you?"

I'm not sure I said anything then. But she reached out and touched my arm, the lightest touch and the warmth of her and the kindness in that gesture would have broken my heart if it hadn't already been lying in pieces on the floor.

I heard her talking again and forced myself to tune back in.

"Why don't we do something tomorrow morning," she said brightly. "Julius and Duncan aren't exactly early birds so why don't you, me, Patrick and Maya go somewhere together? We'll meet you at your place. First thing."

I felt a pressure behind my eyes, constant, tiring. "Sure," I said. "Whatever."

"Great." She looked at me just a second longer. "We're still friends aren't we?"

I looked away from her now, from the beautiful glare of her eyes. "Of course. Friends."

"Cool. See you tomorrow." And she went back inside the room, the door opening for an instant, a glimpse of light and the sound of laughter within. The door closed and

I was left in the gloom of the hallway. I heard steps on the stairs and Patrick reappeared at the end of the corridor.

I started to say something but he interrupted.

"I heard," he said. "Friends."

We walked downstairs. At the bottom we looked at each other silent, unblinking for almost a minute. Eventually he suggested the only word of comfort he could think of. "McDonalds?" and I nodded dazed and we went there and ate through our despair.

12

We dressed the following morning lethargically, unenthusiastically after a fretful night's sleep bearing disillusioned dreams. I was certain that Patrick had been walking around the room again in the middle of the night but still I didn't say anything. Perhaps if I had asked him about it things would have been different. It would have all have been nipped in the bud. Or maybe the seed of whatever was growing inside him had been there too long already and my talking to him about it would have made no difference. Maybe I just want to believe that now. But it's irrelevant in any case. I chose to ignore it and override my unease with other concerns: the thoughts of the disappointments behind us and the frustrations awaiting in the day ahead.

Dressed, this time back in our standard issue jeans and T-shirt, neither of us taking any particular care over our appearance that morning, we went downstairs at a quarter to ten expecting the girls to be even later, expecting Julius and Duncan to have changed their minds and to be there too, for the day to be wet and miserable...

But outside the front of the hotel the girls were waiting for us, alone, and the day was bright sunshine and blue sky. I looked at Sarah and sighed.

"I don't want to go to another art gallery," Maya was saying. "I'm *sick* of art galleries."

"But this is the Accademia," said Sarah soothingly. "It's meant to be the most amazing gallery in Venice. Practically every painting's a masterpiece."

"I don't care," she said stubbornly. "I'm sick of masterpieces."

"*Well*... What would you like to do?"

"I want to go on the boat."

"The water bus? But we can do that anytime. And we'd

take it to the Accademia anyway."

"I want to go on the boat to one of those islands. Mirani or Biryani or whatever." She giggled. It was an infectious giggle and Patrick and I couldn't help but join in.

"*Murano* and *Burano*," said Sarah glaring at her friend but finding it impossible not to smile as well. "They're *really* touristy."

"Duh-*huh*." Maya spread her arms about her. "The whole of Venice is really touristy. Anyway I like being on the water."

"I do too," said Patrick. "I like the little side streets you see from the canals."

Maya's eyes lit up. "They're brilliant aren't they?"

"OK..." Sarah sighed and looked at Patrick and me. "What do you guys want to do?"

"Well," I said. "Sounds like Patrick is into the boat trip as well."

He nodded enthusiastically. It was nice to see him looking happy. And after all, Maya hadn't said *she* wasn't interested... "So why don't Patrick and Maya do that and I'll go with you to the Accademia."

"You sure?"

I shrugged. Torture took many forms, I thought. This would merely be the most exquisite.

"OK," said Sarah. "Well we can take the water bus together part of the way and then you guys go on. We'll meet you back at our place at one for lunch."

We parted company at the wooden bridge at the Accademia. Sarah and I got off at the jetty and watched for a moment as the water bus chugged away, Patrick and Maya waving madly from it.

"They seem happy," said Sarah as we turned and walked into the square in front of the gallery. I looked across at her and she smiled. No awkwardness. Perfectly friendly. She was so much cooler than I was. She was able to behave as though nothing had happened between us. Maybe for her nothing had.

"I think Patrick quite likes her," I said after a moment, to say something.

"I think he does," she said wrinkling her nose happily.

"And does she like him?"

"Oh definitely."

I was surprised at how categorical she was but pleased to have something to talk about. "What about Duncan? She seemed pretty keen on him?"

"Oh Maya likes everyone," she said airily. "And everyone likes Maya. But she's definitely keen on Patrick." We had walked through the entrance of the Galleria dell'Accademia and found ourselves at the ticket counter. We paid our 5,000 Lire to the girl there. "It would be nice if they got together," she continued wistfully. "She could be really good for him. He can be so intense sometimes. And sometimes just really quiet and you don't know if it's you, whether you've done something wrong or what."

I frowned, knowing I should say something. But it felt like a betrayal talking about him even to his cousin. So all I said was, "You two seem quite close. Closer than I am to my cousins."

"I suppose so." We started walking up the broad double staircase to the first room of the gallery. "Even though he lives in London and we live in Leeds. But we're both only children. So he's more like a big brother I guess." She smiled and then gasped as we walked into a large room whose walls were covered with early Venetian masters. The ceiling was high and adorned with carved cherubs and paintings of the prophets. But right in the centre of the room, the thing that caught the eye, was a cross made of silver and rock crystal.

"It's a reliquary," said Sarah reading the Italian description on its plinth. "Made in the fifteenth century. It would have contained a lock of John the Baptist's hair or a piece of Christ's robe."

"Like Polidoro's cross."

"Though that was older wasn't it? And larger?" She walked round it and then peeled away to look at a painting by Paolo Veneziano.

I walked alongside her and started to relax. We milled round the paintings, drifting, stopping, admiring, exchanging comments every now and then. We flowed with the ever-increasing numbers of visitors into Room II which was devoted to eight large altar pieces, panels of exquisite beauty and power painted by Carpaccio and Giovanni Bellini and Cima.

"This is amazing," she said standing before one of them. "*The Crucifixion and Glorification of the Ten Thousand Martyrs of Mount Ararat*. It's based on the life of Saint Ursula. She was a Breton princess who agreed to marry an English prince provided he converted to Christianity and went with her on a pilgrimage accompanied by ten thousand virgins." She twitched her nose. "The whole lot were massacred in Cologne on the way back."

In Room V before the *Tempest* by Giorgione she said to me, "So what do your parents do?".

"Dad's a civil servant and Mum works in a library."

"Sounds nice."

"Sounds boring."

"No, not boring. Comfortable. *Warm*."

"I'm not sure what that means."

She made a face and then shrugged. "It just made me feel safe."

Alongside a Tintoretto I asked her, "So how about your folks? What do they do?"

"I've only got a mum," she explained. "My dad left when I was a baby. I've never even met him."

"Oh right." I felt embarrassed – for her, for me – and I wasn't sure why. I peered at the rich painted velvets on a Madonna and I thought about it and eventually I said, "I bet your mum's really nice though."

"Why? Because she's a single mum?" Sarah raised a combative eyebrow.

"No. Because I assume you take after her."

Her cheeks turned suddenly pink and she said a hurried something about wanting to check out the paintings on the other wall.

We went through three side chambers before coming out suddenly into a larger room dominated by a huge canvas which filled almost the entire far wall.

"That's *The Feast at the House of Levi,*" said Sarah.

"I saw something about that in Shaeffer's notebook." I pulled the small black volume from my daysack and flicked through its pages. "Here we go."

17 January 1915
Today I went to the Galleria dell'Accademia close to the book shop where I bought Polidoro's journal. I visited the museum as a break, not so much from my work – which has fallen in quantity to barely a trickle and has in consequence left me with much free time – but more from the translation of the journal, which is proceeding apace. Unfortunately it came as no break from the rain which pelted me on my way through the streets down to Dorsoduro. I had been told by Colonel Roberts that the gallery made a capital day's outing so I thought I really should take the opportunity to go there even though as you know, paintings by themselves do little to inspire me. At the very least, I thought it would provide me with a place where the dull wet of the day could not reach me.

And for once, Venice has not disappointed. The Accademia is truly a marvellous place and one that you would love, Anna, with your superior understanding of the great painters and their works. Let me briefly describe it to you and also an incident which I found of particular interest. The gallery is set out in roughly chronological succession of rooms in an anticlockwise manner. At the top of the stairs—

"He describes loads of the paintings, but it's not really that interesting unless you're into history of art – no offence." She grinned. "But I'm sure he talks specifically about this painting... Ah, here we go:

In the tenth room which contains many paintings by Paolo Caliari (known as Veronese) my guide was explaining the history of the huge canvas, some forty feet wide by twenty high, called <u>The Feast at the House of Levi</u> which shows a light and airy hall with a long table with diners whilst around is much activity from various characters who are picked out in a splendid array of silks and fabrics, the whole being a highly vivid spectacle.

"Originally," he said to me, "this painting was to be called, <u>The Last Supper</u> and the central figures at the table portrayed Christ and his Apostles, but it provoked much outrage from the Church, who thought it too irreverent, and Veronese was summoned before the Inquisition. They asked him whether he thought it fitting that at our Lord's Last Supper he should paint 'clowns, drunkards, Germans, dwarfs and other indecent things.' Veronese replied that he had used artistic licence and that in any case these figures are not around the table where the supper is being held but on the stairs in front. They said that in Germany and other heretical places such devices are used in paintings to pour scorn on the teachings of the Holy Catholic Church. Veronese agreed that this was wrong, but that he was merely following the line of his predecessors.

"'What predecessors? When would they have ever done anything like this?'

"'Why, in Rome, Michelangelo in the papal chapel painted Our Lord Jesus Christ, St John, St Peter and the entire court of angels naked.'

"'It is not believed,' replied the officers of the Inquisition, 'that there will be clothes or such things at the Last Judgment and therefore there was no call to paint them. Everything in that painting is in the correct spirit. There are no clowns, no dogs, no weapons and no Germans. On this basis do you think you did well to paint this picture?'

"At this point, Veronese showed good sense and backed down though still professing he had intended no wrong. The Inquisition told him to amend the picture and rather than upset the balance of his masterpiece he chose simply to change the title which then satisfied all concerned." My guide chuckled. He was a small man with a bald head and he seemed to enjoy talking around his subject, but now he reverted his voice to a monotone, as was his habit when giving the more basic facts. "Veronese became the official state painter of the Republic when Titian died. His particular specialities were these large canvases with Palladian architecture and decor to set his figures upon." He gave a slight yawn. "He used colour and light well and his compositions often have great allegorical power. Now if you will go over to the other side of this room we can see how Tintoretto..."

But I had stopped listening to him for, on the wall to my left, was a small painting, no more than a foot high, oil on board with a simple gilt frame, of a man in a blue doublet with no ruff and seated at a table. He had dark close cropped hair and his eyes stared from the picture, eyes that suggested they had seen suffering. His face was scarred and on the left side of his neck above the line of his jacket were deep marks as though someone had cut and gouged him savagely.

And on this same side, the neck had contorted outwards into a goitre, a grotesque bulge of scarred flesh as though a hen's egg had been put under the skin. His head was angled so that this side was more visible, hideous though it was. His hands, which were empty and showed upturned on the table before him, were scarred also, scabbed and calloused. Yet he clearly wore his injuries and torments with pride for he faced them forward presenting them to the painter and viewer. In the background was a wooden sideboard and on it a leaden casket. The man looked like he was perhaps fifty years old, but it was difficult to tell for the scarring he had suffered was cruel. His was a compelling portrait but nothing was so compelling for me as the name inscribed below the painting: Girolamus Polidorus, hero of Venice.

We instinctively glanced over to our left but the wall here was covered with more large canvases and though we looked all around there was no sign of the painting anywhere.

My guide was standing impatiently at my side and sighed when he saw me looking at the painting. "A minor hero of Venice only," he said dismissively. "Polidoro received his injuries from the Turks when he went to rescue his master's skin in Constantinople. You have already seen the paintings commemorating the great sacrifice of Marco Antonio Bragadino."

"Yes, I remember. And was this portrait painted by Veronese as well?"

He looked weary. "It has been suggested that it is one of Veronese's last works. The skin was returned in 1580 after Polidoro had stolen it from the Turks and given it to the Venetian ambassador. Polidoro himself, however, was captured by the Turks and did not manage to escape and return to Venice until 1587 or 1588. That was the year that Veronese died. Polidoro was held to be a hero on his return, and since he too was originally from Verona it is thought that Veronese might have been inspired to paint a portrait of him soon after his homecoming. Personally I do not believe that a painter at that stage of his life – he was sixty then – and with his already considerable fame would have bothered with such a subject but who am I to argue with the curators of the museum." He raised an eyebrow as though to suggest he would have been very happy to entertain such an argument with them.

"And the goitre?"

"When the Turks found out what Polidoro had done he was tortured terribly and imprisoned for seven years suffering many privations. Eventually he was ransomed by Bragadino's brother but even then his ordeal was not over for he did not leave the Turks without further hardship and maltreatment. Nothing is known of his journey home other than it took several roundabout months dodging the Turks at every turn and that the last three weeks were spent in an open boat, drifting along enemy shores with precious little fresh water and nothing to eat except seaweed. He was skin and bones when he was finally found by a Venetian frigate, and he had developed a goitre. He recovered well enough after his return though. The goitre eventually went down and he was given a pension by Venice and the sons of Bragadino. He ended his days on his brother's farm in Verona." He shrugged. "But Signor, as I say, this is a minor work only and were it not for the fact that it has been attributed to Veronese – falsely in my view – it would not even be here. Now really we must move on to the Tintorettos." And he walked to the other side of the room.

I paused for a moment before following him and looked at the painting one last time, to view this man whose innermost thoughts I was currently attempting to read and decipher. I stared into his face and saw the pain there, and yet I realised suddenly that I had been wrong about his eyes. For whilst his face showed all the sufferings he must have endured both at the siege and after, and his cheek bones were prominent as though he were clenching his teeth and his brow furrowed, his eyes were gentle and calm and gave him the look of one who was finally at peace.

* * *

We sped through the rest of the collection and then, without needing to discuss it, doubled back to the bookshop in the entrance hall. I picked up a copy of the museum catalogue and Sarah found an illustrated monograph on Veronese and we ploughed through them. But there was nothing.

"I guess the attribution *was* wrong," she mused as we put the books down and ambled out into the sunshine again. "And if it wasn't a Veronese there would have been no reason to keep it."

"But he was an important historical figure."

"A *minor* hero," she said echoing Shaeffer's guide. She looked at her watch. "It's still only eleven-thirty. Shall we just walk?"

We strolled across the wooden bridge, enjoying the sparkles on the bright water, and on the other side we continued through the light-flooded Campo Santo Stefano and Campo Sant'Angelo and then on into the luxuriant shade of the puzzle of alleyways of San Marco. We steered clear of the Piazza. Instead our general route followed the Grand Canal but mazed through the side streets packed with stalls and art shops and booksellers and banks and hotels. Though bustling, the streets were fun and we twisted and turned as we wanted so we could walk down Calle degli Avvocat, Calle del Caffettier and Rio Terrà degli Assassini merely because we liked the names and did not mind that they brought us to consecutive dead ends (though we thought this particularly appropriate for the last). And we could step briefly into churches along the way if we wanted or equally walk on by just enjoying the shade and the cobbles underfoot.

Our route took us up and round the bend in the canal past San Salvadore and San Bartolomeo. Occasionally Sarah would point out something of interest or just something that took her fancy. Like the meat shop selling long sausages made of *asinello*. "Little donkey," she said making a face. Or when we stopped for ages outside a book stall which was selling beautiful hand marbled pages by the sheet and she told me how for a time Venice had been the centre of printing and bookbinding in the world. Or when we came across what looked like a small black metal post box set into the wall, with the slot framed by a lion's open jaws.

"Those lionheads are really cool," she said excitedly. "The Venetians would drop anonymous notes in them informing on people they thought were traitors. Then the Council of Ten would go round and collect them."

"The Council of Ten?"

"They were a cross between the Cabinet and the Secret Police and they took all the key decisions in Venice until Napoleon wound up the Republic in the 1800s. They were responsible for spying and information gathering and dealing with traitors. Suspects would be whisked away in the dead of night, maybe tortured, then tried in private and executed."

"Only a little bit ruthless then?"

"They kind of had to be. For a while Venice was the top state in Europe so it needed to protect itself and to do that the Ten had to know everything that was going on around them. Their spies were everywhere and they had the best code breakers in Europe."

"Sounds like a police state."

"Well kind of. But it was still pretty democratic compared with the rest of Europe. Rather than a royal family, the Doge and the Ten and the Signoria were all selected from nobles whose families were well established in Venice. That's why you see the same names coming up again and again if you look at a list of Doges: Mocenigo, Dandolo, Contarini, Morosini. The man in the street didn't have much of a say in what was going on, but at least he was looked after. There were hospitals and orphanages and support for the poor and the old. The Ten ran Venice with a rod of iron but they ran it well."

Her voice dropped a little. "And when it gets dark round here and you walk down one of these streets perhaps ending in a brick wall or coming right onto a canal, you still look over your shoulder and wonder if the Ten is coming after you." She shuddered deliciously and walked off down a dark alley in search of trouble.

But as well as it being a history tour, we talked about other stuff as well.

"So is it a big wrench finishing university?" she asked me as we passed over the Rio di San Giovanni Christomo, one of the myriad minor waterways which criss-crossed Venice. "I couldn't imagine leaving Manchester any time soon."

"That's because you've only done a year: it's different after three. And anyway Cambridge is quite a small place so I'm pretty much ready to move on."

"What comes next?"

"PhD. I'm going to Imperial to study particle physics."

She chuckled.

"What's so funny?"

"It's just... I can't believe I actually know someone

who's going to do a PhD in *particle physics*. That's *wild*."

"OK," I said feeling hurt. "There's no need to take the piss."

"Oh no, John. I think it's cool, I really do." She put a hand on my arm. "Honestly. I really envy people who do maths and science. They're more definite subjects. More... *objective* than art."

I looked at her through narrowed eyes, determined she was in earnest and then nodded. "They *are* cool subjects. Physics especially. People think it's just about equations and scribbles on a blackboard but it's not. It's about how the Moon goes round the Earth, or how electricity flows, or water falls, or stars are formed. It's about motion and inertia and momentum and energy. It's micro and macro; it's neutrinos and it's the Big Bang. Good physics – *great* physics – is about subtlety and simplicity and... and *symmetry*."

"Physics as poetry."

"Yes. *Yes*." And then I checked as I realised I was getting carried away, but though she was smiling it was a warm smile, an attractive one. "I couldn't imagine doing anything else," I said after a pause, shrugging.

"Like I said: I envy you." We both realised at the same moment that her hand was still on my arm. She removed it and made as if to find something in her pocket.

We continued on for another couple of streets and crossing over a rickety looking wooden bridge we found ourselves in a quarter where the buildings were noticeably higher, seven or eight storeys with the floors packed tightly together. We walked on until we came to a pleasant tree-lined square which was set out with trestle tables and benches and decorated with bunting. At the far end was a podium for a band or a speaker. It looked like there would be some kind of festival later on that day.

We sat down on one of the benches and looking around her Sarah said, "I think we're in the Ghetto."

"Oh are we? It's quite nice. Now I mean. I guess it wasn't back then—"

She smiled. "It is nice, isn't it?" The pretty square was dappled in leaflight and we sat there in a companiable silence. Just thinking.

"You know my feet are killing me," she said at last. She shifted on the bench and, slipping both feet out of her sandals, she reached down and massaged them. "I love Venice. But these cobbles *kill* me."

I smiled as I watched her, a pretty face topped with spiky blonde hair, bleached almost white by weeks in the sun. I breathed in the cool summer air and felt the afterglow of walking with her and talking with her; an enjoyment I hadn't felt all holiday; a warmth which subsumed the heat of when we'd first met; the easy frisson more heady than passion, more potent than anything. I ached with the moment; the thought that it would come to an end. I wondered how I could tell her that.

"You know I'm having a great morning," she said unexpectedly. She had stopped rubbing her feet and was sitting facing me now, straddling the bench. She wore a white blouse today, the top two buttons undone, a glimpse of vanilla skin. Her brown eyes flickered as she watched my face. "And I wasn't lying last night. I do really like you."

"You do?" I felt a sudden and tremendous excitement building inside me.

"Yes. I just don't want to muck everything up."

"You couldn't—"

"I have done already though haven't I? Got you confused and me confused…" She groaned and looked away from me. Seconds passed. A minute. Eventually she looked back, her head to one side. "Would you maybe like to do this again tomorrow? Just the two of us."

I blinked at her, the words engulfing me. "I thought you said it would be better if we didn't see each other?" I said doggedly, not daring to believe.

"We probably shouldn't."

"Then—"

"But it's only going for a walk isn't it?" she said and then with a wry smile, "And we'll take it really slowly."

I laughed. "I'd love to."

"Good."

I looked at her. We looked at each other. Just for a moment, and I felt every nerve ending, every synapse sparkle in me as she smiled at me once again. She smiled with one side of her face more than the other so her eyebrow rose at the same time and it gave an air of such knowing innocence that my mind was wiped of everything except for that moment and the future she promised with her coral lips. I leant forward to her, to kiss her gently, persuasively, but she looked down at her watch before I could get there.

"It's half-twelve," she said as I hurriedly sat up straight again. What can we do that doesn't involve walking for the next half an hour."

I could think of a couple of things. I smiled at her winningly, alluringly.

"Can I take a look at Shaeffer's notebook? The bits you read to me earlier were really interesting."

"Oh. Sure." I put the clothbound book onto the table in front of us. She shifted up until our shoulders were touching.

"So what came after his visit to the Accademia?"

I cleared my throat and read aloud:

<u>20 January 1915</u>

Today, my darling Anna, I am in black despair. That I am not with you I understand; even though the thought of it is still almost unbearable to me. But at least separation from one's beloved wife and daughter is the lot of a man from England in his thirtieth year who has reasonable patriotic feeling and wishes to

serve his country. But therein is the rub, Anna. I wish to serve my country but am stuck still in Venice doing diplomatic and intelligence work for which I am temperamentally unsuited.

When we joined up that day, Rupert and Denis Browne and I, we did so to defend England. But whilst Rupert and Denis have already fought their Germans in Antwerp I have merely been fighting boredom in Venice. Please do not consider I love you less thinking this way. You would surely say that any posting that keeps me away from shells and bullets and poison gas is a good posting and that is why your logical mind proves again superior to mine. But though I know it to be the truth I am still sunk in lethargy and a darkness which hangs over me like a pall. I feel useless here, unable to influence much of anything. And working on Polidoro's journal is not helping me. Here was a man who <u>fought</u> for his cause and risked himself for his friends. And I believed I would do the same, that we would stand shoulder to shoulder and support each other through all trials; that I should be an Ajax to Rupert's Achilles. But it seems that this will not be and however we spend the war it will be on opposite sides of Europe—

"He's talking about Rupert Brooke," she said suddenly. She caught my bemused expression. "You know. Rupert Brooke. The poet. Died in the First World War. *If I should die think only this of me: that there's some corner of a foreign field that is for ever England...* Even you must have heard of that?"

"I guess so..."

"Well anyway," she said not looking the least bit convinced. "Henry Shaeffer must have been friends with him. He's the right kind of age. And the mention of Ajax and Achilles, is just the sort of classical allusion you'd expect from a poet's friend. Fascinating."

She read to herself for a while and I just sat there alongside, warmed through by the sun, happy to watch her.

"He talks about the code a lot doesn't he?" she said eventually, frowning.

"A fair bit. It's quite interesting though."

"It's OK. It's more boy's stuff. Patrick certainly loves it. I hope he's not too into it."

"What do you mean?"

"Oh... nothing." She read on a little bit more and then smiled. "I prefer it when Henry talks about personal stuff:

6 March 1915
1am
My darling Anna – we finally have our orders!

They came through yesterday. It is now one o'clock in the morning and we will be catching a train at eight. Suddenly my head is clear again and the paranoias and frustrations have disappeared. It is crystal clear to me now how this past six months without you has been wasted time indeed. You have written me some two dozen letters in that time which have allowed me your thoughts, but these cannot substitute for a moment with you. And when I look back over this journal that I had started as an outlet for my love for you, I realise that without you to hold me and stabilise me I have drifted. I have become distracted by tedium and grown used to indolence, filling my time with the least of puzzles which is probably incomplete or unbreakable in any case, and points to a treasure no doubt long since removed. And I realise now at my return of clarity, that I did this not to dispel my tedium but to fill the jagged hole left in me by being apart from you.

Since the news of our postings Captain Hargreaves and I have talked earnestly and at length, and I own that I have wronged him in my earlier entries. For he is not the doltard I labelled him. He is just quiet and

solid and he too loves his wife and would be with her.

Yesterday we played a game of deep longing whereby we each gave the other leave for twenty-four hours. What would we do in that time? Captain Hargreaves was shy on this but said he had a young wife and they had known each other for only a short time before they were married and he joined up soon after, so inevitably they would spend their time in bed, twenty-four hours making love punctuated only, he said, by the sandwiches made with the best bacon from her father's farm – and at this we laughed. He is a good man, Anna.

As for me, I said yes we would make love, but perhaps just once, starting with a kiss and an embrace, undressing, feeling your gentle touch on my skin, which is like electricity to me, and then falling together, caressing, and moving, slowly at first, as each discovered the other's body again after our time apart, but then with growing momentum, our long limbs intertwined, my sun darkened skin against you, pale and strawberry fresh, our faces close and consumed with mutual desire. And then we would hold each other for some time, just kissing.

In my mind it is midsummer in Cambridge so that afterwards we would lie together in stillness and calm on the bed with the windows thrown open and a view of green outside, the meadow with its casual flowers and a cool English breeze playing over our nakedness. And then we would talk, just you and I, talk as we have not talked for six months, talk and laugh for our conversations even when on serious topics are punctuated with your laughter and my laughter, yet yours is the more beautiful and matches your smile, and I long to hear and see them again.

And then Frances. She will be eighteen months old now and to have her in front of me, or dandling on my knee would bring me more happiness than I could ever put into words. You say that she is starting to talk. Please, my love, teach her "Papa" as well as "Mama" so that when I am there again she will have a good word for me. When I think of her my heart jumps and I feel a pure warmth inside and I know that even if I am killed or my name besmirched that her love for me will persist as long as she herself has breath; and one day a child of hers will love her in the same way.

But I will not be killed, my love, my beautiful tender darling Anna. I will not die in a foreign field as Rupert wrote in his poem. I promise I will return to you and when I do I will love you every single hour of my life, until one day, and without fear, we both shall die, and then I will be glad for the chance to love you on into eternity.

13

She closed the diary and handed it back to me.

"Read some more?" I asked her. "It was lovely listening to you."

She shook her head. There were tears in her eyes. "No. It all seems to be about the code after that."

"Oh really?" I said in spite of myself and opened it in my lap. "I've not read the end of it. Patrick said Shaeffer got close to breaking it."

She shrugged and smiled at me, then looked up through the leaves at the sunlit sky above.

<u>6 March 1915</u>
<u>3.30 am</u>
My dear Anna
I did not think I should be making another entry into my journal but after the last I was ordering my papers and getting ready to pack them all away when suddenly inspiration struck. It is the clarity which the thought of moving has engendered in me; the same clarity to which I referred before. And this clarity has brought me my breakthrough, and suddenly my vision which was blurred by the lensed jigsaw pieces in their wrong positions has swung into focus and I realise that it is so simple after all. I have broken the code – or rather I know the key and it is so simple that I could almost weep with happiness. And I have discovered the truth in a moment of madness or brilliance that you Anna, dear, dear Anna (I am laughing as I write this, my heart is so gay) would have seen immediately. For there is only one way to make sense of it all: that the coded piece is a letter of course, and then the crib was so obvious as to make me think my idea was laughable. But I tried it nonetheless and though not

enough to tell me the keyword in itself, for it was too short for that, it gave me the first few letters and the rest was suddenly clear.

Dear Anna, how I wish you were by my side now. I look at my watch and see it is almost four o'clock. I simply must rest and catch at least an hour's sleep. But I am so excited. That I should have made such discoveries tonight of all nights when I am but hours away from leaving for I don't know where: it could be France or it could be Africa. I feel like Galois on the night before his duel, desperate to set his thoughts down but plagued also by the constant fear, je n'ai pas le temps. But I have said what I need to my dear, for you will understand and make sense of my ramblings and in any case unlike poor Galois I shall not die in a field without seconds. I shall return to you, I shall be back with you soon on terra ferma. That is the key for me. To be back by your side again to hold you and love you and share these wondrous and exciting discoveries with you.

Now, enough of this or despite my nervous energy I will be tired later on. I am going to put my papers and books away now and I shall rest. Be it only for two hours I will put my head down and shall sleep.

And then the very last entry. I read it eagerly, expecting it to reveal the secret of the treasure. But it was nothing like that.

"You need to see this," I said to Sarah.

"No that's OK," she said still looking skywards. "The code doesn't do it for me."

"No, really. Read it." She was struck by the note in my voice and looked at me curiously.

"It tells you what happened to him," I said and handed her the book.

She read aloud:

<u>6.30am</u>

Colonel Roberts' car drew up outside some half an hour ago and the estimable Signor Mocenigo is supplying him and Captain Hargreaves with breakfast. All my things that I cannot fit into my pack and this diary too will be with you soon: Mocenigo has promised it. Note the date it arrives: I wager a month from today.

This will be my last entry for we shall be away by seven o'clock. The Colonel has finally given me an indication of our mission. Lord Kitchener and First Lord of the Admiralty Churchill are concerned that the Western Front has become static and so Churchill has devised a new way to push the war forward. Attack up through Turkey with the intent of taking Constantinople, thus neutering the Ottoman threat and opening up the supply routes again to our great but poorly equipped ally Russia. What a capital plan and how poignant and wonderful that I shall be rejoining Rupert as we head for <u>Troy</u> no less! I <u>shall</u> be Ajax to his Achilles after all! He has already set sail from England on board the SS Grantully Castle with the rest of the Royal Naval Division and we shall join them in Greece in just three days.

I am desperately excited now for it feels like decisive action is being taken to produce a rapid conclusion to the war. We shall force our way through the Dardanelles and then upwards into Austria-Hungary and Germany. Open another front, break the stalemate, and be back home by the Autumn.

Oh, I hear Colonel Roberts calling to me now. All my love, my darling Anna and to Frances too. Do not worry for me, for I promise I will return. And how could I not for I will be with Rupert again and the estimable Captain Hargreaves and the best forces in the world heading off to the turning point of the war. We will put on a show that will make all England sing our names in years to come, the names of we who changed the course of this great war and fought and won in Gallipoli.

14

She was sitting staring out over the square. It was quiet, just the sound of the bunting above us waving in the breeze to disturb our thoughts.

"We should never have read that," she said eventually. "It was meant to be a private diary."

I nodded, a feeling of guilt rising inside me.

"And how come it was never sent back to his widow? To Anna." She sounded suddenly close to tears; but angry ones. "*She* should have been reading this. Not us. What would she have felt when she heard he'd been killed? She wouldn't have even had his words to comfort her. And poor little Frances?" She looked at me, her eyes glistening, and all I wanted to do was to hold her. "Oh I know it's such a long time ago but Signor Mocenigo or whatever his bloody name was should have sent Henry's stuff on like he said he would. It would just have been something."

There was nothing to say in reply so I sat and stared out as well, watching the shadows of the trees play on the walls opposite. Eventually she sighed loudly and stood up rubbing her eyes with the heel of her hand. "Come on. We've got to go and meet the others for lunch back at your place."

We walked in silence.

I wondered whether I should say anything to try and cheer her up but in the end decided to save it. I'd wait until the afternoon and tell her a joke while we were walking around St Mark's or just brush up against her or maybe even tell her some cool stuff about Relativity. There was plenty of time.

Patrick and Maya had already got back and were sitting with Julius and Duncan on the terrace of a trattoria a few doors down from our hotel. It seemed quite nice though I'd never even properly noticed it before. Somehow, though,

Julius's restaurant radar had detected it. Normally I'd have expected some kind of self-congratulatory burble from him about it. But neither he nor anyone else even registered our arrival as they were in the middle of a fully fledged shouting match.

"*For Christ's sake!*" Julius sounded angrier than I'd ever heard him before. "Will you stop going on about this ridiculous treasure, Patrick! It doesn't exist."

"It *does* exist."

"It *doesn't*. If it did, it wouldn't just be lying around waiting for someone to find. It would be in a museum somewhere by now. *Ergo*, it doesn't exist."

"It *does* exist. The book says it does."

"The book's a fake. Why can't you see that?"

"Well who wrote it then?"

"Who cares? Maybe it was Shaeffer himself. Maybe he was bored. *Who cares?* Just accept the fact that you're wasting your fucking time."

"You think that anything that's not decided by you is a waste of time. Well fuck you." Patrick pushed his chair back and stood up. "Fuck you, Julius. I'm not wasting my time and I'll prove it. Because I know where the treasure is."

"Well why don't you go and get it then."

"That's exactly what I'm going to do," and he turned and ran out of the square.

We looked at each other uneasily. Except Maya that is. "Your cousin's bloomin' bonkers."

Sarah looked like she'd been slapped. "What do you mean?"

"What d'you think I mean? He's nuts."

"Didn't you have a good time together?" she asked in dismay.

"No we didn't. He spent the whole time telling me daft stuff about Polly-bloody-doro and codes and treasure. On and on and on. A total fruit loop."

"Hey! Don't talk about him like that."

Maya shrugged. "Well it's true. He's completely doolally—"

"Don't talk about him like that!"

"Well, someone has to," said Julius now. "He's not been himself for ages. He's been acting really strange this whole holiday—"

"Not strange," I snapped. "Just quiet. He hasn't wanted to talk to you and I don't blame him."

He looked at me in disgust. "Oh grow up for Pete's sake. There's something wrong with him. Can't you see that? And you're not helping by filling his mind with this... this *crap.*"

"Stop it!" said Sarah both hands raised to her face. "If you two weren't at each other's throats all the time, I'm sure everyone else would be fine. Now, Julius, what did you mean Patrick's been acting strange?"

"Well he's always been quiet but now he's up and down and when he's up he's seriously manic. He was practically *jabbering* earlier on about sapphires and gold and Cyprus and God knows what else."

"And what about you John?" Sarah asked me. "You've spent most time with him. Has he been acting strangely?"

I looked at her face racked with concern. My head was addled with molten fury at Julius and torn between loyalty to my friend and the worry that perhaps there was actually something seriously wrong with him. But before I could voice any of this my mind was blanked by an overriding flash of realisation and I jumped to my feet genuinely scared.

"Shit," I said and I felt the blood rush from my face. "He's gone to Bragadino's tomb. He thinks that's where the treasure is."

We ran through the streets to get there. The half kilometre over to the edge of Cannaregio and the Church of Santi Giovanni e Paolo. We jostled past the tourists and into the cool dark of the huge church. Our eyes strayed over the chequered marble floor, wandered between the tall white columns, thinking maybe we'd been mistaken; and that's when we saw him.

"Patrick what are you doing?" screamed Sarah. Her voice echoed around the nave and a hundred heads turned to look at her; then followed the direction of her gaze. Fifteen feet off the ground, Patrick was clambering up Bragadino's memorial, his hands finding purchase on the stone carved coats of arms, inching his way higher using his arms to pull himself up, his legs hanging free.

"Please Patrick." Sarah rushed over to him. *"Please come down."*

From the far end of the church there was the sound of running and two officials in suits and ties pounded over. They started shouting in Italian from halfway across the church. Tourists were starting to gather as well, camera flashes going off. Sarah was sobbing and we others were looking on ashen faced. One of the officials ran from the church and we could hear his shouting outside in the Campo. Inside the noise grew. Patrick reached a hand up to the ledge on which the bust of Bragadino and the urn were sitting. He reached but then almost immediately drew back, clasping at nothing as though he were suddenly unsure of himself. Then his other hand slipped and in an instant he was falling, arms flailing, desperate to slow his descent. His foot caught the bottom of one of the marble columns flanking the inscription and sent him tumbling. There was a loud slap and a thud as he hit the marble floor.

Screams echoed around the church, and then we all rushed forwards. Patrick had got to his feet and was standing dazed. Before the official could reach him Duncan had sprinted between them and started remonstrating in his loud American accent about how he was going to sue the church for emotional distress. Meanwhile Sarah and I grabbed one of Patrick's arms each and when Julius hissed, *"Meet you back at your hotel,"* we sprinted for the huge doorway and out into the square blinded by the sudden brightness.

"Are you OK?" sobbed Sarah.

"I'm so sorry," he said; was saying.

"But are you injured? Did you hurt your leg when you fell?"

"No I'm fine—"

"Then come on!" I shouted. We ran diagonally back across the Campo, ignoring the curious looks from the tourists and just missing a group of Carabinieri arriving at the square as we turned into a side street.

"I thought the treasure was in the urn," Patrick said as we ran.

"They opened the urn in the '60s!" Sarah screamed at him. *"I told you that!"*

"I know that now." His voice was meek, confused. "I didn't know what I was doing."

"Stop!" I yelled at them. More Carabinieri had appeared at the end of the street, their black uniforms menacing. "Back the way we came."

We turned and started back along the street but managed to find an alley to duck into halfway down. From there we zigged and zagged, following some of the streets Sarah and I had taken that morning.

After a while we slowed to a walk as it seemed less conspicuous. We blended amongst the thronging tourists but we were nervous all the while. In the distance was the constant siren from a police launch cruising the canal. And as we got close to the hotel there were suddenly shouts again and we realised we must have been spotted.

We sprinted across the Campo San Geremia and into the foyer of our hotel. An elderly lady mopping the floor gave us a curious look but we ignored her and dashed up the stairs. Along the corridor and into the room slamming the door shut behind us.

"Shit!" I gasped and flopped onto my bed my chest

heaving, breath burning inside me. "*Shit.*"

Sarah collapsed on the floor in noisy exhaustion. Patrick just stood there, his face contorted. "This is all my fault," he said in a low voice. "I don't know what came over me."

"It doesn't matter," Sarah gasped between gulps of air. "It's not important."

"I don't even know properly what happened. One minute I was arguing with Julius—"

"It doesn't matter," said Sarah again, her voice more composed. She stood up and went and put a hand on his shoulder. "Honestly. Tell him, John."

With difficulty I swung my legs round and sat on the edge of the bed. "That's right," I panted. "No worries."

Sarah looked at me gratefully and I felt my heart rate lurch back up to one hundred and fifty.

Patrick was looking distraught and close to tears. Sarah reached her arms round him.

I got up and went to the balcony and cast a swift glance down before hurrying back inside. "They're coming into the square," I groaned.

There was the sound of running in the corridor and I felt myself freeze. A heart stopping bang on the door and then Julius and Duncan burst in. I slumped onto the bed again in relief.

"What the fuck are you still doing here?" said Julius glaring at Patrick. "There are cops everywhere."

"I'm sorry—"

"Do you understand what you've done? Have you any idea how many police are out there? The whole of Venice is *crawling* with them."

"Oh God." Patrick held his head in his hands.

"You can't fuck with their stuff, man," said Duncan. "Not in Italy. They'll send the Mafia after you to cut your dick off."

"I doubt that," said Julius his voice cooler now, though he was flushed, his eyes wide. "But you do need to get out of here. The police are in the square and are starting to work round the buildings. It's only a matter of time before they catch you."

"What happened in the church?" I asked.

"We got in their way," said Julius shrugging and then gave the barest flicker of a smile. "We behaved like clumsy American tourists. Duncan was particularly good at it."

"Fucking A. I was the *meister*."

"Maya is still there. She proved a great distraction for the Carabinieri. They all wanted to take her statement. But anyway you've got to get going before the police start searching the place."

"But if they're in the square it's already too late," said Patrick desperately. "I should just hand myself in—"

"No way," I said grimly. "We can still make it."

"He's right," said Julius. "You've still got time: *just*. Look, pack what you need into your rucksacks. So you'll be able to run if you have to. We'll take the rest of your stuff back to our place." He looked at Duncan.

"Yeah no worries. Just do it quickly or we're all going to wake up with horses' heads in our beds."

"Will you shut up," said Julius but it eased the tension and even Patrick forced a smile. We threw a few essentials into the bottom of our rucksacks shrugged them on and then the two of us stood there.

"I'm really sorry," said Patrick again looking close to tears.

"It's OK," said Sarah who *was* in tears and gave him one last hug. He straightened up.

"Don't worry about it," said Julius. He put out a hand and Patrick shook it and Duncan clapped him on the back.

"Thanks guys," I said awkwardly looking over at Julius and Duncan. They nodded back at me. "Look after yourself," said Duncan.

"You too."

"You guys have *got* to go," said Julius his brow creased

up.

"Where shall we meet up again?"

"I think England would probably be best."

We all looked at each other for a moment.

"Oh this is fucking *crazy,*" groaned Duncan.

"It's all we've got. Get out of here. Now."

I glanced over at Sarah. She put her arms around me. "Look after him," she whispered to me.

"I will."

"And look after yourself too." She kissed me on the cheek and just for a split second we were left looking at each other. Just the briefest of instants. The sweetest moment. "I'll call you," she said.

And then we were gone, Patrick and I, clattering down the stairs. One flight, two flights, half slipping on the wooden steps in our haste, blood pounding again, still not properly recovered from before, God I was unfit, my lungs burning—

I stopped suddenly and Patrick thumped into me. I hissed at him to be quiet. One flight to go, just on the turn of the staircase so that we could see down into the foyer. The old lady was still mopping but Signor Tron was down there as well now and there was another man with him. Tall and dressed in charcoal grey.

"Is he a policeman?" Patrick whispered urgently.

"I don't know. He looks kind of familiar…"

"What do we do?"

The question hung there, sibilant in my ear. What do we do? What do we do?

They were standing by the counter and looked up for a moment but did not see us. Tron said something in Italian to which the other reacted angrily. He banged his hand flat and hard onto the counter and yelled something back at him. Tron tried to hush him looking anxiously over at the cleaning lady but the other would not be silenced.

"Then at least let us speak in English, Loredan, so she

will not understand," Tron pleaded.

"*Count* Loredan!" he thundered. "Do not forget your place."

Tron puffed out his chest. "I am also of noble stock, remember. My forefathers too ruled Venice."

"And now you run a hotel."

Tron shrugged the insult away and put on a placating voice. "Count Loredan, the *Capo* has spoken. I must obey his orders. We are not to interfere."

"But we *must* interfere. We must get that book back."

"If the *Capo* decided to sell it—"

"It was not his to sell! That old fool Galbaio does not understand its worth. It is of value to all Venice, Tron."

Tron seemed to waver but he said, almost reluctantly, "I cannot disobey my orders. He is *Capo*."

"Of course. But then contact Galbaio and tell him to come here. And we will discuss it. But in the meantime that book must not leave Venice."

Tron looked at him and sighed. "Very well." But then he started as he caught sight of movement out in the square. "The police are approaching! Count Loredan you should never have come here. Your activities have not been wise. Someone will end up getting hurt—"

"You will get hurt if I don't get me that book, Tron."

"Do not threaten me." Tron's face hardened. "I said I will get the book. But not for you; for Venice. Now go. You will endanger us all if the police take you."

"I will return tonight," said Loredan and he crossed the hall and slipped outside.

The old woman eyed them, shrugged, and carried on mopping.

"What do we do now?" Patrick whispered in my ear. I half turned to look at him and saw in his eyes he was as scared as I was. How long had we sat there? No more than a minute. Yet we were almost out of time.

"Come on!" I jumped up and ran as hard as I could

down the stairs and I could hear and feel Patrick thumping behind me. Signor Tron shouted after us to come back but we ignored him. Yet when we got to the dirty smoked glass doors of the hotel we saw a pair of burly Carabinieri running towards us. We were too late.

"This way!" Tron was beckoning to us, pointing at a doorway to the right of the counter. "You can hide here."

Patrick and I exchanged a glance. Neither of us trusted him but the police were almost upon us. We had no choice.

We let him bundle us around the desk and through the door. "Don't go anywhere," he said forcing a smile as he closed the door on us. "I need to talk to you when the police are gone."

And then we were left alone, the room plunged suddenly into darkness. Immediately we heard shouting in the foyer and the tramping of boots. "*Polizia! Polizia! Dov'è Loredan?*" I clenched my eyes shut trying not think of what was happening; of what would happen if Tron gave us away; of what would happen if he didn't.

"Look!"

I glanced over to where Patrick was pointing. A vertical crack of light on the other side of the room. A door, but when we tried it was locked against us.

"It must lead directly outside," I whispered. "Out the back. We could get round to the railway station—"

"But it's locked," Patrick hissed. "We can't just break it."

"So do you want to just sit here till the police find us? Or till Tron's friend comes back?"

I could hear his breathing and just make out his face, close to me, pale. He blinked, only once, and then threw himself against the door. I joined him on the second and on the third the door splintered open and we burst into a tiny courtyard. We stumbled, blinded by the sudden daylight.

Behind us the clamour of voices grew louder. We picked ourselves up, and exchanged a glance; but for an instant only. Then we pushed through the gate at the back of the courtyard and ran blinking into the sunlit street beyond.

Part Two

Suns of Home

Summer 2002, London

Julius

15

As usual the Northern Line was execrable on the way home and having taken an hour – mostly stopped in tunnels, part of the time with the lights failed, and all of the time next to a man who had surely not washed for a year – having taken an hour to reach Camden Town from Charing Cross it was decided that our train had gone far enough and would turn around again. It was a fifteen minute wait for the next tube and only a little longer on foot to my place in Primrose Hill. So I got out and walked, glad to be back in the fresh air if the odours of Camden High Street can ever be described as such.

I was late that evening anyway having had to give a group of financiers a private lecture. Their bank was sponsoring my new exhibition and I resented them for it. What did they care about the Florentine Renaissance or Masaccio or Masolino? They wanted nothing save their dilute form of capitalism of which they felt themselves to be the masters but for which they were but small cogs, their lives eaten by the endless pursuit of the deal.

Pitiful.

Though I confess there had been one blonde with a sportily efficient allure who had at least provided fair eye candy.

It was nine o'clock when I opened the front door to the Georgian terrace house where I lived. I sifted through the letters that had been left in the hall, extracted those bearing my name, then skipped up the three flights to my flat. I went inside without switching on the lights, placed the letters on the mantelpiece and walked to my bedroom. Undressed, then out into my living room again and put on some Bach strings. The only light in the room was the green LED phosphorescence from the CD display. I padded to the bathroom and into the shower, the partita still audible to me. I turned on the water and allowed the tiredness and the filth of the Tube to be washed from me.

The door to my flat opened and closed. There was a shouted greeting and a lamp flicked on in the living room, the light spreading like a puddle into the bathroom.

"Madeleine," I called to her, switching the water off. "There's a bottle of wine in the fridge." I stepped out onto the mat and reached for a towel.

Madeleine appeared silhouetted in the light from the living room. She leaned against the door frame as she poured herself a glass of the white burgundy. She was slim but heavy breasted and was well presented as always: her sleek chestnut hair and her mini wrap-around dress and her high boots. "What is it with you?" she said, her voice deep and rich and cool. "If you will insist on living in a shoebox must you keep the door open while you shower? Your flat's like a sauna."

I ignored her familiar complaint and continued to towel. She appraised me, sipping on her wine, inspecting my nakedness. "And are you able to see any better in the dark now? Or are you just saving on your electricity?"

I dropped the towel, water still dripping from me and advanced towards her. She backed into the living room, into the light.

"Now, now," she said. "Be careful of the wine."

Her arms lifted to either side of her as she retreated, moving back until her calves touched the black leather sofa. I took glass and bottle from her, placing them on the floor. Then stood to full height again. In her boots she was four inches taller than me so I put a bare foot between her feet and kicked them apart so that her mouth dropped to my level and then I leant forward and kissed her hard so that it took her by surprise and she gasped.

"You bastard," she said putting her arms around my shoulders and digging her nails in and I pushed her back so that we fell together onto the sofa. I pulled open the poppers on her dress to reveal her long and creamy body and pushed myself against her and into her so hard that we bucked and heaved with desire and pleasure. Her nails tore my back and I devoured her breasts and as we climaxed together she screamed in pleasure so that her cries rang round the flat, *"Julius! Julius!"*

Madeleine was dressing again, smoothing the chocolate cotton of her dress down over her and refastening her poppers. "Julius, you really must learn *not* to rip my clothes off." She stood up straight flattening the material down onto her thighs, inspecting a tiny tear on her hip. "I'm quite happy to remove them for you most of the time."

"Obliging aren't you," I said.

She slapped me playfully. "Let's go. I'm ravenous."

I put on a pair of linen trousers and an open necked shirt. It was a warm night so I didn't bother with a jacket. I picked up my post again from the mantelpiece and followed Madeleine down the stairs.

Outside she pulled out her car keys and bleeped her Mercedes. We got in together, her glamorously long legs flowing into the car after her, swinging deliciously into position with a lifetime's practice.

"So how was your day?" she asked coolly putting the SLK into drive and moving off.

"It was fine. Though lengthened considerably by having to give a lecture to those banking idiots." I started to flick through my post. A couple of bills. A note telling me how desirable an area my flat was in and how, should I wish to sell it, E.g. and Etc. Estate agents would be happy to act on my behalf.

"You see," I said waving the paper at her. "I told you Primrose Hill was the place to be."

"Darling," she said coolly. "I don't doubt that Primrose Hill is a little oasis but the rest of North London is hardly beautiful is it? You should live out West. It's so much more civilised. At least I can get a cleaning lady there."

"I *had* a cleaning lady."

"But then she left. To go to Chiswick or Fulham or Kensington—"

"Well I don't think I need one in any case."

"Trust me darling, you need one. Your dirty plates are building up *again*. You should definitely keep looking."

"Good ones are hard to find. In any case I'm not moving. Having bought my flat six years ago I feel quite happy to stay put and bask in my foresight."

"I'm not convinced you physically *can* bask in a flat your size. At least get a bigger place."

"I can't afford a bigger place."

"Well then move in to mine: it's large enough for both of us." Her voice was suddenly flustered and I felt her watching me. But I chose to ignore both her and her comment and instead opened my fourth letter.

"Oh God," I said pulling out the printed sheet with a coat of arms at the top. "They're inviting us back to a garden party at College." I tossed it onto the dashboard in disgust.

"Is that bad?" she said looking at the road again. "I haven't been to a proper garden party for ages."

"They're not *proper*. Awful food. Worse wine."

"Oh come on, let's go. It'll be fun. I like Cambridge. And you can catch up with your friends."

"Maddie you like Cambridge because you didn't go there. And I don't have any friends from Cambridge. Apart from Patrick. And he's from school anyway."

"Patrick's quite sweet. But I don't believe you don't

have any other friends from there."

"I don't."

"What no one? No one you were close to—?"

"I told you I don't," I snapped at her. Not loud, but she knew me well enough after two years not to pursue it. I looked out the window, my head pulsing with a headache that hadn't been there a moment ago, a pressure behind the eyes that I had no control over. I would be OK so long as she didn't *talk* and thankfully, for the rest of the journey she didn't.

16

On my desk at the Gallery the following afternoon were eight books and one drawing. The drawing was sandwiched between two sheets of glass and the books were all open, most of them showing colour prints of the fresco cycle of the Brancacci chapel. The drawing, a study in charcoal on stained paper was of a crucified figure, his head bearded and bowed with a solid looking halo above his head, naked apart from a loin cloth.

The door to the shared office opened and Robert returned. "Sorry. Too much coffee." He sat at his desk which was at right angles to mine in the corner, trundled forward in his chair and then sat back and crossed his legs, flicking at a speck on his grey suit trousers, straightening his tie against his white shirt. "Where were we? Oh yes: that is not a Masaccio."

"I'm not saying it is," I said irritably. "I'm saying it could be."

"I don't see what you're basing it on apart from blind faith and a dodgy provenance from a similarly dodgy Dutch collector."

"I'm basing it on knowledge of Masaccio." I looked at him witheringly. "Radical as that might seem."

"Have you even confirmed its age yet?"

"Not yet. I'm going to book it in for carbon dating."

"Well, what about the watermark?"

"What about it?" I swivelled round so that I was facing the bright window and held the drawing up before it. A distinct watermark of a bull's head showed through in the bottom right hand corner. "So?"

"So, you can give a rough dating to drawings based on the watermarks in the paper. The paper makers used different marks the same way that printers did. That guy over at the drawings collection at Windsor has done a lot of work on this."

"Really?" I said disparagingly, irked and surprised in equal measure that my *boss* could have made a useful suggestion.

"We've got his book in the library. It's worth taking a look."

"Fine," I said tersely.

"How's your piece for the catalogue?" He gave me a meaningful smile and I gave it back to him.

"I'll be done by the end of next week like you asked."

"Speaking of which," he said checking his watch. "It being half past four on a Friday, *I* am done. What are you up to this weekend?"

I sighed. I found Robert's attempts at camaraderie quite wearing. "Seeing some of Madeleine's friends on Saturday. I've got Sunday on my own as I'm doing a clear out."

"Well, I'll probably do some work on the catalogue on Sunday. And I ought to do some prep for my Italian book expert since he's coming in again next week."

I couldn't be bothered to say anything in response so he continued, "I know he's really over to see the chaps from the V&A but he said he'd drop by. I need to decide whether he can help us later in the year on that printing exhibition. Anyway, he's in on Monday. You should join us for lunch this time. You really need to broaden your mind a bit."

"I will if I've got the time," I said vaguely, having no intention of doing any such thing. "I'm going to get hold of a copy of that book before they shut up shop tonight." And I jogged off to the library before he could say any more.

17

I didn't get round to looking at the book from the library until Sunday. I had woken with a hangover but alone and spread out in my bed luxuriating in the fact that Madeleine was not there. Bliss unconfined albeit filtered through a hangover from the drinks party she had taken me to the previous night. She couldn't understand why I hadn't wanted to spend the night with her afterwards. I thought to tell her that it was because she was drunk and embarrassing but that would have been a bit unnecessary even for me so I gave her a kiss and told her it made sense since we both had early starts the next morning, and would be seeing each other in the evening anyway.

Having lain in for half an hour I made myself some eggs Benedict, adding the pan to the growing pile of washing up that needed to be done – my one vice – and ate them in the living room whilst reading the paper. Yawned and stretched and knew there was no point postponing the inevitable any longer. I went to my wardrobe and pulled out the four large cardboard boxes which took up nearly all the room on the right hand side and took them one by one to the living room.

My parents had recently moved out of the house where we had grown up. They had boxed up some items they thought might be of sentimental value for me and driven them round; my father ignoring my assurances that he should simply take the whole lot to the dump. So I was lumbered with them and they had lain untouched taking up what little space I had for the previous eight weeks. Madeleine's goading about the size of my flat had been the final straw. I put some on some Mahler and set to work.

The first box was filled with toys: soldiers and cars and Lego and I was appalled that my father had thought to save them. I am not a sentimental person and having such things

146

around depresses me. I kicked the box closer to the door as it could go out as it was.

The other three boxes contained books. The first was tatty children's paperbacks and the other two easy adult reads. I extracted a couple of the *Jeeves* books which I thought I might peruse once more before discarding. And then in the bottom of the final box I spotted a brown hardback that had long since lost its dust-cover. I pulled it out hoping it to be one of the *Just William* stories which I knew were very collectable and of which at one time I had possessed at least half a dozen. But the book cover was plain and the leather in good condition though there was no printing at all on the outside. Opening it, I looked at it puzzled. There was no frontispiece or printer's marks and the printed text started after one blank page, the typeface definite, very black, the letters large:

Questo diario e di Girolamo Polidoro, domestico e signorotto di Conte Francesco Bugon di Verona...

I blinked and then started laughing. "Well, well, well," I said. "Well, well, well."

I went over to the sofa and sat down and proceeded to flick through the pages attempting a cursory translation wherever my eye stopped. My Italian was rusty, and the language used was of an antiquated form, but I could still make out the sense of most of the passages I read. Then I came to a section at the end, the closing six pages and saw that instead of whole words there was simply a sequence of capital letters without punctuation.

"The code," I muttered and then laughed again.

The whole book was no more than a hundred pages in length and I closed it and rested it upon my lap. I realised how I must have ended up with it of course. In the chaos of Venice Patrick and his friend John – *John*? What was his surname? – had left many of their belongings behind;

belongings which I had then brought back to England. For some reason John had never come to collect his though he had rung about the book. Maybe it had got lost amongst some of my own things, but in any case I told him I didn't know where it was; which he *had* accepted though it sounded like he didn't believe me. He always had been immature. In any case that was the end of it. His other things had been certainly thrown out long ago. And now here was the book after all.

I opened it again at random and began a halting translation from that point. I nodded with interest as the story of an explosion on-board a ship began to take shape, a ship carrying prisoners from Nicosia. I could see why John and Patrick had been interested in it, though looking at it again now, and feeling the modern leather of the cover, I couldn't understand how they had thought it might actually be from the sixteenth century. That said, the paper inside was not modern as it had not aged the way cellulose paper would have done. My personal hunch was that the book was some publishing folly from the nineteenth century that had been re-bound at some point.

I suddenly had an idea. Flicking through the pages I held them up to the light coming in from the window. It was a grey day but it was sufficient and almost immediately I noticed a watermark on successive pages. It was of a serpent entwined with a tree. I went to my satchel and pulled out the volume on watermarks I had borrowed from the Gallery library on Friday afternoon.

I flicked through the catalogue of paper makers' marks which made up almost half of the book, humming along to the symphony on the stereo. I was in high spirits as I thought I could perhaps use this as the basis of an amusing anecdote at the start of the research paper I planned to write on the Masaccio drawing – as I was convinced it was – later on in the year. I ran my finger down the lists of watermarks, flicking through page after page, becoming increasingly certain I would not find it and that this method was either extremely limited or that the paper used was so new that it did not even register. And then my finger drew level with a symbol on a page in the last third of the catalogue. I stopped my humming and felt my heart pound within me and my hand start to shake.

The mark was there. The serpent and the tree. But it was not from the nineteenth century after all. The watermark confirmed that the book had been printed in Venice. And the date was somewhere between 1570 and 1610.

18

I lay there that evening and watched Madeleine dress, watched her pulling on her knickers and stockings; but I did not really see her at all.

Il panno è caduto dal pacco e improvvisamente una croce dorata è stata rivelata fissato con i gioielli come le stelle.

The cloth fell from the bundle and suddenly a golden cross was revealed studded with jewels like stars.

"You were a bit *languid* today darling. Somewhat lacking your usual *energy*." She put her bra on and turned to look at me straight on.

L'insieme nell'oro era gioielli da dappertutto: diamanti, rubini, smeraldi ed ametisti. E nel centro della croce ci era uno zaffiro, blu quanto il cielo...

Set in the gold were jewels from all over the world: diamonds, rubies, emeralds and amethysts. And in the centre of the cross there was a sapphire, blue as the sky...

"You're not listening to me at all are you?" She stood up in her underwear and stalked over to the chair where her clothes had been carefully folded. She picked up her blouse and gave me a wry smile. "You obviously overdid it during your clear-out. I hope you get some *vigour* back for this evening."

"The thing is," I said looking through her. "Let's say the book really is from when it purports to be: the end of the sixteenth century. So printed only a few years after the events it describes. What does that mean?"

Madeleine heaved a sigh. "I have no idea." She

wandered into the bathroom to do her make-up.

"It means the whole thing could be a contemporaneous hoax… But why would anyone bother?"

"A very good question."

"*Or* it could mean that the treasure *was* hidden and then the Turks – or whoever else – discovered it and subsequently broke the piece up so that it no longer existed in its complete form. But if the Venetians really had buried it, surely they would have done it properly. So… if it *is* true and the treasure *was* buried then…" I felt a shiver run down my spine like ice-water. "Then it's probably still there."

I jumped out of bed and skipped naked into the bathroom and stood behind Madeleine. She thought I'd come to give her a kiss and she turned, one eye mascara'd, the other not. I gave her a peck on the cheek almost absent-mindedly.

"Robert has a chap over tomorrow. An Italian book expert. I'm going to collar him and see what he thinks."

"Oh really darling?" she said coolly, looking back into the mirror, rolling the brush over her long lashes. Staring wide, then blinking wide, then smiling. "How thrilling for you both. And will you be getting dressed at all this evening? Hugh and Daisy like you, darling. Really they do. But I'm not sure they'd want your *pubes* on display over whatever Jamie Oliver bastardisation they're serving up for us tonight."

I looked at her, my head still abuzz but I realised I could do nothing more until the morning in any case. I hopped into the shower, was out again within two minutes and was dressed two minutes after that. Slicked my hair back, slipped on a pair of loafers and was ready at the same time as Madeleine emerged from the bathroom, her cosmetic transformation complete.

"Do you like this lipstick?"

She pouted her lips out for me. They were blood red. *Ruby* red. I smiled. "Yes, very much."

She was pleased. "Shall we go. And you will be good tonight, won't you darling. You will *unwind* and not go on about that book or talk shop about art history. They'll all be lawyers there and they just won't be interested in that sort of thing." She gave me a little kiss and smiled at me indulgently.

She was wearing a pair of slacks and a delicate chiffon blouse through which you could see her lacy bra. It was a good look, a sexy look and, since I could do no more this evening, I decided that I would enjoy her later.

The phone rang just as we were walking out.

"Leave it," she said.

"Let me just see who it is."

It rang twice more before the answerphone kicked in.

"Can we leave it please?" said Madeleine, irritably now. "They're only round the corner so we don't have any excuse to be late."

"*...please leave me a message.*"

"Julius." The voice rang out loud and squawked with feedback from the old machine. "Julius, I hope you're doing fine. Haven't seen you for a few months. But I got an invitation to a College reunion thing the other day, so I assume you got one as well? Just wondering whether you were going or not. Anyway give me a call if you get the chance. See you." And then just as we were actually leaving and the door swinging shut behind us we heard the sound of the receiver being juggled and lifted again at the last minute, and the voice again, embarrassed, "Oh sorry. It's Patrick by the way."

19

By eight o'clock on Monday morning I had taken up residence in a corner of the Gallery library, my mind ringing with the same thought that had occupied me throughout that interminable dinner and the long hours of sleeplessness which had followed: could the book really be genuine?

If it was of the age the watermark suggested then surely it must be. I would show it to Robert's book expert at lunchtime. He'd be able to tell me. I could get the pages carbon dated to be confirm it. And if the book was contemporary with the events described in it then why would it not be a true account? And if it was true, then the cross must have existed; must still exist.

I tried to stay calm.

To go forwards I would need to produce a full translation of the text. Fine. For the moment though I just needed something to prevent my mind from racing. I went to the bookshelves and pulled down Norwich's *A History of Venice*, and *The Venetian Empire* by Morris, and read through the basic story: from the sack of Nicosia, through the siege of Famagusta and all the way to Bragadino's grisly end. Polidoro was mentioned in both. According to Norwich:

...a certain Girolamo Polidoro, one of the few survivors of the siege, managed to steal the skin from the Arsenal of Constantinople and return it to Bragadino's sons, who deposited it in the church of S. Gregorio. From here, on 18 May 1596, it was transferred to SS. Giovanni e Paolo and placed in a niche behind the urn which forms part of the hero's memorial. Here it still remains today ... The niche was opened on 24 November 1961 at the instigation of the leading authority on Bragadino – and his direct descendant – Signora Maria Grazia Siliato. It was found to contain a leaden casket in which were several pieces of tanned human skin. They were replaced in March 1962, after a restoration of the monument.

Immediately there was a discrepancy though. According to Morris:

Finally it [Bragadino's skin] was taken to Constantinople by Mustapha Pasha himself, and presented as a trophy of victory to the Sultan. It was placed in the Arsenal in the Golden Horn, directly opposite the place where, 350 years before, the Venetian forces had breached the walls of Constantinople and begun their imperial history. In 1650 a citizen of Verona, Jerome Polidoro, was persuaded by the Bragadino family to steal it. It was brought to Venice, and laid at last, all torments ended, in the church of San Zanipolo. As for Polidoro, the Turks caught him and tortured him appallingly, but he was ransomed by the Bragadinos, and given a pension of five ducats a month by the grateful Signory.

The names were different, Girolamo versus Jerome, but that was a trivial matter of anglicisation. More to the point the dates were wildly out. If Morris was correct then there was no way that Polidoro could have been a survivor of the siege at all and hence his account as an eyewitness must be a fiction.

On other points the two accounts were in agreement but there was no mention of the Cross of St Peter and Paul – and certainly not its hiding – in either. This did not perturb me unduly as it lent credence to the notion that it was an exclusive gathering who had been present when the treasure was buried. Also, Norwich again:

Nicosia was a rich city, generously endowed with treasures ecclesiastical and secular, western and Byzantine. It was a full week [after the defeat] before all the gold and silver, the precious stones and enamelled reliquaries, the jewelled vestments, the velvets and brocades had been loaded on to the carts and trundled away – the richest spoils to fall into Turkish hands since the capture of Constantinople itself, well over a century before.

So could a treasure such as the cross have existed in Nicosia? Certainly it seemed possible.

At the back of Norwich was a full list of the Doges of Venice with their dates:

List of Doges
726-1797

Orso Ipato 726-737
Interregnum 737-742
Teodato Ipato 742-755
Galla Gaulo 755-756
Domenico Monegario 756-764
Maurizio Galbaio 764-775
Giovanni Galbaio 775-804
Obelario degli Antenori 804-811
Agnello Participazio 811-827
Giustiniano Participazio 827-829
Giovanni Participazio I 829-836
Pietro Tradonico 836-864
Orso Participazio I 864-881
Giovanni Participazio II 881-887
Pietro Candiano I 887
Pietro Tribuno 888-912
Orso Participazio II 912-932
Pietro Candiano II 932-939
Pietro Participazio 939-942
Pietro Candiano III 942-959
Pietro Candiano IV 959-976
Pietro Orseolo I 976-978
Vitale Candiano 978-979
Tribuno Memmo 979-991
Pietro Orseolo II 991-1008
Otto Orseolo 1008-1026
Pietro Centranico 1026-1032
Domenico Flabanico 1032-1043
Domenico Contarini 1043-1071
Domenico Selvo 1071-1084
Vitale Falier 1084-1096
Vitale Michiel I 1096-1102
Ordelafo Falier 1102-1118
Domenico Michiel 1118-1130
Pietro Polani 1130-1148
Domenico Morosini 1148-1156
Vitale Michiel II 1156-1172
Sebastiano Ziani 1172-1178
Orio Mastropiero 1178-1192
Enrico Dandolo 1192-1205

Pietro Ziani 1205-1229
Giacomo Tiepolo 1229-1249
Marin Morosini 1249-1253
Renier Zeno 1253-1268
Lorenzo Tiepolo 1268-1275
Jacopo Contarini 1275-1280
Giovanni Dandolo 1280-1289
Pietro Gradenigo 1289-1311
Marino Zorzi 1311-1312
Giovanni Soranzo 1312-1328
Francesco Dandolo 1329-1339
Bartolomeo Gradenigo 1339-1342
Andre Dandolo 1343-1354
Marin Falier 1354-1355
Giovanni Gradenigo 1355-1356
Giovanni Dolfin 1356-1361
Lorenzo Celsi 1361-1365
Marco Corner 1365-1368
Andrea Contarini 1368-1382
Michele Morosini 1382
Antonio Venier 1382-1400
Michele Steno 1400-1413
Tommaso Mocenigo 1414-1423
Francesco Foscari 1423-1457
Pasquale Malipiero 1457-1462
Cristoforo Moro 1462-1471
Nicolo Tron 1471-1473
Nicolo Marcello 1473-1474
Pietro Mocenigo 1474-1476
Andrea Vendramin 1476-1478
Giovanni Mocenigo 1478-1485
Marco Barbarigo 1485-1486
Agostino Barbarigo 1486-1501
Leonardo Loredan 1501-1521
Antonio Grimani 1521-1523
Andrea Gritti 1521-1538
Pietro Lando 1539-1545
Francesco Dona 1545-1553
Marcantonio Trevisan 1553-1554
Francesco Venier 1554-1556

Lorenzo Priuli 1556-1559
Girolamo Priuli 1559-1567
Pietro Loredan 1567-1570
Alvise Mocenigo I 1570-1577
Sebastiano Venier 1577-1578
Nicolo da Ponte 1578-1585
Pasquale Ciogna 1585-1595
Marino Grimani 1595-1605
Leonardo Dona 1606-1612
Marcantonion Memmo 1612-1615
Giovanni Bembo 1615-1618
Nicolo Dona 1618
Antonio Priuli 1618-1623
Franceso Contarini 1623-1624
Giovanni Corner I 1625-1629
Nicolo Contarini 1630-1631
Francesco Erizzo 1631-1646
Francesco Molin 1646-1655
Carlo Contarini 1655-1656
Francesco Corner 1656
Bertucci Valier 1656-1658
Giovanni Pesaro 1658-1659
Domenico Contarini 1659-1675
Nicolo Sagredo 1675-1676
Alvise Contarini 1676-1684
Marcantonio Giustinian 1684-1688
Francesco Morosini 1688-1694
Silvestro Valier 1694-1700
Alvise Mocenigo II 1700-1709
Giovanni Corner II 1709-1722
Alvise Mocenigo III 1722-1732
Carlo Ruzzini 1732-1735
Alvise Pisani 1735-1741
Pietro Grimani 1741-1752
Francesco Loredan 1752-1762
Marco Foscarini 1762-1763
Alvise Mocenigo IV 1763-1778
Paolo Renier 1779-1789
Lodovico Manin 1789-1797

I scanned down the list till I got to the time of the siege: Alvise Mocenigo, 1570-1577. From my as yet highly unsystematic reading of the journal, I remembered that Polidoro had referred to him as the new Doge. It was at least consistent.

I went back to the shelves and pulled down Volume III

of Hill's *History of Cyprus*. His account of the sieges and the Turkish conquest occupied some one hundred pages in total. I skimmed much of this concentrating on the period between the fall of Nicosia and start of the siege of Famagusta. There was again no mention of the cross. But Hill quoted one source, Paruta, as saying that before the final assault on Famagusta the commander of the Turkish forces, Mustafa Pasha had encouraged his troops by promising them:

> *...the highest honours and prizes for valour: he pictured to them the booty and the spoils, reminded them of the whole regiments enriched by the sack of Nicosia and prayed and implored them to bring no shame on troops so lately victorious, to feel no fear before the arms of men to whom they had always been a terror. He reminded them of their successes at Nicosia and showed them that with equal ease, though with richer fruit, they could achieve another glorious victory, and end the war.*

...with richer fruit... Did that mean that Mustafa knew of the existence of the Cross of St Peter and Paul? Of its removal from Nicosia and journey to Famagusta? I'd read that when Famagusta was finally taken and despite Bragadino's gory end, Mustafa sent his Janissaries quickly into the city to regain order and looting was limited compared with Nicosia. Could he have done this because he was specifically looking for the cross? Could it really have been a treasure of such colossal beauty that he would have concentrated his attention on it in this fashion? And could this explain why he had flown into a rage with Bragadino and had him attacked? The books were not clear on why this had occurred but had offered three suggestions: that it was because Bragadino had executed Turkish prisoners; because he was not deferential enough before the Pasha; or simply because the Pasha was mad. But if mad, why restrict the pillage of the city? And it was surely

commonplace in those brutal times for prisoners to be murdered. So what could it have been that made him so angry? Was it that when honeyed persuasion had failed to elicit from Bragadino the hiding place of the Most Holy Cross of St Peter and St Paul, Mustafa had thought to torture it out of him? But Bragadino kept his secret to the grave and Mustafa left the island empty-handed.

My head was spinning. Too much speculation. Far too much. Back to fact. What did Hill say about Polidoro?

Bragadino's skin and the heads of the other victims were presented to the Sultan, who placed them in the Bagno. Calepio, who was confined in that prison on the charge of being a papal spy, tried, when he regained his freedom, to steal the skin, but was unsuccessful. In 1580, however, a certain Jerome Polidoro, of Verona, at the instance of the Bragadino family, abstracted it from the Arsenal, and conveyed it to the Venetian Bailie, and it was brought to Venice by James Soranzo, ambassador to the Porte, in 1581. At first placed in a pilaster of the Church of San Gregorio, where the Bragadino family were buried, it was on 3 May 1596 deposited in an urn in the church of SS. Giovanni e Paolo.

And in a footnote:

Polidoro, who was frightfully tortured when his theft was discovered and brought home to him, was after some years ransomed by the martyr's brother, Antony, and on 18 Feb. 1588 was granted by the Senate a pension of five ducats a month.

Hill did not refer to Polidoro being a survivor of the siege as Norwich did. However, the dates did at least now coincide and the story was again plausible. Polidoro could have been present at Famagusta. He perhaps returned home to Venice with the other survivors in 1572. Then some time between 1572 and 1580 he set off again to the East to recover his master's skin. In 1580 it was returned to Venice though Polidoro himself was captured and tortured and did not make it back until 1588. He was granted a pension and returned to eke out his final days in Verona perhaps, the place of his birth.

When then did he write the account in the journal? Between 1572 and 1580 or after 1588? Either was possible.

I needed be more precise. His journal was *written* during 1570 and 1571. When was it *printed?*

Surely he would have been asked to submit his journal to the Signoria and more particularly the Council of Ten on his return so that they could glean what they could about the Turks from his account. So perhaps this book formed part of the Venetian State Archive. Perhaps the Ten were also interested in recovering this fabulous treasure. Perhaps this was their prime concern. But then why the code? If Polidoro knew where the treasure was why did he not just tell the Council of Ten where it was hidden? If he was a loyal subject of Venice as he described himself surely it would be his duty to do such a thing.

I opened Polidoro's account towards the back and looked again at the coded pages, staring at them, my eyes seeing patterns in the letters where there was none, *V E L G A S A G A I I...*

I backtracked and looked at the conclusion of the journal proper, translating the final paragraph of the main text:

> *I have recorded this journal for the glory of Venice and the love of God so that even if I do not survive the Most Holy Cross of St Peter and St Paul will be returned to the great and noble Venetian Empire, which was three-eighth's protector of Byzantium. Therefore I write these last pages as a code which I have devised so that only the worthy will be able to understand it and that this great treasure might be kept from unbelievers. Although I did not see the exact hiding place of the treasure, my master Marcantonio Bragadino (may the saints look after him in heaven) told me of its location. Therefore I say, read this code,*

you sons of Venice and then the cross of the true apostles can be returned to Venice where it will stay for all eternity. I set out the directions below and declare that everything I have written in this journal is true, and dedicated to God and Venice, Girolamus Polidorus.

So although Polidoro did not see where the treasure was hidden Bragadino told him where it was. Why? If he had wanted the servants to know the exact location surely he would have told them at the start. Why only tell them later? And when? Before he went to see the Pasha because he thought he might not return? But he surely suspected no foul play or he would not have gone at all. So when? And why tell Polidoro? If he had wanted to tell someone else surely he would have told another noble not his servant who could have gossiped about it to anyone.

I stood up and stretched and walked to the window, exercising my eyes, looking into the distance. It didn't make sense. The Council of Ten would have taken Polidoro's account. If he had told them he knew where the treasure was then why would anything be in code? They would have asked him for the location. First nicely. Then with any of the considerable means of persuasion at their disposal. The Ten were relentless in their pursuit of Venice's interests and quite frequently brutal as well.

I had in my mind a quote about them. My hand hovered in front of the book shelves and then I found it: Plumb's classic account of the Renaissance.

The glass manufacture of Murano, based on secrets learned in the East, was guarded by the Council of Ten: for any workman with the knowledge of its manufacture to leave Venice was an act of treason. The Council hunted him down and killed him.

Relentless.

Along with the monopoly in glass went another – the making of mosaic: this art, derived from Byzantium, was practised only in Venice. Venetian jewellers had no rivals in the late Middle Ages, and emperors and kings sent there for their crosses and sceptres … As the wealth and prosperity of Europe lifted, so the riches of Venice soared. On the threshold of the Renaissance, Venice possessed an unrivalled trade, and a stable and immensely powerful government firmly in the hand of its patricians. It was a city of hatchet-faced merchants. Jacopo Loredan entered in his great ledger: 'The Doge Foscari: my debtor for the death of my father and uncle.' After Foscari had been harried to death and his son killed, Loredan wrote on the opposite page, 'Paid.'

I slipped the book back on its shelf and breathed deeply. The Ten would not have let this rest. That much was clear. So Polidoro must have convinced them that he did not know where the treasure was hidden. And as far as the account in his journal was concerned, he didn't. But it would have given the Ten enough to confirm what they must have already known from Bragadino's dispatches that the cross had been hidden; and enough for them to leave Polidoro alone.

But Polidoro *did* know where the treasure was. Perhaps he had always known; perhaps he worked it out later. Either way he knew. And at some point he decided to go and get it. Surely this would have coincided with his trip to recover Bragadino's skin from Constantinople, 1579 say. But things went wrong and he was captured and when he returned to Venice eight years later he did not bring the cross back with him.

That was almost seventeen years after the siege of Famagusta. He would have been perhaps mid-forties then or maybe even older. He would have been too old and too scarred to contemplate another trip and, besides, the Ten would surely have been watching him. So instead he set the location of the Treasure down in code. Perhaps as a letter which he sent to his brother or to a close friend. The Ten intercepted the letter and in time this also became part of the archive; in time the two got incorporated into the same book, with a linking piece the Ten themselves wrote.

Backtrack. Perhaps Polidoro wrote the coded letter in 1579 just before his trip to Constantinople, in case he did not return. Yes, more likely; but it would be impossible to know for certain without first breaking the code.

But it was starting to make sense now. Why didn't the Ten torture Polidoro when they discovered the letter? Because he would have been rotting in a Turkish jail. And by the time he returned to Venice he was a hero and they would have missed their chance. Perhaps in any case they never believed that a servant could really hold the key to a treasure so profound.

So, the journal and the coded letter were written by Polidoro but not at the same time. The Ten got hold of them both but never cracked the code. Therefore the treasure could still be there.

I blew out my cheeks and tried to keep calm. The librarian looked over sternly.

I walked back to my corner. Could the treasure be there? Who knew about it? Who was present at the burial? Seven servants and six nobles. In addition to Polidoro and his then master Francesco Bugon:

By the torchlight we could see eleven riders: five nobles – Captain General Marc'Antonio Bragadino, Lorenzo Tiepolo, Captain of Paphos, Astorre Baglione, General of the Militia, Count Sigismondo da Casoldo, and Captain Bernadino da Gubio – and their five squires, including my great friend Giuseppe, and finally Alvise who was the head servant of Captain Bragadino's household.

The only servant who saw the cross being buried was the *head servant* mentioned, Alvise. And he had been killed that same day. As had Bugon and Sigismondo. Bragadino had of course been killed by Mustafa Pasha. So that left

Tiepolo, Baglione and da Gubio.

I looked again at Hill. Astorre Baglione had been one of Bragadino's party when meeting Mustafa. He had been killed there and then by the Pasha's guards. Tiepolo had been left in charge of Famagusta in Bragadino's absence. When the Pasha's troops entered the city they caught him and hanged him. That left da Gubio. Captain Bernadino da Gubio. What had happened to him, I wondered.

Hill did not mention him but in the footnotes other sources were referred to: Calepio and Paruta again; and Gatto. Any of these might contain information on da Gubio. There were also references to *Excerpta Cypria*. I had seen this on the shelves and got it down. It was an old cloth bound book rather larger than A4, the cover battered and the titles in faded gold leaf. But inside on the first page the printing was clear: *Excerpta Cypria: Materials for a History of Cyprus* by Claude Deval Cobham. It was a selection of sources that Cobham had translated from the original and there were entries for both Paruta and Calepio.

Paruta's was the official account of the siege of both Nicosia and Famagusta and formed part of the Venetian archive. Calepio, a monk who had been an eyewitness to the siege at Nicosia had been enslaved afterwards and had put together a description of the siege of Famagusta from the accounts he had heard from other prisoners in Constantinople. I knew that what I must do to ensure the veracity of the Polidoro journal would be to first translate it fully and then compare the details he gave with those in Calepio and Paruta and any other contemporary sources I could find.

I glanced at my watch. Ten o'clock. I would meet up with Robert and his Italian in two hours. Until then I would make a proper start on the translation. But before I could begin, something caught my eye in the account by Calepio. A list of the *Christian commanders who died in Famagosta* and amongst them, near the bottom of the page, was Captain

Bernadino da Gubio.

So he had died too.

All those who had seen the burial of the treasure had perished.

So if by some chance Girolamo Polidoro had come to know of the cross's exact location, he would have been the only one alive enough to have done anything about it.

20

"Julius, this is Giovanni from Rome. Julius is one of our curators of Renaissance art here at the Gallery. Giovanni is an expert in the history of Italian printing and processes."

"Giovanni Galbaio at your disposal," he said. His English had an American twang. "How is it I have not met you on my previous visits here?"

"Commitments of work," I said determined not to catch Robert's eye. I handed Galbaio my card and he returned the compliment. We sat down around a small table in one of the meeting rooms. A platter of sandwiches and some soft drinks had been laid out for us there and we helped ourselves.

"Ah I do enjoy these visits," said Galbaio. "If for no other reason than for your sandwiches. Far more civilised than a full and sleep-inducing Roman lunch." He was a tall man in his late thirties, brown eyes, his hair well coiffured and slightly bouffant, dark but with a distinctive white streak flowing through the right side. "Robert has been telling me you are working on a Masaccio problem at the moment, Julius. I have studied the Brancacci frescoes in detail if I can be of any assistance."

"That is very kind."

"Don't mention it." He picked up a sandwich and started eating and I wondered whether now really was the right time for this, but then just shrugged and carried on regardless.

"Actually there might be something you can help me with."

"But of course."

Robert glared at me but I ignored him and pulled out the journal from my satchel. The Italian wiped his hands on a serviette and took it from me.

"What do you make of it?"

164

Galbaio turned it over in his hands. "Unremarkable calfskin cover; certainly a replacement." He opened it and looked closely at the paper. "Aah," he said in a long drawn out breath. "It is *old*. You can tell from the feel of the rag paper, the colour of it, the *smell* of it..."

"How old?"

Galbaio shrugged. "At least three hundred, possibly four. What is it?" he asked taking a loupe from his pocket to inspect the fibres in the paper more closely.

"It's an account of the siege of Famagusta by one Girolamo Polidoro. Are you OK?"

Galbaio had started coughing and almost dropped the book. "I'm fine, I'm fine," he spluttered. "Fine, really." But he took the glass of water Robert offered him.

"My apologies," he said eventually. "Your sandwiches have at last disagreed with me." He gave me a wan smile and then looked back to the journal, reading the opening page. "Polidoro," he said softly. "Girolamo Polidoro."

"So," I said wishing to get back to the point. "You think this might potentially be an old book? It could date from the end of the sixteenth century, say?"

"It is... *possible*. It is certainly possible. I could not tell for sure though without looking more closely at the structure of the paper, running some tests... But it is certainly possible." He fixed me with a stare. "Can I ask you how the Gallery came by this book?"

"Oh it's not the Gallery's. It's mine." I put out my hand and Galbaio passed the book back to me with, I thought, a certain reluctance.

"And where did you get it?" asked Robert no doubt feeling left out.

"I picked it up in Venice a few years ago."

"In Venice you say?" Giovanni looked at me curiously. "Not Rome?"

"It may have been originally purchased in Rome. But I acquired it in Venice. Why?"

"Oh... no reason." He waved a hand.

"And what do you think of it?"

"It is most interesting, of course. The siege of Famagusta is a fascinating story and always has its collectors. Indeed, if you are thinking of selling I would be glad to make you an offer."

"No. Thank you."

"Perhaps I could then at least take the book away and run those tests on it to determine whether it is indeed genuine." He extended a hand to me.

"No, that's fine Giovanni. Perhaps we'll do them some other time." I replaced the book in my bag. "I was just interested, that's all."

He blinked at me. "Of course."

"Do you collect books as well then Giovanni?" asked Robert.

"Yes. Occasionally." For a moment he gazed still at my bag, but then he looked over at Robert, forcing a smile. "My family used to run a book store in Rome for many years and in Venice before that; but sadly it went bust. So I became an expert instead."

Robert continued to laugh long after we had stopped. "Talking with Giovanni today has been very interesting, Julius," he said sycophantically. "He is definitely interested in assisting should we go ahead with the printing exhibition later this year." He gave me a sudden sly smile. "Julius, I see that you still haven't got yourself a cleaning lady?"

I frowned. Looking down at myself I realised that in my haste to get dressed that morning I'd put on a crumpled shirt from the previous day. I flushed in embarrassment and forced myself to laugh with him. "No not yet. Though I am still looking."

"I would have thought your delectable girlfriend would have done your ironing for you."

"I'll tell her that, Robert and see what she has to say." My cool had returned now. "In any case," I said dismissing him like a fly. "I am quite capable of handling my own laundry and any other domestic chores. It is just that I have been extremely busy recently."

"You are really looking for a cleaning lady?" Galbaio asked. There was a rising note of eagerness in his voice.

"Yes," I said puzzled that this could have been of any interest to him.

"Then I can recommend one."

I looked at him in surprise. "*You* can?"

"My brother lives in London," he explained. "He has a domestic. Most reliable."

"I live in Primrose Hill. Is that close to your brother?"

"Oh yes," he said.

"Where does your brother live?"

"I always get these names confused..."

"Hampstead?"

"Precisely."

"That's just round the corner from me."

"Well then, I can ask my brother to see if she will come round to you, if that would be convenient."

"That would be *most* convenient. I am *doubly* obliged to you now. Here is my home address." I took my card back from him and scribbled on the reverse. "That really would be very kind. It's easier to find a new girlfriend in London that to get a reliable cleaner."

"I'll tell Madeleine that and see what she has to say," said Robert with a sneer at me.

"I'm sure she would wholeheartedly agree."

I left them together after we'd finished the sandwiches. Robert reminded me that I had promised him the last section of his catalogue by the end of the week. I nodded vaguely at him, thanked Galbaio again for his help and then returned to the library.

So the book was old. It was from the right period. A carbon dating would confirm it of course but for the

167

moment I was satisfied I was dealing with the genuine article. So what to do now? Robert's catalogue could of course wait. Even the dating of the Masaccio could wait. I needed to get on with the translation which with luck would take no more than a few days.

I popped back to my office at six o'clock. Richard had of course long since gone but he had left a yellow post-it note on my desk telling me that Madeleine had called. The phone rang as I stood there.

"Hi darling. I didn't know whether I'd catch you before you left. Just to say we won't actually be kicking off till seven o'clock so you've got plenty of time. Are you about to leave?"

"I need to work late."

"But I've got a launch tonight."

"Robert's putting me under pressure to finish a piece for his catalogue."

"But why can't you just do it tomorrow?"

"Because there's too much to do. I'll probably have to work late for the rest of the week."

"But Julius, you've known about this for ages. It's the biggest exhibition I've organised and I've told everyone you'll come."

I felt a flash of irritation, but I controlled it. "I'm sorry Maddie. I will try and make it along later."

"But—"

I hung up the phone and went back to the library to continue the translation.

21

The next week was busy. The translation took up most of my time but I was forced to do a few hours preparation for a tour to Paris that Robert suddenly decided he needed. And then there was the forthcoming Renaissance exhibition. I tested the "Masaccio" drawing and found the paper to be from the eighteenth century and promptly lost interest in it. The piece for the catalogue I dashed off in a couple of hours, and gave it to Robert just meeting his Friday deadline. Hardly incisive stuff but Robert received it excitedly and read it one careful sheet at a time as though I had presented him with an essay by Umberto Eco. He was in raptures by the end and thanked me profusely for working late every night to finish it.

Fool.

I did not see Madeleine at all during the week which was a relief but prompted a series of increasingly frantic phone calls from her as the days passed. She had been furious about my not attending her launch. But that had been predictable and after a couple of days she swung around and started being apologetic, saying that she was aware of how hard I was working and that she had not meant to put me under additional pressure. Both her anger and apology were tiresome. I preferred her when she left emotion out of our relationship and was cool and unfeeling. She was certainly sexier that way.

I had agreed to see her at the weekend and stay at her place in Knightsbridge. Which was fine especially as my kitchen was becoming increasingly untenable. Although I was quite able to manage for myself – despite Richard's snide comments, my ironing was normally immaculate – washing-up was something I simply could not abide and in the period I'd been without a cleaner, I had been fighting a constant battle with it; a battle I was beginning to lose.

Since I'd been working late I had let it go completely. Despite this, the rest of the flat was still tidy enough, although there were an increasing number of books and papers covering any available flat surface in the living room.

So, a weekend spent at Madeleine's with her fussing over me suited me fine. She was too docile from having not seen me all week for the sex to be particularly good but then I felt tired anyway. She had *really* missed me though she said. *Really, really* missed me. Not seeing each other all week had *really* made her understand how much she loved me. Apparently.

By that weekend in any case, the translation was complete. A working translation only but satisfactory for my purposes. I knew that the next step would be to tackle the code. But as a reward for having completed the translation I first indulged myself with a bit of research on the cross itself. I went straight to the library again on Monday morning to do some digging. As expected neither Calepio nor Paruta made any mention of the Cross of St Peter and Paul and nor did Sozomeno in his account of the siege of Nicosia. A complete reread of Hill and Norwich and various specific books on art in Venice also yielded nothing.

I adopted a different approach. In Polidoro's account he had Bragadino holding up the cross saying:

Look upon the Most Holy Cross of St Peter and St Paul, the greatest of all the treasures taken from Constantinople.

Taken from Constantinople. Clearly this indicated the cross had been booty from the Fourth Crusade, in which Venice had lain waste to Constantinople and captured a good proportion of its empire in the process. Therefore the cross was most likely 12th Century in style. The sapphire at the heart of the cross had been brought from the Far East which was certainly possible since the trading routes of

Byzantium like those of Venice herself, stretched far into Asia. And the fact that the cross was a reliquary was also consistent with the period.

But what did it look like? I wandered over to the bookshelves once more, returning the librarian's stare until she looked away. Evidently she was used to spending hours in there on her own with no one to witness her lack of industry. I pulled down a large heavily illustrated book on the art and architecture of Venice and flicked to the section on the Treasury of St Mark's. It gave a list of the major pieces within this collection all of which had been looted from Constantinople. Unfortunately there were no crosses there and again no mention of this cross in particular. I was not perturbed. The collection had been broken up during Napoleon's time with much of it vanishing, and it was only under Austrian rule that the collection was reassembled. A full record of what had originally been in the treasury would only be possible by reference to archive material, probably held in Venice itself. I was certain a trip could be arranged for the next month or so: it would not take much to find an excuse that Robert would agree to.

But it still did not answer my question. What did the cross look like? I turned back a page and gazed at a plate of the Pala d'Oro. The work of mediaeval goldsmiths in Constantinople at the end of the tenth century, this altar piece was then further embellished and reset in 1209 and 1345. The upper third showed the archangel Michael surrounded by medallions of the saints, all in enamel. The lower part had at its centre Christ enthroned and was flanked by further enamelled portraits of the prophets, apostles and angels, and the whole framed with plaques showing scenes from the lives of Christ and St Mark. The entire piece, some ten feet wide by five feet high was lustrous with gold, a buttery yellow Byzantine gold, and luminous with the gems which decorated it: rubies, emeralds, pearls, topaz and amethysts. The total effect even in a photograph was breathtaking.

I put the book back and walked to the window but instead of looking out I closed my eyes for a moment and imagined a cross before me, simply wrought yet set about with gems and decorated at the base with a small cloisonné panel of the type I had just seen. The cross was aglow with a soft golden light and at its centre was a single sapphire of the deepest, clearest blue.

22

"Julius, please pick up."

I stared at the answerphone from where I sat at my dining table.

"Please Julius. I know you're there."

It was Thursday. Four days since the weekend. Staying with Madeleine had been all very well but it had made her even more needy and what I wanted now was space and distance from all distraction.

"Please Julius. You've not returned any of my calls since Sunday."

It was embarrassing. She was meant to be a charming and detached adult but she went to pieces whenever I failed to call her. And this had been happening more and more recently. Less and less icy reserve. Less and less chill formality. The very things which so attracted me to her had been melted away in a syrup tide of affection.

"*Please* Julius." She hung up. I shrugged and looked again at the papers before me. I had been studying them since Monday: the six pages of code, evenly printed. I was certain that it represented a letter but that did not help me. I had already tried everything I could think of in order to break it but I had no skill in this field. My mind simply did not work in the right way. I could think laterally about art history and get to the truth, yet felt completely at sea with these codes. They addled and rattled me and however much I read up on them, about *monoalphabetic* and *polyalphabetic* ciphers, the more confused I became. It felt like doing maths at school all over again. That feeling of walking timidly on a slippery floor and losing my footing just as I thought I had grasped a principle. That giddy, nauseous sensation of being unable to control or understand. This code brought it all back and yet with its solution was the possibility of a treasure beyond compare. But to solve it would require someone with a facility for this type of thing; and I was not that person.

There was a knock at the door.

Just for a second I thought that Madeleine had made her last call from a mobile and was now standing outside my flat. But when I crept to the window her car was not there. There was another knock and I shrugged and I went to open the door.

A tall girl, mid-twenties, was standing there. She was Madeleine's height but, unlike Madeleine, she did not carry herself well. Her head was bowed and her shoulders slouched and she looked thin rather than slim, mean-breasted. Her olive skinned face was framed by straggly shoulder length hair which was unattractive both in its cut and its mouse brownness. She was dressed in a pair of blue jeans and a navy sweatshirt, a cheap looking pair of white trainers, the sort you would buy in a supermarket, and in her right hand she carried an orange bucket containing bottles, cloths and aerosol cans.

"People at the bottom, he let me in," she said in a strong Italian accent, hardly looking up.

"I don't want to buy anything," I said frowning at her bucket of pathetic merchandise. "And please leave the building immediately or I'll call the police." And immigration too, I thought. She had an Albanian look about her.

She looked up startled as I made to close the door on her. She had big sad dirty green eyes which when they were wide open like this seemed almost too big for her face. "*Please*," she said, her brow creasing in alarm.

I was getting heartily sick of women saying please to me today and never had time for hawkers anyway so I gave her a look which made my thoughts clear and then shut the door on her. Or at least attempted to. She jammed her bucket in the way.

"Please," she said again meekly, her tousled head

appearing in the gap. "I not sell anything."

"Then what do you want?"

"I sent here."

"You sent what here?"

"No." I had had to open the door a fraction again so I could see her full face, and it was creased with the frustration of trying to make herself understood. "No I *sent* here by boss."

"I don't have a clue—"

"By boss. Signor Galbaio."

"Ah!" A sudden realisation hit me. "You're the *cleaner.*"

She nodded, smiling now, showing her teeth. "I am his cleaner and he say – his *brother* say – you want cleaner too. So he told me to come to you."

"Why didn't you phone first?"

She hung her head. "My English is bad and so telephone no good. Sorry for trouble. Today no good?"

"Well it's not great," I said frowning at her but then, "No come in. You've got to start sometime."

"Oh thank you, thank you." She seemed positively delirious with pleasure and she came two meek steps into the room. "Thank you."

I sighed and closed the door. "What is your name?"

"Francesca Morosini."

"Well Francesca, I am Julius Masters." I put out a hand and she shook it with a grip so limp I wondered whether she would have the sturdiness to unsettle even the lightest dust. "What should I pay you?"

"Two pounds for hour?" she asked tentatively.

"Am I allowed to do that? Isn't that below the minimum wage?"

Her eyes widened in surprise again and then she gave an expressive shrug. "*Minimum wage?*"

I smiled. "Two pounds it is then." She nodded like a dog. "So long as you do a good job. Let me show you the flat. It's not big so I'd expect you to do it in two hours only."

"Two hours fine," she said nodding dutifully.

"OK then. So this is the living room."

"You are writer?" She pointed at the papers on the table and which had recently spread to the sofa as well.

"No. An art historian actually. You know what that is?"

"Art. Yes. In Italy we have lots of art." She laughed at her joke, a not unattractive laugh as it happened, injecting a shot of vivacity into her otherwise lifeless face.

"This room I would expect to be vacuum-cleaned and the surfaces dusted. Do not tidy up or touch any of the papers."

"You have vacuum cleaner?"

"Yes. In the cupboard by the front door. This is the bedroom. Vacuum-clean and dust in here. Do not move anything. This is the bathroom."

"There is no bath. Just shower."

"Yes. You don't need to do the bathroom today but normally I would expect you to clean the shower and the mirror and the floor every week. I want you to tidy up in here each week as well and put the towels for a wash. The washing machine is in the kitchen. If there is any ironing to do I will leave it in here and I expect that to be done as well."

She nodded meekly.

"And this," I said leading her round, "is the kitchen."

She stepped inside and then abruptly stopped, her mouth open and her eyes transfixed by the pile of plates and pans in the sink. *"Madonna."*

I felt my face flush with embarrassment. "You have caught me at a bad moment," I said awkwardly.

She turned to look at me, the natural colouring in her face drained away. "You have party?"

"No. It's just built up over time."

She screwed up her eyes for a moment, muttered something to herself in Italian and then sighed. "OK," she said, pushing up the sleeves of her sweatshirt and lifting a stack of crockery out of the sink. "I start here."

I let her get on with it. I knew I had to go back into the living room and face my papers but as I was currently devoid of inspiration I thought some liquid refreshment might help. I took a bottle from the fridge and poured myself a glass of wine. I stood there sipping the cooling Chablis and watched Francesca. She worked methodically and a stack of washed and rinsed plates appeared on the draining board faster than I thought possible. When working she seemed to have an energy at odds with her subservient and enervated demeanour and her movements were fluid and strangely attractive. Her legs clothed in tight jeans were long and her bottom firm and both moved pleasingly as she worked. Her upper body in her baggy sweatshirt was still a mystery to me but I suddenly felt a greater desire to investigate.

I walked back out into the living room, moved some papers and sat on the sofa continuing to sip my wine and attempting to focus again on the code problem.

Presently the Italian walked back into the living room, her face flushed from the hot water and her sweatshirt damp with suds. "I take this off," she said to me and pulled it up and over her head leaving her in a tight fitting singlet with some basketball logo on it. "I can leave this to dry?"

She held up the sweatshirt and I pointed to the back of a chair. She lay it out and then retrieved the Dyson from the cupboard by the door and carried it round into the bedroom. Her arms were long and slim but lightly muscled so that they flexed agreeably when she moved and her face set on its task suddenly had a certain attractiveness in profile too.

After twenty minutes, during which I did no more than empty my wine glass, she emerged from the bedroom and made a start on the living room. I moved to one of the chairs at the table. She dusted down the sofa and then looked at me, with her eyes slightly lowered. "It's OK if I vacuum here also?"

"Yes. Fine."

She nodded gratefully, plugged in and started cleaning. How to proceed? I wondered, opening the Polidoro journal in front of me at random again and gazing at it. Perhaps I could show the code to Robert and see what he thought. But he was a fool at the best of times and in any case I didn't want to get too many people involved. I imagined again my vision of the cross and thought I really didn't want to share it unless absolutely necessary.

"Sorry," she said banging into me. She switched the vacuum off and then cowered by my side. "Sorry."

"That's OK." Her presence close to me was suddenly appealing. She was flushed from the exertion and abashed from knocking against me. Perhaps there was something to be said for docility after all. I felt the familiar rush of desire.

"That Italian, no?"

I looked at her bemused.

"That book. It Italian, no?"

"Yes, yes." I held up the journal. "Let me show you." She moved closer to me and I put a guiding and innocent hand round her slim waist to point at the book. She was warm and her scent was like a pheromone to me.

"I am trying to decipher a code. You know what decipher means?"

She looked at me and shook her head, her big eyes blinking.

"I am trying to understand what all these letters mean."

She nodded as though she understood and looked at me admiringly. "You very clever man," she said staring into my eyes for a moment, captured by my gaze, but then away again immediately. She turned away from me and I felt a thrill run through me as my hand glanced over her waist and her arm and her bottom. "The vacuum is full," she said looking rather flustered. "It not suck any more."

"You need to take the plastic canister out and empty it."

"I see." She knelt down next to it and I could see the curve of her breast in the singlet she wore. Smaller than I would have normally liked but, as with the rest of her, suddenly imbued with her subservient appeal. She fiddled with the Dyson with studious intent, then suddenly a catch sprang open and the canister which she had been pulling on flew straight at her, showering both the carpet and herself with dust.

"Sorry, sorry." Her voice sounded close to tears, as she scrabbled to get as much fluff as she could back into the container. She shook her head in frustration and took the canister into the kitchen to empty it. She re-emerged a minute later still agitated. She put the canister back in place and then proceeded to finish the vacuuming, cleaning up the mess she had made.

"Very sorry," she said when she had finished, her head bowed.

I was sat still at the table. "That's fine Francesca," I said giving her four pounds.

"I only did hour and half."

"That's OK," I said generously. She smiled meekly without looking at me. Her face, arms and singlet were covered in dirt from the vacuum cleaner. "Look, you can't go home like that. You're filthy. Take a shower before you leave."

She looked at me appreciatively. "You very kind."

"Not at all," I said just reaching out and touching her benignly on the hip; the thigh. "You'll find a clean towel on the shelf."

"You very kind. Thank you."

I watched her padding into the bathroom lost in my thoughts; and then, coming crashing through them, was the answer to my problem.

"Patrick!" I slapped a hand against my forehead. How could I have been so stupid? Patrick would be the perfect

person for this. Mathematical problems were like air to him. He would crack this code like it was nothing. Plus I had not yet returned his call from a few days ago so had the perfect excuse to ring him. I reached for the phone and was about to dial his number when I caught a fragment of a hummed refrain from the bathroom. I couldn't place it: sombre, stately, the *Magnificat* by Vivaldi perhaps? It made me think of her, the water washing over her. The smell of steam drifted through to me, warm, moist, fuelling the flames of my desire.

The humming stopped and I heard the shower being turned off. The bathroom door opened a fraction and Francesca poked out her head. Her dark hair clung to her neck and cascaded over the otherwise naked shoulder which was also visible. She had the air of a Boticelli. Dripping with water she was suddenly quite mesmerizingly beautiful.

"I no could see the towel."

My throat was suddenly dry. "On the shelf like I said. There should be a pile of them."

She blinked at me, her long eyelashes fanning her startling emerald eyes. And then she let the door slowly open on her. Smiled at me. "Why you not come in here and help me find it?"

I grinned at her in return, deciding the call to Patrick could wait an hour or so. I slipped out of my clothes and walked naked over to her, ready to assist in any way I could.

Summer 1571, Cyprus

Girolamo Polidoro

23

Four days after the surrender, Captain Bragadino informed me that he would be taking a party of men to the Turkish camp. The Pasha had requested they meet so he could offer personal congratulations for his handling of the defence of Famagusta. My master said that I was to accompany him and to first help him dress. He would wear his purple robes of office as magistrate and carry the red umbrella which denoted his rank as commander of the city. I myself wore my best remaining tunic with the faded brocade for the Captain General had instructed me that we should put on a show of finery such as we could. And indeed when I stepped out into the main square, in which were gathered the captains and nobles and servants and townsmen who were to accompany us, there was so much show of colour and quality of cloth that it was as though the dark days of the siege had never happened.

The chiefs of the party, along with my master the Captain General, were Astorre Baglione, Louis Martenigo, John Anthony Quirini and many others. Of the high ranking generals in the city only Laurence Tiepolo stayed behind and the city was left in his charge whilst we were gone.

We walked from the city out through the Limisso gate and the shattered ravelin. At a bowshot from the walls we were met by some of Mustafa Pasha's highest ranking officers with a troop of cavalry. With all due ceremony they guided us the league or so to the Pasha's camp. A courtyard area had been formed from the beaten earth. On two sides were the tents of the Turkish soldiers, on a third the ground became strewn with rocks, and on the fourth was a great tent in gleaming *white material at least sixty feet wide and I know not how deep, and this was the pavilion of the Pasha.*

We were led into the courtyard by the cavalry and there we were met by a troop of Janissaries in ornate uniform. They were astonished to see such a resplendent host appeared before them. The Janissaries requested that we remove our weapons as this was a meeting under a flag of truce.

Captain Bragadino, Astorre Baglione, Nestore Martenigo and Antonio Quirini then walked to the front of the camp to the large pavilion which formed the Pasha's residence. I asked my master whether I might walk with him to serve him in some way but he replied that there was no need. The task was a simple one, to pay respect to the Pasha and submit to him formally the keys to the City of Famagusta.

"In any case," he said. "You shall have ample chance to serve me in the future."

And my heart leapt for I had been concerned about what would happen when we returned to Venice, Captain Bragadino being from a fine family and thus having an army of servants from which to choose. I thanked him profusely and for a moment he put his hand upon my shoulder and in his affection for me I felt as close to tears as on the day he had saved my life.

So my master and the others walked to the entrance of the Pasha's pavilion. A pair of Janissaries with halberds stood in front of the entrance curtain but stepped aside as they approached and then they disappeared from view.

We others waited in the courtyard. It was late afternoon and though the sun was close to setting it did nothing to lessen the heat which had been unbearable all day. A light wind had picked up also so that the dust at our feet whipped around us. But we stood there still, our collection of men who still had legs to walk: Italians and Greeks and Albanians. And all the whiles, the inscrutable Janissaries watched us, dressed in their turbans and their fine uniforms.

After we had stood there for almost an hour I heard a groan from beside me and turning I saw Giuseppe swaying on his feet, his whole body ashiver as if gripped with an ague. I stepped to him and caught him in my arms as he fainted clean away. I laid him carefully on the ground and kissed him on the forehead as he was my dearest friend. His eyes opened but they were filled with tears. "I am a useless half man," he whispered to me. "I should have died that day with Count Sigismondo. Like this I am fit for nothing."

"Aye," I said drawing out my skin of water and making him drink a few drops. "But you will be, my friend. You will serve Venice again as will I. Our time will come. Until then you must rest and be strong. I command you to lie there and sup on my water as you need it." I stood back up and smiled with one of my fellows for Giuseppe was well liked amongst all who knew him.

The sun had set by now and it was darkening quickly as was the way in that part of the world, when there came from the pavilion the sound of voices raised in anger. We looked at each other unsure as to what the argument might be as relations since the truce had been cordial enough. The voices turned to shouting. Immediately Janissary guards ran out from the pavilion barking orders in the tongue of the Turks at the other soldiers standing around the camp. In the growing darkness which had not yet been lit by any torch there was the chilling sound of many swords being drawn.

"What is afoot?" I asked Francesco Bognatelli who was close to me and whom I had fought alongside often in the past months.

"Some mischief of the Turks, to be sure." He was a tough man, a man of resilience, but he looked uneasy in the half-light.

And still the raised voices from the pavilion continued and the Janissary guards stood amongst us more roughly with their swords drawn and all the time it got darker and darker.

And then from the pavilion came a great commotion and a host of Janissaries and other Turks emerged bearing torches and dragged behind them were our brave captains Astorre Baglione and Nestore Martenigo bound about the arms. An immediate cry went up from us in the courtyard at seeing our lords so disadvantaged, and we rushed forward to overturn this foul treachery. But in a flash the Turks were upon us.

Francesco was struck on the naked arm by a scimitar. I ran to protect him but the Janissary who had done it saw me coming at him in the flickering torchlight. He caught me a blow in the shoulder and I felt the blood immediately flood from me. I took a step back. Francesco was on his knees and the Janissary finished him right there bringing his wicked blade down on him with great force. I knew that my hour of death was surely upon me when suddenly I stumbled backwards and fell flat on the ground. Giuseppe – for it was him who had pulled me – was knelt beside me and whispered, "This will be my last service for Venice and for you. Do not forget me, my friend." And in a single movement he stood and turned into the path of the oncoming Janissary who had killed Francesco. The Turk cut Giuseppe down with a single diagonal blow and he spun and fell, my friend, into my arms so that he lay face down upon me and his blood and my blood flowed together over my face and hair.

I closed my eyes and lay there with him, my childhood friend dead upon me, waiting for the Janissary to kill me too. But minutes passed and I realised that in the confusion and the darkness he had thought me dead already because of the blood which liberally covered my face and so paid me no further heed and thus was I spared. I knew it was cowardice not to rise up and challenge the Turk in battle. Yet I own I was too scared to open my eyes for fear that I would be seen and because of the screams and shrieks which filled the air. I listened helplessly as the perfidious Turks cut our men down, who had come to them in good faith and under a flag of truce, and I feared greatly for our kinfolk and women in particular who had already embarked upon the galleys the Turks had sent for us.

So I lay there, but when the sounds of movement and screaming about me had diminished I dared open one eye a space. The courtyard was lit only by the torches carried by the Janissaries and thus the full display of the killing was curtailed. Yet the carnage about me was still terrible to behold, a scene of catastrophe: the bodies of my friends and the good men of Famagusta were rudely strewn in a bloody carpet upon the floor, butchered by the enemy. I could not weep for the anger that was in me. Of our leaders I could only guess that they too were dead, but of my dear master Captain Bragadino I had no idea what had befallen him and prayed only that his death had been merciful and speedy; and when weeks later I learned his true terrible fate, I cursed *myself for not being at his side to defend him in his hour of need.*

The Janissaries were over on the far side of the courtyard and hence this was the area lit by their torches at present. I saw that those fiends, not content to kill under the treachery of a white flag, were now further defiling the bodies of our brave men and severing their heads and throwing them in a pile outside the entrance to the Pasha's pavilion. I realised that I was in great danger for they were moving methodically through the dead.

Yet for the moment my location had cover of darkness, so risking all, I crawled out from under Giuseppe, sat up on my haunches and readied myself to run. But when I looked on the face of my dead friend, who had given his life for me, I swore that the Turks would not parade his head for their fancy. So I grasped him under the arms and pulled him as best I could away from the lights in the courtyard and the Turks and the horror of that which I had seen. And I thought all the time that the guards would spy my escape but that if they did I was prepared now for death. But God was with me and I moved unseen to the edge of the courtyard and then further away, on through the outskirts of the camp, until I was amongst rocks and so hidden from direct sight.

There I rested for my shoulder was paining me sorely and it was only after some minutes that I moved off again dragging Giuseppe with me under the cover of darkness, my way lit by the stars only. Though my progress was slow, the sounds from the camp grew gradually quieter until I thought I had come almost a mile, though in which direction I could not have said. By my reckoning a full three or four hours had passed since the massacre. I was weary, and could go no further so I crawled into the cover of some boulders, lay down beside Giuseppe's body and slept.

6 August 1571

When I awoke the sun was already high and I could feel the burning heat of the day. My face was painful and the blood crusted over me formed a mask which made it difficult even to open my eyes. I licked my lips and tasted the dry salt taste there and realised at once that I had great thirst and that I must find water soon or die. I felt the agony of my arm and a great weariness though I had slept several hours.

I knew that I had to move on for fear of being caught in the open and so with great difficulty I sat up and immediately realised I was too late. Squatting in front of me were four Turks, their horses behind them held by a fifth. And they were watching me. I thought for a moment to get to my feet and attempt to either fly or fight with them but my body was too weak and I thought it perhaps God's kindness to me that I could do no more and so I moved closer to Giuseppe's body and waited.

One of the Turks approached and I shied like a coward when he reached into his robes. I feared he would pull out a knife and cut me for sport before killing me as I had heard was their cruel wont. But he merely produced some effects of mine: a container of salt, a leather pouch, and this journal which I had about me always, and I realised that they must have searched me whilst I was sleeping. He waved these at me and addressed me in correct Italian, "Are you from Famagusta?" I nodded for I thought it pointless now to dissemble. "You were at Mustafa Pasha's camp?" I said yes. He looked back at his men and they looked on me gravely. "There was much killing there, yet you escaped?"

"My comrade took a blow for me and died in my stead."

He nodded, understanding, and muttered some words in Turkish to his men. They talked amongst themselves a moment before he turned to me again. I feared he was at last going to kill me or worse, return me to the camp. Finally though he spoke:

"Much has happened which should not have happened. Too many have been killed already and the blood spilt last night was unworthy of both victor and vanquished. Yet there could be worse to come, for the Pasha Mustafa has set his heart on some terrible vengeance and he cannot be persuaded against it." He sighed heavily. "But Allah, in his mercy, is all-seeing and will not allow such cruel acts to go unpunished."

I was much surprised by his words and his gentle tone. He handed me back my effects. "We will bury your comrade and then we will escort you to the hills where you may seek refuge in one of the villages there. In this small way can we make amend for the disgrace which Mustafa Pasha has brought upon us."

He stood and in his height and bearing I could see now that this was some Turkish prince before me. He motioned to his men and they helped me to my feet. They buried Giuseppe where we were for there seemed no reason now to take him further and then they gave me water to drink and with which to wash my face which had become sore from the blood and the dirt. Finally one of them dressed my wounds with gentle hands and applied herbs which were unfamiliar to me but were wonderfully fragrant and gave me immediate relief from the pain in my arm. Then they helped me onto one of the horses behind this Turk who I took to be some kind of doctor, so skilled was he, and we rode all of us two leagues till we reached the start of the hills and then further on until we were at the outskirts of a large village. There they lowered me carefully from the horse, gave me food and wine and water to take with me and bade me farewell. I watched them as they rode away, moved and uncertain at such kindness.

In the village I was looked after by a Greek family. Whilst I was recovering news arrived of the final days of suffering of my good and kind master. Of this I shall not write for it caused me to weep openly and the pain of it and of my inability to prevent it will never leave me.

After a month I was well enough to walk and use my arm freely. The Turks did not molest us in this time and, whether or not this is the truth, I believed it to be because of the intervention of the Turkish prince that we were left alone.

A further month passed and then I heard that a boat was sailing for Crete from one of the smaller ports and I crept upon it and was hid aboard with a Venetian family. We arrived safely in Crete and, two months after that, I was back in Venice.

Summer 2002, London

Patrick

24

I was so pleased when Julius rang as it had been almost two weeks since I'd left the message on his answerphone. He'd apologised about not coming back to me sooner and though he hadn't been too keen on going to the College reunion – which I understood completely – he did really want to meet up. And I said I thought that would be great and when I put the phone down I just felt really happy. Because Julius was my oldest friend.

He suggested we meet midweek at a pub called the Landsdowne. I got there a little early and bought myself a pint and sat at the bar and read my paper. It was really nice to be out of the office for once, drinking beer, eating olives and getting time to read something other than the business pages. And Julius was hardly late at all when he showed up and I just felt this great throb of happiness at seeing him again. We ended up sitting on a brown leather sofa in the corner.

"Can you believe it's nearly a year since we actually met up?" he said. I groaned and started to apologise but he waved that away. "It's no one's fault. It's just that life's too busy. How's accountancy treating you? You must be a partner now?"

"No," I said grinning bashfully. "Well, almost. And what about you? How's it going at the gallery?"

"Oh fine. My boss is an idiot but he lets me do my own thing. And we've got a couple of exhibitions in the pipeline. One in Paris. One over here. You must come along. I'll get you tickets for the opening."

"Thanks," I said impressed.

"That's what friends are for. And how are your parents?"

I felt bliss enter me, engulf me, the soft brown leather of the sofa and the bar sound, conversation from fifty different people washing out in waves, lapping over me and most of all my oldest friend before me. Who asked about your parents these days? It was only those with the connections – the school friends, the university friends, the long rooted and deep entwined histories – they were the only ones who knew enough and cared enough to ask. "They're fine," I said my face flushed with simple happiness. "And yours?"

Connections. Points of contact. We sat and drank and talked, getting on to teachers at school like we always did, and it was just so easy and friendly and comforting that by the time we were being kicked out he was insisting that I should come over to his place for Sunday lunch because there was still loads we had to catch up on. And I said yes, definitely, and the knowledge that I would see him again in just a few days meant more to me than I could possibly say.

The following day I sat in my office and sighed. It had been a long morning after the long evening of drinking and now in the early afternoon I felt drowsy and heavy and thought maybe I should have gone out to see a client rather than attempt to review accounts. But there I was stuck in the office and I forced myself to concentrate for the nth time as I stared at the draft papers before me, the numbers and words merging, swimming together.

There was a knock at the door and John poked his head in holding up a black lever arch file. I beckoned him into the room grateful for the distraction.

"I've made those changes you asked for," he said, handing me the binder.

"Oh brilliant. Thanks, John."

He smiled wanly and turned to go.

"I met up with Julius last night."

He looked round with narrowed eyes. "God. I haven't heard that name for a while." His face relaxed into blank neutrality. "When did you last see him?"

"Almost a year ago. It was great to catch up."

"Well, you two always were pretty close."

"I guess so. I'm going over to his place for lunch on Sunday if you want to come along."

"I can't," he said briskly. "I've got to do some revision this weekend. My exams are coming up soon."

"These are your finals?" I whistled. "It seems mad you're still doing them."

He shrugged. "Still doing them. You're pushing partner and I'm still trying to qualify."

"Oh I'm sorry, John. I didn't mean it like that. And they'll be finished in no time, you'll see." I nodded at him reassuringly. "Well, what about the College reunion? Have you made up your mind about that yet?"

He gave a hollow laugh. "Can you really see me going along there and telling everyone I'm a trainee accountant. At *thirty-one.*" He raised an eyebrow. "I need to get some other stuff finished. Door open or closed?"

"Keep it open. And John?"

He poked his head back into the room.

"Could you get me the files for the holding company as well please. You've only given me the trading company at the moment."

"I thought that was the one you wanted."

"No, I need them all. I'm sorry I probably didn't make it all that clear—"

"No, that's fine." He blinked at me. "I should have time to do them."

"That's great. Thanks, John." I smiled at him and then returned to the accounts.

25

At Julius's on Sunday he greeted me with a warm handshake.

"I've always thought this was a nice flat," I said as he showed me into the light and airy living room.

"It suffices," he said with a nonchalant wink. There was the sound of metal on metal from the kitchen and a strangled cry of frustration. "My cleaning lady," he said rolling his eyes. "Look, I've had a busy morning, a bit of work that needed doing..." He waved vaguely at the table which was covered in papers.

"If I'm interrupting—"

"No, no. It just means I won't be cooking for you. We can go to the Engineer down the road. Just give me five minutes to change. And have a seat." He indicated one of the chairs at the table and I sat down whilst he disappeared into his bedroom.

As I waited I found my eyes wandering over the table before me. There were books stacked up at the far end, but covering most of its surface were scribbled pages torn from an A4 pad and, closest to me, six photocopied sheets. On them were printed line after line of capital letters. None of them grouped into words; all of them individual. I felt a sudden thrill of excitement as I looked at them; and something else too. A flicker of recognition.

Julius re-emerged, changed into a pair of smart trousers and a polo neck. "I see you've been taking a look at my current problem."

"I'm sorry Julius, I didn't mean to pry—"

"Don't be silly. There's nothing secret there."

"What is it? It looks like a code."

"We think it's a coded letter between Veronese and Tintoretto. It's been in the collection for years but no one's ever looked at it properly."

"How fascinating."

"Kind of. I'm hoping it will establish that they collaborated on a particular painting."

"Sounds really interesting. What does it say?"

"Ah-hah. That's the tricky bit. We don't know yet. I've been looking at it for a week now and have got nowhere and no one at the Gallery has been able to help either."

"Well, what have you tried so far? Caesar shift? Monoalphabetic substitution?"

Julius looked at me blankly. "You've lost me already. What did you just say?"

I grinned at him and then had an idea. "Why don't I give you a hand with it? I *love* codes. Always have. Let me have a go at cracking it."

"Patrick I don't want you to waste your time. You're far too busy—"

"No really. Let me take it away and have a look. I can't promise anything but I'll give it a go."

"Gosh." He looked stunned. "Thank you. Any sort of lead would just be so helpful. Take those copies. I can always make others."

I took the papers and stared at the first few lines. "You know… it's ridiculous but this reminds me so much of the book John and I picked up in Venice. That time when I… when I kind of lost it."

"You didn't *lose* it, Patrick. It was just one of those things." He shrugged. "It could happen to anyone. Anyway," he said curiously. "You always said that those days in Venice were a bit of a blank for you. That you don't really remember what happened."

"I don't." I felt suddenly confused. "I *can't*. I mean…" My voice trailed off and then, to do something, I shrugged and laughed. The way I'd always done. I folded the papers and put them in my pocket.

The door to the kitchen opened and a tall slim woman in her mid-twenties stepped out. She was dressed in faded jeans and a T-shirt. She looked exhausted yet she had a beauty about her, a certain elegance.

"I finish the washing up," she said yawning. "You need house vacuum today?"

"No, that's fine. Patrick this is Francesca, my cleaning lady."

"How do you do?" I said shaking her hand. She started as though she recognised me though I was sure I'd never met her before; then she smiled at me awkwardly and looked like she was thinking of something to say.

"You help Julius with his work?" she said finally, pointing at the papers in my hand and those on the table and laughing at the same time to disguise her awkwardness with the language. I thought she was lovely.

"Patrick is going to help me with working out what the code says." I was surprised to see Julius suddenly put his arm around Francesca and kiss her on the cheek. "Do you remember when I told you about the code?"

"Yes, yes," she said impatiently. "Why you like this code so much?"

"Because it leads to treasure." Julius winked at me and I laughed. Francesca broke free from his grasp and looked at him, eyes lowered.

"I go home now. I come again Wednesday?"

"Of course." He kissed her on the lips and she smiled at him shyly, waved politely to me and then walked to the front door.

"Wow," I said when she was gone. "She's beautiful."

"Is she? Really? Isn't that strange. I think she's a bit bony myself. And she's a touch too obedient to be really interesting."

"Oh right. And are you two an item?"

"Oh God nothing like that. I *am* sleeping with her if that's what you mean but it's nothing serious. I'm still seeing Madeleine after all."

"Of course," I said nodding. "I'm impressed."

"It's just double the hassle believe me. Now you put these papers away," he said pointing to the sheets still in my hand. "And I'll buy you lunch."

26

The next couple of days were busy, so I didn't have a chance to look at the code until Wednesday evening and even then I got home from work late. I made myself a microwave meal of chicken korma and rice and went straight to bed.

I was glad it was Wednesday. The large audit I'd been working on was pretty much over and the partner, Derek, had been so pleased with the work we'd done he'd taken us out to lunch. So all that was left was the closeout meeting on Friday when the last issues would be discussed. But that should just be a formality and I smiled when I thought about it, and I smiled when I looked down at the pages of code which I'd spread out in front of me, because it made my mind buzz at the memory of seeing Julius again.

But looking at the code gave me something else as well. A kind of tingle, a prickle of febrile excitement, a shiver of passion. I had not looked at a brain teaser or a mindbender and certainly not a code for years. I felt rusty but at the same time almost giddy with excitement at the puzzle before me. The thought that I would find meaning where there was presently none, this would have been enough for me, but combined with my thoughts for Julius it made me eager to begin.

So I looked at the papers before me. Six pages, numbered so that the order was clear. Each page had twenty-five lines and each line had 39 letters; apart from the last which had twenty lines, and the last of these had 9 letters. So in total there were 5625 characters, certainly enough to work with. A code needs to be of sufficient length for it to be vulnerable. For with length comes structure and with structure repetition, and with repetition the cipher is weakened; vulnerabilities can be found and the code can be cracked.

And so the code itself. How do these things start? How did this thing start?

V E L G A S A G A I I...

Again that vague feeling that I had seen these letters before, that what I was about to do had echo in my past. But it was momentary only, inevitably swept aside by my surge tide of anticipation and the thrill of the problem before me.

V E L G A S A G A I I...

What could I tell from looking at those raw coded letters? Letters distributed as though at random. Surely nothing. No structure. No meaning. Yet there were clues even then. Even at that first sighting.

V E L G A S A G A I I...

What could those letters tell me without being decoded? They told me that just the letters of the alphabet were being used. No punctuation of course. But also there were no numbers. There were no symbols, no stars, no moons, no star signs. Perhaps this seems like no help at all but for me it was information rather than just observation. All these were employed in codes. All included for the purpose of complexity. Yet in the end they did no more than undermine the code, pointing the code breaker in the right direction. Layers of intricacy are hints in themselves; the overlaps have weaknesses that can be probed, interstices to be penetrated.

And the letters were pure and identical and unmarked. No extra flourishes on an *F* or a cross on the stem of an *I*. There were no dots above any of the letters and no bars under any others. I stared at the printing closely under my halogen bedside light. The photocopy was good and the light was pure bright white and I examined closely and found nothing. Just the letters of the alphabet.

I noted all these things carefully and locked them away for later when I might need them, and smiled to myself at my precise approach. And so to begin:

V E L G A S A G A I I...

Begin at the beginning.

Caesar Cipher. One of the simplest forms of code. The kind a child would use. Each letter of the alphabet is shifted by a set number of letters, so if *A* is shifted five places to become *F*, then *B* would be *G*, and *C* would be *H*. A simple code and easy to test. I drew a grid and smiled when I thought that *my* Julius was not even aware of this easiest of codes made famous by his namesake.

Since each code letter is formed by moving the same distance from its original plain text letter, by simply shifting each letter back by the same amount we could discover the plain text again. So if it were a Caesar Cipher one of these lines on the grid should read like proper Italian.

I drew my grid and wrote out the first few letters at the top and then on the next line I shifted each letter by one so that V became W and E became F. And on the next line I shifted them all once more so that W became X and F, G and carried on, cycling through till I had got back to the beginning again:

V	E	L	G	A	S	A	G	A	I	I
W	F	M	H	B	T	B	H	B	J	J
X	G	N	I	C	U	C	I	C	K	K
Y	H	O	J	D	V	D	J	D	L	L
Z	I	P	K	E	W	E	K	E	M	M
A	J	Q	L	F	X	F	L	F	N	N
B	K	R	M	G	Y	G	M	G	O	O
C	L	S	N	H	Z	H	N	H	P	P
D	M	T	O	I	A	I	O	I	Q	Q
E	N	U	P	J	B	J	P	J	R	R
F	O	V	Q	K	C	K	Q	K	S	S
G	P	W	R	L	D	L	R	L	T	T
H	Q	X	S	M	E	M	S	M	U	U
I	R	Y	T	N	F	N	T	N	V	V
J	S	Z	U	O	G	O	U	O	W	W
K	T	A	V	P	H	P	V	P	X	X
L	U	B	W	Q	I	Q	W	Q	Y	Y
M	V	C	X	R	J	R	X	R	Z	Z
N	W	D	Y	S	K	S	Y	S	A	A
O	X	E	Z	T	L	T	Z	T	B	B
P	Y	F	A	U	M	U	A	U	C	C
Q	Z	G	B	V	N	V	B	V	D	D
R	A	H	C	W	O	W	C	W	E	E
S	B	I	D	X	P	X	D	X	F	F
T	C	J	E	Y	Q	Y	E	Y	G	G
U	D	K	F	Z	R	Z	F	Z	H	H
V	E	L	G	A	S	A	G	A	I	I

I read across the rows looking for meaning, looking for
words which might show that I had discovered the secret;
but there was nothing, just pieces of words, fragments of
Italian, gobbledegook. I gazed at the grid but found no
overriding meaning, no compelling form. This was not a
Caesar shift.

And I felt relief that it was not. A puzzle should not be
too easy or else it is just a disappointment. It needed to be a
challenge and should not yield its secrets too easily.

So to the next step and I felt the tingle again down my
spine at the thought of what lay ahead. Monoalphabetic
substitution cipher. Could it be? Where each letter in the
original text is substituted for one other so *A* might become
J but *B* need not become *K*, but could be *S* or *R* or *B;* and
just because *A* is coded as *J* need not mean that *J* is coded

as *A;* it could be any of the letters. But there are bounds, there are rules still, so that each original letter may only be represented by *one* code letter so if *A* is coded first as *J* it will *always* be *J*. And each code letter can only represent one original letter so whenever a *J* is seen it will always represent *A*, not *Q* and not *X*. It is a close coupled relationship, a one-to-one mapping, a generalisation of the special case which is the Caesar shift cipher and throwing up so many possibilities that to the uninitiated it must surely seem unbreakable. For every A has 26 possible encipherments and every B then 25, and every C 24 and so the total number of encipherments is 26 x 25 x 24.... which gives a total of 403 million million million million. This is the number of different codes available. So surely it must be impossible to break such a code? And yet I smiled when I looked at it and cracked my knuckles in gleeful anticipation. For the code *was* breakable. And it was breakable because of a trick, a sleight of hand which would neuter the 403 million million and so on different possibilities at a stroke. A thousand years ago this trick, this skill would have made me a sought after man and one who would have been able to name his price to governments and kings. For a device such as this was power indeed if it allowed you to read the secret thoughts of subjects and enemies.

Yet the trick is so simple and it works because all codes have weaknesses, all of them betray something and the clues are lodged in the intricacies of the language of the original text, some subtle, some blinding, clues which stem from keen observation of the code and understanding of the language it encrypts; clues like whether one letter is always followed by a particular letter, or never followed by another; whether a letter is often found to be repeated; and most of all, most important of all, most powerful yet most simple: *how often does each letter appear.*

That one piece of knowledge, easily achieved by a series of counts on the coded text will by itself place you on the edge of cracking the code. And why? Because every language has its own characteristic structure, its fingerprint based on the frequency of occurrence of its letters. In English the letter E appears most frequently. If you take a sample of English you would normally expect to come across the letter E 12.7% of the time, so roughly one letter in every eight will be an E. T appears 9.1%, A 8.2% and so on.

So all that is needed is to count the letters in the coded text and the most frequent letter is likely to represent E, the second most a T and so on. The method is called *frequency analysis*. Of course there are subtleties since in a given passage there might be a preponderance of other letters because of particular words or names or just because the sample is small; and of course in this case I was dealing with Italian which had its own frequency fingerprint. But I had confidence because it was a powerful method and simple and for me even fun; and best of all I had a laptop to help me.

I fetched my computer, plugged it into the phone line and got back into bed. I switched on, my fingers drumming against the case as I planned my course of action. The first thing I needed was to find the frequency of letters in Italian. I got onto the internet and did a search for the information and got back the ordering of the most common letters: $A E I L O...$ as opposed to $E T A O I...$ for English. But it didn't give me the frequency percentages. So I went into an online version of the *Corriere della Sera* copied a few pages of text and dumped them into a word processing document and used a word count on each letter in turn to produce an approximate frequency table. A bit rough and ready I thought but it would do.

In order to use the method I first needed to count how many times each letter appeared in the coded text. Rather than do this by hand I decided to type in the six pages, one hundred and forty-five lines, five thousand six hundred and twenty-five letters of the code and then get the computer to do it for me. I could normally type nearly fifty words a minute, maybe 250 characters but here with no word structure, no aid to memory, and with constant checking necessary to ensure I had made no mistakes, I was much slower and it was nearly one o'clock by the time I had typed it all in. But I didn't mind because that was where using a computer now came into its own. With all the data in its memory I simply ran another word count on each letter until I had a table showing me the relative frequencies. And that was when I sat back in surprise.

For instead of a table showing letter frequencies similar to the one I had made from the *Corriere della Sera*, a kind of mountain range with peaks at *A* and *E* and *I* and *L*; instead of that, five letters didn't appear at all, and the frequencies for the rest were practically identical.

27

I was exhausted the next day and sat in my office staring at the file in front of me. I had slept only fitfully, my mind awhirr, trying to make sense of the code and the results of the frequency analysis.

The first part had proven to be simple: the five letters which did not appear at all were *J, K, W, X,* and *Y.* Although these letters were used in modern Italian they were only found in foreign words that had been introduced to the language. Thus the core alphabet consisted of only 21 letters.

However, the second issue was more troubling. All the letters appeared with roughly the same frequency. What did this mean? Obviously the comparison with the frequency analysis tables was pointless but what did it *mean*? What structure did it imply for the original text? What clues did it throw up?

All night the ideas had gone through my mind. All night I had gone through the options and proposed ideas and counter ideas to impose order on the seemingly random characters. These thoughts had prevented me sleeping, the problem had taken over, but so quickly that already it was a part of me, occupying a part of my brain so that even while performing other conscious actions it was there whirring away in the background and yet when the switch to subconscious was needed it sprang forward, it took over, and the blank screen of my closed eyes became back projected with $V\ E\ L\ G\ A\ S\ A\ G\ A\ I\ I...$

Already it was ingrained. It flowed where my blood flowed, it spread into the spaces between cells, it moved like lymph. It had taken over so quickly that I was shocked and however hard I shook my head and tried to get on, it returned, a voice to the letters, a picture to the text, patterns forming where there were none.

What did it mean? It meant it was not a simple monoalphabetic cipher. Of that I was sure. But then what? What were the options out there? What else could this code be? How to explain the even distribution of the letters?

Before I went further forward I went back. I revisited the Caesar shift grid altering it for the shorter alphabet: could this perhaps be the answer after all? And where before I would have been disappointed with a Caesar shift solution now I would have been mighty relieved for the initial shot of pleasure I had got from the code had faded leaving only the aftertaste of compulsion, a tang of obsession which lingered and grew.

So I reset the grid, but all I got was:

V	E	L	G	A	S	A	G	A	I	I
Z	F	M	H	B	T	B	H	B	L	L
A	G	N	I	C	U	C	I	C	M	M
B	H	O	L	D	V	D	L	D	N	N
C	I	P	M	E	Z	E	M	E	O	O
D	L	Q	N	F	A	F	N	F	P	P
E	M	R	O	G	B	G	O	G	Q	Q
F	N	S	P	H	C	H	P	H	R	R
G	O	T	Q	I	D	I	Q	I	S	S
H	P	U	R	L	E	L	R	L	T	T
I	Q	V	S	M	F	M	S	M	U	U
L	R	Z	T	N	G	N	T	N	V	V
M	S	A	U	O	H	O	U	O	Z	Z
N	T	B	V	P	I	P	V	P	A	A
O	U	C	Z	Q	L	Q	Z	Q	B	B
P	V	D	A	R	M	R	A	R	C	C
Q	Z	E	B	S	N	S	B	S	D	D
R	A	F	C	T	O	T	C	T	E	E
S	B	G	D	U	P	U	D	U	F	F
T	C	H	E	V	Q	V	E	V	G	G
U	D	I	F	Z	R	Z	F	Z	H	H
V	E	L	G	A	S	A	G	A	I	I

And I did what I'd done before and circled what I thought might be clues and hints but were in fact nothing but the coincidences that language throws up. None of these lines was recognisable Italian. They meant nothing. So it was not a Caesar cipher. There could be no more doubt about that.

How then to proceed?

I sat at my desk. Open in front of me was the file of accounts and Derek's last few questions which needed to be cleared by tomorrow's meeting. But as I looked down at the notes to the accounts showing director's remuneration and depreciation and tax, I thought only of the code, *V E L G A S A G A I I...*

What did it mean? It meant the code was more complex than I'd first thought. But from the nebulous possibilities open to me only one seemed likely, possible, probable. A code so simple yet powerful that it sent my head spinning, running desperate for alternative solutions rather than this one, this code, the thought of which made my stomach cramp and my breath get short. For I knew the code they must have used, in my gut I *knew* it, but it made me scared even to think it. For I believed the code was the *Vigenère* cipher; so powerful when it was first devised in the sixteenth century that it was known as *Le Chiffre Indéchiffrable*, the undecipherable cipher.

It was no longer a monoalphabetic cipher but *poly*alphabetic: each original letter could be represented by more than one character. So *A* might be represented as *G* and *M* and *Z*. But it was more powerful than that because *G* might not always represent *A*, sometime it might be *K* or *L* or *F* or even *G* itself. There was no longer a one-to-one or even a one-to-many relationship between letters of the original text and the code letters. The relationship was many-to-many. And this was what made the code so hard to crack since if you found three occurrences of the letter P in the code text you simply had *no idea* whether they all represented the same letter in the original. Hence frequency analysis on its own would not work and if tried would throw up a roughly even distribution of letters.

Yet the Vigenère cipher was also beautifully simple to use so that coding and decoding text was a relatively easy process. All that was needed was a key word or phrase, which was known only to the sender of the message and the recipient. I sketched out an example on the back of the draft accounts as I sat there. The keyword was *PIZZA* and the message was *Io sono Italiano*. I wrote the keyword above the message, repeating it as required:

P	I	Z	Z	A	P	I	Z	Z	A	P	I	Z	Z
I	O	S	O	N	O	I	T	A	L	I	A	N	O

For each letter in the message which had a *P* above it a particular code alphabet would be used to encrypt it, for each with an *I* a different code. Thus the letter *O* would be encoded in three different ways even in such a short message. The code alphabets could be chosen arbitrarily but to make things simpler they were normally taken from a so-called Vigenère square. I wrote out the square for the 21 letter Italian alphabet which was simply made up of successive Caesar shifts of the entire alphabet.

To encode the first letter of the message I moved across the top of the square until I got to the column starting with the letter to be enciphered, *I*. Then ran down the left hand side of the square till I got to associated keyword letter, *P*. Then read off the code letter from where the two lines crossed, *A*:

A	B	C	D	E	F	G	H	**I**	L	M	N	O	P	Q	R	S	T	U	V	Z
B	C	D	E	F	G	H	I	**L**	M	N	O	P	Q	R	S	T	U	V	Z	A
C	D	E	F	G	H	I	L	**M**	N	O	P	Q	R	S	T	U	V	Z	A	B
D	E	F	G	H	I	L	M	**N**	O	P	Q	R	S	T	U	V	Z	A	B	C
E	F	G	H	I	L	M	N	**O**	P	Q	R	S	T	U	V	Z	A	B	C	D
F	G	H	I	L	M	N	O	**P**	Q	R	S	T	U	V	Z	A	B	C	D	E
G	H	I	L	M	N	O	P	**Q**	R	S	T	U	V	Z	A	B	C	D	E	F
H	I	L	M	N	O	P	Q	**R**	S	T	U	V	Z	A	B	C	D	E	F	G
I	L	M	N	O	P	Q	R	**S**	T	U	V	Z	A	B	C	D	E	F	G	H
L	M	N	O	P	Q	R	S	**T**	U	V	Z	A	B	C	D	E	F	G	H	I
M	N	O	P	Q	R	S	T	**U**	V	Z	A	B	C	D	E	F	G	H	I	L
N	O	P	Q	R	S	T	U	**V**	Z	A	B	C	D	E	F	G	H	I	L	M
O	P	Q	R	S	T	U	V	**Z**	A	B	C	D	E	F	G	H	I	L	M	N
P	Q	R	S	T	U	V	Z	**A**	B	C	D	E	**F**	G	H	I	**L**	M	N	O
Q	R	S	T	U	V	Z	A	**B**	C	D	E	F	G	H	I	L	M	N	O	P
R	S	T	U	V	Z	A	B	**C**	D	E	F	G	H	I	L	M	N	O	P	Q
S	T	U	V	Z	A	B	C	**D**	E	F	G	H	I	L	M	N	O	P	Q	R
T	U	V	Z	A	B	C	D	**E**	F	G	H	I	L	M	N	O	P	Q	R	S
U	V	Z	A	B	C	D	E	**F**	G	H	I	L	M	N	O	P	Q	R	S	T
V	Z	A	B	C	D	E	F	**G**	H	I	L	M	N	O	P	Q	R	S	T	U
Z	A	B	C	D	E	F	G	**H**	I	L	M	N	O	P	Q	R	S	T	U	V
A	B	C	D	E	F	G	H	**I**	L	M	N	O	P	Q	R	S	T	U	V	Z

Repeating for the rest of the message would give:

P	I	Z	Z	A	P	I	Z	Z	A	P	I	Z	Z
I	O	S	O	N	O	I	T	A	L	I	A	N	O
A	**Z**	**R**	**N**	**N**	**E**	**S**	**S**	**Z**	**L**	**A**	**I**	**M**	**N**

So for example in the final coded message there are two *S's* but one represents an *I* and the other a *T*; and of the four *O's* in the original message, two were encrypted as *N's*, one as a *Z* and one as an *E*.

I doodled on the back of the accounts, drawing a swirl of letters running this way and that, interlocking and interlacing. It was still possible to break this code. The easiest way would be to find the keyword or phrase, but there seemed no chance of that as it could literally be anything. However it might be possible to find the *length* of the keyword. If the keyword was, say, five letters long then the 1st, 6th, 11th etc. letters would all be encoded using the *P* line in the Vigenère square. The 2nd, 7th, 12th etc. letters would be encoded using the *I* line and so on. Thus the polyalphabetic cipher would have effectively been broken into five monoalphabetic ciphers upon which frequency analysis *could* be used.

How though to find the length of the keyword or phrase? Again it all came down to the structure of the underlying message and, in particular, repetition. Short words in Italian like *una*, *sono*, *con* would be expected to appear frequently in any text. Because they are short it is quite likely that sometimes the reference letters used to code them will be the same as earlier in the document and so the same word could get encoded identically:

P	I	Z	Z	A	P	I	Z	Z	A	P	I	Z	Z	A	P	I	Z	Z	A
C	O	N				C	O	N						C	O	N			
R	Z	M				B	N	N						R	Z	M			

So when looking at the coded text it should be possible to spot sequences of characters which repeat again and again. This is an indication that a word has been encoded identically. Crucially it gives a clue that the code breaker can use. If counted from the start of one repeated phrase to the next that number will have to be a multiple of the length of the keyword or phrase. In the example I was playing with it was 15 characters between the repeated phrase. And so the key word or phrase must be either 3 or 5 or 15 letters long. By doing this for other repeated fragments it would be possible to find other examples which could narrow things down so that the length of the phrase could be ascertained exactly. And then frequency analysis could be used to do the rest.

And so what I needed to do now was to analyse the text in detail to find those repeated fragments to see if they would reveal the length of the key. But the code was at home in my flat and I knew I would have to put it out of my mind for the rest of the day and get on with finishing off the accounts for Derek. But when I looked down at the figures all I could see before me were the letters of the code, *V E L G A S A G A I I...* I wanted to start the analysis now. I wanted to search for the repetitious structure which would solve the riddle for me.

I stood up abruptly and paced around the small office. This was ridiculous. I had work to do. I could not let something like this take control. To occupy my thoughts so entirely that it stopped me functioning. I was stronger than that. I sat down again at my desk and took a deep breath. Then picked up a pen and looked again at the accounts. I saw the doodles I had made on the back and flipped the pages over. I needed to concentrate now, just a final read-through for mistakes, to make sure nothing was missing, or that none of the accounting notes had been repeated.

Repeated.

Repetition was the key I was sure it was. If only I had the text in front of me now I could probably solve it in half an hour.

I threw down my pen. My palms were sweating and my face felt hot. I needed to do something active. I couldn't read at the moment, my mind was buzzing far too strongly for that. I needed some alternative problem to occupy my mind. There was a trainee called Simon working on the directors' remuneration note. I could help him with that. There were other things I needed to do as well, but it was still only three o'clock. If I spent an hour with Simon it would calm me down. Get me back on track. I found myself breathing shallow and fast. I got up again and felt dizzy. I went to the closed door and stood there for a moment to regulate my breathing. To give it more structure. Structure was the key. What *was* the key? If only I could guess that then the code would unfold in a moment—

I stepped outside into the open plan office. Smiled at my secretary Susan. She had a message for me, she said. The closeout meeting was tomorrow at 12 o'clock in Derek's room. The finance director and MD would be coming in for it and she had booked us in for lunch afterwards. Derek wanted to sit down at 11 to run through the final points.

I smiled and thanked her. My ears were buzzing like I was in a pressurised capsule and though I could hear her, she was indistinct, the nuance to her voice lost. But it was good to be out. Everyone saying hi and smiling; James, another manager, talking and laughing with me about... about what? The football? Yes. Talking about the football so that I could just nod at him and laugh with him as he talked about... what now? I moved on, touching his arm, saying *Yes, I definitely would* (would what?) and smiled at another secretary Julia who was my friend and liked me and she wanted to talk but I had to walk on. I just needed to find Simon so I could fill my mind, which was buzzing louder now, angry buzzing wasps and bees, *V E L G A S A G A I I...*

I stepped into the student area where the trainees hot-desked until they had passed their exams and been assigned a permanent place in the office. There was no sign of Simon but John was there.

"John?"

"Oh, hi Patrick. How's it going?"

I nodded at him. "Yes fine, fine." I was distracted and glanced back over my shoulder.

"You OK?"

"Yes, of course."

"How was Julius?"

I frowned. The thing was that modified frequency analysis would not be easy. There were no guarantees.

"Patrick?"

I just nodded now, hoping that would answer his question and then laughed because people always want you to laugh at what they've said, don't they. An appreciative audience. Well I could be one just as much as the next person. "So," I said skilfully changing the subject. "Is Simon around?"

John was staring at me but then just shook his head. "He had to go to the dentist. But he said he'd left some files for you. I think with Susan. He said he'd finished everything."

"Yes I'm sure." I turned abruptly, needing to get back into my office. And yes there were the files sitting by Susan and I picked them up and went inside again and closed the door. Sat down. I suddenly felt very hot and was sweating profusely. I wiped a hand across my forehead and loosened my tie. Simon had finished the work. He had even left a yellow sticky to say it all tallied. So he didn't need my help. Well that was good. All I needed to do was to look at those accounts. Just one last check before I spoke with Derek tomorrow morning. One last thing.

I got up again.

I had come to a decision.

I would do it tomorrow. I would get in early. It was only one last thing and would take no more than an hour if I looked at it with a clear head. I had no other meetings today. I deserved an early finish. I'd been working too hard. I felt ill.

I snapped my briefcase closed, grabbed my jacket, looked unseeing around my room, biting the inside of my lip, sweat pouring from my face. Go home. Do the code. Finish it off. Come back tomorrow morning. Fresh. Early.

I told Susan and she agreed. She said I didn't look well. I said I was fine, just wanted an early night. She said I needed it. And John was there at the lift too and he smiled at me oddly in the way he can sometimes. He'll need to lose that chippiness if he wants to progress, get anywhere, not stay at his level for the rest of his life and I just smiled back at him. Nothing to say. Nothing to say. Nothing to say.

28

It had been light.

It had been light and now it was dark.

I sat on the floor, laptop by my side, printouts before me, around me, pages of letters with lines highlighted and fragments circled and underlined. Thirty, forty sheets of paper surrounding me, covering the floor. Where was the meaning in all this? Where was it leading? Where was the truth?

I had rung Julius late. Twelve o'clock. One o'clock. It was light and had got dark. But there were things I had to know.

"Julius, it's Patrick."

"Patrick? *Patrick*? What's going on? I'm in bed. I'm heading off to Paris first thing—"

"I've been looking at the code."

"Have you solved it?"

"Not yet, but I'm close. I need to know a few things."

"Are you OK Patrick? You sound strange. And *Christ*, it's one o'clock—"

"I need to know when was it written?"

"When—? I don't know exactly. Between 1580 and 1600 maybe."

"How can that be? Veronese died in 1588. I looked it up."

"Oh. Of course." He sounded confused. "I mean between 1570 and 1588."

"Fine. That's OK then."

"What's OK?"

"The cipher they used," I said impatiently. "It would have been in existence then. But no one at the time could have broken it."

"Not even the Council of Ten?"

"No one."

212

"Then when you break the code you'll be the first person to read what they wrote. What else do you need to know?"

"Nothing more. I'm on the verge. I made a partial breakthrough a couple of hours ago. I know the keyword is ten letters long. But I can't get the frequency analyses to yield anything. Having ten of them makes it so much harder: the sample sizes become so small it's hard to work out the distributions accurately."

"I don't really understand..."

"It doesn't matter. I've got to go." I hung up. So it was almost certainly a Vigenère cipher. So what? How did that help me with finding the key? I looked around me. I had ten frequency analyses to do. Ten different problems to make sense of. So much data. I was surrounded by data.

I slept where I was.

It was dark and it got light.

I woke up in the early morning, the thoughts still there, angry bees, swarming around me, $V\ E\ L\ G\ A\ S\ A\ G\ A\ I\ I$... I slept but had no rest. I was exhausted and felt feverish. I was ill, I was sure I was.

I looked again at the papers and it started again, comparing the frequency analysis plots with the frequency tables for the letters in Italian – maybe this was wrong, maybe this was the problem. I went onto the internet again and downloaded page after page of Italian text, hundreds of pages, and did revised letter counts on them, but the results were not markedly different. The problem was me. I was too tired to think straight, to do this properly yet I could not stop. I could not leave it. It was eight-thirty. I should be in work. I had to do the last bits and pieces for Derek. And then we were to have the final meeting. I had to go in. I simply had to.

Eight-forty.

Nine o'clock.

I rang up Susan.

"I'm sick," I said. "I can't move. My head hurts."

"You didn't look well yesterday. You should stay at home. What do you want me to do about your meeting with Derek?"

"I'll ring him later."

Ring him later. To explain. To tell him. It had been a good audit. It would be a shame to spoil it. I should ring him now. But now I was too busy and I had to go through the printouts again. There was a clue there. I knew there was. It was in there. I wouldn't ring him now. I needed to keep going just for another couple of hours. That was all I needed and then I'd be done. I might even make the final meeting. I looked at myself. I was still in my suit. I hadn't changed last night and had slept in it. I went downstairs and outside. The morning was hot and sticky. I walked quickly to the newsagents two roads down, blinking and talking to myself, going through permutations, trying to understand how it would all fit together and then suddenly I stopped.

I looked round sensing something, someone, following me. I thought I had heard... But there was no one there.

I went to the newsagents and bought five cans of Red Bull and a bar of chocolate. I drank a Red Bull the moment I got outside and felt the rush immediately. My tiredness vanished. I felt clarity return. The ability to focus on many problems at once, multi-tasking, compartmentalising my mind so it worked for me on ten different tracks, sub divisions assisting each other, a collective. I would solve this now, I knew. I would do this. I walked back slowly but then in a flash I ducked behind a hedge, because this time there was definitely someone there following me, always following me even though I twisted and turned and looking out onto the street I saw him I thought or her was it? and then no one and I was alone again. I ran back to my flat ignoring the looks from my downstairs neighbour, ignoring her looks, and slammed my front door and drank another Red Bull and ate half my chocolate, a big bar of Dairy Milk and I ate it piece by piece and then I had to start again, I forced myself, I was drawn in, sucked. I was there amongst the paper. It was light and the day became hot.

At eleven the phone rang.

"Patrick, it's Derek. I heard you're ill."

I blinked down the phone at him.

"Patrick are you there?"

"I'm not well."

"Quite. Well I hope you get better soon. Are you up to just talking through a few points?"

"I feel quite sick, Derek."

"OK, well not to worry. There was hardly anything anyway. Look, you rest. I'll get Simon to come along to the meeting. They like him anyway and it'll be good experience."

"Thanks."

"That's fine. Can I give you a call during the meeting if there's anything particular we need to know?"

"Yes. That's fine. That's fine." I would be done by twelve. I was almost there now. I was sure I was. I had letters in place in the document but didn't know more than a few words in Italian so couldn't be sure. I couldn't be sure of anything. The papers had their own power now. And there were so many of them, stacked against me, arrayed in force. But I knew I was almost there. What was I missing? Why couldn't I do this? There must be something simple. There had to be.

The day got hot and bright light flooded into the flat so that when I stepped outside onto the balcony I thought I was drowning in it, lightfall splashing over me, blinding me. And then I saw him again, the one who had been following me that morning, watching me from outside. And then another on the other side of the road. There were two of them studying me. From behind the trees. I ducked back inside and drew the curtains. Drew all the curtains. Cool and dark was how I worked best anyway. Cool and dark.

The phone rang again.

"Patrick." It was twelve-thirty now. "I'm sorry to disturb you but can you help us with a question about depreciation policy."

I knew nothing about depreciation. Or Derek. Or any of them. The frequency plots were all I cared about. The different possibilities and permutations, the different attempts at interpretation and meaning.

"...so it's really to find out what you think about that idea."

And yet what did I know? What could I show for it? My work. I was so close but at present what did I have? I had nothing. "Nothing."

"I beg your pardon?"

"Nothing. I know nothing now. At present. Any more."

My thoughts filled the silence and I put the phone down and then took it off the hook and switched off my mobile. I sneaked a look into the street and they were still there watching me though I couldn't quite see them. I closed the curtains and pushed my hands into my hair and began again because I was so close.

I drank milk at lunch.

I finished my chocolate in the afternoon.

The day was hot and stayed hot.

It was light outside then began to get dark.

And suddenly from nowhere at a complete tangent to my thoughts I knew how to do it. And the moment I thought of it I was sure it would work. I rang Julius but there was no reply. I remembered he was meant to be in Paris and tried his mobile. He picked up after only one ring. "Patrick, what's up?

"I know how to crack the code."

"How?" He was suddenly shouting at the end of the phone. *"How?"*

"How does an Italian letter start?"

"How does what—?"

216

"How do you say *dear* in Italian?"

"Oh. *Caro.* Or *cara* if it's to a woman. But why—"

"I'll ring you back."

Because it was a letter of course. There was information I had not used, structure I had disregarded, clues I had ignored. Because it was a letter. And letters start with *caro* or *cara* and this was a letter between Veronese and Tintoretto. It would start with *caro.* I knew it would and that little would be enough. I tore out a piece of paper and wrote down the letters of *caro* and beneath them the first few letters of the code, the angry bees:

C	A	R	O							
V	E	L	G	A	S	A	G	A	I	I

C must have been encoded as *V,* and *A* as *E* and so on. It was so simple, so beautiful. I took my Vigenère square and read back from it what the first four letters of the keyword must be and wrote them above, starting the repeat above the 11th letter:

T	E	R	R							T
C	A	R	O							O
V	E	L	G	A	S	A	G	A	I	I

I rang him again. "What was Tintoretto's first name?"

"Why?"

"Tell me!"

"He was called Giacopo. His real name was Giacopo Robusti. But—"

Giacopo. Caro Giacopo. Surely that's what it must be. I knew it had to end in an *O* in any case.

T	E	R	R	R	I	A	E	L	S	T
C	A	R	O	G	I	A	C	O	P	O
V	E	L	G	A	S	A	G	A	I	I

"What does *Terrriaels* mean?"

"I doesn't mean anything."

"Then this letter wasn't to Tintoretto."

A pause. "How do you know?"

"I know from the code. The key will be a word or a phrase. It has to be."

"Then..."

"It's ten letters long. It starts with *TERR–*. Give me some Italian words."

"Terra– something, maybe? *Terrazza*? No that's only eight. *Terribile* – that's nine... I don't know. Wait. *Terracotta*. What about that?"

TERRACOTTA. I tried it and knew immediately it was wrong.

T	E	R	R	A	C	O	T	T	A	T
C	A	R	O	A	O	C	M	D	I	O
V	E	L	G	A	S	A	G	A	I	I

"Come on Julius. There must be something else."

"*Terra–*... *Terra–*... *Terraferma!* T-E-R-R-A-F-E-R-M-A. It *must be.*"

"Why must it be?"

"Because that's what the Venetians called their land empire. Verona was part of it as was Padua and... Try Terraferma. And Patrick? *Patrick—?*"

The phone dropped from my hands. *Terraferma.* It made sense. It had to be. I suddenly slowed. Could this really be it? I paused and just breathed. The phone rang again and I took it off the hook. *Terraferma.* I set out yet another grid:

T	E	R	R	A	F	E	R	M	A	T
C	A	R	O							O
V	E	L	G	A	S	A	G	A	I	I

I looked at my Vigenère square and read off the letters one by one, carefully, precisely, taking my time.

T	E	R	R	A	F	E	R	M	A	T
C	A	R	O	A	N	T				O
V	E	L	G	A	S	A	G	A	I	I

Deliberate action. Care was required now I was so close. Concentration was needed to prevent a mistake being made.

...O...

...N...

And then the last of the letters in there and by coincidence the eleven letters I had always had in my mind, my angry bees, formed words entire and I sat back and admired them.

T	E	R	R	A	F	E	R	M	A	T
C	A	R	O	A	N	T	O	N	I	O
V	E	L	G	A	S	S	G	A	I	I

Caro Antonio. Dear Antonio. This wasn't a letter to Tintoretto at all. And a tiny shiver of memory pricked me. Dear Antonio. But what I remembered was *My darling Anna.* Who was Anna and why did I think of her now? I shook my head. No matter.

I felt suddenly exhausted, relief and tiredness washing over me simultaneously. The code was defenceless now. I had the key. I could break it any time I wanted. But suddenly my eyelids felt like lead and I thought I would rest first. I could afford to rest now. I had earned it. I put some music on and I lay down on the sofa and closed my eyes.

* * *

When I opened them again the room was dark but the music was still on and loud. Louder. I sat up immediately, disconcerted, discombobulated, not knowing what time it was. I was breathing heavily and when I stood up and saw the papers around me, I stared at them, confused as to where they had come from.

And then suddenly I knew I was in great danger.

There were noises outside, noises I couldn't explain, grating through the sounds in the room, the sounds in my mind, so that I had to do something about them, I couldn't just ignore them or all would be lost. I ran for the door, to where the sounds were loudest – scrapings and scratchings – and got to it just in time to pull the chain across and bolted it just as the banging began.

I grabbed a chair and put it there, flimsy defence perhaps, but another two and the barricade was looking stronger and all the while the banging went on and on, so loud in my head.

Until it stopped.

Then the voices came, whispering low, their plotting even more terrifying, their numbers uncertain. I ran back to the living room and over to the balcony thinking I could escape that way. But he was there outside already waiting for me.

"I'll never tell you anything!" I shouted at him looking around frantically for some other way of escape. "Help me!" I shouted into the night. *"Police! Help me!"*

I was on the balcony.

Screaming.

It had been light.

But now it was dark.

And I stood there on the balcony with the close air about me. I had nowhere to go. He was coming towards me and I backed into the flat. There was so little time. They would get in eventually, that much I knew, but I wouldn't make it easy for them. I cleared the papers from my desk, and slid them into the drawer and away, out of sight. Then turned the music up louder, all the way, so they would not hear me, and hid in the wardrobe, pulling the door to so that through the crack I could see just a slivered glimpse of the room behind.

"Patrick! Patrick!"

How could they have known my name? A shiver of fear jangled me and now the shouts were from all sides above and below, the sides of the wardrobe reverberating with their attempted entry, their forced rhythms, and I screamed over the top to drown them out to make myself heard and beyond it all I heard sirens wailing, a growing ululation, a sonic crush. And then there were lights, blue flashing, and I saw red and green also, all manner, but when I screamed my hardest the sounds were subdued and when I closed my eyes, no one could touch me.

February 1915, Rome

Henry Shaeffer

29

<u>10 February 1915</u>
My darling Anna
This is my first journal entry for two weeks. The work has been busier since the return to Rome and we are seeking to order the papers built up in Venice over the last six months.

Polidoro's journal is translated as I said in my last entry and I have made further attempts at breaking the code in which is written the assumed directions to the treasure. But still with no luck. I am certain of a few things, however: it is not a Caesar shift or a monoalphabetic substitution cipher. I therefore must surmise that it is some type of polyalphabetic substitution cipher. Although very simple to construct – even a child could do it with ease – this would have been an extremely powerful cipher in Polidoro's time. None of the contemporary intelligence services, not even the Ten themselves, would have had the skills to break it.

I was in the Forum, looking for inspiration amongst the ruins when I came to this conclusion that the code had to be polyalphabetic. And I own I felt a surge of energy at the revelation. For though such a code is devilishly difficult to break it is not impossible. Charles Babbage had indicated the way forward using a form of modified frequency analysis. I remembered seeing a paper he had written on the subject and decided to head back to the embassy and look it up without delay.

On standing, however, I noticed that a man had been in the ruins with me, a raven-haired man in a dark suit. Whether he had been there the whole time or whether he had just arrived I could not tell, but when I looked in his direction he turned away almost immediately as though he had not been interested in me at all.

I took a couple of steps towards him but he proceeded to walk off in an unhurried fashion. I wondered whether I should follow and challenge him, for we had been warned that agents of Germany and Austria Hungary were in operation in Rome just as we were; but I thought better of it. After all, the Forum was a public place and he had been doing nothing wrong by being there. Instead I shrugged my shoulders and proceeded in the opposite direction, picking my way through the stones over to the Colosseum.

It was becoming dark, the time being close to five o'clock, and torches were burning around the Colosseum lending an eerie impression to that extraordinary building. I stopped to admire its shadowy splendour when the sound of a footfall caused me to turn and I saw through the gathering gloom that the black-haired man was approaching. Now there could be no doubt that he was following me, as he had been headed in an entirely opposite direction only minutes earlier.

My heart pounding, I resumed walking, moving anticlockwise around the amphitheatre perimeter. Behind me I heard the man's continuing tread, even and distinct through the otherwise quiet evening. When I stopped, he stopped; but when I walked on he did the same and from the quickness of his steps it sounded like he was gaining on me.

I increased my pace and moved nearer to the walls so that the massive curves of the arena would prevent him getting clear sight of me. When I reached the north side, which is the side closest to the road, I ducked into the dark shadows of an archway so that the man, continuing around, would have to emerge in front of me and I would be able to surprise him and ask him his business.

But he did not come. I waited there for some minutes my heart beating fast inside me, my mind racing. But he did not appear and the sound of his steps faded to nothing. Frustrated, I re-emerged from the arch and looked around and, even though I peered deep into the darkness, there was no sign of him.

I was on my guard all the way to my lodgings but saw no more of him. Back at the hotel I described the man to Signor Mocenigo and asked whether he had seen him in the vicinity before; but Mocenigo merely shrugged his shoulders and said he had not. Noting my concern he did however say that he would keep an eye out for him and would challenge him should the situation arise.

20 February 1915
My darling Anna
My sojourn in Rome is almost over. I have been told that I will be given orders in the next two weeks. Until then my time is my own. Or at least it would be if I had never picked up this wretched journal. If only you were here, your intelligence and wit would surely break the code in a matter of a day or two whereas I have been working on it now for weeks with progress so slow that it hardly merits the name.

I have been looking for repeated fragments in the text which might tell me the length of the key which governs the cipher and am now convinced that it is ten letters long. Yet this work took me nearly a month whereas you would have probably seen it instinctively and immediately. My task is now one of modified frequency analysis à la Babbage but it is desperately dull and the results difficult to interpret given the relatively short lengths of the text.

I will own to you that the code has frustrated me. My room is strewn all over with the papers bearing my feeble attempts at decipherment. And I am running out of time. Soon my posting will come through and where but a month ago I was longing for the event now I wish only for a few days more to make headway.

28 February 1915

My darling Anna

I have been unwell these past few days, gripped by a nervous malaise which seems to energise and enervate me at one and the same time. My mind races yet goes nowhere, meaningless aggregations of letters coursing through my mind to no effect, **V E L G A S A G A I I...** The code has me, and my lack of usual diversions means I am thrall to it. Most of the day is spent looking at it and it feels like there are but few moments when I am released and clarity restored. These come mostly at night and even then I am feverish during them in an effort to marshal my thoughts while I have the ability to do so.

I have become difficult of late: I know it. Short with those around me and not willing to spend time with them. A poor show in the circumstances. Yet it feels like every second spent away from the code is a second wasted and still I have not made the breakthrough. Only my posting will end this and set right my state of mind, yet I have heard nothing more on it.

I tried to escape today by leaving my room early and walking in the clear air. I wandered aimlessly for

more than two hours visiting everything yet seeing
nothing until I came to the Trevi Fountain and there,
suddenly, was the raven-haired man again. Or perhaps
he had been following me all along. But the moment I
noticed him he disappeared and so many people were
around that I could not be sure and as my head has not
been clear I thought it likely that I had been mistaken.
Yet it occurred to me then that if the journal were true
and the cross existed, then surely I would not be the
only person looking for it. Would not the forces of
Venice also be on the hunt for it? Would not their
agents be abroad and searching?

I was unsettled by the thought and returned to my
lodgings immediately but was brought up short in the
doorway.

Someone had been in my room.

Looking around at the papers strewn all over the
bed and the desk and the floor it would have been by
no means clear to any other observer that a visitation
had taken place. Even I could not properly explain
how I was so sure, for the papers themselves did not
appear disturbed and the mess was, as far as I could
tell, the same mess I had left there before my walk. But
something was altered in the room, whether it was a
depression in the bedclothes or a change in position of
the chair or even the faintest, most tantalising, scent
left behind. Perhaps it was one of these things or all of
them or none; for I could not put my finger on exactly
what had changed.

But I knew, Anna. I knew as I am writing to you
now, that someone had been in my room.

I went downstairs and spoke sternly with Signor
Mocenigo who assured me in hurt and voluble tones
that no one had access to the rooms of the hotel except
himself; and that no one had been into my room on
this or any other day except when I had specifically

requested a maid to come and clean.

I shook my head and went back to my bedroom and locked the door and, having moved all my papers to a pile on the desk, I lay down. I was wrong when I wrote I wished for more days before my posting. I want only for it to come through now so that I can leave this all behind.

2 March 1915

I awoke last night convinced I had heard the sound of footsteps in my room. I lit an oil lamp immediately yet there was no one to be seen. I lay down again on top of the covers, my breathing shallow, my eyes straining to see further into the shadows and the dark recesses of the room. After five minutes – which I counted by the beats of my heart – I got up again and became the boy I had once been, tiptoeing into each corner of the chamber and dispelling the demons which hid there. And, though it shamed me to do so, I knelt and peered under the bed. Then I walked to the wardrobe. It was nonsensical I thought to myself, that anyone could be hid there, yet it took me three aborted attempts before I pulled open the creaking doors and saw the truth inside: clothes and nothing. I laughed in relief and foolishness and lay back down once again.

My mind slowly emptied and sleep came upon me.

I fell into a dream immediately in which I was lying on sand, the dark ocean before me, rising and falling in time with my breathing. From the green sky, heavy with cloud and impending storm, I heard a beating of wings and there in front of me appeared a great winged lion, its fur and feathers lustrous gold. It opened its maw and I backed away but no sound came from it, no roar, just a silence that was all-engulfing.

I woke with a start and sat bolt upright as I heard the rattle of the door handle, someone outside attempting to turn it. This time there could be no doubt and I jumped from my bed and leaped to the door yanking it wide open.

There was an exclamation of surprise and Mocenigo, a lamp in his hand, tumbled into the room.

"What were you doing?" I asked angrily as he hauled himself to his feet. "Snooping around here in the middle of the night?"

"Middle of the night?" said Mocenigo recoiling at my fury. "Captain Shaeffer, it is only nine o'clock."

I was flabbergasted and consulted my watch. But he was correct.

"I did not know whether you were even returned for the evening," he continued. "So when I hear noises in your room I come up to investigate."

I had lost track of time, lost track of reason. Mocenigo looked at me strangely and said, "I can see that you are in, so there is no need for me to worry further." And he walked off down the corridor shaking his head.

I closed the door and sat down on the bed.

My body was cloaked in sweat. My hands were trembling. Only nine o'clock and the whole night still to endure.

There was no danger in the room, nothing to be frightened of, yet I felt scared in a way I had not since I was a child. I wished with all my soul that you were in bed with me to hold and comfort me. But you were not. You were far away. So my solace and protection had to come from a different source. And when I finally went back to sleep it was with my service revolver cocked and ready at my side.

Summer 2002, London/Cyprus

Sarah

30

When I was small, Mum and I stayed with Aunty Jean and Uncle Malcolm and Patrick every time we came down from Leeds; always in the summer and Christmas, and often at Easter and in the half-terms as well.

At first we'd come by train, long journeys with a packed lunch and Connect 4 and super-percussive games of snap. Morning would turn to afternoon as the endless scenery flashed past us, the weather often changing from sun to cloud to rain and back again as we hurtled south.

Then Mum passed her test and we came by car, a Fiat 126, the smallest car I'd ever seen. But I loved it. I felt so proud that we had a car just like other families. We came down together, just the two of us, for years, me in the passenger seat, singing or joking or chatting till I was too tired or too old and then I sat in stony silence or snoozed against the cool glass letting the spots of rain fleck the window and my breath smoke it till its transparency was gone and all that was left was the interior of the car, Mum and me.

We drove down together till I was eighteen and then we stopped. I went to University and we never made the journey together again. There was no argument which precipitated this break, no sea change in attitude or affection, it just happened that way and after Uni I was living in London anyway so I carried on seeing my uncle and aunt for a while, but for some reason now always in a cafe or a restaurant or even back at Mum's. But I didn't see them that often and the visits became no more than annual and then, six years ago, they stopped being even that.

They lived in Highgate and, on the evening I was to visit Patrick, I walked from the Tube taking the short cut through Queen's Wood. In winter the Wood was open to the sky, the trees branching up to twiggy nothing; but now in summer it was overgrown and dark green and dusty. Patrick and I had played there a lot when we were young; yet it was only walking through again that I remembered how much.

The path from the Wood emerged onto a street of large Tudorbethan semis and I followed it to their house nestled into the corner where the road curved round. It looked just the same: the windows still diagonal leaded, the front door still shiny white, the whole well looked after. I'd loved that when I was little, a marked contrast to our place in Leeds where every bit of external paint that could peel did. Uncle Malcolm took care of all that here, he'd always been good at DIY. I'd envied Patrick that. I'd envied him his house, the Wood, and most of all his father, near-silent Uncle Malcolm. Memories of envy. They took me by surprise.

The windows were dark and there was a delay after I rang the bell during which my heart surged with relief. *I did my best, Mum* – I rehearsed the conversation in my head – *I went round there but no one was home...*

Then I saw the downstairs net curtain twitch and a couple of seconds later the front door opened and there was Aunty Jean and she threw her arms around me, shouting, "Sarah, Sarah." Uncle Malcolm was there as well and he gave me a kiss. They led me into the living room, and Aunty Jean wouldn't leave my side and she kept on saying how lovely it was to see me, and how good it was of me to come over, but she'd been sure I would. All the while she was crying her eyes out.

I just sort of smiled back, but all I could think of was that Aunty Jean was *tiny* and how had I never noticed it before. And Uncle Malcolm's moustache, which he still had against all the odds, had turned grey, and the room we sat in, the living room, was the room they had always reserved for visitors, for *grown-ups*, so Patrick and I had played elsewhere. It was cream and bright yet I could see a cobweb on one of the lamps, and for some reason it made me want to burst into tears.

"John found him. Patrick's friend John from Cambridge? I don't think you know him dear." Aunty Jean had sat me down next to her on the sofa and was stroking my arm, dabbing freely at her eyes with a tissue. "Patrick had been behaving strangely at work so John went round to his flat and..." Her voice faltered and she looked at Malcolm.

"He wasn't himself. Let's just put it that way."

Jean nodded. "And the police were called by his neighbours because he was making such a din. And by the time we got there he was babbling away nineteen to the dozen about all sorts: codes and intruders and everyone being in danger. And now he just lies there upstairs, hardly saying a word, like he's terrified. But what can he be scared of?" She stared at me, her eyes wide in appeal but she continued before I could even think to answer. "And the doctors say there's nothing they can do."

"What's the point of them, if *they* can't help," growled Uncle Malcolm.

"And John's been round again and they talked for ages and we thought maybe things would be better but afterwards he was just the same. We're at our wits' end. We just want to know what caused it and whether it was anything like the last time—"

"It's completely different to last time," said Uncle Malcolm.

"But how can you know that?" she said shrilly.

"Because," he said in a weary voice, his part in a conversation they had clearly had many times. "Then it was a reaction to his Finals and starting a PhD. He's not been under that kind of pressure this time."

"But he *has* been under pressure," said Aunty Jean shaking her head at him and turning back to me. "He's been working far too hard. I've been telling him that for months. And now he just lies there all day long and we're really worried…" Her voice accelerated into it, "that he might try and... you know..." She started crying once more.

"Kill himself," said Uncle Malcolm gravely.

"And he doesn't want to go out," she sobbed. "Just refuses point blank. Even for a walk. I don't know what to do but I thought if he saw you then everything would be OK because he's always been so fond of you."

Oh God. "Look, Aunty Jean, I'm not sure I can do anything. I really don't. I mean we haven't been that close in the last few years—"

"But he was always so fond of you, darling. We all are. Please just go up there and talk to him. We'd really appreciate it."

I knew I had no choice and in any case just looking at my Aunty Jean and seeing her stare wide-eyed back at me with hope and trust and love almost broke my heart.

The stairs I remembered, though predictably they were smaller, less steep, less Everest-like. I had memories of the house from when I was a teenager but the dominant ones were from earlier, when we were properly little: memories of running down the stairs with Patrick; of trying to jump the bottom few steps with Patrick; of squeezing through the gaps in the banisters to escape from Patrick. A host of Patrick related memories, and it wasn't that I'd forgotten them; it was just that they weren't memories I carried around with me. They'd been archived, here, in this house. Remote storage to be accessed when I returned.

We walked together up the two flights to the attic conversion. Aunty Jean tapped on the door. "I'll go in first," she whispered to me and went through. I felt Uncle Malcolm give my arm a squeeze. For courage? I wondered.

Aunty Jean came out again, her eyes lowered, tear filled. "Go in dear. We'll be downstairs if you need us," and with a sidestep she was past me and I was at the door and the next moment I was inside.

It took me a moment to see where he was. The room was done out chalet style, the joists and sloping walls all in pine. To the left as I looked in was a little dining table, straight in front of me was a two-seater sofa and TV, and in the corner on the right was a low bed. And it was on this that Patrick was lying.

He was on top of the covers, curled up in the centre of the bed, his head propped up on a pillow and he stared out through one of the large Velux windows set into the roof.

"Your mum asked me to pop up and see you," I explained after a few seconds during which he'd done nothing to acknowledge my presence. "To see how you were." I smiled at him, praying for some kind of reaction. But there was nothing.

"So..." So what? "So it's been a nice August, right? Warm... It gets pretty hot up here though doesn't it? Being at the top of the house and with all the windows, I guess…" I pointed over at the patio style doors leading onto a small balcony. "Do you mind if I just open the doors for a bit of air."

Silence.

OK. I didn't actually have anything to say to him. I sighed heavily, caught myself doing it, then stared down into my lap wondering just how long before I could go down again.

"You shouldn't have come."

I jumped at the suddenness of his voice. Patrick was staring right at me. His face was gaunt, his eyes in deep shadow.

"Your mum asked me to," I said after a moment.

"She shouldn't have." His voice was no more than a whisper. It made my own throat feel dry to hear it.

"She thought it would help."

He looked away from me back to the wall. "Well it hasn't."

I blinked at him feeling like I'd been slapped. "Fine," I said. "*Fine*. But there's no need to be rude about it. I've come after work to visit you. If you want me to go just tell me."

"It's too late now."

"What is?"

He shrugged again and I felt a wave of tiredness and irritation pass over me. I was definitely not the right person for this kind of thing. I didn't have the patience. I took a breath. "Look Patrick—"

He sat bolt upright in bed so quickly that I jumped again. "It's too late," he said looking straight at me. "Because they'll have seen you."

"Who'll have seen me?" I said my nerves jangling.

"The people who tried to break into my flat. Who tried to get the code from me."

Ah yes: Aunty Jean had mentioned a code. I blinked at him. "Are they in the room now?"

Patrick looked at me like I was mad. "Of course not."

"So where are they?"

"Outside. You must have passed them on your way up here."

"And what do they want?" My stomach felt like I was in free fall. I so did not want to be having this conversation.

"They want to break the code too."

"What code?"

"The one that Julius gave me. *Julius!*" He clapped a hand against his forehead. "Julius is in danger. They'll come after him as well. Maybe they've got him already—"

"I'm sure Julius is fine."

"You don't understand." He started rocking backwards

and forwards, his hands clamped firmly round his knees. "They've linked me to the code." Rock forwards. Rock back. "So they'll know about Julius as well. It stands to reason. You've got to warn him. I've tried. But he wouldn't listen to me. He thinks I'm mad." He looked at me directly, full in the face, so that I had to look away.

"Julius isn't in danger," I said as gently as I could. "No one's in any danger."

"Of course we're in danger. We're all in danger. But no one'll listen to me. *Why won't anyone listen to me?*" He sighed and shook his head and subsided into sulky silence.

I didn't want to go on with this. I couldn't help. I stood and walked to the patio door. It was stiflingly hot in the room and all I wanted was to be outside. I pulled open the door and a gust of cool air swept over me. I breathed it in and then I stepped out onto the balcony. Behind me there was a crash of a knocked-over lamp and a shout and then Patrick was suddenly standing just inside the door and waving at me furiously.

"Sarah, come inside! Come inside! They'll see you!"

I stared at him in shock.

"Come inside," he hissed. He started banging on the glass with the flat of his hand. "They'll know you've been talking to me."

Tears started to roll down my face. Tears of pity for him and Aunty Jean and *me* and tears of anger that I was so unable to make any difference to him. To help him in any way. "There's no one there," I said my voice choking. "There's no one in the street." I walked forward to the parapet.

"Come back Sarah!"

I looked out into the road below and it was empty, all the way back up to the Wood.

"Sarah, please."

I turned to look at him, at my cousin, a grown man, his face contorted like a child's, his hands shaking with fury and suddenly I knew what I had to do and I didn't know whether it was right or wrong but I just had to do it.

I walked back to the patio door. Patrick seemed to calm himself a little. "Will you come back in now?" he beseeched me.

"Yes," I said and I put out my hand so he could help me. He reached to take it and then my hand closed on his, tight, and I yanked him outside. "*Yes*," I said dragging him to the balcony. "But not till you see for yourself that there's no one there—"

"Help me!" he squealed but I held him tight and pushed him right up to the parapet.

"Look!" I yelled at him. "See for yourself—"

"Please Sarah, it's too dangerous. They'll see us—"

"*Who'll* see us?" I grabbed his chin and forced him to look. "Patrick, *there's no one out there!*"

He fell suddenly quiet and I let go of him. His body relaxed next to mine and he looked down into the street and up the road. He edged forward and peered down closer to the house and then he looked up again, gazing all around. There was silence, just a quickening breeze, cooling, fresh.

"I don't understand," he said at last, his voice small. "Where are they?"

"They're not here, Patrick. There was never anyone here."

"But..." He stared at me and out into the street again and then suddenly it seemed as though his whole body sagged. He turned and limped back inside. I followed him and watched as he lay back down on his bed.

"It's OK," I said gently, sitting down beside him, putting out a hand to stroke his hair. "You're safe." He lay there for a few seconds almost motionless and then suddenly his eyes flicked open.

"No. I'm not." And I felt a shiver like ice water down my spine when I heard him. "Because, believe me or not they do exist; and, what's more, they're coming back."

31

By the time I got home that night the only thing I wanted to do was to have a soak. Maya's mum had given me some lavender bath salts as a house warming present and I put some in and ran the bath as hot as it would go and then just lay there for an hour.

Eventually, when the water had grown tepid I lifted myself out and sat on the edge of the bath while the water emptied behind me. I felt drained, enervated by the heat and the steam and the time spent with Patrick and work and the new flat and everything. Everything was a chore. Everything had to be done, be fitted in. And I didn't know what this patchwork of duties was heading towards. Hours at work and hours on the Tube didn't make for a particularly satisfying tapestry. I shivered as I sat there, the droplets of bathwater cooling on my shoulders. I needed to get up. I needed to eat something before I went to bed. Food as a chore. Something was definitely wrong in my life.

I went to the bedroom, dried my hair and put on pyjamas, then padded barefoot to the kitchen. My tiny kitchen. I stood there, wondering what I should eat. It was ten-thirty and anything at all was going to take effort. I had thought I would make pasta, maybe spaghetti with pesto. But now, confronted with the task, I baulked. I didn't want to have to wait for anything. I wasn't even that hungry.

I wandered back down the hallway. Got the phone and lay on the bed. It was too late to ring Maya – she'd been going to bed at nine ever since Amita had been born. And I knew Katy was out. So there was no alternative, no chance of getting out of it and I let my fingers do what necessary and dialled a number that my mind had long forgotten.

"Hello?" a voice answered.

"Julius?"

The name was unusual enough that it still gave me goose-bumps whenever I heard it, even when I used it myself.

I'd heard it first when I was thirteen; first seen him when we were still at school; first kissed him when we were on holiday together; first slept with him back in England in the bedroom of my skanky house share in Manchester; first held him, stroked him, loved him then.

Everything stemmed from then, from my memory of him, vivid drops of gorgeous colour, always those moments to mind, the first days of laughter and longing and tender embraces and time spent together, every minute, every day, and long calls when apart. The thought of him, of us then, still made me smile now, my face replicating the look I gave him as I remembered the look he gave me, an eye thing and a mouth thing, love I guess, thoughts of him that I had thought before. However imperfect we had been with each other, however disastrously it had all worked out as we'd grown tired of each other, as we'd grown up, however deep the hurt, however far the fall, he was still there inside me, my first real love, my always.

"Sarah?"

His voice was uncertain. Julius was never uncertain. Even when we were falling apart, a year on and the commuting between Cambridge and Manchester and London had become too much for both of us and in our youth not enough to keep us together, even then he wasn't uncertain, the time he told me that he loved me, and for the first time I'd really believed him, just a week after I'd slept with Francois and knew I was in love too, really in love, enough to go and live in Paris for a year with him; knew then that Francois was the love of my life; but I was wrong and Julius was right and we came together again once more, briefly, in a whirl, two years later, a high energy confluence before the head-fuckness of it all spun us apart; yet even when I told him about Francois, dizzy with nausea at what I had done, there was only momentary uncertainty and then he was coolness itself, whereas now there was a tentativeness in his voice. Perhaps I'd interrupted him; perhaps he'd been expecting the call. "It's been a while," he said.

"I know. I'm ringing about Patrick. He said he'd spoken to you."

"He did. His parents rang as well. It didn't sound good. But I'm in Paris at the moment with work. Have you seen him?"

"I saw him today. He's talking about people watching the house and everyone being in danger. You especially."

"He said the same when he rang me."

"He said you gave him a code?"

"Ah." I heard him sigh. A single exhalation. The same sound as when I'd told him about Francois all those years ago. "It's my fault Sarah." There was a pause and I waited for him to find the words. This was not his normal way.

"I let him have something to work on that I thought he'd enjoy. A code from a book we found in Venice. Do you remember when we first got together?" A memory of falling into his arms exhausted, a glimpse of his face next to mine, my cheek on his, and finally a kiss as natural as breathing.

"Is that the thing that Patrick got so excited about when we were inter-railing?"

"Yes. I shouldn't have let him take it from me. I should have realised it could trigger another incident."

"Julius, he's a grown man. He's the only one that can trigger anything. How could you have known—?"

"I should have known. His parents said he was practically suicidal." His voice shook. "How can I live with myself?"

"You can't think like that. Patrick's been sensitive his whole life. If it hadn't been this it would have been something else. Sorry. I shouldn't have said that about him." I was tired anyway but talking to Julius was making it worse, an ache, a longing, not for him, but for someone, *anyone*. "I'm worried about him. When are you coming back?"

"Tomorrow. I'm going to visit him in the evening. Will you come too?"

"I told Aunty Jean I would."

"Good, good. It'll be nice to see you again whatever the circumstances."

"Sure. Take care of yourself Julius. See you tomorrow."

The phone went dead and I lay back on the bed in the darkened room and thought of the last time I had seen him, at a gallery opening, a few months before, just a Hi and a Bye, other people to see, and for the years previous the same, two, three times a year; no time to talk, nothing much to say in any case, easy chat, catalogues and exhibitions and PR, laughter with third-parties and warm white wine. The last time I'd really seen him was five years ago and even then it's not like we'd talked, it had hardly been the day for that. And thoughts of then flooded me as I lay on the bed in the darkness of my bedroom; we were already long over by then but Julius had wanted me to come anyway, for him he said, as a favour, one last favour, not that he had any owing but I'd said of course. So I went along and stood by his side and all I can remember is the rain and the heavy charcoal itch of my tweed suit and the crispness of my blouse, looking down mostly seeing its white cotton blaze more than anything else, trying not to look around, not wanting to catch anyone's eyes, certainly not the family, so I looked down at my suit and my blouse and the sodden green brown of the grass and felt Julius next to me, the blackness of his suit and the blackness of his tie, his whole body trembling so that I put my arm around him just to do something to stop his pain and all the while the fat drops of rain teemed upon us as they lowered him into the ground and the priest spoke over the drumming water and Julius's trembling became more violent, like he was cold or had a fever, shivers that would not pass however tightly I held him, insistent, persistent, memories that will never leave me, forever with me, vivid like it was yesterday, of the only time I ever saw him cry, the day of Duncan's funeral.

32

I was on the Northern Line after work the following day, on my way to see Patrick, when the lights went out.

The train had already stopped in the tunnel between Old Street and Angel and it was stiflingly hot in the packed carriage. I was standing squished in the aisle between the two rows of facing seats, not even enough room to fan myself with my Evening Standard. I slipped a foot, bare and sore, out of its new flip-flop – unspeakably beautiful with a saffron coloured flower over the toe, but somehow also excruciatingly painful.

"I like your shoes."

A little girl was looking shyly up at me. She was about six and to my mind quite beautiful with a sleek black bob and almond shaped eyes. Her skin was pale but with a hint of something in it. Maybe her dad was Japanese, because the lady she was holding tightly to was as white as me. I smiled at the girl and then at her mother. She was looking tired and I noticed suddenly she was pregnant. Just starting to show. My first reaction was the raw and envious biological rush I always had these days; the second real anger that no one had offered her a seat.

I scanned the seated commuters around us. One guy, not much older than me, was sitting right by me in his City suit reading a novel. Kind of pale looking but quite cute actually for all that. I decided to glare down at him all the same until he got the message.

He obviously got something because he looked up and was then so taken aback that he dropped his book. It flew out of his hands, a big thick chunky number and landed spine first on my bare foot. I gasped at the stab of pain. And that was when the lights went out.

Absolute darkness.

A hundred feet down.

In a tunnel.

It was like ticking things off: how dark can we make it? I closed my eyes and thought it actually got brighter.

The little girl started crying. Not howling but small scared sobs. She just wanted to get out of there. We all did.

Eventually the lights flickered back on again and, true to form, the carriage jolted. We were all packed in so tightly that there was no suggestion of anyone actually falling over but it did mean a stagger and a wrench to the shoulders as we grimly hung on to retain balance. A low rumbling and then the train started moving forward. Slowly.

There was a scrambling by my side as the pale-but-interesting man got up to offer his seat to the pregnant mother. Getting up itself wasn't that easy because of how squashed together we all were, but he managed it gracefully enough. She squeezed past him and sat down, the little girl, her tears subsided, immediately hopping into her mother's lap.

The man was now standing next to me. He was tall and brown haired. Slim build. Nice skin: maybe he shared my Clarins obsession. I smiled at him but he turned away from me and looked apologetically and gravely at the lady with her child.

At Camden the carriage exchanged one set of passengers for another. The little girl said goodbye to me – *so* sweetly – and I thought you could do worse than having a kid like that. Maybe I needed to find someone Japanese? My hairdresser was Japanese.

It was still packed in the carriage and I was still standing in the aisle feeling more and more tired. It was only when we got to Archway that some seats came free.

"Do you want to sit down?" It was the guy with the book. I'd forgotten all about him but he was still there indicating a seat in front of us.

"No, you take it," I said. "I'm getting off at the next stop."

He looked a little surprised at that. But he didn't sit down either and so the seat was left empty for the seven minutes and twenty seconds the train took to limp between stations. Awkward.

At Highgate I got off and stopped for a minute on the platform to let the crowds thin out. But when I looked up the guy was right in front of me, so close that it made me jump.

"Hey," I snapped at him.

He jumped in turn. Gratifyingly.

"Sorry," he said stepping back a pace. He looked like he was summoning up the courage to say something. Almost like he was going to ask me out or something. Not that anyone ever *had* asked me out on the Tube. Although I had flirted a little every now and then, but *not* on the way back from work and not with... well, he was actually very good looking, great cheekbones, but he was *so* serious. Why was everyone so serious these days?

"Are you going to Patrick's?"

My improbable train of thought skipped a rail and went ploughing into a cornfield. "How did you—?"

"You're Patrick's cousin aren't you? Sarah?"

I squinted at him. There was something familiar about him, *kind of*, he sort of reminded me of someone I was at school with...

"It's John," he was saying. "My name's John. Patrick's friend."

I remembered what Aunty Jean had said. "Right." Patrick's friend from way back. I put out a hand to shake. "Nice to meet you."

He took my hand and tentatively shook it. "We *have* met before you know."

"I don't think so," I said patronisingly. "Although a lot of people think I look like—"

"We met in 1992." He blushed. "In Venice. We were all inter-railing..."

I smiled kindly and began to explain that he was mistaken when the swinging weight of a memory long forgotten smacked me in the head; a cascade of images, thoughts from a hot summer's night, ten years ago, of me with him, unmistakably him, the two of us together. In bed.

I looked startled and felt a flush of warm red blood engulf me, my face and neck and all points south. My ears buzzed and when I looked at him, he flickered in and out, a flurry of visuals and instants of sharp salt emotion.

"Of course we did," I said woozily. "I mean, of course I remember you." And then… silence.

I knew I couldn't just leave it there. I knew I had to say something but there was simply nothing to say, my mind was empty, sluiced through by the deluge of embarrassment brought on by being in the company of someone I had once almost slept with. He was saying something about going to Patrick's and I nodded in a way I hoped make sense as we got on to the escalator together and shared the long, *long*, ascent to ground level, through the ticket hall and out onto the road and still I hadn't said a word.

I think he was talking normally, I'm not entirely sure, and I desperately wanted to say something, *anything*. So I said, "You're looking well," and cringed at the startling unoriginality of it.

He nodded politely and said, "You're looking well too. But I was asking if you'd already seen Patrick?"

I blushed again so hard that it felt like the blood would burst out and I shook my head and said, "Yes", in a way that must have made him think I was a nutcase. We were approaching Queen's Wood and I knew I had to say something sensible to prove that just because I'd once seen him naked didn't mean that I couldn't continue a perfectly normal conversation with him. So I coughed and said, "What are you doing these days?"

"That's what I just asked you."

We stepped off the pavement and onto the path

through the trees and I let a branch smack me in the face to hide my embarrassment.

"So what *are* you doing these days?" His voice was deepish, kind of cool sounding. Had it always been like that?

"I'm in PR." My voice squeaked when I spoke but sounded reassuringly human. "Arts PR."

"What does that mean?"

Question. Answer. Question. The makings of a conversation. "It means doing gallery openings and getting people to come to exhibitions. That kind of thing."

"You did art at University, didn't you," he said ducking an overhanging branch.

"History of art and Languages. How did you remember that?" I asked genuinely impressed. "I don't remember what you did."

"I did physics," he said flatly.

"Wow. That's cool."

"I think that's what you said ten years ago." My mouth fell open but he carried on. "It was OK. I did it for eight years. Just physics. And then I gave it up and became an accountant." He gave a hollow laugh which was also a tiny bit creepy."

"Well accountancy's OK," I said though I couldn't actually think of anything worse. "So why did you give up physics?"

"Needed the money. Needed a change."

"You needed a change so you became an accountant?" I grinned at him but he stared back at me seriously and the chuckle died in my throat.

"That's life isn't it," he said neutrally, no emotion in his voice. "We don't always end up doing what we love."

He had quickened his pace, striding forward through the narrow corridor of trees, thick leaved, shadow heavy, and then out suddenly onto the street again, blinking in the bright summer evening's light. I had to skip after him to keep up. "Well why don't you change what you do if you don't enjoy it?"

"It serves its purpose."

"You sound like a Vulcan," I said. "Surely you've got to try and enjoy your job a little more than that?"

"Do you enjoy your job so much then?" He slowed and looked at me full on and I stared back defiantly.

"Of course." Which of course I didn't but I found his defeatism exasperating. I wasn't going to tell *him* quite how pointless I thought the whole thing and how I was looking around right now for something different. "Yeah, I love it. You should do too. You spend most of your waking hours at work—"

"That depends on how long you sleep."

That was such an infuriating thing to say. I opened my mouth to give him a piece of my mind when I realised we were at Patrick's and he'd already rung the doorbell.

The door opened and Aunty Jean greeted us. She looked tired but at least she hadn't been crying this time. "He's still much the same," she said wearily. "But just go on up you two. Julius is with him already."

John narrowed his eyes but said nothing and we started up the stairs with him racing ahead again, up to the top floor, and after a cursory tap, into Patrick's room.

Julius was sitting by Patrick's bedside and looked round as we entered. He stood up and walked towards us and John practically collided with him halfway into the room. "I can't believe you're here," he snarled jabbing a finger at his chest. "Haven't you done enough damage already?"

Julius ignored him, instead leaning to me and kissing me on both cheeks. "Hi Sarah, it's been too long. You're looking lovely as you ever did." Only then did he slowly turn to John. "And nice to see you too John." He coughed. "You know I would normally engage in some pleasantries with someone I hadn't seen for ten years—"

"Cut the crap, Julius. If you hadn't given Patrick that

code none of this would have happened."

"It's not his fault," I said.

John glared at me. "Of course it's his fault."

Julius held out his hands, palms up. "Of course it's my fault. I *am* to blame."

"You're not," said Patrick and we all started.

He was sitting up in bed, his eyes sleep-filled, his hair tousled. He shifted so that he could lean against the wall, the effort of speaking seeming to sap what little energy he had. "It was my fault," he said, his voice barely above a whisper. "I saw the code and really wanted to solve it."

Julius sat down next to him again. "But I should never have allowed you to. I knew the code wouldn't be good for you. That's why I didn't tell you who the letter was really written by just in case it got you... *over-excited."* Julius's voice trailed off and he bowed his head.

Patrick took his hand and patted it. "It's OK," he said softly, his voice no more than an extension of his breath. "It's OK."

"You can't let him off that easily! Julius knew exactly what he was doing. And where did the code come from in the first place? From a book he stole from me, that's where."

"Be careful John." Julius's eyes were suddenly glittering. "I didn't steal anything from anyone. I found the book a few weeks ago when I was going through some old junk."

"Oh really?"

"Really. I recognised it immediately and I wanted to return it to you. But Patrick was ill and I had no way of contacting you. So in the meantime I arranged to take it to Oxford this weekend to have it carbon-dated."

John blinked at him. "But it's mine."

"Of course it's yours. But I thought it would be useful to establish categorically whether it's genuine or not. Would that be OK?"

"Well... I guess so..."

"Good. Then I'll let you know on Monday what the conclusion is." Julius smiled at him but John scowled and looked away.

There was a creaking behind us. Patrick had hauled himself up and was walking over to the bookshelves. We watched as he took down a stuffed A4 card folder. He returned to his bed and slumped back down on it. "I'm knackered," he said; but there was the faintest glimmer of a smile on his face, the first I'd seen. "Julius, this is the work I've done on the code: notes and explanations and so on."

"We don't need to think about that now," said Julius uneasily.

"No I want you to have it. I obviously haven't actually decoded it yet—"

"Really," said Julius hurriedly. "I don't want to talk about it. I'll take the file if you want me to but I'm not going to look at it till you're feeling better." He stowed the folder under his arm.

"But don't you even want to know—"

Julius held up a hand. "I mean it."

"OK." Patrick shrugged; but then almost immediately seemed troubled. "You will be careful won't you?"

Julius raised an eyebrow.

"I mean…" Patrick leant forward and whispered confidentially. "There are people after this."

My heart sank as I heard the words. "Patrick," I groaned. "I thought we went through this yesterday. There's no one after your stupid code."

"Yes there is, Sarah!" His suddenly raised voice shocked even himself. He looked confused, frustrated, then turned to John. "You believe me don't you?"

John closed his eyes and opened them, a long blink, no more than that. "Yes."

"Oh, come on! Patrick, he's just humouring you." I turned to John bewildered. "You were the one who found him. How can you indulge him like this?"

"I'm not indulging him," he said quietly. "I just don't think it's completely beyond the bounds of possibility—"

"Oh *please*." I turned to Julius. "Tell him: he'll listen to you."

Julius regarded me and then Patrick. "Sarah's right," he said. "There *is* nothing to worry about. There *is* no one looking for this book. Why should there be?"

John opened his mouth to say something but then closed it again.

"But there have been people following me. I'm sure of it."

"Perhaps there were," said Julius gently. "But not any more. There really is nothing to worry about." He smiled and put a hand on Patrick's arm.

Patrick nodded, deep in thought.

"Look," said Julius eventually. "I'd better get going."

"But we've only just got here," I said.

"I know. But I think it's better if I did." His eyes flickered to John. "I'll come round on Monday night," he said to Patrick. "When I'm back from Oxford. We'll know then one way or the other whether any of this is true."

We heard his steps receding down the stairs. I turned to John. "So what's this book Julius is meant to have stolen from you?"

He stared back at me unblinking. "We found it in Rome when we were on holiday that time. Girolamo Polidoro's journal. It got left behind in Venice when Patrick and I had to get out quickly."

"Well I certainly remember that."

"But wasn't there another book as well?" said Patrick. His voice had a spark in it all of a sudden and he was sitting up alert. "A soldier's diary?"

"Yes. Henry Shaeffer's notebook. It found its way into my rucksack but somehow not Polidoro's journal."

"Did I read it?" I asked frowning. "It seems familiar somehow."

He looked back at me, directly at me. His eyes were grey-blue, a steel and flint kind of colour. "Yes," he said. "You read about his last days in Rome and of how he went round the Accademia —"

"That's it!" I was surprised by the intensity of the memory. "That Veronese portrait of a man with a goitre. We went round the whole place looking for it."

The barest shadow of a smile crossed John's face.

"We walked round Venice together didn't we?" I said bemused as the scenes came back, synoptic sparks, each one overlaying the last, a three dimensional holographic past, satisfying, colour saturated. "Why was that? Where were the others?"

"Patrick and Maya had gone to Murano and Julius and Duncan were still in the hotel."

"Yes that's right." He watched my face as though sharing in my glimpses of recollection. "I remember. Shaeffer's notebook was really interesting. Do you still have it?"

"I still have it," and, as surprising as anything that had happened that day, he blushed, his whole face turning in an instant to rose pink. "I carry it with me," he said looking defiant, expecting a comment but I said nothing, intrigued as he pulled the small clothbound notebook from inside his jacket. He hesitated and then held it out. I took it from him. Feeling the fabric cover against my fingertips, I remembered something else, of how we had sat together in the square and read portions of the diary; such sadness, I recalled. "He died at Gallipoli didn't he?"

John nodded, his face grave. I opened the notebook close to the end and started to read.

And then Frances. She will be eighteen months old now and to have her in front of me, or dandling on my knee would bring me more happiness than I could ever put into words. You say that she is starting to talk.

Please, my love, teach her "Papa" as well as "Mama" so that when I am there again she will have a good word for me. When I think of her my heart jumps and I feel a pure warmth inside and I know that even if I am killed or my name besmirched that her love for me will persist as long as she herself has breath; and one day a child of hers will love her in the same way—

I snapped the book shut feeling my eyes prickle with tears. As I had ten years before. A lifetime ago. "His family ought to have this," I said softly. "His wife must be dead but Frances could still be alive..." I looked up and found John watching me uncomfortably. "You know don't you?"

He frowned. "Perhaps."

"What does *perhaps* mean?"

"I mean…" He drew breath and looked from me to Patrick and back again. I found his face impossible to read, no softness at all, a facts and figures face. How could anyone love a face like this?

"I mean I have looked into it," he said. "I found out from the Public Records Office that Anna Shaeffer – his wife – died in 1976." He sighed. "Frances is still alive or was two years ago. She'd be eighty-eight now."

"Have you contacted her?"

"No. All I did was a directory enquiries search in Cambridge which is where Shaeffer was from. The number they gave me is for a private line at an old people's home called Darnley.

"Then there's Henry himself. The PRO couldn't tell me exactly when he died even though I told them it was some time in 1915. They were having problems with their First World War records when I went there which is a shame because if we knew the exact date we could work out which bit of the campaign he died in. He was in the Royal Naval Division which led an attack up the coast from ANZAC Cove. But later on they joined the 29th Division who were pushing up from Cape Helles at the bottom of the Gallipoli peninsular. Most likely he died here during the summer of 1915 as the fighting ground into stalemate—. What's wrong?"

I'd been staring at him so hard that he'd had to break off. *"What's wrong? I'll tell you what's wrong.* You're more interested in your military facts and figures than you are in real people. Who *cares* which bit of the campaign he died in? What matters is that his daughter is sitting in an old people's home and you've got something that belongs to her."

He frowned. "The book belongs to me."

"It *does not*. It was meant for his wife and daughter. You should return it."

"She's right you know," said Patrick his voice again taking us by surprise. "We should go and see Frances and give her the book."

"Assuming she's still alive," said John coldly.

"Well then we'd better do it soon, hadn't we? Jesus, don't you have any feelings at all?"

He glared at me, his breathing heavy but in the end he just said, "Fine," and looked down at the ground.

"Great," said Patrick and I was astonished to see a smile had broken out on his face. "Well let's do it this weekend. Have you got the info on Frances?"

"I'll text it to you," he muttered. "When I get back home."

"Great. Well, let's talk tomorrow then and we'll aim to go up on Sunday—"

"Hang on Patrick," I said. "You're not going anywhere."

"Why not?"

"Why not? You're not well. You've been lying here for *days* hardly saying a word and now you suddenly want to take off for Cambridge? You need to take it easy."

"But don't you think it would be good for me to get some fresh air?"

"Of course, but—"

"And you proved to me yesterday that there's no one following me so there's nothing to be afraid of outside." He smiled innocently. "So it's settled. This Sunday?"

He looked at me and John and when John sulkily nodded I realised I had been out-manoeuvred and, having suggested returning the book in the first place, I could hardly back down now.

I frowned at him. "OK, but you stick with me the whole time."

I made to give the notebook back to John, but he shook his head. "You and Patrick seem pretty certain about what should happen to it," he said bitterly. "So you take it." He looked at me and there was real anger in his eyes. But it lasted only a split second and then he had turned for the door and was gone.

33

Aunty Jean was over the moon when I went over there to collect Patrick on Sunday. "He's been so much better the last couple of days," she said. "Talking and laughing. It's like he's back to normal again. I don't know what you all did for him but it really helped." She put her arms round me and hugged me and there were tears in her eyes which put tears in mine. I was happy for her, of course I was, but I was uneasy too.

Patrick really was transformed though. "I think it's a very important thing we're doing," he said chirpily as we faffed around before we left. "We'll be helping someone by doing it. That's really key. If you help somebody you help yourself."

Which sounded a bit New Age to me but he was grinning when he said it and just generally looked so happy that I didn't have the heart to rubbish it. It was as though the breakdown had never happened, and he was the Patrick I'd always known again. I was as willing to buy into that as anyone.

Leaving the house was when the reality of our trip seemed to dawn on him though. He said walking up the road felt like wading through treacle, and I caught him a couple of times snatching glances over his shoulder; but he managed to hold it together and once we got into the Wood, he seemed more relaxed. After that it was only a few minutes further to the enclosed safety of the Tube.

We met John at King's Cross and he was as lacking in personality as he had been a couple of days previous. He hardly said a word and made no attempt to respond to any question beyond yes or no. He didn't seem at all cute any more, just impossibly rude.

The journey was spent sitting opposite him. Luckily we were on the fast train – well, fast for a Sunday anyway –

which was so noisy that it made conversation almost impossible. Patrick and I took turns looking at Shaeffer's notebook while John just stared stonily out the window.

At Cambridge station we got a taxi and were driven through wide yellow-brick streets, the roads tree-lined, leafy, until we reached Darnley residential care home, a large Victorian mansion with a modern extension on one side. We walked in silence up the broad gravel path and straight in to reception. A lady in her forties in a nurse's uniform greeted us.

I looked at the boys and realised that I was expected to do the talking. I summoned a smile. "We're here to see Frances Shaeffer. We've got an appointment."

The nurse peered into a big desk diary then nodded and called over a girl in her mid-twenties. "Margret can you show these visitors to the Sunshine Lounge please."

Margret led us down a dark hallway with doors on either side, through a TV area where a number of residents were dozing in front of the afternoon matinee, then round a corner, past a dining room from where a waft of institutional cooking hit us – no nostalgia in that smell, just mince – and finally into the lounge. There was a small conservatory at one end where glass doors opened onto the gardens. There were a dozen people sitting in the conservatory all quite elderly looking, most in wheelchairs, enjoying the sunlight which streamed in through the glass roof. Margret sat us down at a small table a few metres away from them and went to get Frances. I smiled at the residents who were watching us with interest and then felt a jolt inside as I realised that they were all female.

"Have you come to see me, my dears?" a lady in a wheelchair called over in a frail voice. She must have been about ninety and looked at us hopefully. I stared back at her my eyes wide, biting my lip, doing anything to hold back the sob which was building inside of me. I was wondering what I was going to say when I heard a voice beside me.

"We've come to see one of your friends actually." It was John. His voice was different to the way I'd heard it before. It was deep yet extremely calming, no edge or chippiness to it any more, just soothing warm honey. And then he had stood up and was walking over to her. He waved a sunny hello to the other ladies as well most of whom waved back and then he knelt down by the lady's wheelchair and started talking with her. She listened enraptured and then giggled and whispered something back to him. The lady nearest to her was craning forward to catch their conversation. John turned so that she could hear as well and she giggled and then leaning almost out of her chair she said something to them both and the three of them burst into laughter.

Margret re-emerged through the double door on the right with an elderly lady walking beside her using a stick. She was dressed neatly in a blouse and cardigan and a pair of slacks and she walked steadily if slowly.

John returned to us, giving his new friends a parting wave. They waved happily back.

"What were you talking about?" I asked him astonished.

"Oh I couldn't tell you." He said looking at me sombrely and then his face split into a grin. "It's far too rude."

Frances shuffled over and we stood up to greet her. She looked at the three of us in turn and then back at Margret.

"I don't *think* I know any of them Maggie. But I might be wrong..."

Again it was John who spoke, his voice gentle, kind. "Miss Shaeffer—"

"Oh please call me Frances."

"Frances." He smiled at her holding her gaze. "You're right, you don't know us. We're here because we have some information which we thought you might find interesting. About your father."

"My father's dead."

"I understand. But we have something which we think

used to belong to him."

Frances looked uncertainly at Margret for a moment but then there was a shout from the group by the windows. "Oh listen to what he's got to say, Frances. He's come all the way from London and he's lovely." There was much laughter from that end of the room. John turned pink.

"Mind your own business Elsie!" Frances called back; but we caught her giving a stagey wink as well. "Fine then," she said turning to us once more. "It's not like I get many visitors so I can't look a gift horse in the mouth. What are you called, dear?" she asked me.

"Sarah."

"Oh I like the name Sarah. I'm going to sit next to you." She came forward and took my arm. "I like you already. Aren't you pretty? Don't you think she's pretty?" she said to Patrick and John. I felt myself blushing profusely. "You two boys sit down there," she said pointing at the couch opposite. Margret disappeared again to get some tea.

"And what are you called?"

"Patrick."

"John."

"Good. Now we all know each other." She frowned for a moment. "I'm so bad with names and faces and everything these days. I can't remember if you've been before. Are you from the school again? Because I don't really get any visitors these days. That's the problem with not having any children you see. Everyone else either forgets about you or gets too old. And who'd want to come to a place like this anyway? Unless they want something…" She looked down at her lap, musing. I cast a glance at John but he nodded at her hand holding to my arm. I gave a little sigh.

"Did you never get married then Frances?" I said tentatively.

She looked up again. "What was that dear?" I repeated the question. "Oh no. Funny isn't it."

"Did you never meet anyone you liked?"

"Not really. Not after Howard anyway."

"And who was Howard?"

"He was my sweetheart. Just before the war, dear. Just before. I was only twenty-six then. Can you believe it?" She looked at me, her face crinkled and old. "Can you believe I even was twenty-six once? I can't."

"You look very good for your age."

She smiled at me happily. "Oh thank you dear. You're very kind. I knew I was right to sit next to you. You should look after her," she said staring at Patrick admonishingly. He looked back startled, his head nodding obediently.

"Is he your boyfriend?" she whispered to me coyly.

I giggled. "No he's my cousin."

"Oh is he?" She sounded disappointed for a moment but only for a moment. "He does look like you, you know. He's quite handsome just like you. You're all good looking you know. So young," she said, smiling at me warmly, her eyes almost disappearing in a mass of wrinkles but sparkling happily, holding tight to my arm and giving it a little shake. "So much time."

"And Howard," I said gently, hoping the dread I felt didn't show through. "Your Howard, what happened to him?"

"Oh he was my sweetheart. So lovely. Always funny and such a lovely moustache. Can't ever see a man with a nice moustache and not think about him."

"But you didn't get married?"

"No dear." Her voice suddenly became grave. "He wanted to. Everyone was doing it you know. It was such a dangerous time and he was flying missions over France and Germany. Girls were getting married all the time, sometimes to fliers they hardly knew. Yanks. All sorts. And I'd known him for months already, and he wanted to but I thought it best to wait. I didn't want to have a baby with him and then for it to grow up without a father."

I felt I suddenly understood her and I exchanged a glance with Patrick and John.

"But I wish I had now. Not for the baby but just for Howard. It would have made him so happy. It wouldn't have made any difference of course. They'd still have shot him down. But he would have been so happy. Everyone always says it's the happiest day of your life and I'll never know." She looked at me, not sadly, just matter-of-factly. "But there's no point dwelling on these things is there. You just get on don't you. My mother did when Papa died. You just make the best of it don't you? Oh thank you Margret."

Margret had returned with a steel pot of tea, cups and a plate of biscuits. She poured the tea for us and one for herself and then sat down on her own chair to one side of us but just within earshot in case anyone needed her.

"Do have a biscuit, dear," Frances said offering me the plate with a shaky hand. "It's always lovely when we have visitors because they bring out the *nice* biscuits."

I politely took a bourbon from the selection on the plate which seemed less special than the range I always had back in my flat, and then handed the plate on to the boys.

"So," said Frances, holding her cup with both hands and blowing at the steam. "What was it you were here for dear? I'm sorry if you've told me already. I can't really remember anything of anything these days."

I took a deep breath. "We came here because we have something of your father's."

"My father? But you're too young to know my father. He's dead you know."

"Yes we know. We – well, John here..." I looked at him to see if he wanted to tell the story but he waved at me to go on; but smiled at me as well to show he thought I was doing fine, and I felt buoyed by it. "John here found a notebook – a diary really – a few years ago when on holiday in Italy. We think it belonged to your father."

I pulled it out of my bag and handed it to her. She took

it curiously and opened it and saw the name inscribed on the inside cover. "But this *is* Papa's," she said, looking at me her eyes wide with wonder, and I felt a surge of relief and happiness flood through me. "This is Papa's writing and this is his name. Henry. Arthur. I always thought if I were to have children and if it was a boy then I would call him either of those names. Kings' names. Oh what a pleasant surprise dear. Where did you get it did you say?"

"John got it from Italy. I believe your father was posted for a while in Italy during the First World War."

"Well of course he was dear. Of course he was." She flicked through the pages stopping here and there and smiling. "But he's talking about me here," she said tears coming to her eyes. "He's talking about me. *Little Frances.* That's me isn't it?" We nodded at her. "That's *me,*" she said in a tiny voice now flicking on. "Oh how he loved Mama. He loved her so much. She would have so loved to have seen this you know."

"It must have been very hard for your mother when your father died."

"I remember how upset she was straight after. Distraught she was."

"But how could you remember that?"

She looked at me sharply. "Young lady, I might not be able to remember what happened five minutes ago but I can remember that. I can remember my mother crying for days on end."

"I'm sorry," I said gently. "It's just that you would have been so young then."

Frances smiled at me again now. "So kind," she said to the boys. "She's so kind to me. I *was* young then I suppose," she said dreamily.

"And did your mother remarry after... I mean when your father died."

"Oh no, dear." She looked at me quite surprised. "Oh no. She would never have done something like that. She so loved him you know. So much. She would never have dreamed of marrying someone else."

"So she spent all those years on her own."

"I suppose it was a long time wasn't it when you look at it like that. Fifteen years?" she ventured uncertainly.

"Sixty years," said John.

"Oh no dear," she said confidently. "I don't think it was that long. Or maybe..." She looked a little confused. "Could it really have been as long as that? Everything becomes a little hazy when you get older and I never was much good at dates and arithmetic any way. Never any good at it. You're probably right. But it was so many years to be without the person she loved. Her best friend she always said. But she had her memories of course."

"And she had you."

"Yes. She had me as well. We were great friends Mama and I. I know your generation thinks we were all very starchy and proper but we were great friends Mama and I."

"From what we read in your father's diary she sounded like a very intelligent and very caring woman."

"Oh she was. She was. I still miss her you know." Her voice was sad now.

John cleared his throat. "It's hard isn't it when you lose your parents. Mine died a few years ago. It can be very tough."

"Oh dear, that's very hard for you. Give me your hand dear." John reached over and she gave his hand an sympathetic squeeze. "And you're so young too. Always harder when you lose your parents young. I was lucky in that respect."

"You lost your father early though didn't you?"

"Oh yes but not as young as you dear."

"I think you were even younger," I said to her gently, trying to keep her mind on a level.

"Oh maybe you're right," she said shaking her head.

I looked over at Patrick and John and they returned the

same sympathetic smile. I thought I'd get back to a safe topic. "But like I was saying your mother sounds lovely."

Frances perked up again. "Oh she is dear. Oh what am I saying. She was." Her face suddenly screwed itself up as though she were about to cry. I looked over at the nurse in sudden alarm. Margret was poised to get up but then Frances' face relaxed again. She was silent for a moment and then she said, "It's hard being old sometimes. Often it's like waking from a dream and you tell yourself that you're seventy-something or eighty-something and you can't believe it. And suddenly you remember something and it's as though you've heard a piece of news for the first time and it's so vivid it makes you want to cry. But you were saying dear. My mother *was* lovely. You're right. Did you know her then?"

"Oh no."

"You weren't one of her children by any chance?"

I was taken aback. "No, Miss Shaeffer."

"Frances dear. Please."

"Frances. *You're* one of her children."

"Well of course *I* am." She was amused by this. "I was wondering whether you were as well."

I blinked at her and cast an unsettled glance at the nurse. She gave the minutest shrug of her shoulders back at me. "How many children did your mother have?"

"Oh... hundreds."

I laughed at this but Frances looked at me seriously and then slightly worried. "Oh dear have I made another mistake."

"No it was just funny the way you said it. So were you from a very large family then. I thought it was just you and your mother?"

"Oh yes dear. Just us. And Papa of course."

"Then the children you mentioned?"

"Oh yes hundreds of them in the end. Maybe even as many as a thousand. All Mama's little children." She nodded at me proudly and I smiled, feeling my eyes start to tingle.

"Of course," I said

"But it was so sad when Papa died," she said the smile fading from her face again. "So sad. We all felt it. And Mama said that after he died it just seemed like it had all gone so fast. The years were like days she said. Gone so fast. Years like days. But of course I feel like that as well now."

Suddenly I found it hard to breathe. I felt a hotness behind my eyes, and my head was constricted. I hurriedly stood up. "We have to go now, Frances."

"Oh really dear. So soon?"

I nodded and saw John and Patrick were on their feet as well. My face was screwed up whilst looking in their direction so that Frances would not see it. John took a half-step towards me but I signalled that I was OK. I took a deep breath and looked back to Frances who by now was standing, resting on her stick.

"I'm sorry we have to leave so soon," I said, forcing a my face into composure.

"Oh that's all right dear. I understand. Thank you all very much for coming over here to talk to me. And thank you very much for my book. I shall enjoy reading this. Yes I shall. What a lovely present."

"You're welcome," I said softly, just wanting to be out of there.

"But I want you to have something too. For coming all this way. I've got a little something for you." Frances reached up and grabbed my arm again. "Come with me my dear. What was your name again?"

"Sarah."

"Sarah. Such a pretty name. Come with me. I have something I'd like you to have."

"Oh I couldn't," I said nervously. "Really I couldn't."

"Oh I insist. Come on dear." She started walking,

pulling at my arm with surprising force.

"But... I mean shouldn't Patrick and John come with us as well," I said hopefully to her.

She giggled suddenly. "Well, it's my bedroom dear. I can't have young men in my bedroom with me. I'm not sure whether Maggie would allow it."

Margret looked at her smiling. "If you want to I'm sure it will be fine. I'll come along too."

"No that's fine, Maggie. I just want my Sarah." She raised her voice slightly. "The boys can stay here and keep Elsie entertained."

I cast one last appealing glance over at John and then allowed myself to be dragged round the corner through the double doors and down a corridor, Margret following at a discreet distance.

The door to Frances' room was unlocked and she went inside whilst I stood in the doorway.

"I won't invite you in properly dear. It's a bit of a mess at the moment."

I looked around the tiny room. It was spotless inside and immaculately tidy. A single bed by the near wall, made, the sheets carefully turned back square. A writing desk with a single hard wooden chair at it on the right hand side with a bookcase beside it filled with books, most of the shelves double stocked. On the facing wall was a window and a radiator and then on the left hand side was a mahogany wardrobe next to the bed and in the corner a dark wood chest of drawers. It was to this that she walked.

"It's just a little something dear. Just something I think you'd like." She smiled at me for a second more and then turned to the chest of drawers. On top of it was a wide old box two feet by one foot and six inches deep. The top was plain dark wood but the sides were of metal, brass or bronze perhaps, a dull golden glow showing through the dust. Brightly coloured crystals were set into the metal but on the side facing forwards was a recess the size of hen's egg from where one of the baubles had long since been lost. Apart from the books it seemed to be her only possession in the room.

She opened the box and pulled out various items from within: mostly papers, but also an old fashioned necklace, an enamel square, and a few pairs of earrings: the scant remnants of a lifetime.

Eventually she took out a handful of envelopes, tied with red ribbon. She looked through the bundle and then selected one letter, putting the remainder back in the box. Then she took a brown envelope from the top drawer of her writing desk, slipped the letter inside it, sealed it and presented me with the package.

"This is for you, dear."

"But it's one of your old letters—"

"Of course it is. But I want you to have it. It's the last letter Papa wrote to Mama from the Great War. I think he would have liked you to read it and she would too."

"No really I can't take it. It's far too precious a thing to give to a stranger."

"Well then," she said with a suddenly sly look in her eyes. "Why don't you just borrow it? Why don't you take it away and read it and then when you come back here to visit me again..." She looked at me hopefully. "When you come back you can bring me the letter as well."

"Well, I'm not sure..."

"Whether you were going to come back? Oh I understand dear," she said breezily.

I felt tears in my eyes. "No. I mean I'd like to come back."

"Oh would you? Would you really?"

I nodded. "Of course I would. If you want me to."

"Oh yes dear. Please come and see me again." She forced the letter into my hands. "I have so enjoyed speaking with you. But don't if you're busy. I will understand."

I was choking to hold back my tears and just shook my

head. "I'll come," I said eventually. "You can count on it."

"Oh thank you dear. Thank you so much." There were tears in her eyes as well. And then she leant forward and gave me a kiss and she held me close and she felt old and smelt old and I thought my heart would break.

I went back through the lounge, without saying anything to the boys, to anyone. I just had to get out into the fresh air. And the moment I was outside I started running down the gravel drive, faster and faster, until I'd passed through the gate and was stood on the pavement of the world beyond; and then I just sobbed.

34

We got the slow train back. Stopping at what would normally have been an interminable list of hick East Anglian villages: Foxton, Meldreth, Shepreth. But today the longer the journey the better. It was insulation against the real world.

We didn't speak about the visit on the way to the station. In our own ways all three of us were processing or reflecting or running from it. And now, resting my head against the cool glass I emptied my mind of everything except the succession of brown and yellow fields flashing through my vision.

Patrick had fallen asleep almost immediately the train started moving. He leaned against me, his head swaying as the train swayed. I felt very fond of him in that moment and was happy he slept. He had always had a tremendous capacity for sleep when travelling, but this was something else, exhaustion from being outside again, of overcoming his fears.

In the seat opposite me, John read his book. I recognised it as the same one he had dropped on my foot, a thick black and yellow Penguin Classic. I tilted my head to read to spine: *The Count of Monte Cristo*. Is that how he saw himself I wondered? And then decided probably not as he was only a third of the way through it. He yawned and looked up and smiled at me and I found myself smiling back.

"How are you feeling?" His voice was low and composed: attractive.

"I'm fine now. Thank you."

"You were very kind back there the way you spoke to Frances."

I shrugged. "She was just a nice old lady. A bit lonely; and a bit confused." I felt a sob threatening to rise inside me but I choked it back.

After a pause he said, "You were right about wanting to give the notebook back. It made a difference to her. Thank you for overruling me." He smiled at me and for some reason it made me feel a little better.

A couple of minutes passed, a station came and went, and then, our conversation beating time with the easy progress of the train, he said, "You seemed really upset when you came back from her room. Did anything happen?"

Passing trees. Passing fields. Cows and green. Birds and air. Free as a cow. No one ever said that. But a cow would do. "No. It was just me. Just being there with her. The thought that her life had been reduced to the contents of that tiny room. The whole ageing thing. It scares the shit out of me. I find it scary enough just the thought of turning thirty."

"Aren't you thirty yet?"

"*Hey*," I yelped; but I was happy to go off at a tangent, away from that room. "You don't have to sound quite so surprised. It's *weeks* away. I don't *look* over thirty do I?"

"I *guess* not," he said and I glowered at him and he laughed. "*Definitely* not." He considered my face for a moment or two until it made me feel uncomfortable, shy almost. "What?" I said. "What are you thinking?"

"Just thinking how you'd changed since I first saw you."

"You can't remember surely."

"Yes," he said innocently. "I can."

"Oh," I said flattered. "I can't really remember you. Well maybe a little."

Maybe a little more than that. I remembered his eyes, grey-blue, piercing, and remembered his body and his hands on mine. I remembered his touch against me, his lips, his tongue. I remembered our laughter and the stupid drinks we drank and the sudden realisation of attraction crystallised in an instant and then back, walking with him on a black night, memories rolled in passions rolled away, thoughts that made me happy. I grinned at him. "So what do you remember about me? How have I changed? Fatter right? I used to be a size 8 when I was nineteen. Can you believe it: *size 8*. Now I'm size 12."

"Is that bad?"

I eyed him suspiciously.

"But, OK, your hair's different. You were blonde back then."

"God! Yes. That holiday was the only time. Boring brown now though."

"I like your hair brown. And you were a vegetarian."

"Was. Pretty much lapsed now."

"And you smoked a lot."

"Oh God did I? I've been trying to cut that down. It's only social now."

He laughed. "But you do look older."

"I do?" I said taken aback.

"Yes. Around the eyes you have some lines now."

"Oh don't say that. *Please* don't say that."

"But they suit you. They're very… womanly."

"I doubt that," I said feeling my cheeks go warm at the compliment. I smiled at him and he smiled back. It felt friendly and easy talking to him all of a sudden and I wondered which of us had changed.

"So..." he said. "Are you going to have a big party for your thirtieth."

"No way. I just want to forget all about it. I hate birthdays." I sighed and made a face as I thought about Frances again.

He leant forward and touched me on the knee. "You brightened her day you really did."

I blinked at him, pleased that he had known what I was thinking, surprised at his gentleness. "But anyway," I said after a moment, "if anyone brightened up that place it was you. Those ladies *loved* you."

He laughed bashfully. "Women of a certain age..." he said grinning. "They can't get enough of me. Fifty-five and above and they're *mine*."

We were both amused by that and we looked in opposite directions to quell our laughter. Next to me Patrick stirred, his eyes opening for a second, almost surfacing then closing again. I stared out through the glass, the pleasant giggle in me fading to a dull ache, the fields fading to concrete and a sea of brick houses and industrial estates and roads seen from the rails, long lines of street lighting and fast cars moving backwards.

"I'm sorry about your parents," I said after a while, my heart thumping in me, hoping he wouldn't take it the wrong way, reaching out and touching his knee the way he had touched mine, feeling a ridiculous charge at so chaste a gesture.

He looked at me, studied my face for seconds that felt like minutes, our eyes meeting and holding and then he nodded at me. "It was a few years ago but thank you." I nodded as well and we both stared out of the window together.

Eventually, he asked, "So what did she give you?"

"Frances? A letter. She said it was the last one that Henry wrote to his wife from the War."

He raised an eyebrow. "He must have written it during the Gallipoli campaign. Have you read it yet?"

"No. And maybe I won't. It was the last thing he wrote before he died." I made a face. "It wasn't meant for us. Do you know what I mean?"

"I think so…"

"I know you must be interested having had his diary for so long. But the letter really is too private a thing to have given to strangers. I'll return it to her when I see her again. She probably won't even remember she gave it to me, poor dear."

"So you will go back?"

I felt myself about to cry again. "Yes. She hasn't got anyone else. And she was really nice. I did genuinely like her. She's just a bit... just a tiny bit *disconcerting* at times."

"You know, I told Elsie and her friends that I'd pay them another visit too."

"Really? They must have been over the moon about it."

He gave an embarrassed smile. "They were quite pleased. I thought I could coincide it with a College reunion that's happening in a few weeks. Patrick had wanted to go and I hadn't been too keen... But maybe it would be a good thing to do. Lay some ghosts to rest." He smiled and then said, his voice a bit more hurried, "You know I'm allowed to bring a guest. Would you, maybe, like to come? We only need to stay for an hour or two and then we could head over to the old people's home and you could see Frances again."

"Are you asking me on a date?"

He looked suddenly very embarrassed. "I suppose so – but I mean Patrick would be there too. I mean it was just a thought—"

"You're asking me on a date... to an *old people's home?*" I stared at him and then we both started laughing, loud happy laughter, and the more we looked at each other the more we laughed.

We got in at seven and had a quick drink at the pub in the station, all fake mahogany and cigarette burned carpet.

Patrick, fully rested, did most of the talking, and he was eloquent and funny yet not so loud that it made me worry about him. But it really was just a quick drink, no more than an hour, and at the end, having first of all checked he would be OK to get home – John said he would go with him – I said goodbye to Patrick and gave him a kiss and said I'd see him the following night for Julius's big reveal on the carbon dating of the journal. I hesitated, then gave John a kiss on the cheek as well.

"Thank you."

"For what?" he said surprised.

"Just for coming along."

He looked at me and laughed, but then said "I'll see you tomorrow," and I nodded and he gave me a kiss on the cheek as well and the tiniest of hugs, no more than his hand brushing my side, the barest touch, but with it a wealth of warmth and a thrill that I couldn't quite explain but which had passed through me from head to toe by the time I'd walked away.

35

That night I thought about him.

I thought what I would say to him when I saw him again. And I thought what he would say to me. I wondered what he would be wearing – a suit I guessed, it being a weeknight: not *very* interesting. So I wondered what I would wear instead, what he might like.

I thought about what we had said on the train and how he had been kind and how he had laughed.

I thought about being with him, our being together, now, and then, and I wondered why I had never rung him like I'd said I would. Back then. Way back then. A sudden ache of guilt, a bruise on my conscience long forgotten, because I should at least have rung him. A prick on soft skin, a stab against bone, pain either way. I should have rung him. Even if just to say *nothing*.

Because of course Julius and I were together by then, my fantasy made flesh, and he was all I needed, wanted, desired. Everything else was awkward and superfluous and was best left; so I left them, small acts in the main of indifference and cowardice, let them fade into memory and then beyond memory.

And now I wondered if I had rung him how things might have been different. I wondered whether I should apologise. I wondered whether he was single. And I wondered whether he was thinking about me. At all. A little bit.

I hoped he was.

I'd got off work a bit early so had managed to go home and change before coming out, my linen suit and white shirt combination, three buttons casually undone, going rather well with supercool retro Golas. I headed straight out again to Aunty Jean's and was surprised when Patrick himself answered the door.

"Mum and Dad are going out tonight."

"We'd arranged it weeks ago," said Aunty Jean appearing from the living room, Uncle Malcolm behind her. "Now you will be OK dear?" she asked Patrick anxiously.

"Of course, Mum." Much kissing and hugging and anxious farewells later and we were left alone. "Thank goodness for that," Patrick said as we walked up to his room and he crashed out on the bed.

"Well, you can't blame them for worrying," I said sitting cross-legged on the floor.

"But I've been feeling fine for days now. What's there to worry about?"

He was looking good, it had to be said. He was dressed and shaved and looked like he'd been eating. There was a spark back in his eyes and his conversation was entirely normal, not a trace of paranoia. And yet, and yet...

"So when are you going back to work?" I asked.

He got up and switched on the TV, lying back down again with the remote control on his chest. "Maybe not for a while."

I raised an eyebrow. "They have to take you back you know. You've got rights."

"Don't worry. It's not like that. I just don't know whether I want to go back."

"How come? I thought they were about to make you a partner?"

"Perhaps. But I'd have to work like a dog to get it."

"Well I'd work like a dog if I was about to get paid—" I broke off realising I had no clear idea how much someone senior *not* working in crappy old PR would be on. "Well, whatever it is, I'm sure it must be stacks."

"I don't care about the money. I just don't want to work so hard anymore. Not lunchtimes and evenings and weekends anyway. Life's just passing me by. I haven't been out with anyone for almost two years and even that wasn't

277

serious. I only see John at work. I hadn't seen Julius for months. And when was the last time I saw you?"

I shrugged. The description of his life was uncomfortably similar to my own.

"And now because of my…" He waved his hands around him searching for the right word.

"Incident?" I helped him out politely.

"*Breakdown*," he said firmly. "Because of my breakdown, I've had time to stop and think about what I want to do. And I don't think it's accountancy."

"Then what?"

"I don't know yet. Just something different. Something that would help people. If you help somebody you help yourself."

"Is that your catchphrase now? It sounds like someone's been hiding crystals in your room."

He laughed. It was a nice sound. I liked to hear him laugh. But then he said, "Maybe you need to think about doing something different as well. I get the feeling you're not exactly *wild* about your job."

"It's fine," I said immediately, defensively, having no desire to let anyone pick my life to pieces: God knows I could do that easily enough if I needed. "What time are the guys turning up?" I said hurriedly.

"I haven't heard from Julius. I hope he hasn't forgotten."

"He doesn't forget things. He'll be over. How about John?" I said as casually as I could.

"He rang about half an hour ago to say he couldn't make it."

"*Oh*," I said deflating obviously.

"Just kidding." Patrick grinned. "He should be over any time now. I thought you might be looking forward to seeing him again."

"Not particularly," I said feeling my cheeks colour.

"Oh right. So do you normally have that many buttons

undone?"

"Yes," I said instinctively reaching to my chest and doing one of them up again. "It's called *fashion,* Patrick."

Over the sound of his laughter I heard the tring of the doorbell.

"That'll be him," said Patrick lying back, hands behind his head.

"Well aren't you going to get it?"

"No. I think I'll let you do that." And he gave me a big stagey wink that had me punching him hard and laughing out loud at one and the same time.

The doorbell went again and he really wasn't intending to move so I groaned and got up, rolling my eyes at him, "I don't *believe* you," I called back over my shoulder despairingly as I walked down the stairs, one flight, two flights, and I felt a sudden skitter of nerves at the thought of seeing him again, and I let out that third button, because it was summer after all, and *PR slutty* was a pretty good look.

The bell went a third time and I called out "I'm coming," and I skipped to the front door thinking I should have kicked off my shoes as bare feet were even sexier and turned the lock and started to open the door, my heart thumping out of my chest, and saying, "Hi John," in as cool and clear—

The door smacked into me and I spun round and hit the wall hard,

My shoulder

My face,

And then the floor.

I was on the floor. Crouched down. I tried to get up but was shoved sprawling again.

There were shouts behind me and now I was pulled to my feet.

My mouth was full of blood and I tried to struggle free but was pinned against the wall.

Shouting. A hand gripped my head so that my face was squeezed into the wallpaper. Straight on not allowing me to turn profile.

Shouting. My head pressed against the wall. I couldn't breathe or scream. My body pinned there by the force behind me.

Shouting. An order. My hair was yanked back and a band of cloth brought down in front of my eyes; but I squirmed and the material slipped.

Then I felt a punch. A thump of incandescent pain. I almost passed out there and then. The material, a scarf, was brought back up to my eyes, yellow, a repeat pattern, Hermes-style my fashion mind thought, a one inch repeat motif forced onto my face, deep gold on lighter yellow, a hundred winged lions, coming home to roost.

We were moving. I gasped for breath as whoever it was behind me pushed me along the hall, another of them in front of me, I realised as I bumped into them. *"Patrick!"* I yelled up the stairs in warning. *"Patr—"*

And then more pain. I didn't even know where I was hit this time. I was on the floor again. Gasping. Pain and air. Air and blood.

I was shoved along. Rolled down the hall. Voices around me. Not English. Maybe Italian. I knew Italian. But the voices faded in and out and my mind wandered.

Then the stairs. In my blindfolded state I banged into them and stumbled. Whoever was in front reached back and dragged me by the hair so that I screamed at the white heat pain. "I'm coming," I screamed, I cried, tears soaking my blindfold. "Please don't hurt me." I staggered to my feet and started up the stairs, pushed from behind, my shins hitting the steps as I went. Such a little thing. But pain each time. Bruise on bruise.

More stairs. Up to the top of the house. My head lolled. Eyes open. Eyes closed. Blackness either way. Shuddering at the pain. Cowering from it. Why were they doing this?

Who was doing this?

A door banged open and I was thrown into a room, Patrick's room. The shouting started again. Patrick's voice. Other voices. Two. Three maybe.

I didn't care. I was facedown on the carpet. My cheeks and forehead resting on the soft pile. Ignored for the moment. Glorious freedom.

"Leave her alone! Sarah are you OK—?"

"Then tell us what we want to know."

"I don't know what you're talking about—"

A dull sound. The sound of hard stuff on soft stuff, bone on flesh. I lay there. They'd forgotten about me. I could stay there forever. I could sleep for a hundred years.

Patrick's scream rent me. But I could do nothing. And I was glad it wasn't me.

"Tell us the key."

"I don't know the key."

"The girl," he said. He, the leader.

Suddenly fear. Not of pain but that the carpet warmth might be taken away from me.

"Hurt the girl."

The words before the actions.

"No! Leave her alone—"

"Then tell us what we want to know."

The words before the actions. I felt the carpet beneath my hand. I clutched at the softness, the kindness. My heart banged.

Suddenly I was being lifted into the air and my feet set on the ground. I was forced forwards and put my hands out to stop me hitting the inevitable wall. But I felt nothing save fresh air and I knew immediately I was on Patrick's balcony. It had started to rain, hard, the fat drops pelting me. A sudden sear of light. A flash of lightning. Yellow through my blindfold. The winged lions of St Mark lit up before my eyes.

"Tell us or we kill the girl."

"OK, OK—"

"Throw her over!"

No time for fear now.

"I said *OK!* I'll tell you."

A pause. All silent. Just the rain coming down on me.

"Terraferma."

There was a cry from him. The leader. And then suddenly I was being dragged back inside. *Hurt the girl*, he had said. Now it would start. Whatever they had in mind. Fear swept through me.

"Come sono stato cosi cieco?" Definitely Italian. *"Come non l'avrei indovinato per tutti questi anni?"* Desperate for some escape my mind translated. *"How could I have been so blind? How could I have missed it all these years?"*

I was forced to my knees and then there were shouts below, from downstairs and frantic steps on the stairs. *"Dobbiamo affretarci. Una macchina èd arrivata fuori."* We must hurry. A car has drawn up outside.

"OK. Kill them and let's get out of here."

"But Count Loredan you know the Capo's orders."

"The Capo is soft. Who's in charge here?"

"You of course. But we have what we need. They are not a threat—"

"We need to go, Count. Now!"

There was a bellow of frustration from him, the one in charge. *"Very well!"*

"Quickly Count. Down the fire escape."

The hands gripping my arms were suddenly released. I reached immediately for my face to loosen the cruelly tight scarf which bound me around the temples. Oh the relief to have it fall from my eyes.

Patrick was on the floor nearby, leant against the bookcase, blood dripping from the side of his mouth. I turned my head and saw *him*, tall, dressed in black. There were two others leading the way onto the balcony but he was unquestionably the leader.

"How did you find me?" Patrick called after them.

The leader paused a moment in the doorway. Lighting flashed, illuminating his handsome face. "That is what we do." He laughed and with his hand he drew an X in the air, unmistakeable, and then he was gone.

The door to the room burst open and John appeared.

"What—?" His hand going to his face as he saw us, hesitating as to which one to attend to first.

"The balcony!" shouted Patrick. "They're going down the fire escape—"

John ran out into the teeming rain, right to the parapet, peering over, but then was back within a few moments, already soaked through. "They're gone."

"Thank God," I said. "The leader wanted to kill us."

"Jesus." John came over to me and helped me upright, his face so close to mine that I could feel his breath on me. He touched my face with the back of his hand, an action of such gentleness after the violence that I began to cry. But I didn't want him to see me like that so I shrugged out of his embrace and got to my feet, unsteadily, holding onto the back of the sofa for support. "Who the hell are they Patrick? What did they want?"

"They wanted the key," said Patrick. "I had to tell them." His voice was high pitched, his eyes bulging. He stared from me to John. "I knew they would come for it. I said they would."

"But you don't know the key," said John.

"Of course I do."

"But..." John looked at him dismayed. "I didn't realise you'd cracked the code..."

"Well I haven't exactly. But I worked out the keyword so the decipherment should be easy. It's a letter you see. Though it'll be in Italian—"

"Did you tell Julius the key?"

"It was in the notes I gave him."

"Then they could be headed over there as well. Or

maybe they went there before and they've got to Julius already."

"But who *are* they?" I asked, my head and body aching.

"I thought I recognised the leader," said Patrick.

"You did," said John, but before we could ask him any more he had sprinted to the door. "I'll explain on the way to Julius's."

The rain lashed us as we drove, heavy drops beating down too fast for the wipers to cope, the windscreen a constant film of water, smearing the brake lights and headlights of the cars ahead into daubs of violent colour. I sat in the back. Patrick was in the passenger seat.

"The leader's name," said John gripping the steering wheel, his eyes on the blurred road ahead, "is Count Pietro Loredan. And Patrick and I have seen him before. On our last day in Venice. He came to get Polidoro's journal back. But the police arrived before he could make his move. We thought the police were after us. But they weren't. They were after him."

"But who is he?" asked Patrick punching numbers into his mobile phone.

"He's from one of Venice's oldest families, a descendant of a Doge of Venice. He's also a terrorist. The Italian police have been after him for more than fifteen years. He's part of a group called the *Lega de Dieci* who want Venice to break away from Italy and become an independent republic again."

The winged lion, I thought and shuddered.

"He was responsible for a bombing campaign in Venice in the late 80s and early 90s. He targeted foreign shops and government offices. No one was killed but that was down to luck more than anything."

"But why was he after Patrick?"

"He wanted the key to Polidoro's code."

"But why?"

"Because the Cross of St Peter and Paul is a potent symbol of Venice and he evidently believes the code will lead him to it."

"No one's answering," said Patrick, the phone to his ear. "Julius was definitely meant to be back from Oxford today, right?"

I nodded and then immediately regretted it as my neck spasmed with pain. I massaged the back of it, rocking my head gently from side to side.

John eyed me in the rear view mirror. "You OK?"

"OK enough." I was feeling nauseous but I knew we had to get to Julius's. "How do you know all this stuff about Loredan?"

"I saw his name in a newspaper article a few years ago when I was… researching something… and I remembered him from that day in Venice. He's not been active for years, had kind of disappeared from view. He must have been hunting the books. But I don't understand why he chose this moment to get to Patrick – we'd have been easy enough to track down. He could have done it years ago. It's like he knew somehow that Patrick had cracked the code…"

"But I've given him the key," said Patrick. "That should be it shouldn't it? There's no reason for him to go after Julius as well?"

"Maybe," said John grimly. "But I reckon Loredan would want Polidoro's journal back as well."

We pulled up in front of Julius's building in Primrose Hill and bundled out into the crashing rain. We sprinted across the street to the front door and were wet by the time we got there. Patrick stabbed repeatedly at the buzzer but there was nothing, no sound at all above the continual throb of the rain around us.

"Come on Julius!" he yelled desperately and hit it again, one last time then drew a long breath and looked from John to me. "What do we do now—?"

"Hello?" The intercom squawked into life.

"Hello," said Patrick excitedly.

"Who is that?" An angry electric female voice.

"It's Patrick: Julius's friend. That's Madeleine isn't it?"

"Patrick? What are you doing here?"

"We wanted to see—"

"I can't hear a thing through this. Come up." An abrupt click and a buzzer sounded. We pushed on the door and ran up three flights of stairs. Julius's girlfriend was standing in the doorway dressed in a bathrobe, her hair up.

"Well if I'd known we were having a party…" she said sardonically as she saw the three of us, out of breath, dripping water onto the sisal matting in the hallway. "I was in the bath," she said. "Looks like you were too…"

"Is Julius OK?" Patrick panted.

She raised an eyebrow. "Fine I should imagine." Then she squinted at him, at the dried blood on his face; at me, the bruising on my cheek. "What happened to you two?"

"Nothing," said Patrick impatiently. "Where's Julius?"

She stepped aside and indicated the interior of the small flat. "*Not* here. He's not back yet."

"From Oxford?"

She looked puzzled. "What makes you think he's in Oxford?"

"He said he was going there this weekend."

"Well I don't know why he told you that. He's gone on holiday. Back in a few days. Though precisely *when* is a bit too much detail for me apparently."

"Where's he gone?" asked John.

Madeleine appraised him carefully as she crossed one bare leg in front of the other, leaning herself against the door frame. "I don't know you do I?"

"I'm John," he said briskly. "Where's Julius gone on holid—?"

"I know *you* of course," she said turning to me, fixing

me with a smile that was icy its pearly whiteness.

I smiled politely back at her. "I didn't know you two were living together now."

She frowned and shrugged. "As good as. I have a key. So practically living together. And while he's away…"

"Away where?" John persisted.

"Ah yes," she said dreamily. I saw through the open door a half-finished bottle of wine and a single glass on the coffee table. "He's gone to Cyprus."

The colour drained from John's face.

"There must be some mistake." Patrick looked like he was going to be sick. "He told us he was going to Oxford to get a book carbon dated."

"Then Julius has clearly told you a bigger load of boloney than he normally tells me," said Madeleine bemused.

"When did he leave?" asked John. His voice was utterly expressionless.

"He headed off Saturday lunchtime. And don't ask me why Cyprus: I have no idea. It came out of the blue, but is certainly in keeping with everything else at the moment. This place has been a complete madhouse the last couple of days. First of all this Italian book chappy from Julius's work turns up – on a *Sunday* for Pete's sake – I mean why whatever it was couldn't just wait till Monday? – and when I tell him that Julius isn't around he says he needs to talk to the cleaner – of all people. Who then turns up. Did I mention it was a Sunday? And they start whispering like they've got some great secret. And then I go out and come back and find that nosy bitch going through Julius's things: brazen as you like. She doesn't even pretend she isn't. Just because he's screwing her she thinks she can take liberties."

She stared at me, challenging me to say something. In what? Sympathy? Empathy? Or maybe she thought he was screwing me too.

"But anyway," she continued, "I wasn't standing for

R P NATHAN

that. So I fired her. At which she laughs and says she has
what she needs anyway. So I make her turn out her pockets
as I was certain she'd been thieving and then kick her out.
But then this afternoon the book guy comes back with
three more Italians who wanted to know where she was. I
wouldn't be at all surprised if they turned out to be her
pimps. And even while I'm standing there they launch into
a blazing row – Italian being yelled to the rafters and then
the book guy storms off and the pimps storm off and I say
to hell with the lot of them."

"And what time was this?" asked John.

"About five. Six maybe."

"So they did come here first, Patrick. They must have
known Julius had obtained the key to the code: his cleaning
lady was clearly keeping an eye out for them. But when they
came to pay him a visit he'd already gone. So they went
after you instead."

"Lucky for Julius then," I said, "that he decided to go on
holiday when he did."

"Lucky, yes," said John darkly. "But he's not on
holiday."

"As fascinating as this conversation undoubtedly is,"
said Madeleine yawning loudly, pointedly. "My part in it
seems to be over so I'm going back to my bath. I assume
you can let yourselves out."

We walked downstairs. The rain was still lashing down
so we stood in the hallway with the front door open waiting
for a suitable moment to make the dash to the car. My body
was feeling achy now, not pain, more like I'd been sleeping
in a funny position. But my head was cloudy and befuddled.
And I still didn't understand what was going on. "What did
you mean Julius isn't on holiday?"

"He meant that Julius lied to us," said Patrick. "He's
gone to Cyprus to look for the cross."

"But Loredan must be heading to Cyprus too," I said
anxiously.

"Exactly," said Patrick. "Julius doesn't know what he's got himself into."

John shrugged. "If they catch up with him then Julius only has himself to blame."

"But we can't just wash our hands of it."

"I'm not washing my hands of anything," he snapped. "Julius double crossed us and now he's going to get what he deserves."

"But we can't do nothing." I frowned as I felt a searing pain in my left temple. I closed my eyes for a second against it and saw Loredan wreathed in lightning, a winged lion perched behind him. I said, flustered, "Whatever Julius has done we've got to help him."

John looked at me straight in the eyes, unblinking, emotion-free, this face which was capable of such kindness, such humanity, which seemed to be capable of love, even; this face which was now cold and angry and hard.

Then he suddenly smiled; not a nice smile. At all. "OK," he said. "Maybe you're right. Maybe we're not too late."

"Not too late for what?" I asked him suspiciously.

"To help Julius. He only left for Cyprus on Saturday and Loredan at the earliest can only leave tonight. We've still got time to get out there as well."

"Yes!" said Patrick. *"Yes!* That's what we need to do. We need to go to Cyprus to warn him. If you help some—"

"Hang on!" I said. "What I meant was we should call the police."

"The police won't do anything," said Patrick. "They'll never believe us for starters."

"Loredan wanted to kill me," I said affronted. "Of course they'll believe us."

"Well good luck with that. But even if they do they're hardly going to send anyone to Cyprus are they?"

"So what would you suggest?"

"We go out there."

"But how do you even know where to go? Have you

decoded this letter of Polidoro's?"

John opened his mouth to say something but Patrick cut in before he could speak. "No. But that's fine. I have the key. And you speak Italian—"

"No. *No.*" I put my hands to my head. "Patrick this is all wrong. It's the code which caused your breakdown in the first place. You mustn't get involved in this again."

"Don't patronise me. We haven't got time for that. Julius is in danger."

"I know he's in danger but the best way we can help him is to go to the police. If John is right about Loredan then wouldn't they be able to stop him travelling? Isn't that what the police do? Circulate his description or something?"

"It would take too long," said John coolly and Patrick nodded. "The only way is to go out there."

"Why on earth are you so keen to go out there? Loredan's guys are serious about this. They tried to kill us. And for what? A cross that doesn't even exist."

"It does exist!" John's eyes blazed. "Of course it exists."

"Oh yes. I forgot you were a believer too. Well I've got news for you: your precious Cross of St Peter and Paul is a figment of the imagination—"

"The Cross of St Peter and Paul is buried in the sand where Bragadino left it."

"Based on Polidoro's diary?"

"Based on everything, goddamn it. It's there."

"Of course," I said, suddenly seeing it. "That's why you want to go to Cyprus isn't it? You don't give a stuff for Julius or Loredan or *anyone*. You just want to be the first to the cross."

"And you think your precious Julius is any different?"

"No, I'm sure Julius is just the same. But at least he's consistent. I can't read you at all."

"You don't *know* me at all."

"Well I was just starting to wasn't I? Christ, I was even

starting to *like* you."

"Oh well. What a fucking *honour*."

I stared at him absolutely furious with him; with myself. He sneered back at me.

"What a one hundred per cent, copper-bottomed honour for you to decide to like someone." His voice dripped sarcasm and I wanted to slap him. I stepped forward but stopped myself. I hugged my arms about me.

"It's pointless. I can't talk to you."

"I don't want you to talk to me."

I looked at him with tears in my eyes. Tears of frustration and anger and... My voice dropped and I sighed. "John, you're such a nice guy. How did you ever get so *obsessed?*"

He didn't answer this time. He just stared at me for a moment, his face and eyes hard to me, and then blinked and looked away.

There was silence for seconds that seemed like minutes. And then Patrick said, "*So...* What are we going to do?"

"We're going to go back to your house and get the police round like I said."

"But—"

"But nothing. We'll call the police and give them the information we've got."

"And if they don't believe us?" said Patrick. "Or won't do anything?"

"They will," I said briskly now. "They have to." I looked at John. "Are you coming with us?"

There was a flicker in his eyes and the tiniest shake of his head.

"Fine." I wasn't surprised. "Fine."

"But I can drive you there if you want."

"That's quite all right." I was trying my hardest to stay polite. "We'll call a cab."

"Suit yourself." And with that he walked out into the still pouring rain.

"Whatever." I fumbled in my handbag for my purse and pulled out a minicab card from it; handed it to Patrick. "These guys are usually pretty quick. Let's get back over to your place and call the police from there."

We didn't talk on the cab ride back to Aunty Jean's. The driver had the radio tuned to a Turkish music station, and we just sat on the backseat as the songs filled the silence.

I ached from the attack and the flashback grip of fear. The winged lion. Loredan. I felt like I was on the verge of tears, welled with a disappointment I didn't properly understand. All I knew was I didn't want to talk or think about anything or *anyone*. I just wanted to stare through the dirty glass at the beating rain and darkness.

We hit traffic and got caught in a long queue in Kentish Town. All I wanted was to get back to Patrick's house so we could call the police, and then they could come and inspect the crime scene – because that was what it was – and then I could get back to my own bed as soon as possible. But it wasn't to be and we just sat there with me getting crosser and crosser. The driver had turned the music louder as well which didn't help my mood. Every few minutes Patrick tried getting my attention but I refused to talk to him.

Eventually though when we had been there for nearly twenty minutes, no way forward or back, cars ahead, cars behind, I had to listen to what he was trying to say.

"We need John when we get the police round, Sarah. He's the only one that really knows anything about Loredan."

He was right of course. I knew he was right. But I shot him a black look all the same. "He had his chance to come with us." I looked straight out ahead past the driver's shoulder and out through the windscreen. The rain continued to pour down. Wash me away, I thought. Wash me away from here.

"We should have insisted. And anyway if it hadn't been for your stupid argument maybe he would have—"

"Stupid?" I blinked at him, my blood hot in me instantly. "How can you say that? How can you…" I wrestled with my overheating emotions. On the verge of tears. Just the *unfairness* of it all, the disappointment, the whole fucking thing.

But he was still talking. "You shouldn't have said that stuff to him about being obsessed. I think you need to apologise to him and then he'll talk to the police with us."

"Apologise? For what? The only thing he cares about is finding that stupid cross."

"Not the only thing, Sarah. He cares about you. He always has."

I heard him speak the words and it felt like he'd thumped me. The wind was knocked out of me, and I could say nothing. Just the words in my head. *He always has.*

"We're not going anywhere here." Patrick's voice was like a nagging headache. "Let's ask the cab driver to take us over to John's place."

"You want to go somewhere else?" the driver asked his eyes still on the road.

"Come on, Sarah. We may as well."

"They've dug up the road further on. I was stuck here for an hour yesterday."

"You see."

Suddenly I couldn't fight it any more. I shrugged and sighed. "Sure. Why not."

"Great." Patrick sounded delighted. "Can you take us to Highbury Fields please."

The driver looked just as pleased as he glanced over his shoulder. Behind us a small gap had formed. We three-pointed and then suddenly, as if breaking free, we were moving again.

* * *

It was almost eleven by the time we reached John's place. Patrick had been there before and led the way up the front steps of a converted Victorian villa overlooking Highbury Fields. He rang one of the six doorbells, spoke to the intercom, and we were buzzed into a dirty hallway, the worn black and white floor tiles strewn with mail. I trailed behind Patrick as he trotted up the tatty carpeted stairs to the second floor. A door was flung open by a guy a bit younger than us, early twenties, in a long stripy shirt worn outside tight jeans.

"Hey Patrick," he said delighted, high-fiving him. "Haven't seen you for ages man. Hi," he said expansively to me. "I'm Jed." I really wasn't in the mood and gave him a lukewarm smile in return. "Come in," he said eagerly to us both.

"We wanted to talk to John," Patrick said as we walked into the living area. Another guy who looked a lot like Jed was kneeling in front of the TV, Playstation controller in his hands. He shrugged at us and looked back at the screen.

"He's gone out," said Jed sitting down cross-legged and picking up the other controller. "About an hour ago. For food, I guess. You're welcome to wait. Help yourself to a beer from the fridge—. Oh come *on*. I wasn't ready."

I exchanged a glance with Patrick as Jed pummelled the controller in his hand in an effort to catch up in the racing game they were playing.

"You want a drink?" asked Patrick.

"No." I had a headache already and didn't need to add to it. We sat there on the sofa for a few minutes while they played; like we were their parents or something. But John didn't show and they kept upping the volume until my head was splitting.

"Guys," I said. *"Guys!"*

Jed looked round, the game paused, the car on his side of the split screen frozen in its inexorable spin towards a crash barrier.

"Could we wait in John's room, maybe? Might be a bit quieter."

"Don't see why not," he said looking back immediately to the TV. "It's that door on the right."

We got up and walked over to it. There was the realistic sound of a crash behind us and I raised my eyes to the ceiling. God, I felt old.

"I wonder what time he'll be back," said Patrick.

"Soon I hope," I said reaching for the door handle. "He can't be too long if he's just gone out for food."

"I guess not."

I turned the handle. "I don't really care so long as it's quieter in here." I pushed the door open and switched on the light. "So long as—"

I stopped.

Blinked a few times.

And we both just stood there for a long time.

Not saying a word.

Just trying to take it all in.

36

"What the fuck is all this?" Patrick breathed out at last.

I shook my head. I'd never seen anything like it. There were books everywhere: on the shelves, on the desk, round his bed, and piled on the floor beside it. Books on Venetian life and literature and art and history; multiple Italian dictionaries and primers on grammar and Venetian dialect; Venetian biography and books on the Venetian empire; travel books and maps on Crete and Rhodes and the Peloponnese. But most of all books on Cyprus. *Loads* of books about Cyprus. A library section's worth. Four volume histories, personal memoirs, travellers tales, even cookery books. Books everywhere.

But even more than the books was what was on the walls. They were covered in A4 and A3 sized photocopies, enlargements of pages from more books. So many that the room itself had become a continuum of words. The underlying blue paint was barely visible, papered over by the dizzying expanse of white and grey, at a distance featureless, disorientating, like fog, like snow, but as we got closer form appeared and structure surfaced from the flat landscape and we saw book extracts and diary entries, handwritten and typeset and, as we walked around the room, names began to jump out at us: Polidoro and Bragadino, Nicosia and Famagusta, Loredan and the Cross of St Peter and Paul.

Some of the pages were from Shaeffer's diary: in part faithfully transcribed and word processed and printed out, in part still in the original, Shaeffer's copperplate enlarged to twice or four times its original size, its regular beauty rendered lumpy and careless by the rigid typesetting around it, all the passages in the room being spoken at once, literal overload, whiteout.

"I take it back," said Patrick after a few minutes more.

"He *is* obsessed."

"Have you been here before?"

"Not in his room. Not ever I don't think." We were circling round each other, our eyes on the walls reaching out to the words but both afraid to touch anything, engendered by a feeling of deep unease. It was like the lair of a psychopath.

We stopped by his desk. Above it was a gap in the papering, just the crusty pieces of blue tack left on the wall, the sheet which should have been pride of place torn down, lying on the desk in front of us.

"Why's he taken that one off?" Patrick gingerly picked it up. It was different to the others on the wall. The words here were dense on the page, single spaced in a small font.

"Do you think we should even be in here?" I glanced over my shoulder as I thought I'd heard a sound. "I mean what if he comes back now?"

"Well we're waiting for him aren't we?" He shrugged, immune to the weirdness now, totally absorbed by the paper in his hands. And then he let out a shriek that had me jumping out of my skin.

"What Patrick? *What?*"

"This is Polidoro's code. This is his letter. Look it starts, *Dear Antonio.*" He stared at me, his eyes wide. "Which means that John has cracked it too. Decoded it. Translated it. Maybe ages ago. Why didn't he tell us?"

I didn't know. I didn't even want to think about it. I gave my head a little shake. "That doesn't matter now," I said trying to sound decisive, but my heart and head were pounding. I took a breath to calm myself. "The important thing now is what does it say?"

37

Dear Antonio

I write because I am soon to leave Venice. You know that I have not settled since my return from Famagusta, the pain from that time never leaving me. Yet I am also still bound to that place so that your ever-patient offers to join you and your dear son in Verona have fallen on deaf ears. You have supported me these past seven years and my gratitude to you is undying. Yet though the money you have sent me has kept me physically, my sorrow cannot be assuaged.

The dead of Cyprus haunt me.

I see their faces in my dreams and my waking. Often now I stand by the Lagoon and look out to sea, and I know I must return to it if I am to throw off my cloak of sadness. Even if it kills me; for I am not alive now. I am a ghost. I am air. Yet not so light as air.

Three days ago the sons of Bragadino came to me with a proposition. And it coincided so well with my own thoughts that it left me overjoyed. They want me to bring back the remains of my dear master. To seek him out, even to the Sultan's Court itself, and recover what exists still of Captain Bragadino so that he might have a final Christian resting. They have promised me money but it is not for that I would go. I go for the love of my master and the chance to repay the kindness he once showed me. A ship leaves in ten days and I shall leave with it.

There is another motive too. To see once again the stone which we have talked about. To look again upon beauty such as I have never seen in woman; a depth of blue which makes me cry even at the memory of it. To return with my liege's body will remake me as a man in men's eyes; but to look into that overwhelming blue again will heal me for myself.

But if I bring this thing back I will not do it for Venice. Venice has failed me, Antonio, and those like me. Why could they not have raised the effort they did for Lepanto in order to save Cyprus? And why should we poor survivors of Famagusta fester forgotten whilst the scions of the Golden Book receive glory? That is why I will not tell the

Ten where this treasure is hid, even if they put me on the rack for it.

They suspect me, of course, for my lord Bragadino sent word to Venice that the cross had been hidden. And the Ten took the journal I wrote on that bloody isle, no doubt in the hope of finding news of the treasure within it. Yet they will be disappointed for I did not understand then where the treasure was. But seven years have passed. Seven long years when I have walked heavy-hearted through the streets of Venice and have thought of nothing else but the events of those days in Cyprus.

And now I know.

Though I have told the Ten otherwise, now I know.

I retraced my steps. We rode for three hours that night. But by my reckoning we travelled no more than three leagues for we were careful and did not use our torches, travelling by moonlight alone. So three leagues. And then we were blindfolded and descended a gentle incline until the ground below our feet became paved. And I thought then what place would have a paved courtyard? Surely not just some remote village.

Standing there I heard the sound of many buzzing bees, yet thought nothing of it at the time. It was only many years later when I heard that sound again while walking through the gardens of Sant'Elena that it occurred to me where we had been taken that morning: a monastery, for monks favour honey greatly. And then everything became clear. We must have been at the monastery dedicated to the icon of the Virgin. And so I had my starting point.

When we walked from the monastery through the trees I remember a cooling breeze kissing my right cheek and it did not vary so although difficult with roots and branches the path must have been straight. We walked for two hours, a distance I judged as being nearly four miles, until we reached the beach. Then, when we were made to stand parallel to the shoreline with the sea on our left, the rising sun shone straight in from that direction so I knew that the beach faced east. Also I am sure the breeze had not changed direction and now blew directly into my face. So the wind was from the south and we had walked east from the monastery.

And yet there was a final piece of information that I had known all along. After the cross had been shown to us and we had been blindfolded again, mine had been put on slightly too high so that I could see a fraction out of my right eye. Risking all, I raised my head just for an instant and there to the right saw three rocks, giant granite boulders placed there by God's hand and standing sentinel to the beach well above high tide. Five paces to the left of the largest, Captain Bragadino's servant Alvise was climbing out of a hole. I looked down to the ground again immediately and no one suspected me.

So now you too know the secret. If I do not return, then perhaps one day, when the world has changed, you or your son Gianni that I love so much, may go there and recover the treasure for yourselves. And, if you do ever find yourself in that cove, dig down into the fine sand and you will come upon a wooden box and, inside that, the most magical of treasures.

Farewell then my brother.

I do not expect to return from this voyage. I am not sure even whether this letter will reach you for the Ten have been active recently. No doubt they will intercept and try to read it but I am sure our childhood code is too strong even for them. I trust you retain the wit to read the letter should it make it to you. If the Ten question you then you should say I am mad or you should tell them the secret: whichever you wish. But if you can, tell them I am mad for they want to believe it in any case.

I trust that God will protect you and that one day we shall meet again and, if not, that one day you and your Gianni will benefit from the blood that has been shed for all Venice. Wish me luck on my quest, which I undertake for both my lord and myself. And pray for me. So that one day, if I should somehow survive, I will be able to settle and need walk like a ghost no more.

Your loving brother
Girolamo

38

Patrick sat down on the bed and stared at the piece of paper in his hands. When he finally looked up at me, there were tears glistening in his eyes. "It's so sad. For Polidoro, I mean. After all he'd been through at Famagusta to then come back and feel so isolated and unhappy."

I sighed. "It must have been like US soldiers coming back from Vietnam. Everyone wanting to pretend it never happened. And then there was the huge victory at Lepanto and everyone celebrated that instead."

"What *was* Lepanto?"

"A massive naval battle. Soon after the fall of Famagusta. It checked the expansion of the Ottoman Empire."

"So Polidoro and the other survivors of Famagusta would have been forgotten?"

"Right. Who cares about a defeat when you've had a big victory… But Polidoro cared. He couldn't forget about the people he'd left behind. He was haunted by it. So, years later, he goes off to bring back Bragadino's skin and the cross." I started pacing round the room.

"That must have been around 1578," said Patrick. "He mentions seven years in the letter."

"And he recovers the skin but he then winds up in a Turkish gaol for another nine years." I grimaced.

"And the thing he really wanted, the thing that would have really made him happy, the jewel, eluded him. When he finally came back he was empty-handed."

"And sick," I said, remembering the description of the Veronese portrait from Shaeffer's diary. "He'd been tortured and he was starving and had developed a goitre."

"What's a goitre?" asked Patrick.

"It's caused by iodine deficiency. Your thyroid gets overactive and makes your neck swell up."

"Ugh. But at least when he got back they'd have treated him well, wouldn't they? At least he was a hero."

"Maybe," I said. "Though I bet the Council of Ten still had him under surveillance thinking he knew something about the cross." I frowned and looked at my watch. We'd been there nearly an hour and it was pushing midnight. "When's John going to get back?" I muttered.

"And where's Julius right at this moment?" sighed Patrick. "Why did he have to go out there on his own? Where *is* he?"

I shrugged. "Why don't we find out." I pulled down an atlas from the bookshelves and flicked through the pages till I came to a double sheet showing the Eastern Mediterranean and Cyprus. "OK, here's Famagusta on the eastern side of the island. Now, they rode three leagues that night, right? That's nine, maybe ten, miles. So if we draw a circle ten miles around Famagusta, what places does that throw up?" I stood over the map, pencil poised and then felt a sudden shiver down my spine. There was a circle there already, about an inch in diameter, faint as though it had been rubbed out. "John's done this before us," I said.

Patrick blinked at me. "Go on. We need to go on."

"OK." My voice was shaking now. "OK so let's see what's in the circle..."

"How about *Agia Napa?* That's about the right distance. Pass that book on Cyprus. The one by your foot."

I handed it to him and he flicked through the pages.

"There's a monastery there: '*Located in the centre of Agia Napa, the monastery was built in the 14th century around a cave where a miraculous icon of the Virgin Mary had been discovered many years earlier. The church of the Monastery was originally the cave shrine but was later extended to its present form.*' This is it. It must be."

"Agia Napa? Is that the same as *Ayia Napa?*" The thought hit me like a train. "As in the tourist resort? Club Central?"

He turned back a couple of pages and nodded and then looked up at me his eyes wide. "Julius? In Ayia Napa?" We burst into nervous laughter. "I almost feel sorry for him."

"Yeah. I've been there and believe me he won't know what's hit him." But the laughter died on my lips, my feeling of unease returning. I looked again at my watch. "Where *is* John?"

"You know what…" said Patrick looking around him; and even as he was saying it I saw it too, what I had failed to notice when we'd first entered the room, blinded by the pages on the walls and the full-on weirdness of it all: the open drawers, the clothes on the bed, the wardrobe door wide open and obvious gaps in the items hanging there.

"He's gone too hasn't he?"

I heard Patrick's voice as though from a long way off but the words found echo in my mind. He's gone too. I nodded. Of course he had. "He's gone after Julius." I heard myself speak the words this time and felt chilled by them.

"What will he do when he catches up with him?" asked Patrick. His voice was scared, a small voice.

"Nothing," I said blinking. "He wouldn't. He's just gone to find the cross."

"Sarah look around you. Look at his room—"

"He's a nice guy." I screwed my eyes up against what I could see, against what he was saying. I just wanted to think of the John I'd been hoping to see that evening.

"Sarah listen to me. We've got to do something. I'm really worried for Julius. He's got Loredan *and* John on his tail now—"

"John wouldn't do anything. I *know* him—"

"You don't know him."

"I do." I stared at him. "Coming back on the train. We connected. I understand him."

"Do you understand this?" His arms were outstretched towards the walls. "Who knows what's going through his head."

"Well what can we do about it anyway?"

"There's only one thing we can do." His eyes sparkled. "We've got to go after them."

39

The night was black and we could see no further than the sweep of the headlights on the road and the gently curving line of cats-eyes caught in its beam. The view ahead hardly changed, a constant flow of grey through our fan of light, the tarmac surface bleached by it, over-exposed and then fading into the distance, the deeper monochrome, an endless hypnotic continuum.

Half an hour on the internet told us John must be taking an early morning charter flight out of Stansted or Luton. There were a couple of possibilities but either would get him into Larnaca at ten o'clock on Tuesday morning. So all that was left was to work out what to do about it.

"This is madness," I said, my head in my hands. "We can't just head off to Cyprus. What do we do if we come up against Loredan?"

"We'll be ready for him this time."

"How? *How?* He could have killed us Patrick—"

"It'll be different this time. And we have to go out there. We need to help them. *Both* of them. *If we help somebody we help ourselves.*"

I shook my head at him furiously. "Even if we wanted to go, there are no seats until tomorrow afternoon. At best we'll be seven or eight hours behind John."

Patrick shrugged. "If that's the best we can do then it's the best we can do."

"And what about work?"

"Just call in sick," he said firmly. "There are more important things at stake than work. If anything happens out there and we could have prevented it we'd never forgive ourselves."

No sounds but the bumps from hitting the ruts in the

road. The headlights brought them out in stark relief, mountain valleys, great scars across our way, but the tyres took them with just a little jolt each time, and the rhythm soothed me, slow struck beats, keeping time with our journey.

We couldn't get a flight till six on Tuesday evening. It was a charter packed with holidaymakers heading away for sun and cheap booze. I tried to doze against the backdrop of noise from a stag party in the row of seats behind and the fevered racing of my brain. Patrick, beside me, was poring over the translation of Polidoro's letter and a map of the Ayia Napa area.

"I think I may have been there," I said after fifteen minutes of frowning at the incessant clamour around me. "I remember a beach the way Polidoro describes it from a holiday I went on. Years ago with Maya. It had rocks, huge rocks on the sand. It was a few miles from Ayia Napa, round the coast near Protaras." Patrick gave the map to me and I looked at it a moment, at the pale blue sea washing up against the uniform yellow marking of the beaches. "It's one of these, I'm sure it is."

Patrick marked the area with a little pencil cross. "We'll get a car at the airport and drive straight there."

"What about getting to a hotel and getting some sleep?"

"We're already half a day behind John and two days behind Julius. We can't waste any more time."

"But it'll be the middle of the night when we get there."

"Well they're not going to dig it up in broad daylight, are they?" His voice was sarcastic but he looked at me anxiously.

I turned away from him not wanting to get dragged down by his worry, ensnared already by my own. I leant my head against the plastic pull-down window blind and closed my eyes. I was almost asleep when I heard the sound of party poppers in the row behind and loud and very raucous laughter.

"I think it's this turn-off here," said Patrick. For once he was not asleep but alert and awake beside me in the passenger seat. Probably more alert than me after the long flight and an hour on the road. I couldn't believe it when I'd got lumbered with the driving. Patrick had just shrugged at me in the airport. "I never passed my test," he'd said.

I yawned and slowed down. The headlights illuminated the turn-off.

"Are you sure?"

"I think so. If you're sure about which beach it is."

"I'm not *sure* but..." I'd already started turning the wheel to take the corner. The road became a single lane track after a few hundred metres, the road markings disappearing. I kept the car in second as I picked a careful way round the potholes.

"I think we're being followed," Patrick suddenly hissed at me.

I caught my breath; but when I checked my mirrors there was nothing but the empty night behind. "There's no one there. There hasn't been anything on the road for the last twenty minutes."

"I can feel it."

"Calm down." *I* needed to calm down. "Everything will be fine. We'll get to the beach and no one'll be there. Julius and John will be having a drink together somewhere. Everything will be fine." I heard my own words through the night. High-pitched. Thin.

The dirt track petered out after another quarter of a mile at a signpost. We got out of the car and felt the sea before we heard it. The cool breeze hit us, freeing us from the warm night. We picked our way carefully along a stony path. The only torch we had with us was a tiny Maglite so we moved slowly in single file guided by its pencil beam,

Patrick in front.

"We should have waited for daylight."

"We can't wait," he said. "Something's happening now. I know it is."

"How do you know?"

"I just know. And, by the way, we're still being followed."

"Will you stop that." I shivered and forced myself to look back down the path, peering through the darkness. "There's nothing there."

"I can hear them."

"You *can* not. There's no one there—"

"Look!"

I jumped and then, my heart pounding wildly, my eyes followed the beam of his torch. He illuminated a purple motor scooter propped up against some rocks on the side of the path and just beyond it a red hatchback car. And then suddenly, unmistakable in the night, came the sharp crack of a gunshot.

I felt my heart lurch inside me.

Patrick and I exchanged a glance and then we were running headlong down the path towards the rocks. The sea came into view, a dark mass against the dark sky, but mottled with wash and flecked with foam. The path curved round taking us to the top of a flight of wooden steps which led down to the beach. But we didn't take them. We were transfixed by the scene like a nightmare below us.

A police jeep had been driven onto the sand and its headlights were illuminating a wide sector of beach. To begin with all I could make out were two policemen standing in the light. They were no more than fifty yards away but they had their backs to us, hands raised above their heads, the short sleeves of their sky blue shirts falling down around their shoulders. There was a shout from beyond them, a barked order, and then they stepped forward and to one side and suddenly the full scene was revealed and I screamed in horror as it became clear to me.

Standing in front of the policemen was John and he had a pistol in his hand. He waved it to keep them back. At his feet, lying face up and motionless in the sand, was Julius, a huge red blood stain covering his white T-shirt. Behind them, close to a boulder, a hole had been dug in the sand and on the ground nearby was a discarded pair of shovels.

"Julius!" I made to run down the steps but Patrick held me back.

"No Sarah. You can't go down there."

I struggled against him but he was too strong. *"Julius!"* I called again. The policeman on the beach were looking up at us by now. John had turned as well, the pistol moving with his body until it was pointed straight at me; but I didn't care.

"How could you do it?" I yelled at him, tears streaming down my face.

He just stared back, the gun still pointed straight at me. The policemen on the sand were shouting too but I couldn't hear them clearly.

"How could you?"

"We've got to get away," hissed Patrick.

One of the policemen was waving his arms.

"Would you have killed us for the treasure too?"

The other policeman broke suddenly and made a run for the pistol.

John's eyes were still on me.

I felt Patrick tugging at my sleeve.

I heard the sea.

And then John laughed and pulled the trigger.

I felt an explosion of pain in my head and, after that, nothing.

Part Three

A Richer Dust Concealed

Summer 2002, London/Cyprus

John

40

It is from *sappheiros*, the Greek for blue, that the sapphire gets its name.

Originally it was used to denote any blue gem such as lapis lazuli or aquamarine. But over time it came to refer to a particular stone, corundum, the hard crystallised form of aluminium oxide. Pure corundum is colourless but when impurities of ilmenite appear in the regular structure the crystal takes on a blue colour. But not just any blue. Rather a blue so vivid that the ancient Persians believed it was a sapphire which lit the sky, shining from a jewel so strong that the stone was worn by kings to protect them from harm.

Unlike their cousins, the rubies, sapphires can occasionally grow to great size. The Star of Asia at the Smithsonian Institute in Washington is 330 carats while the Star of India weighs 563. They are both examples of star sapphires where a further impurity, rutile, lends the stone a milky quality and, due to the alignment of its microscopic fibres, reflects incoming light into a star shaped pattern which seems to hover above the surface of the stone. Such sapphires are usually cut and polished into a dome shape, a cabochon, to enhance this effect. This was a cut used in antiquity.

The jewel at the heart of the Most Holy Cross of St Peter and St Paul would have been a cabochon. But although certainly of great size, perhaps over 100 carats, it was not a star sapphire. The stone was unadulterated by rutile and hence free from asterism; its beauty lay in its colour alone.

It was a gem from the East, perhaps from Burma or Kashmir or Sri Lanka. A gem of great size and quality and almost unimaginable value. The 62 carat Rockefeller sapphire was sold in 2001 for over three million dollars. The sapphire of the cross would have been bigger than that and more handsome still. A huge cabochon of extraordinary brilliance, set in a golden cross with historic and intrinsic value of its own.

But to even think of price is beside the point. When Girolamo Polidoro of Verona stared into the stone with the morning sun shining on it, he did not see its value in gold reflected back to him. I am sure of that.

So what did he see when he looked into the jewel, into its crystal heart? What did he *see* as he surveyed the latticed arrangement of molecules within? Did he see busy electrons shunted from one quantum state to another absorbing all light but blue? Photons penetrating, cascading, colliding, dying? Or did he see something deeper, something beyond the essential atomic arrangement, the crystal structure, the colloidal dispersion; something beyond analysis and reduction?

What did you see, Girolamo? What did you see?

No matter. One day soon I shall see for myself.

41

Five years ago my life changed. I'd just started a new post doctoral assignment and had been working late at the university. I came home that evening to an anxious flatmate and two policemen who sat me down before breaking the news that my parents had been killed in a car crash.

There was no mystery to the way they'd died. On the way back from a day out in Oxford they had been driving down the M40, the day clear, no fog, when a lorry driving in the opposite direction had burst through the central reservation. Two other cars were hit before the lorry got to my parents' old Sierra. It hit them a glancing blow spinning them into the path of a van which struck them head on. That was what killed them, along with the driver of the van who hadn't been wearing a seatbelt. The drivers and passengers of the first two cars died as well.

Only the lorry driver himself walked away from the scene. He maintained throughout his trial that he had not been asleep at the wheel, that his loss of control was due to oil on the road and, in the end, the jury believed him.

Why is this of importance? The story itself is not. In the second car hit by the lorry were a mother and father. They were both killed leaving a nine year old daughter who had been spending the day with her Aunt. If there was a story from that afternoon surely it was hers. My loss might not even be objectively considered a tragedy. Not compared with that little girl. Nor with the van driver who left a pregnant wife. Nor with Duncan, dying from throat cancer at the age of twenty-six.

So why do I choose to tell my story?

Because it *is* my story.

Because my parents might have had a *good innings* but they were fit and healthy and I loved them and I was not ready for them to die. Mine might have been the minor tragedy on that afternoon, but my life changed as a consequence, and the emotional overspill has coloured me ever since.

In the days and weeks that followed, my life fell apart. The feelings of loss were so profound and unexpected that everything stopped, for a while even eating and sleeping. I existed in a kind of stasis. Lying in bed with the curtains drawn was all I could manage and the semi-darkness of the room seemed to sum up the shade that I felt had been cast over my life, the monochrome filter that had been snapped in front of it.

The emptiness stayed with me long after I had roused myself upright; and into this vacuum I allowed to be sucked my life, so that my research foundered and the beauty I had once created in fermions and bosons and super symmetry turned to dust overnight. I sat and watched a dry wind blow my research to nothing around me.

I had to look elsewhere for sustenance and purpose.

I didn't find it in love.

But after twelve months of drifting I found what I needed to survive: the code.

I viewed it as a challenge, an old fashioned quest, and one I could conduct alone. Something I could pursue without people around, without my needing to interact. Something I could wrestle with whilst ducking the real issues in my life.

And so for hours I would stare at Shaeffer's notebook, at the carefully hand-transcribed pages of code, seeing patterns where there were none, looking for messages hidden in randomly juxtaposed characters, *V E L G A S A G A I I...*

It was a labyrinth in which to lose myself but one where the positions of the walls themselves were uncertain, branching passages in the pitch black. I walked amongst

them for a couple of years, content just to be there, to be
lost; at the heart of me scared at what I should do if I were
to ever find my way out.

I began the way Shaeffer and Patrick had begun, trying
Caesar shift and monoalphabetic cipher in turn, before
realising like them that it must be polyalphabetic. At this
point my immersion became entire and I spent evenings
and weekends for weeks and months with reams of paper
around me, trying to make sense, trying to make a
breakthrough.

But I found I could no longer concentrate the way I had
once been able. I was no longer equipped to build the
structures in my mind necessary for decipherment, to hold
the framework in place long enough for my analytical
processes to bear fruit. Instead my mind wandered, far
from the work in hand and away to Venice and Cyprus and
my parents' side.

Yet still I persisted. Shaeffer had cracked the code and
had written of the moment in terms of joy, with emotion
that I imagined for myself should I be able to repeat his
success. So I looked through his diary to find some hint or
clue to this most enduring of riddles. His words thrilled me
when I read them, the energy in his discovery on the very
eve of war:

**I have broken the code – or rather I know the key
and it is so simple that I could almost weep with
happiness. And I have discovered the truth in a
moment of madness or brilliance that you Anna, dear,
dear Anna (I am laughing as I write this, my heart is so
gay) would have seen immediately. For there is only
one way to make sense of it all: that the coded piece is
a letter of course, and then the crib was so obvious as
to make me think my idea was laughable.**

And so he had cracked it. Yet where was the evidence of his victory? *Where was the key*? Surely he was not so intoxicated with the thought of seeing Rupert and Denis again and finally entering the theatre of conflict that he would not have taken the simple precaution of preserving his discoveries on paper.

That I should have made such discoveries tonight of all nights when I am but hours away from leaving for I don't know where: it could be France or it could be Africa. I feel like Galois on the night before his duel, desperate to set his thoughts down but plagued also by the constant fear, je n'ai pas le temps. But I have said what I need to my dear, for you will understand and make sense of my ramblings and in any case unlike poor Galois I shall not die in a field without seconds. I shall return to you, I shall be back with you soon on terra ferma. That is the key for me. To be back by your side again to hold you and love you and share these wondrous and exciting discoveries with you.

He was aware of the danger he faced; the talk of Galois meant he knew he might not survive despite his reassurances. So where was the key? Why had he not written it down?

And then, after two years, on the point of giving up, I realised he had. That Shaeffer had left nothing to chance after all. That he had left two clues for Anna, one discreet, one head-turningly obvious, and yet I had seen neither until my own moment of clarity.

For Shaeffer loved his wife. And regarded her as more than an equal to his own intellect. Therefore he left her a clue which was subtle, yet would be clear as a bright star to her, one half of their tight unit, between whom their terms of familiarity would have been long established.

I re-read the entries leading up to this one and each started the same way, a greeting to his beloved wife, *My darling Anna*. Not once was there deviation, not once did he use another term of affection. Yet in this entry he departs from convention and calls her *Dear Anna*. Could this just be coincidence? Or was this a clue left for his wife, a crib that she might pick up on when she received the book. I cannot be certain on this but what I am sure of is *I* saw it, late one night, after a couple of beers with friends, the first time in ages I had been out, and I lay there as the realisation flooded me of the meaning of Shaeffer's words:

Only one way to make sense of it all: that the coded piece is a letter of course, and then the crib was so obvious as to make me think my idea was laughable.

The code was a letter and now I had the crib to hand. But even more than that, before I had a chance to use it to deduce the keyword, the *other* clue leapt out at me and I almost wept that I had not seen it till now, so obvious was it; yet my tears turned to elation almost immediately, peals of loud and happy laughter, congratulatory guffaws at the sheer audacity of the man, that he could have been so bold in his writing:

But I have said what I need to my dear, for you will understand and make sense of my ramblings and in any case unlike poor Galois I shall not die in a field without seconds. I shall return to you, I shall be back with you soon on terra ferma. That is the key for me.

42

When I embarked upon my quest I had initially worried as to how I might feel once it was done. Whether I would be left searching for some other proxy for real life. Yet when I finally made my breakthrough I did not feel bereft that my constant occupation for two years had been reduced to a simple question of translation. I tentatively examined myself and found myself not to be as fragile as I had thought. Two years had passed; and a corner had been turned. Far from merely unlocking an obscure piece of sixteenth century code, what I had really unlocked was myself.

Once I had the key, decrypting the text was a relatively trivial affair. To translate the resulting Italian I enrolled in evening classes and hoped that I might meet some people in the process. I thought eventually I would travel again, to Italy or wider. And maybe once I had learnt Italian, Spanish and French would follow.

Other changes were being wrought in me as well. I decided to give up research. I'd been as good as useless for some time in any case. And in looking for alternatives I spoke with Patrick and he got me a job in his accountancy firm, an essential break with the past.

All the while I worked on the text, gradually improving my Italian proficiency until, a year after I'd first found the key, I had finally translated it. I read Polidoro's words and was touched and saddened by them. But by then I had moved on. My true life had grown around me. It felt like I was standing again outside in the sunshine, in a world of colour and light and that Polidoro's words – the search for which had helped me fill the darkness left by the death of my parents – were no longer intended for me.

So I put the letter aside. And though I thought it all to be true, I did not feel there was any rush to go and discover the location of a treasure quite possibly long-since looted. But I hung on to my keepsakes: the papers on the walls reminded me of darker times and made me laugh now to see them; and Henry's notebook I kept. That spoke to me of treasures even less tangible than some mythical cross; it spoke to me of love. And that was only reawakened in me truly the day I saw Sarah again.

Seeing Sarah again, what can I remember of that moment?

Our eyes met. I'd remembered her eyes as being brown yet, when looked at close, they bore flecks of green and red and black. I looked into her and she looked into me but only for a moment before there was darkness.

Our eyes met. For me it was not a turning point in itself but the confirmation of one. And for me the moment had an importance far beyond anything that Sarah could have felt as she looked at someone long forgotten. For I felt that our lives had touched again and our stories were intertwined once more, even if only for a moment. Our parallel journeys had converged even if I alone recognised it.

And strangely I had just been thinking about her. I had not spent the previous ten years thinking of her I should say, probably hastily. But I'd thought of her from time to time, a happy memory, someone I had connected with, albeit long ago. And I happened to be thinking about her then, not constructing some athletically demanding sexual tableau for the two of us, simply *thinking* of her.

When I saw her, I knew her at once, my recognitive faculties taking no more than an instant to process the changes and return a match. I looked up and she was standing there. Looking like she wanted to kill me, but there nonetheless.

I saw her and she was no longer a girl. Her hair was bobbed now and natural brown instead of spiky dyed blonde; her figure filled out, but the more desirable because of it; her feet reddened from the flip-flops she wore, bare and blistered and sexy.

All of this registered in a single split second. Mentally the message had got through. Unfortunately, my faculties processed physical recognition in an altogether different way. A jolt inside. A kick to the heart. And a mad muscle reflex leading inevitably, embarrassingly, to my book ending up on her foot. She yelped, which was an entirely understandable reaction and then the lights went out.

My process of reawakening, already under way, was accelerated by her presence. And when, through strange circumstance, we were afforded time together, we connected, just as we had in Venice. I loved her company and I allowed myself to believe that she liked mine. I felt an electricity when she was near that I believed could only occur when the other person felt the same, a mutual charge, a static energy that could power an interaction through frisson alone.

But I was wrong.

She didn't feel the same way.

She thought me an obsessive.

She had said so to my face.

Having left her and Patrick waiting for a cab in Primrose Hill, I returned to the empty lounge of my flat-share and pondered her words. The room was dark and my thoughts amplified themselves in the blackness. I closed my eyes against them, against my disappointment, but the thoughts clamoured around me. How could she have been like that? She knew that Julius had gone to Cyprus. So why couldn't she believe the cross existed? Why didn't she believe me? Because she did not trust my motives?

Maybe she was right not to. I *was* an obsessive. How could I ever have thought that she would be interested in me? I held my head in my hands.

But it lasted seconds only and then I set my face like stone. I had been fine before I met her and I would be fine again. In the meantime there was unfinished business to take care of. Julius business.

I had surprised even myself at how intense my loathing was for him when I met him again at Patrick's. The moment I laid eyes on him I knew I'd forgotten none of the put-downs or the patronising glances; nor the fact of his relationship with Sarah. All felt fresh, all rankled. And his smooth manner, his easy eloquence and his *confidence* – all honed by the intervening years – were enough to make me realise quite how much I still hated him.

And now he had betrayed us. He had flown to Cyprus to steal a priceless treasure from under our noses. Did he really think I would just let him?

My flatmates returned from the pub and switched on the lights. Blinking in the sudden white glare I knew what I had to do.

I had not spent three years of my life trying to locate the Cross of St Peter and Paul simply for Julius Masters of all people to get there first. Only Sarah could have held me back, persuaded me against this course of action. But she had made her feelings clear. So there was no reason not to go after him now; no one to stay my hand when I finally caught up with him.

Unless of course Loredan got to him first.

Either way, I promised myself, this time Julius would pay.

43

The earliest flight I could find was leaving Stansted for Larnaca at 5.40 am and my only way of catching it would be to crash at the airport overnight.

I threw a few things in a bag and headed off to Liverpool Street from where I caught the Stansted Express. I sat in a corner of the carriage and tried to think rationally.

Today was Monday.

Julius had left some time on Saturday.

Flights were either first thing in the morning or late in the afternoon. He would have taken the latter arriving in Ayia Napa in the small hours of Sunday morning. Potentially he could have struck out the moment it got light to identify the beach but he would have been in no hurry. He would have not expected anyone to follow him out there. If the treasure had lain hidden for four hundred years, another day or two would make no difference. He would have orientated himself on Sunday, perhaps visiting the monastery, with the intention of locating the beach today. And then maybe he was not intending to make an attempt on it until the following night. Tuesday. So there was still time. Assuming he *was* taking things easy.

But what if he wasn't? What if he had arrived on Sunday morning and was ready to recover the cross that very night. He could have found it already. Touched it. Held it. If that were the case there was nothing I could do about it and Julius would have won.

At least until Loredan caught up with him anyway.

I collected my tickets from the tour operator desk at Stansted from a girl in a too blue uniform. "Check in starts at 3.40am," she said. "All the delays are over now so you should be leaving on time."

"Delays?"

"The dispute with air-traffic-control in Cyprus. Nothing coming in or out for the whole of Saturday."

I smiled at her, at the best news I could have heard. Julius was only a day ahead of me after all.

Outside a shuttered Dixons I found a place to hole up for the next few hours, three seats in a row, airport regulation hard plastic, but room enough. I lay out, my holdall tucked firmly under my head acting as pillow.

It was way past midnight but the airport was still awash with noise: tannoy announcements; cleaners cruising along in their electric sanitation carts; strains of conversation and laughter from those travellers around me who couldn't or wouldn't sleep. I lay there looking up at the high terminal ceiling, at the grey struts and beams and lights and the black sky beyond. I wondered where Julius was at this precise moment. Patrick. Loredan. Sarah.

I closed my eyes.

I was woken by bustle around me. It was four o'clock. The check-in desks had opened and people were on the move. I stretched and tried to shake the grogginess from my head, then ambled over to join my queue.

Larnaca airport, once I got there, was heaving. I decided not to wait for the coach transfer but to get a cab. Four hours in a cramped charter flight seat was enough as far as I was concerned and though I had slept it had been fitful and I had left the plane feeling as dog-tired as when I'd got on.

I walked out of the airport and the heat from the Cyprus morning hit me like a wall. I stood blinking at the super-bright images beyond the shade; then forced myself towards the taxi rank. When my turn came I stumbled into the back of the cab, showed the driver the name of my hotel in Ayia Napa and tried to relax. But there was no air-con and the black back seats were hot and sticky to the touch.

We took an inland road, anodyne and featureless, and every inch of grey tarmac and concrete section reflected the heat back at me. I hadn't brought sunglasses so I kept my eyes half closed against the glare of the Cyprus day outside.

The drive took an hour and by the time we reached the hotel I was feeling sick and dizzy. I got my key from reception and went straight up to the room. I pulled the curtains closed, kicked off my shoes and socks and felt the tiled floor luxuriously cool beneath my bare feet. The room wasn't dark, the strong sun still glowed through the curtains turning the whole room a muted orange. But I didn't care. I took off my clothes, leaving them where they fell, and lay out face down and naked on the bed.

At that moment Julius and Loredan could have been holding aloft the Cross of St Peter and Paul between them and I wouldn't have cared. I just needed to sleep.

44

I awoke at one o'clock and felt better.

I lay there for a while in the cool bright room and just stared up at the ceiling, breathing deeply; and for an uncomplicated moment felt as happy as I had in a long time.

I had a reasonable idea where the cross must be from Polidoro's letter. What I didn't know was whether Julius or Loredan had got there ahead of me. All things considered, Loredan was best avoided so number one priority had to be to track Julius down.

And for that I had a plan.

I figured that he would need to rent a car: the cross itself was big and he would need tools to dig it up. So I would visit the car hires in Ayia Napa, my story being that I had found a wallet belonging to Julius Masters and inside had been a receipt with the car hire company's name on it. I wanted to return the wallet and thought they might be able to give his address on the island. The phone directory listed over fifty car rental companies in Ayia Napa and I knew it was a long shot. But I thought I would try the largest few and if I had no joy then I would strike out for the beach instead.

But I was in luck. After only an hour and five hire shops I stumbled on the right one. *Charles and Henri's Vehicle Hire* it was called, and while it didn't sound very Greek, and the twenty year old behind the desk didn't seem very French, when I enquired there he said, Yes, they had had a Julius Masters visit them. Yes, he had hired a car: a small red hatchback. And, Yes, they could tell me where he was staying: the Hotel Eleganza, which was on the other side of town. I figured I might need some transport of my own so I hired a scooter while I was there, a shiny purple Vespa.

By now it was four o'clock. I rode over to the Eleganza

which was an identikit modern hotel from the same mould as the one I was staying at. I paused in front of reception to get my story straight but was distracted by the loud music blaring from the pool area fifty yards away. I took a few steps towards it and saw on the deck a line of bikini clad girls of varying ages and sizes engaging with a row of young men in swimming trunks, bananas being passed orally between them, all supervised by an expertly tanned rep in a T-shirt which declared he was *100% Up For It*.

As I turned back to go into reception I froze in surprise. I could hardly believe it. Julius was right there in front of me. He was seated at a shaded table, surrounded by sun loungers and their slowly reddening occupants. He stared vacantly out across the pool at the antics on the opposite side. They were all trying to do press-ups now and the rep was helpfully decanting orange jelly over their rising and falling buttocks.

The blood pounded in me at seeing Julius again and I strode over to his table and sat down. He didn't make any movement so I rapped on the zinc top to get his attention and when he looked round I gave him a menacing stare. "I bet you're surprised to see me!"

Julius smiled faintly. "Nothing surprises me about this place any more."

"What?" I blinked at him disconcerted.

"This place. It's... *extraordinary*. It's..." He gazed at me, his eyes searching deep into me. "It's *hell*. The things I've seen... Oh..." His voice trailed off in a low moan.

I was irritated by his lack of combativeness. I'd been expecting a full blown shouting match with him. This was just plain weird. "Why, what have you seen?"

"The town, last night." He rolled his eyes. "It was like there was some kind of epidemic. People being sick everywhere. I mean vomit absolutely *everywhere*. And urine. Drunken English girls lying in the gutter with drunken English boys taking a piss right by them. They couldn't walk and they couldn't talk." He looked close to tears. "The music is so loud and I just don't understand what any of them are doing here."

"Julius, this is Ayia Napa. The clubbing capital of Europe. What did you expect?"

"What did I expect?" His voice rose to a shrill whine. "What did I *expect?* I'll show you what I bloody expected."

He pulled a blue book from the satchel by his side and read from it. *"Ayia Napa is a quiet fishing village with many sandy beaches. Good local seafood and a beautiful monastery in the centre of town dedicated to—"*

I snatched the book from him and looked inside the front cover. "Julius your guidebook is from *1976*. Didn't it occur to you things might have changed since then?"

He wrung his hands. "It's my uncle's book. I had no idea. Simply no idea."

"Well what about the girls here? I'd have thought you'd have been in your element." A pair of twenty-year-olds walked past in their bikinis, pretty and tanned.

"Oh be careful," he said, his voice trembling. "They look luscious don't they? I tried my hand with a couple, to help me settle in, to calm my nerves. But I couldn't understand them. If they'd been French or Italian that would have been fine. But John they were from *Britain*. From Newcastle or Scotland or some other Godforsaken place. I couldn't understand their *accents* and their weird *youthspeak*. I have no idea what anyone around me is saying or doing."

His left leg started shaking and he laid a hand on his thigh to control it. I couldn't believe what I was seeing. There he was before me, a quivering shambles of a man. The man I had hated my whole adult life.

I sighed.

"Look, Julius, why don't we get out of here and have some food and a chat."

Hi eyes widened. "John, please, yes. I'm starving.

Everywhere I look are inedible pizza and kebabs and English breakfasts with signs in four different languages, none of them Greek. Where are the tavernas and family run restaurants selling fresh fish and seafood?"

"I'll find you one Julius."

"You will?" He reached out and touched my arm. "Truly?"

Half an hour later we were sitting in a quiet restaurant on the edge of town. Julius had already had some calamari and was now tucking into a huge plate of sardines. I watched him uneasily and picked over a simple Greek salad, having little appetite. Only when the fish was gone and the plate wiped clean with the last piece of bread did Julius sit back in his chair. He sipped on a glass of red wine and breathed deeply. There was a light again in his eyes.

"John, I want to thank you." His voice was calm, in control once more. "I lost it a little bit back there, but I think I'll be fine now."

I looked at him warily. I trusted him better when he didn't look so self-assured.

"You're probably wondering why I came to Cyprus?" He lowered his glass to the table and ran his finger around the rim. "I mean why I came without telling you or Patrick."

"It's obvious isn't it? You wanted to find the cross on your own. You've worked out the code, I take it?"

"Naturally. The key was in the file Patrick gave me. I hadn't intended to do anything with it until Patrick was better. But to be honest with you the temptation was too great. By the end of that evening I'd decoded the whole passage and there was the letter in front of me."

"Was your Italian good enough to translate it?"

"Mostly. Plus I'm fortunate enough to have an Italian *friend* at the moment. A lovely girl if a touch shy." He took another sip of wine. "She helped me with the areas I was uncertain on. By Friday I was done."

"So why didn't you just call Patrick?"

"John, I had a dilemma. The last thing I wanted was to get Patrick excited again after his breakdown. God knows I feel guilty enough about involving him in the first place."

"What about me?"

"You're right. I should have contacted you."

I was nonplussed at the frankness of his admission.

"The thing was that once I had the text I couldn't stop thinking about it. I'm sure you of all people can understand that; the feeling of having Polidoro's actual words in front of me. So I read and re-read it and surmised that it was the monastery at Agia Napa that he'd been taken to on that morning in 1570. You know all of this of course. When did you break the code?"

"A couple of years ago."

"And you did nothing about it? You take the notion of delayed gratification to the limit."

"Well I didn't think there was any rush," I said embarrassed. "I didn't realise you'd head off to steal the cross for yourself."

"I think *steal* is a bit harsh."

"Weren't you intending to find the cross?"

"Of course. But not *steal* it. I wanted to recover it and document my findings for posterity."

"Yes but with posterity noting that you were the one that found it. Julius alone. Master archaeologist, perhaps?"

"Nice ring to it," he said unruffled. "Look, I'm not going to lie to you. I certainly do want to find the cross. And be the first one at that. But my main reason for not telling Patrick about it was that I thought it would be too much for him."

"So you thought you'd just dash off over here at the last minute. You thought that would help Patrick more?"

"We all make mistakes. In any case I was always intending to see Patrick the moment I return. Come to think of it…" He frowned. "How did you even know I was out here?"

"Madeleine told us. She was staying at your flat."

"Was she now?" He raised his eyebrows. "Well that's something to sort out when I get back. Look, John," he said lowering his voice, "we're not kids any more. I want to find that cross. The very idea of it gives me a thrill I find very difficult to control. And I'm as selfish as the next man. I want to be the first. There's nothing wrong in that. I mean, what exactly are *you* doing out here? Did *you* tell Patrick you were coming?"

"No of course not."

"Of course not. And you're out here why? Just to stop me finding the cross? Or so you can find it instead of me?" He gave me a sly little smile. "I mean you've studied this thing a lot longer than I have. God knows if anyone deserves to find it it's you."

I frowned at him and tried to frame my reasoning for being there. "I just… I mean…"

He held up a hand. "It's OK, John. It doesn't matter. We're not so different the two of us. We want the same thing. To find the cross and prove it's real. What we do after that is where we might differ."

I looked at him uncomfortably. He poured himself another glass of wine and raised it at me in salute.

"Do you think it's there?" I asked him eventually.

He smiled at me and his eyes sparkled. "Oh yes." He sat forward in his chair and his voice dropped to a whisper. "I'm certain of it. Everything I've read points to it. It's all consistent. The description of the cross, Polidoro's journal, the fact that he didn't want to reveal it to the Council of Ten. It all makes sense. It's there I'm sure of it. What about you?"

"I'm here aren't I?"

He sat back in his chair. "Yes you are." He considered me for a moment and then nodded. "OK, John, how do you want to play this? Do you want to do it together or separately?"

"Why should I want to do anything with you?"

He shrugged. "No reason, of course. It's clear you don't like me."

"Or trust you."

"OK, that's clear as well." He smiled. "But I've got a day's head start on you. So maybe I'm further ahead in the game than you are."

"So why would you want to help *me?*"

"Because it's *your* game. You found the book originally. Even I acknowledge that. If you want to come with me then the least I can do is let you. If you want to do it on your own then that's fine as well."

"What about wanting to be the one to find it first?"

"That's no problem. We can both have our names on it. At the end of the day I'll get more attention because I'm part of the art world already."

"Well, that's certainly honest."

"I'm just being realistic. That's the way life works. But you aren't doing this for the fame. You're not even doing it for the money. If it's anything like the way Polidoro describes it, the cross is priceless; but that's not why you're here. You're doing it because you just want to know whether this whole thing is real or not."

"Why I'm here is nothing to do with you." I scowled. Then sighed. "What do we do with the cross when we've found it?"

"Present it to the Cypriot authorities at a press conference. Unless you had some other plan in which case I'm happy to listen?"

"No. That's the right thing to do." I frowned. "You know we're not the only ones looking for this don't you?"

"To whom are you referring?"

"A man called Loredan. A Venetian terrorist." Julius raised an eyebrow. "He's been looking for the cross for years. And Madeleine said some book guy you know is also involved. An Italian. They'll both be here by now."

"Who? *Galbaio?* What the hell's he got to do with this?"

Galbaio. The name triggered something in my mind, but just out of reach, not quite accessible. It'll come to me, I thought.

Julius was talking. "This would be the most significant find in Byzantine art in two centuries; of course there are people hunting it. I'd be more surprised if there weren't."

"They're serious though. Loredan's men roughed up Patrick and Sarah—"

"Are they OK?" He sounded suddenly anxious.

"Yes they're fine."

"You're *sure?*"

"Of course I'm sure." I don't know why but his display of concern really irritated me. "I was *there*. Anyway, Loredan and his goons know you're here. And if I managed to find you they will too."

"Let them find me. It's of no concern. By tonight we'll have the cross and by tomorrow lunchtime we'll have publicised it. And then they'll be too late." He shrugged and I shrugged too. And then a thought occurred to me.

"When we find it," I said coyly. "Who gets to lift it out of the hole?"

Julius laughed. "We'll take it in turns. Holding it up to let the morning sun shine on it. Just like Bragadino did. To stare deep into the sapphire at its heart. Just like Polidoro. That's what you want isn't it?"

I didn't say anything.

"I know that's what *I* want." He smiled at me and drummed his fingers on the table. After a moment he said, "If you want, you can take the cross out of the hole first. But to the press we say we did it *together*."

"OK," I said and put out my hand. He shook it and laughed. I just nodded at him. He divided the last dribble of wine between our two glasses and we clinked them and drank them back in one.

"So," I said wiping my mouth. "How close are we?"

"I think we're almost there. I visited the monastery yesterday after I arrived from the airport. Before this place freaked me out…" His eyes glazed over momentarily; but then he gave his head a little shake. "From the monastery I followed the route that Polidoro had described. The monastery's in the centre of town now. But if you go east from it you do go through some forest. Then keep heading that way in the direction of Protaras. You take a track which is a turn off from the main road and it leads you right to the beach." He leaned towards me. "John, it's just the way Polidoro describes it."

"The three rocks?"

"They're there." He thumped his hand down on the table. "Three huge rocks just the way he described. Great granite boulders. God knows how they got there. The beach faces east and the shoulder of the cliff around it is low the way he said it would be. There's no doubt about it. This is the right beach."

"Did you go down onto it and check it out close up."

"Not quite. I felt... let's say a little awkward."

"How come?" I asked suspiciously. "You've come a thousand miles and you're feeling awkward all of a sudden?"

"It's a nudist beach."

"Ah."

"I felt a touch over-dressed just to waltz down there in shorts and T-shirt and go digging an exploratory hole whilst surrounded by all that flesh. In any case it wouldn't be prudent to attract too much attention now that we're so close. I was planning to take a trip out there this evening."

"What time?"

He flashed me a grin. "Well why don't we just be traditional and say midnight."

45

Julius drove ahead whilst I followed on my scooter. It was pitch black once we got off the main road, the warm darkness of the Cyprus night enveloping us. All I could see was the red of Julius's rear lights and the tiny patch of dirt track illuminated before me by the Vespa's headlamp.

Somehow it had made sense to have my own transport: I still didn't trust Julius and I didn't want to be stranded by him. Though it has to be said he could have given me the slip at any time; yet he diligently kept his speed down so that I could keep close.

The road petered out at some rocks and continued on as no more than a footpath around a corner. Julius parked right there and I pulled the motorcycle onto its stand just behind it. He opened the car boot and took out two shovels, two swivel-headed torches, a leather satchel and a plastic bag. He threw me a shovel and a torch and we followed the path past the rocks and round to the top of a flight of steps leading down to the beach.

We killed the torches and stood for a few minutes to let our eyes adjust. We could hear and smell the sea and, as time went by, see it as well, the white wash from the waves and the dark mass of it, a complete blackness next to the sky which was deepest, profoundest blue. There was no moon but the stars were out and bright. I could taste the salt water of the sea in my mouth and feel the warmth of it in the breeze around us.

The beach itself was deserted. There were no lights and we stood there for nearly five minutes checking for movement. But there was nothing.

We climbed cautiously down the wooden steps, no more than a ten feet drop to the sand and, once on the beach, we split up to do a reconnaissance of the area. Julius cut away to the left and I went right towards a shoulder of low cliff.

It gave way about fifteen feet from the water and beyond it I could see another beach, deeper and wider than our one, and could just make out a road at the far end of it which came all the way on to the sand. But it too was deserted. Wherever the beach parties were happening that night, it wasn't here.

I turned and walked back towards Julius. He had set his light up, twisting the head round so that it was like a lantern. The light from it illuminated a huge mass of hard dark rock, some fifteen feet high. In the thin light I could see another pair of similar rocks beyond it.

"All clear," I said setting my light down in the sand next to his.

"Me too." He peered at the area of sand lit white-yellow by our torches. "I guess this is it?" He sounded suddenly nervous.

"I guess so."

"There's only one thing to do, then." And he picked up his shovel and lifted it high in the air, the lights glinting off the brand new blade, a gleam of fanaticism in his eye. He swung it and I stepped back in alarm, but the steel end came crisply down onto the ground, biting deep into the sand. "It's time to dig." He grinned and heaved a spadeful of sand over his shoulder.

I blinked at him and then took up my shovel as well. I stood to his left so that we were actually digging two holes right next to each other and as we got deeper and wider they joined in the middle. We dug non-stop for an hour at which point we were four feet deep and the hole was ten feet across: a kind of crater rather than a well. We seemed to be making good progress so decided to take a break, threw our spades down, walked a few steps from the site and collapsed onto the sand.

"How are your arms?" he asked as he massaged his shoulders and biceps.

"Terrible. God only knows how Bragadino's servant

managed to dig the hole *and* fill it in again so quickly."

"They were made of sterner stuff in those days. God, I'm tired." He lay back on the sand, but then sat up again almost immediately. "Better not get too comfortable otherwise we could find ourselves waking up with the nudists." He chuckled and reached for the plastic bag he had brought with him. "Cold water," he said chucking me a bottle. He drank from his. "Well cold-*ish* anyway."

"Thanks." I gratefully took a draft.

"And I've got bread, sausage and cheese here as well," he said laying out some food. "Help yourself."

"That was good thinking."

"I got my confidence back after we'd eaten lunch." He pulled a Swiss Army penknife from his pocket and unfolded the largest blade. "I thought we'd need some provisions if we were to keep going." He cut the slab of cheese into slices and was doing the same with the sausage when he let out a scream of pain and jumped up.

"Julius?"

"I've cut my hand!" He was waving it around hopping with pain.

"Let's take a look," I said picking up one of the torches and shining it at him.

"I've fucking sliced it open—"

"Show me."

He held out his clenched fist and slowly opened his fingers. Immediately his palm was full of bright red blood. He gurgled at the sight of it. I picked up my bottle of water and poured it over his hand. He yanked it back, his face contorting. "That stings!"

"It's only water." I pulled his hand back to me and examined it under the light. For a moment before it filled again with blood I could see the wound clearly. It was deep and ran the width of his palm and looked clean enough. But it was bleeding heavily.

"Look Julius we're going to have to put something on

that. There's a first aid kit in the scooter. I'll go and get it. But you've got to stop it bleeding."

"How?" he yelped in irritation, his hand clenched, the blood dripping freely from it.

"Hold it against yourself." I took his hand again, clenched it, and pressed the fist into his opposite armpit against the white cotton of his T-shirt. "Just keep it there. *Tight.* I'll be back in five."

I returned with the small green box of the first aid kit. By now the blood had seeped under his hand and into a large scarlet patch which spread from his armpit across his chest. I took his hand gently, cleaned it with an antiseptic wipe which made him wince, but silently; and then dressed it with a piece of sticking plaster, wrapping the whole thing round and round with a length of crepe bandage. "There," I said finally, allowing him to take back his hand.

He reclined on the sand opposite me and gingerly flexed and unflexed his hand, then nodded. "Not bad," he said approvingly. "Not leaking any more anyway. Thank you."

"You're welcome," I said smiling at him briefly before putting the first aid kit away in its box. "Will you still be able to dig?"

"Left hand," he said. "Should be fine."

"Good. Well, let's have ten minutes rest and then start again. I reckon there's another hour's digging max."

He nodded and reached for some bread and cheese. He ate them hungrily whilst I just sat there sipping my water. After a while he said, "John?"

"Yes?"

"Why is it you dislike me so intensely?"

I caught my breath; he was immediately apologetic.

"I'm sorry, John. I didn't mean to make you feel uncomfortable. It was just an observation, that's all. Your antipathy has surprised me. And I'm not certain of the reason. After all we got on well enough on that holiday."

I spluttered into my bottle. "Which holiday do you

remember? We were at each other's throats the whole time."

"Well maybe there were a few fights—"

"It was constant warfare. You kept calling me a geek."

"You *were* a geek."

"I *was* a geek. But that was no reason to call me one." I frowned at him, at *myself*, at my suddenly pumping heart and hot face as I felt all the old injustices come flooding back. "You know I hated it. You did it on purpose."

"Did I?" He sounded surprised, though then he nodded sagely like I had revealed a great truth to him. "You're right of course. But John, we were all a bit rough around the edges back then. It was ten years ago after all. Yet when we met up again at Patrick's, it wasn't just a few old scores: you *hated* me."

I felt myself blush. "Well," I said awkwardly. "You'd taken Polidoro's journal."

"Oh it was worse than that. You were hostile before you even knew I had it. Was it because you thought Patrick liked me better than you? Because he doesn't—"

"No, it was nothing to do with that." I looked across at him, his face half illuminated by the torch and sighed. "It was because you went out with Sarah and I never did."

Julius's eyes widened and then he raised his head in thought and let it fall into a nod. "I *see*. You liked Sarah too."

"I was there in Rome when we met her, remember? I thought she was wonderful. But she ended up going out with you."

"She was young and had a crush on me." He shrugged. "And there was a *moment* after you and Patrick had gone. That's all."

"But you went out for ages."

"No, only a year. I was in Cambridge and she was in Manchester and it started to fizzle almost immediately. Then she went off on her year abroad and met the new man of her dreams; some silly frog called François. *Bâtard*. I was devastated."

"*You* were?"

He looked quite affronted. "Is it so difficult to believe that I might have actually felt something?"

"Sorry, Julius."

He looked away down the beach. "I felt *that* I can tell you. I was so in love with her."

"*Really?*"

"You've got to at least *try* and keep the surprise out of your voice," he said throwing a handful of sand at me. "I'm not completely cold you know. Anyway this is all ancient history. What about you? Sounds like you're quite keen on our Sarah?"

"*Was* keen."

"Surely you must still be otherwise you wouldn't bear a grudge against me?"

That was logic hard to argue with, so I said nothing.

"And does she like you as well?"

"She thinks I'm weird," I said flatly.

"You are weird."

"That's a bit harsh."

"Well you're here aren't you?"

I opened my mouth to protest but then nodded. "You're right." I sighed.

"But… Despite your undeniable strangeness, you're a nice guy. And she goes for guys like you these days."

"You think so?" I said in spite of myself. I eyed him suspiciously, but he seemed sincere enough. So I said, "And how about you, Julius? Do you still like her?"

"Of course. But in the final analysis not even my *mother* would consider me a nice guy so I'm not really in the frame."

I shrugged. Again it was difficult to argue with.

"Not jumping to my defence? No, fair enough. I can be pretty unlikeable. I really need to change. At the moment

I'm awful: sexist; borderline racist too I reckon."

"Way over the border I'd say… Homophobic?"

He considered. "No. Not actually homophobic."

"Well, there we are then. Something to build on."

He caught my eye, and suddenly it seemed very funny. I tried to keep a straight face but began to giggle; and then he started to laugh as well.

"Come on," he said getting to his feet. "Let's get on with it." He put out his good hand and, after just an moment's hesitation, I took it and he helped me up.

We grabbed our shovels and began to dig once more. As we got deeper the base of the hole grew smaller and more awkward for both of us to be in there at the same time. So one of us stood in the bottom of the hole and shovelled out to the other standing three feet higher and to one side. This one on the higher ground would move the sand completely clear of the hole. We took turns doing the deeper digging as this area was more confined and proved much harder work. But even so after only half an hour we had deepened the hole to six feet. We rested for a moment on our shovels.

"Polidoro didn't say how deep," I panted. "But it can't be more than a man's height down."

"Well, that's where we are now. And there's no sign of anything."

"What do you think?"

"Well our hole is only three foot across at the bottom," said Julius standing in it, putting out his arms. "We could be above the wrong spot. Maybe we should widen the area. Out to at least six by six? That way we've definitely got it covered."

I looked at my watch. "It's three o'clock Julius. The sun'll be coming up at six. And we're going to be getting tired soon. If we widen the dig area that much we could still be digging come morning."

"What's the alternative?"

"Well… it's been in there four hundred years, right? The

level of the sand on the beach could well have risen in that time. Maybe we just need to dig deeper."

"Fine. But how much deeper? Three foot? Six foot?"

"I don't know." I looked into the hole, my spirits sinking. I sighed. "Look, we can only do what we can do. I say we dig down another three feet. If we don't find it we widen the hole. The cross was buried in a box four feet by two so we ought to stand a chance of hitting a corner of it at least."

"And if we still don't find it?"

"Then we fill in the hole again. It'll take us an hour to refill it. So that means we have to stop by five o'clock."

"So we just give up?"

"No way. We'll come back tomorrow with a metal detector and rip the place apart."

He shrugged. "OK."

We swapped places so I was in the main hole and Julius was on clearing duty. My back and shoulders were aching constantly by now and my arms and wrists were sore. But I kept going. Concentrating each time simply on the next spadeful of sand. In, lift and throw. Then again. And again. And above me I could hear Julius wearily doing the same. We had no choice. We were running out of time.

"John."

I looked up and Julius was crouching down, a finger on his lips. He had killed his torch and I immediately did the same and was left blinking in the deeper blackness.

"I thought I heard something," he whispered.

"What?"

"I'm not sure. It sounded like an engine."

"Well can you see anything?"

He raised himself on his haunches so his head was just above the line of the outer hole, silhouetted against the stars. "There's nothing there."

"Maybe you imagined it."

"No, I definitely heard something."

"But if there's nothing there... Come on Julius, we're wasting time. We need to get on—"

"Shh. There it is again."

This time I heard it as well, the low rumble of an engine and the scrunch of sand under tyres; then a metallic sigh from brakes as a car came to a halt. In the hole I had no idea where it was, how far away from us. All I could see was Julius's outline above me, peering out.

"What do you think?" I whispered.

He ducked down so that his face was close to mine. "It's a jeep, stopped about twenty feet from us. It's facing in our direction."

"Could it be Loredan?"

"He would have driven right up, wouldn't he? It's probably just a couple looking for somewhere to get passionate. At least they haven't got their lights on, so they can't have seen us."

"So what do we do?"

"We'll have to sit it out."

"Well what happens if they stay there till it gets light? We should at least get out of the hole and hide over by the rocks."

He made a soft clicking sound with his tongue, weighing up the options. "Fine. You're right. Let's go. *Quietly.*" He helped me out of the lower hole and then leaving our shovels where they were we climbed cautiously up to beach level.

"I need to get my bag," he hissed. "It's got Polidoro's journal in it." Keeping low he started to move across to his satchel when the night exploded. The dark sky disappeared and was replaced with searing white. I gasped and covered my face, green and red retinal burn torching the black of my closed eyes.

"Police! Halt!" A megaphoned shout came to us across the beach. I wanted to run but I couldn't see a thing.

"Stay where you are!"

Squinting into the headlights from the jeep, I could just make out two policemen in black trousers and short sleeved blue shirts advancing on us across the sand. I looked over to Julius five feet away from me. "Shit. *Shit,*" he fumed. I caught his eye but there was no time to talk, no chance to get our story straight.

"What are you doing here?" the taller of the two asked us, looking from me to Julius and then back again. "Why are you here?"

Neither of us answered.

"You have been digging. Why?"

I looked down at the sand.

"Answer me! Why are you digging? You are planting explosives, yes?"

"No." I looked up in alarm but at the same instant the policemen's hands went to their sides and they both pulled out their pistols and pointed them at us.

"Put you hands up."

"Oh shit," said Julius looking very pale in the headlights. "Look, there's no need for any of this—"

"Hands up."

"Fine, fine," he muttered, doing as he was told. "But let me just explain—"

A pistol was brandished in his face.

"There's no need for this." He took a step forwards and then everything happened at once. The nearest policeman shouted, then lurched at him, bringing his gun down on the side of Julius's head. He crumpled to the ground.

"Julius!" I ran at the officer who had hit him. We struggled, his gun pointing in the air. It fired once, harmlessly into the sky, the noise of it sudden and loud in the night, surprising us both, and then I got my leg round his and tripped him onto his back. The other cop came at me but suddenly, almost inexplicably, he was on the ground as well. I kicked one gun away into the hole, picked up the other, and then I was standing there pistol in hand pointing

it at the two policemen sprawled on the sand in front of me.

I looked to my left and Julius was lying there face up, his head to one side, a red mark on his temple where the policeman had struck him.

"Fuck." I spoke it aloud, breathing hard, looking back at the police. This was madness. I gave my head a shake to get it clear. "Get up," I said to them. *"Get up."* They hurriedly stood up.

"Look." I pointed the gun at them. "Look, I'm going to give this back to you." I waggled the pistol. "You understand? There's been a mix-up here. We haven't done anything wrong." They stared at me blankly.

"I'm going to give this back to you now. And then I'm going to check my friend is OK."

They made no movement, and no sound to indicate whether they had understood me or not. My heart was thumping in my chest and I felt nauseous. I extended my hand holding the pistol, just wanting to return it to them. Just wanting this all to end. But there was a shout from the steps over to my left and I spun round.

"Julius!"

For a moment I didn't understand what was happening: other players had appeared in a tableau that to my mind was already too crowded. A further distraction when all I wanted to do was to give them the gun back. Get its cold black hardness out of my hand where it surely did not belong. Give it back. And then wake Julius up and get us the hell off this beach.

"Julius!"

The scene snapped into clarity. Sarah was standing at the top of the steps screaming down. Patrick was standing behind her. Yet still I didn't understand. How had they got there? And could Sarah not recognise me in the darkness? Was that why she was shouting for Julius?

The policemen started shouting back at her. I wanted

them to stop. I wanted everyone to stop *shouting* so I could think. So I could work this out for all of us. And then I realised the police weren't shouting to Sarah at all. They were shouting beyond her and Patrick because running along the cliff line towards them was another figure, tall, moving fast. He was heading straight for them. I was about to call out, to warn them but she beat me to it.

"How could you? Would you have killed us for the treasure too?"

I looked over at Julius lying there in his blood-soaked T-shirt. Suddenly I saw what she saw and I understood; but it was too late. On the ridge the third policeman had almost reached them. Against the starlight I could see he had drawn a baton and raised it ready to strike.

There was no time to explain to her, no time for anything. I raised the pistol and fired a warning shot above the ridge, above their heads. But it was too late and the policeman brought his baton onto Sarah's head and she went down and even as I screamed and Patrick screamed he was hit too and disappeared from sight.

I ran towards them, to get to the steps, to reach them, but the two policemen on the beach rushed me, knocking the gun from my hand and I sank to the sand under a flurry of blows.

46

A fire had been lit and a man was crouching in front of it. It had been a warm night but now, an hour before dawn, the temperature had dropped right down and the man was on his haunches close to the flames. Unlike his colleagues he wore plain clothes, dressed all in black, but his face shone pale yellow in the firelight.

He was leafing through Polidoro's journal, his head nodding while he turned the pages as though reacquainting himself with a once familiar text. His long fingers caressed the paper but apart from that his body was still. In the ten minutes I'd been watching him he had barely moved at all; only once did he look over in our direction, blink, and then turn back to the book.

It was Loredan.

To the right I could see one of his men standing by the side of the hole, pistol in hand, looking desultorily out to sea. The other was in the hole and digging. The one at the top occasionally kicked at the sand landing by his feet but otherwise made no effort to assist.

I felt curiously removed from the scene yet I was seated only yards away from them. My wrists were tied to my ankles, my legs bent up before me and there was a painful stiffness in every joint of my body. And I was tired. *So* tired.

I rested my face forward onto my knees and then hastily took it back again. My cheeks were tender and puffy and my mouth salty with blood. If I moved my head to the right, I could see that all four of us were there in a line – Sarah next to me, then Julius, then Patrick – all tied up in the same way. And, on my left, if I forced my aching neck to look that way, was the sea.

I sat there shivering, content to do nothing more than watch the activity on the beach while my tongue investigated the swollen surface of my lower lip. The sound of the water was rhythmic and strong, the rush onto the sand and inevitable retreat, and I felt my eyes closing again, lulled by its soothing cycle.

After a while I became aware of whispered voices coming from my right, the hissed words blending with the sea sounds; but staccato, not the lilting beat of the waves on the shore. With an effort I opened my eyes again and cautiously turned my head. Patrick was speaking.

"It's definitely him."

"You're right," said Sarah. "I can see him better now."

"But why are the police with him?" Julius hissed.

"They're not police," said Patrick. "They're Loredan's men."

"So why haven't they questioned us or tortured us or *something?*"

Patrick shrugged. "Because they know what they're looking for. They're just getting on with it."

"And then what?" asked Sarah. "What happens to us when they find it? Will they just let us go again?"

"Sure," said Patrick. "Why not." But he said it too quickly, and even he didn't sound convinced.

Sarah hung her head. "What are we doing here?" she muttered wearily.

I licked my lips and swallowed and then, my voice no more than a low croak, whispered, "What *are* you doing here?"

"Oh. You're awake now. How are you feeling?"

I shrugged. "I feel quite *bruised*. How are you feeling?"

"OK. We got a whack on the head each. I think you copped the worst."

"I guess." I was drowsy still, my mind unclear, and it felt like a struggle to make sense of the situation. "I don't understand why you're here," I repeated.

"Same reason as you."

"What I mean is, why have you brought Patrick with you? He shouldn't be here."

R P NATHAN

"I'm OK, John. Really I am. We were worried that something would happen. We thought—" Patrick stopped abruptly and, even in the dancing glimmer of the firelight, I could see the awkward look on his face.

Sarah helped him out. "We thought you and Julius would... would come to some harm,"

"From each other," added Patrick. Sarah glared at him.

The thoughts registered dully, echoing earlier thoughts. "You thought Julius was in danger from *me?*" I said eventually.

"We didn't know what to think," said Sarah looking suddenly distressed. "You headed off here on your own. And we saw your room…"

"Ah." I nodded. "The room's not *me*. It was once but not any more."

"I know that now." She tried to edge towards me, struggling against her bindings. But in the end she gave up. "I know that now," she said again, her voice low.

"Well," said Julius. "I agree with John on this one. I think it was pretty irresponsible of you to let Patrick come along."

"Irresponsible?" she echoed in disbelief. *"Me* irresponsible—"

"Dragging Patrick over here—"

"I *didn't*—"

"No one *dragged* me anywhere—"

"Whatever," said Julius imperiously. He turned to me. "Are you sure you're OK, John? Your face looks pretty bad."

I shrugged. "I'm OK. Are you OK?"

"Sore head, but otherwise fine."

"Since when did you two become such good friends?" Sarah muttered irritably.

"Just trying to get on," said Julius.

She glared at us in turn and opened her mouth to say something more but just then there was a whoop of delight from the hole. We heard excited chatter between the two police officers. The one at the top shouted and then jumped into the pit himself.

Loredan ran over in time to see them reappear, manhandling an oblong wooden box between them, four feet long by two feet wide by a foot deep. They carried it away from the hole to a flat area of sand illuminated by the campfire; laid it down carefully and then made way for Loredan. He knelt over it, brushing the stray grains of sand from its surface.

"So it's true," sighed Julius. "It really exists."

Loredan blinked his eyes closed, like he was saying a prayer, and then lifted the lid of the box. It opened outwards, hiding its contents from us.

There was a moment's silence, a silence which gripped the whole beach so that even the sea fell suddenly quiet and the only sound was the barest whisper of the wind.

A moment.

Two.

Then a scream and the lid of the box was flipped back so hard that it broke away and landed with a thump on the sand. Loredan was revealed, kneeling there still, his face contorted in fury and even in the flickering yellow half-light we could see the interior of the box now as well: empty except for the twelve flat stones arranged inside.

Loredan stood up, his face contorted with rage. His men were peering into the box, their faces distraught. They picked over the stones, cursing. An angry exchange. Raised voices in Italian.

Sarah caught her breath. "They're saying we've taken it. They're saying we've taken the cross!" All three men were looking in our direction, and we stared back petrified. They started walking over, Loredan in front.

"Where is it?" he yelled at us.

"We don't know what you're talking about," said Julius.

"Where is it?" He was incandescent with rage. "What

have you done with the cross?"

"We don't know where it is," said Patrick. "We swear."

"Silence!" He screwed up his face and bellowed with frustration. It was starting to get light and I could see him more clearly, tall, dressed in black and when he opened his eyes again, I could see them flash with anger. He seemed to be struggling to bring himself under control and then he turned and muttered something in Italian to his two henchmen. Sarah flinched.

He turned back to us. "If," he said in English. *"If you do not tell me what you have done with the cross then I will be forced to kill you one by one. Start with him."* He pointed at Patrick.

"But we only just got here," said Sarah desperately. "How could we have taken it—?"

Loredan clicked his fingers and his men walked over to Patrick, picked him up between them, swung him high and then threw him to the ground. Patrick gasped as the air was knocked out of him.

"No!" Julius did a forward roll towards them, trying to catch the closest one off guard. But he easily jumped out of the way and gave Julius a savage kick in the stomach. He writhed in agony. "It's nothing to do with Patrick," Julius moaned. "I got him into this. *I'm* responsible—"

The uniformed man kicked him again and again until he fell silent.

"Tell me where the cross is," said Loredan. "Tell me where it is and you all will live."

"We don't know," sobbed Sarah. "Please leave us alone—"

"Do not take me for a fool." He grabbed Patrick by the hair and shook him. "Tell me what you have done with it."

"We... haven't... done... anything…"

"Tell me!" He let Patrick go so that his head fell back hard onto the sand. Then he drew a pistol from inside his jacket, bent down and pushed the muzzle into Patrick's

face.

"Oh God," groaned Julius.

"Let us go!" I shouted.

"Tell me where the cross is and I let you go. I count to three and then he dies."

Patrick closed his eyes.

"One."

"Please," screamed Sarah, the tears rolling down her face. "Please don't hurt him—"

"We don't know anything—"

There was a click as the pistol cocked.

"Two."

"Please—"

"Leave him." A voice from behind us, strong commanding. *"Let him go."*

There was the sound of footsteps and three policemen ran into view, guns drawn. They pushed Loredan away from Patrick and took his pistol.

"Release them," the voice said again, still out of view, a woman's voice, clear and cool. The policemen who had just arrived pulled out knives and cut the ropes binding us, helping Patrick up to a sitting position, helping us all up as we gabbled our thanks to them.

They sat us with our backs resting against the largest boulder, facing down the beach to the sea. As well as the three who had helped us a further three police were standing on the shoreline, two women and a man. The sun had risen and we squinted into its glare to make out their faces.

"Thank you," Sarah called to them, massaging her wrists and ankles.

"Thank you so much," I chorused. "You came just in time. They're not real police." I pointed at Loredan's men. "They're impostors."

"Of course they're not real police," said the woman in charge, the one in the middle of the three uniformed figures by the water's edge. "Neither are we."

The smiles faded on our faces.

She took a couple of steps up the beach. "There is no need for guns here," she said waving at her three men who had liberated us and who were guarding the others with drawn pistols. They holstered their weapons. One of them walked to the box and inspected its contents.

"It is empty, *Capo*," he said and held up one of the smooth stones from inside. "Just these."

"Under whose authority was the box opened before I arrived?" the woman asked.

"Under my authority." Loredan stepped forward, brushing past those guarding him. He walked down the beach and stood before her. He was taller but she was in now way cowed.

"You have no authority here, Loredan. You should not even be here."

"I would not be here if left to you. Luckily young Galbaio knows where his loyalties lie."

"You'd asked me to alert the members of the Ten, *Capo*." It was a policeman standing on the shoreline who spoke, the anxiety clear in his voice. "I hope I did nothing wrong. I did tell Uncle he was to wait—"

"*Wait*," sneered Loredan. "I *wait* while the *Capo* comes for the cross herself. How convenient. And how ironic when I am the only member of the Ten who ever placed any credence in the old stories about this treasure."

"Not the only one, Loredan," she said. "And I asked you to wait behind for a reason."

"Because you wanted the cross for yourself—"

"Because you are too impulsive; as your family has always been. Your activities in our name have drawn attention, and made things more difficult for us all as a consequence."

"A real *Capo*—"

"I am a real *Capo*, Loredan—"

"—would understand that I have done what I've done to keep the spirit of Venice alive."

"Bombings. Terrorism. Your methods provoke anger and outrage. Times have changed. So must we. There are other ways to get what we want."

Loredan snorted. "You are weak like Galbaio's father. He gave the books away when I was on the point of a breakthrough. *You* let them come here and try and steal this treasure out from under our noses."

"I am here aren't I?"

"Too late it seems. Is this how you will free Venice?"

"Venice will not be freed overnight. It will require patience."

"Patience is what destroyed Venice."

"Patience helped Venice endure for a thousand years. You should learn its strength."

"Strength comes through action."

"Yet for all your *action* nothing has been achieved thus far. That is why a new approach is needed."

He scowled and spat. "You and your *politicians*. I am already tired of your *new* approach."

"Then you are tired of being part of the *Ten*."

"The Ten. *The Ten.*" He gave a hollow laugh. "We are but a shadow. And now you will destroy us entirely."

"You doubt my leadership, Loredan?"

"I doubt those who put a *girl* in charge."

"I am *Capo* because of who I am. And because of what I will do. Look at me Loredan."

Loredan had turned to walk away.

"Look at me!" Her voice was deep and suddenly commanding and Loredan slowly turned to face her. She drew herself up to full height. "I may be a girl, Loredan, but never forget who I am. I am Francesca Morosini, descendant of Francesco, Commander Doge, Scourge of the Ottomans, Defender of Crete, and Conqueror of the Peloponnese. I am *Capo* of the Ten, elected to serve all

Venice. And I will have your allegiance whether you like it or not."

Then she put her hand out to him and, her voice grown soft, she said, "One day, Loredan, our Venice *will* rise again. You know it to be true."

He grimaced. "One day," he said. "*I* will be *Capo*. Then things will be different."

She shrugged. "When you are *Capo*, you will have my loyalty. Because, my dear Loredan, until the World has changed, loyalty is all we have." She smiled at him and he looked at her and nodded. He gave her the tiniest of bows and then strode back to the jeep with his two colleagues running behind. He started the engine and they drove away.

The four of us looked at each other blinking, not quite sure what we had just witnessed.

After a while the man standing by the empty box said, "If the cross is not here, then where is it? Was it Polidoro after all?"

"Polidoro?" She laughed clear as a bell; but cold like one too. "Polidoro didn't have the cross. He thought he was so clever with his code but the Ten were waiting for him on his return and he was *thoroughly* interrogated. Let me assure you, Polidoro did not bring the cross back with him. Nor did he ever make any further attempt to retrieve it: he was watched by the Ten till the day he died."

"Then who?"

She looked at the man and I thought that I had seen him somewhere before. "Tron," she said, "four hundred years have passed since it was buried. *Four hundred* years. It could have been taken by anyone in that time." She sighed. "There is nothing more to be done here. We will take the box with us as evidence."

The man tipped the rocks out and, slipping the empty box under his arm, he walked back over the beach to the others.

"Hey," called Julius. *"Hey!"*

The leader turned to face us haloed still by the sun.

"Do you want to tell us what's going on here? Who the hell are you?"

"Who am I?" she said and then started laughing. "You mean you *still* haven't recognised me?" They all started laughing now. She took off her cap and shook out her hair. "You mean you really don't know who I am, Julius?"

I saw his face suddenly stiffen.

She took a step forward and for a moment she blocked out the sun and we saw her clearly: tall and willowy and beautiful.

"Julius," said Patrick, his eyes narrowing. "Isn't that your cleaning lady?"

Julius stared at her. "It can't be..." he muttered disbelievingly. *"Francesca?"*

"And what about me?" called one of the men also walking forward. He too was tall, his hair dark but with a blond streak through it.

"Galbaio," murmured Julius. "Giovanni Galbaio."

"That's the guy who sold us the book," I said excitedly.

"At your service," he said bowing low.

"Or me," said the other woman, dark, her hair a curly brown. "Carlotta Contarini."

"Or me, Nicolo Tron."

We blinked at them as they stood there, handsome in the glittering morning sun.

"But…" said Julius eventually, his voice dry, his eyes blinking, still struggling to understand. "Francesca, who *are* you?"

She smiled at him gently now, kindly. "Were you not listening, Julius? We are the Council of Ten."

"But how can you be? The Ten were dissolved two hundred years ago when Venice fell to Napoleon."

"Did you think the institutions and structures of so great a nation would just disappear? That they would simply die? No, the Ten survived and has survived ever since. In secret we continue to protect Venice from her enemies and campaign for her liberation. Some would say we have little influence now but one day the Republic will be remade and Venice will rise again; and when that day comes we will be ready."

"And Loredan?"

"A rival Julius. A *dangerous* rival. There are always factions are there not and different camps? Loredan does not respect me. But he respects the *Capo* of the Ten. While I am *Capo* that is enough."

"But why did you want the cross?"

Now she laughed. "We have survived two hundred years, Julius. How do you think we have done that? By selling what fragments and artefacts we had to bribe and cajole to keep the memory and power of Venice alive. The Most Holy Cross of St Peter and St Paul would have kept us going *forever*. But no matter. We must manage without it. You have Polidoro's journal with you?"

"His journal?" said Julius, reddening.

She looked at Galbaio who walked over and picked up Julius's satchel from where it lay on the sand, checked inside and then held it up. "I have it," he said.

"Good. Then we shall go."

"But, but..." Julius stuttered. *"Francesca,"* he called to her, looking at her, his eyes wide. "It's just that you're so different. You're so... *strong.*"

She laughed and walked up the beach to him. "I was always strong. I desired you and I had you." She bent down and kissed him hard on the lips. His arms dropped limply to his sides. She pulled his head back from her by his hair. "Goodbye, Julius," she said. "I have enjoyed my time with you."

She stood tall again and ran down the beach to the others. She drew a pistol from the holster on her belt and the others did the same. "You will not see us again," she said and all six of them levelled their guns at us. "Shut your eyes."

We closed them and I felt a sudden rush of fear that it should end like this after all. We heard the barking of their pistols and we fell backwards into the sand.

But after the shock of the moment had passed we realised they had fired over our heads and we were unhurt. We scrambled back to our feet but, by then, the Ten were already gone.

47

It was seven o'clock and the sun had fully risen. We had lain on the beach for almost an hour after the Ten's departure. Then, of one mind, we had silently refilled the hole. It seemed smaller in the daylight and, with four people working, it had taken no more than half an hour. The sand was level there now, a patch slightly darker than the rest if you looked closely enough.

When we were done we sat and ate the remains of the bread and cheese and stared out across the sparkling water. My mind was empty, my thoughts elsewhere, and I was happy just to be sitting there squinting against the brightness, savouring the morning breeze.

Over to my right Julius and Patrick were talking.

"When we get back," said Julius, his hand on Patrick's shoulder. "I want to spend some time together. Properly I mean. It's been too long. You should come over," he said including Sarah and me in the invitation. "I want to make amends."

"Hey," said Sarah, "apart from almost being killed a couple of times, it's not been so bad. I mean, look where we've ended up. On a beach. A beautiful day." She had her knees drawn up to her chin and she looked happy as she sat there, pretty with the sun shining on her. "I've been working so hard I haven't been on holiday for two years. *Two* years."

"I haven't been on holiday for seven," I said shaking my head. "Can you imagine that?"

"I can imagine that." She laughed at my look of surprise; but she put out a hand and stroked it against my shoulder and then gently away again. She smiled at me almost shyly and then lay back on the sand. "It's so peaceful here," she said. She closed her eyes and breathed deeply, blissfully. "I need to do more of this."

"Well I think I've had enough time off," said Patrick.

"What will you do when you get back?" I asked him.

"I'm not sure yet…"

"Not back to the firm?"

"No. Probably not that."

"A charity maybe?" asked Sarah. "*If you help somebody…*"

Patrick grinned at her. "*Maybe.* Or maybe something exciting."

"But not too exciting…" said Sarah. "And whatever happens, you'll go and see your doctor again?"

"I will."

There was a big sigh from Julius. He was staring forlornly out to sea.

"What?" said Patrick.

"Oh. I was just thinking about Francesca." He looked wistful. "Wasn't she *amazing.*" He looked at us seriously and we collapsed into helpless laughter. "What? *What?*"

"Oh don't," I groaned, sitting up again. "My face hurts."

"Let me take a look." Sarah knelt down beside me and I turned my face to her. She winced as she saw my bruised cheek and swollen lip in close-up. "You definitely got the worst of it." Her face was only inches from mine; so close that I could see every fleck in her eyes and every long lash. "I've got a tissue," she said. She sat back on her haunches and poured some bottled water on the paper and then knelt back up to me and delicately dabbed my cheek and lip with it. It felt cool and delicious and kind.

"Thank you," I said. She was so close that I could see the soft down on her cheek illuminated by the sun and the specks of sand in her hair.

"You're welcome," she said softly. She blinked and each lash seemed to move separately in infinite slo-mo.

"No, you're welcome," said Patrick.

"No, *you're* welcome," said Julius. We looked over and the two of them were pouring water over each others' heads, cackling with laughter. Sarah looked at me and shrugged and then leaning forwards she kissed me on the lips in a movement so deft and sudden that it had me gasping with surprise.

"I still think you're kind of strange," she said arching an eyebrow; but then she grinned the most gorgeous, sexy grin imaginable and I pulled her to me and we kissed for an everlasting instant.

Apart once more I was aware of the continued laughter from down the beach, Julius and Patrick still horsing around. We exchanged a glance.

"Let's get those bastards," she said and we raced over to them and pushed them over and sat on them until they submitted. Then we rolled out onto the sand again and lay there warming ourselves through our gradually subsiding giggles.

"You've got to wonder, haven't you," said Julius eventually, staring up at the sky.

"Wonder what?" said Patrick.

"Well... I mean what *did* happen to the cross? Who took it?"

Sarah shrugged her shoulders against the soft sand. "Four hundred years *is* a long time..."

"But who else knew about it? Polidoro went to live in Verona with his brother after he came back with Bragadino's skin. And never left again."

"Well maybe his brother went and got it?" said Patrick. "Or maybe *his* son Gianni, Polidoro's nephew, the one he liked so much?"

"That would have been nice," said Sarah.

"But..." Julius sat up. "I don't see how a farmer from Verona could have organised such a difficult expedition. Venice's sea power was failing anyway and Cyprus was in the hands of the Ottomans until the Twentieth Century."

"Who took over after the Turks?" asked Patrick.

"The British," I said. "We annexed Cyprus in 1914 when the Turks came out in support of Germany."

"Was there fighting on Cyprus?"

"No, but wounded soldiers from the Dardanelles were taken there. To Famagusta."

"Dardanelles? As in *Gallipoli?*" Patrick looked suddenly excited. "Then Shaeffer, dying at Gallipoli, could have told another soldier about it. And *he* could have been brought to Famagusta and found the treasure—"

"Maybe," I interrupted. "But it would have been a hell of a deathbed message."

"I agree," said Julius. "We have to face facts, Patrick. Polidoro didn't get it. Shaeffer was killed at Gallipoli. So at some point, someone *else* dug up the cross."

Patrick made a face but then sighed. "I guess you're right," he said, resigned, and picking up a flat pebble he threw it hard at the water so that it skipped and bounced three times before it sank. One, two, three, and before the stone disappeared beneath the surface I understood. I looked up and found Sarah blinking at me and I knew in that instant of synchronicity that she was thinking exactly the same thing.

"We got it wrong," she said softly.

We'd had it wrong from the start.

Received knowledge taken as fact colouring all we had heard and seen.

Assumption transmuting to reality, steering us the wrong course, further and further from the essential truth.

"What if Henry Shaeffer wasn't killed at Gallipoli?" she said.

"But he was," said Patrick.

"But how do we know?"

"Because everyone says he was."

"Who everyone? The people who sold you the book? The Ten? Maybe they'd just *thought* he was dead too. Maybe he wanted them to think that."

"But we spoke to Frances," insisted Patrick. *"She* said he died in the First World War. She said—"

"What did she say?" said Sarah her eyes shining. "She never said he died in the War. *We* said that to *her*. *She* said her father died fifteen years before her mum. That would have been 1961."

"But she was confused—"

"No. *We* were. We were so certain that we didn't listen to her. She was trying to tell us but we just assumed she was talking nonsense; and in the end that's what she thought too. Poor Frances." She looked like she was about to cry. "Poor *dear* Frances."

"I don't understand," said Julius. "Are you saying—"

"I'm saying that Henry Shaeffer didn't die at Gallipoli. He came home from the war after all."

"But then..."

But then... Slow blink, a look from face to face, wheels turning, inexorable motion, the truth approached, close now, so close.

A thought occurring to us all together, a joint epiphany.

The collective realisation glistening like gold before us.

"The letter," I said; but she knew it before the words were out of my mouth and was already on her feet sprinting to their car.

"I've got it with me," she called back. "I'm sure it's still in my bag."

"What letter?" asked Julius.

The letter from Frances, Patrick explained. I watched his mouth moving but heard nothing save for the blood in my head and the sound of the sea. I looked from him to Sarah running back to us, a brown envelope in her hand. She was in T-shirt and shorts, sand spilling up and down her bare legs as she cantered across the beach, her movements youthful and beautiful, reminding me of a girl I had once loved; reminding me of her.

She knelt down on the sand before us and tore the end off the envelope and slipped out the smaller ivory coloured one inside. She held it up to us. The last letter that Shaeffer had written his wife from the War. The last piece of the jigsaw dropping in place, snapping tight with its mates. "Look at the postmark," she said.

Cyprus 1915.

The last piece.

What if he wasn't killed at Gallipoli?

What if he was only injured there. What if *he* was brought to Famagusta.

Click.

With trembling fingers she took the letter from its envelope and carefully unfolded the four handwritten pages of yellowed paper within. She skimmed through it for a minute, two, and I saw tears forming in her eyes. She looked up and saw me watching her and smiled and nodded and I wanted to say a million things to her, then and after, but she silenced me with a finger from her coral lips to mine; there was time, for us, and said, to all of us, "Listen."

<u>10 October 1915</u>
My darling Anna.

I am coming home to you. Our sentence of separation is ended at last. I was told by the doctors and my commanding officer this morning that I am to return to England on the next ship. It departs in a matter of days. So at most it will be but another month before I see you again. Before I can take you in my arms and hold you as I have longed to do in the year since I last saw you. This longest of years.

Oh how I have missed you. You know this for I have written of it in every letter I have sent you. But my longing has not grown less with time and has indeed been sharpened by the thought that I really will see you again. And this time when I return to you it will be forever.

I have written already of what you should expect of me bodily, of my catalogue of wounds which have left

me scarred and physically lessened. I am not the man whom you waved off a year ago. I am <u>reduced</u>.

But my mind is changed too and you will need to be patient with me. Be kind to me, my love, even if I am not so to you and be gentle even if my mood seems hard. For I am changed in other ways as well as physical. I am gripped with bouts of anger which shake me at times, and my manner is unsettled and unpredictable. On occasion I feel a hate in me which knows no bounds and leaves room for nothing else. I am changed by the war my love. I am burdened with dark thoughts and try as I might they will not leave me.

I am visited every day by thoughts of Rupert and the wasted way in which he died, felled by such a petty assassin, a mosquito, a nothing. And my heart rages that one so strong, so magnificent, so <u>beautiful</u> as he could die in such a way, before I could even be reunited with him. How can it be that the light of our heroes can be extinguished in such a careless manner? What have we done that the fates should so conspire against us?

And what of Hargreaves? Poor Hargreaves. I still cannot commit to paper the details of that day at Bulair. I cannot though they are burned into my mind forever. I shall not forget the way in which he died nor how he held tight to my hand at the last. Dear, gentle, Hargreaves. What harm had he ever done to anyone? And what future good will he be able to do lying cold in the ground. Oh my love! The horror and the pity of it. The memories that do not fade, that will not release me from their grasp.

Oh my darling, I am sorry to spill my anguish upon you again. This letter was meant to be joyous yet it turns to tears so quickly. This is how I am now. This is how events and my absence from you have weathered

me, turned me misshapen and ugly, awkward in
company, and prone to melancholy. How I long to see
you! So that in your arms and your breast I can take
full refuge from the endless night thoughts which
pursue me through the day; so that your kindness can
dilute the fear and the hurt and the guilt I feel. The
guilt above all. That I am alive when they are not. Only
you will be able to make sense of these feelings. Only
your love will make me whole again.

I shall write no more of such matters to you for it
disguises the true joy I feel that soon I will be with you
once more. So let me instead finish this letter by
lightening your heart – and mine – with the telling of
the final part of the tale I began in Venice regarding
the journal I found there.

You will already be acquainted with the story from
reading my notebook which you would have received
some six months ago. You may recall that on the night
I left for the Dardanelles I had finally understood how
to break the book's coded message. It was a Vigenère
cipher and the key phrase as I hinted in my journal
was Terraferma. No doubt, you will have decoded and
translated the letter already my dear with your superior
intellect and understanding of the Italian language.
(Oh, what a capital school mistress you will make; and
I do approve of the idea: passionately!) For me the
process took me such time as I would have been
ashamed to admit to you. But of course time was what
I had.

I have already written to tell you that for long weeks
I lay in my hospital bed in Cyprus not knowing
whether I was entirely alive or entirely dead. I lay there
and when I was not dreaming of you and Frances my
sole amusement was to work through the copy of the
coded letter I had made when I left Italy. To work

through it, to decode and translate it. And when I had succeeded in my task and I finally read Polidoro's words I felt a sympathy for him that was wholly unexpected. For here was a man separated from me by over three hundred years and yet I understood his mind entirely. His words struck a resonance in me. He spoke of loss and torment and regret. He spoke of the bitter emptiness of defeat when victories are still being won. He spoke of feeling like a ghost. Well I was a ghost as were so many of my brothers who lay there in the hospital with me. I understood Polidoro. I was Polidoro.

And then one day I was better and though still weak I was allowed to walk about. I was shown around the compound and I asked the nurse what place this was as I had not cared to know before and she said Famagusta. I stopped still for a moment in silent surprise and breathed in the same air that Polidoro had done.

Then one afternoon they took us on a trip, a few miles south of Famagusta to the monastery of Agia Napa. We went up into the courtyard and, it being a hot day, we all drank from the well. And at that moment I felt a shiver of realisation down my spine. I was within touching distance of Polidoro's beach I realised, and I had all the instructions of how to find it.

Later that week I spoke to my nurse. She let me slip out and I made my way back to the monastery and from there through the woods and then finally to the beach. And it was just as he had described it. There was the golden sand. There were the three boulders. I ran over to the largest and dug down as Polidoro had instructed and eventually struck something in the sand. I pulled out a box flat and wide and opened it excitedly, yet immediately felt a wave of disappointment close to nausea on looking inside.

For the cross was there. By all that is still beautiful the cross was there. Yet incomprehensibly, sacrilegiously, it was broken into four pieces and the centre of it, the stone that Polidoro had described with such longing, the sapphire of deepest blue, was missing.

I sat back, trying desperately to make sense of what I saw, those shards of beauty arrayed before me; and gradually it came to me. All became clear that should have been obvious from the start. A truth which had escaped even the vigilant gaze of the Ten. That Polidoro had recovered the treasure he wanted after all.

My belief is that on his way back from Constantinople, freed at last from his Ottoman prison, Polidoro made the perilous trip to Cyprus. And, somehow evading the Turks, he returned to this very beach where he knew the treasure had been buried. Perhaps waiting for nightfall, he unearthed it and looked upon the great jewel entire in its moonlit splendour.

But only for a moment and then, taking a knife from his pocket, he prised the sapphire from the centre of the cross. It was for this incomparable stone and this alone that he had risked all. Polidoro had never coveted the cross itself, nor its body of gold and rubies and relics. For he had wanted only peace; and some find that in the love of our wives or children and others in a blue fist-sized stone in which a broken man can begin to see a future again.

So Polidoro removed the sapphire. And he brought it back to Venice concealed so that not even the Ten would find it. The Turks had cut him cruelly during the years of his torture and, into a flap of skin in his neck which had never closed or healed, he secreted the stone. And then he set off for Venice. It took him several weeks journey in an open boat and when the authorities found him they were not surprised to see him ill. He'd eaten nothing but seaweed for days and was half-starved and disfigured with a goitre. Yet how could we have been so foolish, the Ten and I? How could he have developed a goitre when seaweed is so rich in the iodine which is used to treat it? How indeed. It was with a ruse as simple as this that Girolamo Polidoro outwitted the mighty Council of Ten.

So he returned with the stone hidden in him. And Veronese painted him with it; perhaps he knew the truth as well and enjoyed the joke against the authorities. Afterwards Polidoro retired into obscurity in Verona, living out his days on his brother's farm, watching his favourite nephew grow to a man. And whenever he was torn or bitter or filled with the emptiness and dark tears of war's aftermath, he knew he could look into the sapphire and believe in himself once more.

Of course this is no more than conjecture. All I *knew* was what lay before me, the contents of the box. But seeing them and having divined as far as I could Polidoro's mind and deeds, I laughed aloud, my disappointment gone, my spirits soaring, and I shouted his name around the cove so that for a moment he might live again.

I busied myself for a time after that and when I was done the box was replaced in its hole, and the pit refilled with sand. I returned to the hospital, a sackcloth bundle containing the shards of the cross held tight under my arm. And then I slept as though I had never slept before; and for that while I too was at peace.

That is the end of my story, my darling, and this

will be my last letter for I shall see you again soon and my heart beats so at the promise of it. Give little Frances a hug from me and tell her I will be bringing her a worthy souvenir of my adventure. But for you my darling Anna, I shall simply bring myself.

Your ever loving husband
H

October 2020, London

John

Afterword

My story – *our* story – has been out there for a couple of months now.

I ended up publishing it on the internet as I couldn't get any agents or real publishers excited by it. I guess the tale of a shadowy group keeping the notion of Venice alive isn't really of interest, especially twenty years after the events occurred. There hasn't been even a sniff of terrorism from the Ten in that time. And though I've kept my eye out for Francesca Morosini popping up in Italian politics I haven't spotted her.

But I guess she was always the type to work in the background.

Anyway I'm sitting back out in the garden again.

It's been a tough year. We've been luckier than most I'm sure – none of us have had Covid yet – but it still feels hard. And now, as winter approaches, infection levels are rising again and it looks like we're heading for another full lockdown. The house feels increasingly claustrophobic as the rules on seeing people start to tighten once more and I'm filled with foreboding. And if that's what I'm feeling then I'm sure it's even worse for the kids. Just at an age when they should be looking forward to broadening their horizons they're being narrowed. At least they're back at school for the moment. But we can all see what's coming. They must dread the coming winter. I know I do.

So we're making the most of days like these, the last of the pleasant ones, when a few rays from the sun can still warm you. I'm sitting in a deckchair which is getting increasingly hard to get into and out of as my middle-age embeds; not helped by my lockdown attempts to do the first handstand of my life at the age of fifty. I'm not sure my left shoulder is ever going to recover from that.

As I sit here I have to say I'm disappointed that few seem to have read my story so far. It has not become an internet sensation. It is not the lockdown novel everyone is talking about. A few copies have been sold. But I'm not even sure to whom as there's no one to talk to about it.

Still. It's out there.

And that's liberating on many levels not least because it proves once and for all that I'm not afraid.

Sarah's just come out into the garden with the post. It often just sits on the mat for days on end now. There's little in it to get excited about. We take a weekly turn at sorting it.

She's forty-eight now, and she's well wrapped up in a fleece as the afternoon starts to cool.

She's still lovely.

It's been a good marriage.

The usual ups and downs. This past year lots of downs of course.

Furlough and the uncertainty of what will come next.

Us all being stuck at home.

(At one point no one in the house was talking to anyone else. That's a lot of permutations of antagonism.)

But the love is still strong.

And as she walks towards me carrying some letters I'm reminded of that morning on the beach in Cyprus all those years before.

The late sun catches her face like the early sun did back then and she's still so beautiful.

We'll go back, I tell myself.

We'll go back there, and other places too.

The kids may have left home by then, but we'll still be together.

We'll survive this time.

She catches me staring at her and she smiles.

"What?"

I shrug. (God my shoulder hurts.) "Nothing," I say.

She shrugs as well and tosses the post in my lap as she lowers herself into her deckchair far more gracefully than I did. Our two seats are side by side, facing away from the house, staring forward – always forward – at the short strip of lawn and a rose covered wall. But above us is sky.

"Just a couple of charity magazines and a letter," she says reaching down for the bottle of gin.

"We should really tick the box to say we can receive these by email…" I'm saying this but my attention is drawn by the envelope of the letter. It's handwritten in a black copperplate which seems somehow familiar. We hardly ever get actual letters these days, certainly not outside of Christmas. I hold it up to Sarah.

"It does seem familiar doesn't it?" she says. Her interest is piqued but she's also scrabbling around to find the tonic. "Open it."

Inside is a single fold of A5 with the same handwriting and a playing card. The letter says:

Dear John

I know we've always had our differences and haven't actually spoken in years. But I'm in danger and I really need your help. Your book has stirred things up. And maybe a few things I've done as well. They sent me this. I've been trying to get hold of you. Please call me as soon as you can.

Julius

"Julius."

"God! What does *he* want," she says extending an arm. I hand the letter to her.

"It says he's in danger…" I'm distracted by the absurd pleasure of knowing that Julius is aware of my book. I wonder if he bought a copy? I wonder what he thought of it.

"Danger." She rolls her eyes and flaps the paper at me.

I'm turning the playing card over and over in my fingers as I wonder why on earth it should matter what Julius thinks of me after all these years.

"That man has always been so dramatic."

Well I can't argue with that.

"Though now I come to think of it… when I was talking with Mum last week she was saying that Aunty Jean had been saying…"

In my hands the playing card slows and I see it properly for the first time.

"… that Patrick had been saying that Julius had gone on a trip somewhere…"

I'm staring at the card.

"…which isn't easy at the moment so something's going on…"

It's become like lead in my hands.

"What's with the card?"

I blink and hold it up to her. Show her both sides. It has the usual red patterned back but when I turn it over instead of spades or hearts or whatever there's just a large capital X.

In my ears I suddenly hear the blood pounding like waves hitting a beach.

Because of course it isn't an X.

It's a Ten.

If you've enjoyed this book (or even if you haven't) do you think you might be able to leave me a review on Amazon? *A Richer Dust Concealed* took me seven years to write, and fifteen years to publish, so each review I get means so much to me personally. A review only takes a few minutes and whether the verdict is "good", "bad" or just *"meh"*, it will help new readers to find my work and will also encourage me to continue writing in the future. Thanks so much in advance: it really does mean more than I can say.

And if you *did* enjoy this book you can keep up to date with news about my writing, upcoming releases, and receive exclusive extracts and short stories by joining my Readers' Club at
rpnathan.com

ACKNOWLEDGEMENTS

I got the first germ of an idea for this book when I was travelling around Italy in 1998 with my then girlfriend (now wife). We were having dinner with Milanese friends up in the old town in Bergamo. There on the wall, keeping a close eye on us, was carved the winged lion of St Mark; but we were a long way from Venice. Later I learned how Venice had once been the pre-eminent power in Europe and about the shady dealings of the Council of Ten; and over the next few years a novel gradually took shape. But the seed of it was planted in Bergamo, so the first thank you is to our dear Italian friends for that dinner and so many others, for numerous day trips and happy times: Paola, Beppe, Sara, Lorenzo, Anna, Lorenzo, Allegra, Alessandro, Monica, Camilla, Lorenzo, Carlo and Filippo.

And then I am hugely indebted to several authors whose works of scholarship have allowed me to tell this story with a degree of plausibility. In particular I would pay tribute to *A History of Venice* by John Julius Norwich (to whom there is a clear homage in this novel) and *The Code Book* by Simon Singh. But I would also mention: *The Venetian Empire* by Jan Morris; *A History of Cyprus* by George Francis Hill; *Excerpta Cypria* by Claude Delaval Cobham; *Forever England, The Life of Rupert Brooke* by Mike Read; *Art and Architecture in Venice* by R Shaw-Kennedy; *The Italian Renaissance* by J H Plumb; *Gallipoli* by R Rhodes James; *The Great War and Modern Memory* by Paul Fussell; *The Blue Guide to Venice, 1976 Edition*.

I want to thank Anne Dewe for loving this book and trying so valiantly to sell it for so many years and for believing in me when no one else in the publishing industry did. And thanks too to various friends who have been unfailing in their encouragement for my writing over many, many years. In no particular order: Gordon, Anne, John, Karol, Jonno,

Monica, Edwin, Darryl, Jenny, Chris, Karen, Alison, Richard, Trevor, Alice, Joe, Will, Simon, Ali, Rachel, Matt, Catherine, Martin, Stuart, Eric, Swapnil, Mike, Kish, Dorian, Bal, Pav, Danny, Denise, Giles, Sarah, Neil, Julie, Piers, Sally, Simon, Pete, Claudia, Qun, Francesca, Guy, Steve, Piers, Paul, Kate, Cagdas, Ezgi, Tim, Nigel, Ben, Vicky, Rose. (If I seem to have forgotten you, don't worry, I'll be thanking you in person.)

A huge thank you to my parents and sister who have always supported me, whatever; and to my own pair of sapphires Dominic and Rosa.

And finally to Hilary without whom I would not have been able to write this book nor would have wanted to:

Testamentum est libri huius amica mea.

R P Nathan, April 2021

Also by R P Nathan
and available from Cassiopeia Publishing

THE SECOND BEST MAN

When Alan gets asked to be best man at his friend's wedding he should be delighted. Only problem is he's got a morbid fear of public speaking and is in love with the bride-to-be…

What readers have said:

> *"I have just finished The Second Best Man and loved it! It made me laugh and laugh and laugh! I want to start reading it all over again."*

> *"I devoured it within 24 hours. Perfectly paced. Made me laugh out loud as well as cry."*

The Second Best Man is a sparkling romantic comedy, an everyday story of life, love and lobsters…

All author royalties received from the sale of *The Second Best Man* are donated to Comic Relief.

THE COLLABORATORS

It is December 1942 in Occupied France. The Bertrand family are hiding their daughter's Jewish fiancé in a secret room in their apartment. The Resistance is planning to get the couple to freedom but the Germans have been tipped off by a collaborator.

The family's worst fears are realised when German captain Karl bangs on the door and begins to ransack their apartment. But all is not what it seems because, as the heartbreaking plot unfolds, we realise that what Karl is really looking for is redemption.

What readers have said:

"Combines a captivating plot with beautiful emotion"

"Treachery, friendships, and search for meaning: a heart-warming and absorbing tale."

"Powerfully written, heart wrenching and tender, quietly devastating and uplifting"

"A really amazing read – so immersive, emotional and powerful. The time structure made it uniquely complex and really added to the dramatisation as the plot was unravelling and puzzle was piecing together in my mind, making the story all the more captivating."

An exhilarating literary thriller from the author of *The Second Best Man*.

NOW WE ARE ANIMALS

What would you do if the human race suddenly got deposed by a higher species who set about colonising our planet, eradicating all semblance of our culture, and farming us like cattle?

Set in a dystopian near-future *Now We Are Animals* takes the form of a pair of journals written by Cara contrasting her isolated existence as a pet, with her traumatic experiences from a year earlier, when the normality of her life as an A Level English student was swept away by the arrival of the Colonists…

The journals capture how Cara's feelings of resignation turn first to resentment and then to resistance, the very act of writing awakening in her the human creativity that the Colonists have sought to suppress. Cara herself is no natural rebel, just a normal teenager with all that that entails, but in her exciting, funny and at times moving commentary on her plight, we are reminded why humanity might just be worth saving…

The first book in *The Colonists* trilogy, *Now We Are Animals* will change the way you think about animals – and each other – forever.

Printed in Great Britain
by Amazon

10405072R00222